LONG DIVISION

Also by Sarah Harvey

Misbehaving
Fly-Fishing
Split Ends

LONG DIVISION

Sarah Harvey

HEADLINE

First Published in 2001
by HEADLINE BOOK PUBLISHING

10 9 8 7 6 5 4 3 2 1

British Library Cataloguing in Publication Data

Harvey, Sarah
Long division
I.Title
823.9'14[F]

ISBN 0 7472 6992 0

Typeset by
Letterpart Limited, Reigate, Surrey

Printed and bound in Great Britain by
Mackays of Chatham plc, Chatham, Kent

HEADLINE BOOK PUBLISHING
A division of Hodder Headline PLC
338 Euston Road
LONDON NW1 3BH

www.headline.co.uk
www.hodderheadline.com

For Terry, again . . . and again . . .

Acknowledgements

Thanks as always to the usual motley crew of family and friends – I am fortunate in that each can easily fall into both categories; to Luigi, John and Amelia at Sheil Land; to all at Headline, in particular Clare, and Sherise for her help, good humour and advice on tanning; and thanks also to Germ, the Btart and GoGo for being such a constant bad influence, and the Bearded Wonder and the other Fat Bird for the light entertainment.

Chapter One

Life is a peppered steak, I muse, toying with the charred remains of cow on my plate. You think you want all the crap on top, all the garnish, but does it actually make the thing taste any better?

I look up, up and across at my fiancé Richard sitting opposite me.

He is talking down to the waiter.

Richard talks down to everybody, an excellent trick for someone who is such a small person. Small in stature, small-minded, and dare I say it small . . . Well, let's just say small in other *rather* important departments.

Richard is my pepper sauce, my garnish, my piece of curling Lollo Rosso lounging on the side of the plate. Looks appetisingly good to the eyes, but tastes remarkably bitter. As a small person Richard likes to surround himself with large things. Large apartment (penthouse, of course), large car, large wallet, and large matching ego.

He is a prat, but my mother loves him. It has taken me exactly one year, eight months, six days to realise that I do not. I look at my watch. Make that one year, eight months, six days, three hours and thirteen minutes. I won't go into seconds, I've wasted enough time already. I stand up, and reach for my handbag.

Richard looks away from the waiter and smiles briefly, anticipating another trip to the Ladies' in order to titivate for his pleasure. He is what I would describe as an ego-hedonist, interested only in his own pleasure. A pleasure-seeker not a pleasure-giver, Richard's main aim in life is . . .well, Richard.

He has dedicated a lifetime to pleasing himself, and expects those around him to follow his example and please him. Tonight, I do just that. He has decided that I am looking rather voluptuous.

Titivate: the word pleases him, arouses him. This whole

scenario, the candlelit restaurant, the expensive wine, is the charade he believes is his key to the latter part of the evening, the important part of the evening, the sex part of the evening, his reward for enduring the rigmarole, the boredom, the tedious niceties of courtship.

I open my handbag. Amongst the flotsam of used tissues, loose change, keys, half-eaten lipsticks, and dried-up wands of mascara, lies a packet of condoms.

Ribbed.

My mind also moves forward to the latter part of the evening. The sex part of the evening, where I usually have to attempt to coax Richard's small prick into being Richard's slightly bigger prick while he lies back with the same smug look on his face, as though he is bestowing a great favour by allowing me to do this.

My resolve deepens. I take a deep breath, feel in my bag for the keys to Richard's place, the keys to Richard's life.

'Richard,' I rehearse in my head, 'I don't love you, and I'm leaving.'

I open my mouth.

'Richard . . .' I can hear myself speak, but my voice sounds somewhat detached. 'I don't . . . er . . . I don't.'

'You don't what?' he snaps at me, annoyed by my dithering interruption of his complaint about his meal.

I open my mouth but this time no words come out at all.

'Well?' he presses irritably, anxious to get back to berating the poor harassed little French waiter.

'I don't want any dessert, and I'm going to the Ladies'.'

The words come out in a breathless rush as I push back my chair and stride across the restaurant like my backside is on fire, although in reality the only cheeks burning are the ones on my face.

Inside the Ladies', I press my hot forehead against the mirror, and watch my breath form warm pools on its smooth immaculately clean surface. Through the vaporous reflection I can see my face, familiar yet totally alien. Why does one never look as one imagines oneself to look? Sometimes I will walk past my own reflection and smile because the person looking back at me seems vaguely familiar. I stare at the strange dark eyes, which stare rather hazily back at me. Is that really my face? The only thing I recognise is my own fear. A fear of being single. As part of a couple one is regarded as a normal human being. As a

2

single person one suddenly becomes a statistic.

What would life be like without Richard? Was there ever life without Richard? Sometimes it doesn't feel as though there was. Is there life after Richard? Like life after death, this is an unknown phenomenon, although what I am certain of is the fact that I'm too young to die. There may well be life after Richard, but if I attempt to explore this unknown terrain, then my mother will kill me.

I think I have the standard disease of the decade.

I know I want something, but I don't really know exactly what that something is. Something better? Something different?

I ponder for a moment. Somebody better, something different . . . definitely something bigger!

I snigger aloud at this thought.

The Ladies' attendant, having replenished the loo roll in number two cubicle, is now sitting in her dainty paisley-upholstered Queen Anne replica chair, engrossed in her favourite Barbara Taylor-Bradford novel.

She glances up upon hearing my snort of laughter, disturbed from her tale of street girl made good, and looks disapprovingly at the dark-haired girl loitering in her scrubbed and lemon-scented domain. The attendant has an inferiority complex longer and more structured than the Severn Valley Bridge. When somebody laughs, she automatically thinks they are laughing at her. Her world is in this tiled corner of this ladies' loo in a smart restaurant in a smart part of town. If it weren't for the row of four white cubicles upon the right-hand wall, you would think that you had wandered into someone's private parlour by mistake.

She glares at me from behind a rather funereal arrangement of hedonistically creamy lilies. I rummage in my voluminous handbag for a lipstick as a ruse to appear unaware of the attendant's disapproving gaze. Life is so restrictive, I muse as I run Beautiful around my mouth. You can't even laugh out loud nowadays without someone looking at you like you're mad. Perhaps you are mad, my reflection mocks me, mad to want to give up a comfortable secure future for the unknown, give up something familiar in the hope of finding something better. But then again, any future is unknown, even the anticipated one. I ostentatiously place a £5 note in the attendant's small white saucer. For some reason, this makes us both feel a lot better.

I return to the table. My pepper sauce has cooled and congealed, just like my love life really. It's now or never. I take another swig of Burgundy, steel myself, brace my back and open my mouth.

'Richard . . .' I begin again.

'Richard? Richard Trevelyan!'

A sleek brunette dressed head to toe in Versace, in the process of being shown to her table by a waiter, stops mid-sashay and peers across the dimly lit room towards our table.

'Why, it is, isn't it?' With a toss of her raven head, she pushes past the waiter, who steps backwards on to another diner's foot, and practically stampedes across the restaurant towards us, dragging a rather good-looking, obviously embarrassed man in her wake.

'I thought it must be you. Didn't I just say, that looks just like Richard Trevelyan, Alex, didn't I?' she gushes to her companion. 'Well, long time no see . . .'

She swoops down upon Richard and kisses him firmly just to the left of his mouth, leaving a big red lip imprint. She'd have caught him full on the lips except for the fact that he moved his head slightly. I know he only did this because he's been eating garlic. It's OK to blow it all over me, but never another member of the female sex.

'How *are* you, darling? Still a dangerous shark in the sea of corporate law?'

She laughs, one of those cultivated laughs that's supposed to sound all light and melodious, like the tinkling of a glass bell, but is as false as the nails on her slender elegant hands. Richard laughs too. He also has a false laugh, a sort of boom, one of those deep, hearty, I'm-a-jolly-good-chap-really laughs, the kind that resonates around a room like a rubber ball, and has been known to break the odd glass on occasion with its velocity.

'Well, I never, Katherine the Great – what a wonderful surprise. You look bloody marvellous, but then again you always did.'

Richard makes a show of getting to his feet and kissing her hand. (The garlic again, he's not at all chivalrous usually.)

'And, Alex. How are you, old man?' Richard turns to her companion, taking his outstretched hand with both his own and pumping it vigorously, convinced as he is that the strength of one's handshake reflects the strength of one's personality.

4

'So good to see you both. It's been far too long.'

The man called Alex is smiling at me, waiting to be introduced, but Richard isn't that polite. He's been known to hold a lengthy conversation with an acquaintance with me standing right next to him, and not so much as mention my name.

Curiosity is obviously too much for Alex's wife, however.

'Who's your little friend then, Ricky?'

Ricky! Despite the fact I've just been interrupted at a pretty important moment in my life, I only narrowly suppress an outburst of laughter.

'This is Felicity,' he says.

The woman's elegant hand is extended graciously. I notice she has rings on all of her fingers. I once read that this is a sign that a woman wishes to be dominated by a man. There are so many diamonds on this hand she must be wearing a whole field full of carats. It gives the effect of an outrageously extravagant knuckle-duster, hardly an indication of a weak nature unless that nature includes a weakness for expensive jewellery.

'My fiancée,' Richard continues.

The hand immediately shoots back and, flustered, toys with her dark brown hair which is so glossy she could be on the vitamin pills my father feeds his Labrador.

I can see genuine shock on the girl's far-too-perfect features, but it doesn't take her long to regain her composure.

'Why, you sly old dog,' the affected lightness has returned, but the voice is noticeably strained, 'and you always said matrimony wasn't for you.' She tries the laugh again, but it's even more false than the first time. 'But I knew you'd get caught sooner or later.'

Richard is smirking. I don't know why but I get the feeling there's an exchange going on here that isn't purely verbal.

'Every dog has his wedding day,' he says brightly, trying to be witty. 'You know, it really is great to see you, Kat. It seems an age since we last met. We've a few years to catch up on, haven't we? Tell you what,' he rubs his hands together like Scrooge contemplating riches, 'why don't you join us?'

I groan inwardly. At this rate I'll never pluck up the courage to call everything off; I can hardly announce I have no intention of marrying Richard before an audience.

To my horror, Katherine beams and begins to accept.

'Oh, what a lovely idea . . .'

5

This time her husband steps in. He must be more intuitive than her; either that or he spotted the look of dismay on my face. He must think me so rude.

'Thanks, Richard. It's really very kind of you but perhaps on another occasion,' he says. He has a nice voice, warm but not too hearty, educated but not clipped or false.

'That would be nice,' I say quickly, apologetically, smiling gratefully at him.

'Yes, we really ought to get together sometime.' Kat addresses Richard as she says this. I get the feeling the invitation doesn't include me. 'As you say, it's been *far* too long.' She says this with great emphasis, and a flash of incredibly small straight white teeth, to match her incredibly small straight nose.

'That would be *nice*.' Richard echoes my words, but the tone of his voice is very different. 'We really must stay in touch now that we've met up again. In fact,' he looks over at me, his smirk is now so wide that by rights his oh-so-chiselled jaw should begin to crack, 'I've just had the most marvellous idea.' He stretches his arm across the table and puts a hand over mine. I look down at it in shock, as though I've just discovered an unusual and very unexpected growth there.

'Why don't you come to the wedding?'

'Wedding?' The laser beam smile flashes on and off again.

'Well, that's what usually follows an engagement.' Richard laughs.

If only you knew, I think to myself.

'August the twenty-fifth – only seven weeks to go, eh, Fliss darling? Seven weeks tomorrow to be precise.' He smiles at me affectionately. Now I know there is something very odd going on here.

'You must come, I insist upon it. If you give Fliss your address she'll send an invite through, won't you, darling?'

Two darlings in the space of twenty seconds. This isn't the Richard I know and loathe.

'Alexander and Katherine Christian, 16 Belvoir . . . very nice address.' I read the card a very disgruntled Katherine Christian presented to Richard with a whispered 'Call me' that could be heard by her husband, half the restaurant and myself.

'Nice girl, don't you think?' says Richard, as soon as they are out of earshot.

I don't think, but I'm not going to give him the opportunity to misinterpret my instant dislike of Katherine Christian as jealousy by saying so.

'Who is she, Richard?'

'An ex.' He attacks his *haricots vert* with surgical precision.

Well, that much was pretty obvious.

'How ex?' I'm not bothered, just curious.

'Oh, a few years ago now.'

'What happened?'

'She wanted more than I was prepared to give at the time.' He looks up at me with clear brown eyes, his mouth full of beans and sole. 'She was devastated when I finished the relationship,' he adds.

He's waiting for a reaction. I refuse to give him one and stay silent.

He tries again. 'She used to worship me, you know.'

If you're that wonderful then why did she marry someone else? I think furiously.

'Of course she married on the rebound,' he states smugly, unconsciously answering my unspoken question.

I look over towards their table; Alex Christian catches my gaze, and smiles. He has a very nice smile. He also has a very nice face, fit body – lean and muscled, and is wearing an impeccably cut dark grey Armani suit extremely well.

'He looks very nice,' I challenge, sneaking another look and deciding that I wouldn't mind rebounding from Richard on to someone like Alex Christian. How on earth did Katherine manage it? Yes, she's beautiful, but from what I can make of her in the short space of time I've known her that beauty is about as deep as the lightest of paper cuts. I may be wrong, of course, I suppose it's not really fair to make snap judgements about people you barely know, but having been a teacher for the past four years, I've come to find that my first impressions of people are usually pretty spot on. Although I have been known to be wrong. A major example of this is currently sitting opposite me, of course, agreeing rather reluctantly it seems that Alex Christian is indeed a very nice man.

'Oh, he is,' concedes Richard. 'Decent chap really, quite successful, runs a small but rather good publishing company.'

He always measures a person's worth by their status in life, but is usually reluctant to acknowledge anyone's achievements

7

but his own. A 'quite successful' from Richard would equate to 'very successful' in anyone else's book.

'Why on earth did you invite them to the wedding?'

'Why not? They're old friends after all. Come to think of it, I really should have put them on the guest list some time ago. What's the matter, Felicity? Don't you want one of my exes at our wedding? You're not jealous, are you?'

Oh, he'd like that, I can tell you. A little jealousy always bolsters his self-esteem which is already unwarrantably high.

'She's a stunning girl, isn't she?' He's really stirring now. 'Quite a beauty.'

'If you like that sort of thing,' I murmur nonchalantly, running my finger along the blunt blade of my butter knife. 'I actually thought she seemed a little bit plastic. A bit false. You know: false nails, false eyelashes, false laugh, false smile. It makes you wonder about other parts of her . . .' I indicate my own very real cleavage.

'Oh, I can assure you, *they're* all her own.' Richard smirks. 'I know, I have prior knowledge.'

'Carnal knowledge more like,' I reply glaring at him, angry not because he's provoking me but because he *thinks* he's provoking me.

'Ooh, we are jealous, aren't we!' he crows happily, then adds rather patronisingly, 'Never mind, darling, you've just got to remember that it's you I'm marrying.'

'That's what you think,' I long to shout back at him, but my already wavering courage has gone as cold as my rejected peppered steak and the moment for revelations has therefore passed. I steadily drink my way through another bottle of wine as I wait for Richard to finish the rest of his meal. He always chews his food one hundred times before swallowing. He reminds me of a square-jawed bovine monotonously chewing cud. The waiter has sourly carried away my untouched food with the air of the much maligned. This is such a renowned restaurant it's probably the grossest of insults to leave the majority of your meal on the side of your plate, but I'm so disappointed by my own cowardice that I've completely lost my appetite.

Finally, after pudding, which I didn't have, and coffee, which I should have had considering the amount of wine I managed to consume waiting for Richard to finish eating, he signals for the bill. He hands the waiter his platinum card with a flourish, and then states that he's just going to say goodbye to Katherine and Alex.

I can see him smoothing his very clean brown hair in the large gilt mirror on the far wall as he makes his way through the tables toward them.

As far as I'm concerned Richard is the personification of vanity. He has a major league love affair with mirrors, and spends more time in the bathroom getting ready to go out than I ever do.

I can't deny that he's a very attractive man, as he walks across the room several female heads turn to look, the problem is I find him about as attractive as week-old cottage cheese. What are you doing with the man? I hear you say. How can a girl find herself engaged to someone who, instead of inducing undying love and devotion, simply makes her want to punch his stupid face in?

Well, apart from pointing out that we all make mistakes, what girl hasn't got a few embarrassing exes in her closet, a few photographs she really ought to burn before anyone sees just what she managed to get involved with at one mad moment in her life? All I can say is it hasn't always been this way.

When I first met Richard he really kind of swept me off my feet.

Richard is a barrister.

I'm a teacher.

I'm also a terrible driver.

He represented me when a minor car accident turned into a major lawsuit. By the final court hearing, he'd somehow managed not only to convince the judge that I was the innocent and injured party, but also to convince me that I should promptly fall into bed with him as a jolly good way of expressing my gratitude.

I have to admit he's very impressive in court.

Shame he wasn't so impressive in bed, but at the time I was so swept up by the whole knight-in-shining-armour thing, I was even prepared to overlook the fact that the first time we hit the mattress together he kept on not only his socks but his stupid curly white wig as well. Despite this, and the fact that his come-to-bed line was a pretty crass 'the courts may have found you innocent, but I find you guilty of stealing my heart', which

9

at the time I thought was dreadfully romantic but now makes me cringe with embarrassment, I am ashamed to admit that I was a pretty easy lay.

The ease with which Richard lured me into bed might also have had something to do with the fact that I was always the girl at school who never got the boys. I had plenty of great mates, but definitely no hot dates.

Going to an all girls' school didn't really improve the odds, but considering I left when I was eighteen and at twenty-six Richard was really the first man ever to show more of a permanent interest in me than, say, the odd drink, or a drink with an Indian and a quick grope to follow on a second date if I got lucky, then maybe I couldn't be blamed for thinking that there was something wrong with me (an opinion regularly voiced by my wedding groupie mother), and jumping at the chance of a relationship with someone who on the outside at least seems to have everything a girl wants.

For the first time in my life I was able to bask in the warm glow of maternal approval, an emotion never really radiated by my mother before. Not in my direction anyway.

Her overweight, under-achieving daughter had finally got herself a man. And not just any man, but one who could actually be boasted about to friends and family.

Unfortunately, although Richard seems to have everything a girl wants – looks, charm, wit, success, relatively good taste – none of it has ever really been aimed in my direction. He's the kind of guy who will lead you on to the dance floor and pull you into his arms to smooch to a slow romantic record, then spend the entire song gazing over your shoulder at someone else.

I don't suppose I can put all the blame on him. After all, as they say, it takes two to tango. Maybe I haven't made him as happy as I could have done. Maybe I didn't turn out to be quite the person he thought I was either.

Maybe it's him, maybe it's me. But there are no maybes anymore when it comes to whether we should be together. That, my friends, is a definite no.

He takes half an hour to say his goodbyes. I'm getting crosser and drunker by the minute. You can hear the false tinkling laugh and the false hearty boom simultaneously at regular intervals.

10

Alex Christian is noticeably quiet, although it's hard from where I'm sitting to tell if he's excluded from the conversation by the other two's ignorance, design, or his own choice. Finally Richard returns to our table, smiling like a Cheshire Cat.

'Nice couple, shame we lost touch. Must have them round for dinner sometime.' He picks up their address card, which is sitting by the side of my empty glass, and puts it in the breast pocket of his suit jacket.

I'd love to have Katherine and Alex Christian round for dinner.

I could pot roast her, and eat him.

Eradicating any trace of my own identity, I lie back and think of Richard Gere in a white uniform. He is carrying me into the bedroom, all ten stone of me, without a murmur. He lays me back upon the king-sized bed and admires my magnificent body (cellulite does not exist in celluloid). He bends to kiss me, and his features dim and pale. He becomes the familiar unknown stranger, with the invisible face and the passionate embrace. Is this fantasy figure the someone that I'm searching for? How can I recognise someone with no face? My eyes blink open, the real Richard trembles for a moment above me like a persistent Jack Russell mounting a Red Setter.

He tenses, sighs, and then falls away. He is asleep within seconds, leaving me gasping in frustration like a landed fish. It may be madness to give up something good, but it is utter stupidity to hold on to something bad.

I reach for the glass of wine beside my bed. I don't smoke so I allow myself the vice of drinking too much on occasion. Tonight is one such occasion. I'm trying to build up that wonderful sense of bravado that normally appears after too many glasses. Two shared bottles of excellent Burgundy over dinner, and now halfway down a bottle of Sancerre, I am beginning to feel marvellously brave and liberated again, ready to throw off the shackles of boredom and compliance to convention, and head for freedom.

Richard-free freedom.

I look across at him, vulnerable in sleep. Whereas I used to feel tenderness, now I feel nothing but tedium. Richard is a bad habit I'm determined to break. I reach for my ever-present tardis of a handbag, which is at the side of the bed. I don't have a pen or paper, but I manage with a credit card bill envelope and a dark pink lip liner.

I'm not sure what to write. After rehearsing my speech in my head for weeks my mind has now gone rather blank. The one and only thing in this whole mess that I am totally and utterly sure about is that Richard and I aren't meant to share the rest of our lives together.

I'd made up this wonderful speech about different values and a better future for both of us if we went our separate ways, but that all sounds terribly trite at this particular moment in time. And far too kind.

Like a typical woman I usually take the blame for everything that has gone wrong and apologise profusely for any inconvenience. I'm a nicer person when I'm sober, but at the moment I'm far from sober and ready to ignore completely my own poorer qualities and blame the whole banality of our relationship on him, fair or not.

Richard, you are the weakest link. Goodbye.

The final message is short but satisfyingly sweet. I read it back aloud and snigger to myself, but not too loud, I don't want to wake sleeping boorish. Getting quietly from the bed, I pad across the shag-pile carpet on my size five feet. Richard's bedroom is opulent yet impersonal, dominated by the king-sized oval bed which sits in the centre of the room on the sort of dais you expect to see a pair of thrones mounted upon.

I've always been surprised that he doesn't have a mirrored ceiling. He's a mirrored-ceiling sort of person. He can't walk past a shop window without having a look at his own reflection and smiling smugly, although he is also pretty orgasm-driven. I suppose having to stop every five seconds to gaze at his perfectly honed body in the mirrors above would put him off his stroke a bit too much.

A door pretending to be a cupboard door actually leads to a white en suite bathroom with a white-tiled floor and gold fittings. It's very sparse. Safari for Men sits upon the glass shelf below the large bathroom mirror in various guises: aftershave, deodorant, body lotion, shower gel. These bottles and several thick white towels are the only proof of human existence within the room. There are no hairs blocking the plughole in the sink, no empty loo roll holders floating around the floor, no abandoned underwear bundled in a corner. The toilet seat lid is down, and the towels are folded neatly on the heated rail.

I splash cold water on my face, squirt my armpits with Richard's aftershave, and rub a finger laced with toothpaste across my front teeth, then purely for the hell of it wipe my still plum-coloured lips – Richard rarely kisses – across the snow white of a virgin towel, a long red glare, the despoiled virgin now.

I have been seeing Richard this long yet there are still none of my possessions in his flat. Sorry, *penthouse apartment*. He's never actually banned me from bringing my own touch to the place, but he's never verbally invited it either. I know most people wouldn't worry about being asked and would make sure they had at least enough stuff in situ for convenience and comfort, but for some reason I never have brought anything over. Not even a toothbrush. I go back into the bedroom and pull on my clothes. As I sit down on the bed to put on my shoes, Richard, disturbed in sleep, rolls over, pulling all of the duvet on to his side of the bed with an iron grip, and farts noisily.

It's gone three in the morning. The streets of Oxford are practically deserted. The Indian taxi driver plays Bangra music all the way back to my place. My head throbs in time with the frenetic bass beat. The cab smells of stale sweat and cigarette smoke. Every time we round a corner an abandoned lager can rolls across my feet, spilling dregs and ash. I live just on the outskirts of Oxford in what used to be a village but has now been swallowed up by urban sprawl – a small fish living in the belly of a whale. My flat, my home, is the total antithesis of Richard's apartment; it is small yet very personal. The place is a mess. I don't really like it that way, but after twenty-eight years of an oppressive mother-dominated life, untidiness is an easy way to assert one's own independence.

Feeling guilty but liberated, I ignore my usual ritual of showering and religiously removing make-up, and collapse on to my bed fully clothed, eating a cold Mars Bar straight from the fridge. For some reason I'm always ravenous when I'm pissed.

I know I shall wake up in the morning looking like a panda with my mascara, my plum eye-shadow and black eyeliner streaked around my bloodshot eyes, but for once I don't care. Sod the regime of trying to retain my looks for the sake of my love life and future, hopefully wrinkle-free, happiness – what I have of looks anyway.

Some kind soul once said to my mother, 'Fliss could never be called pretty, but there are moments when she looks beautiful.'

Isn't it funny how some comments, no matter how carelessly voiced in the first instance, can stick with you for a lifetime?

I've tried to capture one of these rare moments when I'm not looking pretty but could be described as beautiful, and re-create it at will, but it never works. You think I'd have had more luck recently what with all the pampering I've been subjecting myself to in preparation for the 'Big Event'. All of the manicures, the cathiodermie, the anti-cellulite massages, the increasingly more intimate waxing, the pedicures, the sea-weed wraps, the agony that is tweezing . . . hell, my mother even tried to persuade me to go for a course of Botox injections a couple of weeks ago, although I suppose I was lucky she didn't suggest full-blown plastic surgery.

She has been training me – well, attempting to train me more like – for the one moment when every girl is expected to look radiant, her wedding day – *my* wedding day – since birth. It was her idea to call me Felicity, a girly name if ever I heard one. It doesn't really suit me, I'm not a girly girl.

I think this is probably one of the main reasons why we've never really got along.

She wanted a little doll she could dress in pink, with curls and an angelic smile. Someone she could show off, and be dreadfully proud of, and take to ballet lessons.

Instead she got an ungainly tomboy who sprouted faster than an undetected garden weed in the best spot in the garden, lived in jeans, was occasionally mistaken for a boy in her younger, more androgynous years, and was happy to motor along at an average scholastic level instead of attaining the heights her mother dreamed of.

A tomboy who rebelled at just the thought of pink, organza or gingham, singing lessons, piano lessons, deportment, and practically everything else that Mother thought the right ingredients for a proper girly childhood.

For quite a long time I wished fervently that I'd been born a boy so that I could go fishing, or get up to my armpits in mud in the garden with my father – his two favourite pastimes – without incurring any maternal wrath. Then at about fourteen I

14

discovered boys in the form of a very uncontrolled crush on Bono from U2, and was suddenly very glad that I was a girl.

My mother is one of those women who just missed the sexual revolution. She was brought up in an era when women were expected to finish school then marry. That was it, no career, no choice, and no particular say in the future of the one life you had been given. It was drummed into her from a very young age – although I don't think she ever quite believed it enough, hence the resentment – that women were only good for one thing.

Marriage.

Well, most women anyway. I'm a different story.

My mother has always despaired of ever getting rid of me.

Unlike my younger sister, Sally-Anne, who is pretty, delicate and feminine in every way, and has had a string of male admirers since first learning to flutter her long black eyelashes at the tender age of three, I am slightly too tall to be fashionable, totally addicted to chocolate which I store in my fridge and on my hips, totally devoid of that wonderful gift feminine guile, and according to my mother a hopeless case.

That's why she loves Richard so much. It's like entering your daughter in a beauty contest expecting her to come in a dismal last, and then finding out she's actually won first prize. That first prize being Richard Trevelyan.

When I met him my mother couldn't believe her luck. He has everything she thinks a man should have. She loves him, my younger sister Sally loves him, my wonderfully sensible father thinks he's an arsehole but since when has Dad's opinion ever been taken into account? I think my mother would marry Richard herself if she could.

I can't believe I ever thought I would marry him. Full white wedding, the works, done up like a raspberry Pavlova in some wonderful creation my mother picked. It's hanging there now, there on the back of my door, mocking me like the ghost of Miss Havisham from *Great Expectations*.

Not that I ever had any Great Expectations about life with Richard. He is the easy option, the sensible choice, but what about happiness, that ecstatic sense of euphoria you should feel when you're about to marry the man you love? The Mills & Boon factor? The beating hearts, the bursting bodices? I'm afraid it's just not there.

15

When I think of Richard, I don't feel the urge to write poetry or move mountains, I don't want to bear his children, I don't even want to launder his dirty underwear – a true test of love.

When I look at Richard, I don't want to cover his face in kisses, I don't want to throw him on the floor and rip off all of his clothes. In fact, what I really want to do is wipe the ever-present smug-git smile off his face with my fist.

Not surprisingly, I've come to the conclusion that I don't love him.

The only sense of euphoria I have felt in a long time is when I look at that dress and finally realise I won't have to wear the bloody thing after all.

Just the sight of it used to fill me with foreboding. Sad, isn't it? A wedding is something one normally looks forward to, especially one's own. What was I doing agreeing to marry the man, I hear you ask, if just the thought of him breathing makes me want to punch his lights out?

I think part of it is my sense of self-esteem, or rather lack of it. I'd actually begun to believe that nobody would ever want me, my mother had drummed it into me for so long. So when Richard proposed – eligible, successful, short, dark and handsome – I grabbed the opportunity with both hands, and when you want so very much to be in love, it's so very easy to convince yourself that you are.

And why the change of heart now? Self-preservation has a lot to do with it. I'm like my little village being swallowed up by the whale of the town, losing its own individuality, or the steak being smothered by pepper sauce, congealing and covering, taking away its own identity. Only somebody threw me a life belt and hauled me to shore.

That somebody is Caro.

I'm a teacher at the local girls high school. I've been there for about four years now, tutoring, or should I call it torturing, a reluctant upper-fifth through their English GCSEs. Caro is the new drama teacher.

She is also a very old friend, last seen before our recent reunion as a skinny horse-mad eleven year old. I lost touch with her when her father, who's something rather splendid in the diplomatic corps, took a posting to Hong Kong. She is four years older than me, and used to boss me around dreadfully, but I adored her with a reverent passion, and cried for weeks when she left. Things haven't changed very much since our childhood, only now she is not so much bossy as emboldening.

Since her return into my life Caro has given me a new outlook on life. She is now very happily married herself to a wonderful man called David who farms some beautiful land just on the border of the Chilterns. He is fifteen years older than Caroline. Together they have two teenagers from his previous marriage, one dog, a flock of geese in their back garden, and the most wonderfully idyllic partnership you could ever imagine. I have other friends who seem to be happily married, but Caro and David just have that extra something.

They are the best of friends. They tease, they talk, they complement each other – two very different people. Caro is outgoing, vivacious, artistic; David – solid and reliable yet sensitive and imaginative – a rare breed of man. They go together like pepper and salt. Just seeing them together made me realise I want more.

I want someone who will sit up with me until dawn discussing shared passions; someone who will cook an amazing dinner for his wife and her friend, and then sod off without enjoying any of it so that they have some privacy to talk; someone who will dance with me in the moonlight.

The last time I stayed with Caro and David it was a hot balmy summer's night, the sort where you throw off your duvet at midnight and lie with the window wide open, just letting the softest of breezes caress your naked body, and listening to the gentle sounds of the night.

Well, that night the gentle sounds of the night were rudely but pleasantly interrupted by the sound of Sarah Vaughan playing on an old gramophone. When, enticed by the music, I padded barefoot across the polished floorboards and leaned out of the window, there they were, in each other's arms, dancing in the orchard, illuminated by the light through the open French doors like a spotlight on the star couple in *Come Dancing*.

David was stroking Caro's golden hair with one hand while his other hand rested gently but firmly on her backside. I could hear him singing 'Misty' to her, along with the record. The orchard was raining blossom on their heads like confetti at a wedding.

Corny? Maybe.

Appealing? Definitely.

It was at that moment I made my decision. I want someone who'll dance with me at midnight to old songs, who'll sing sweet words to me, who'll treat me like a friend and a lover, the most precious object in their world. Am I asking too much? Perhaps, but I know now that Richard and I don't have that, and that I'm worth more. More anyway than a no-hope relationship with someone whose idea of a balanced relationship is ninety-nine per cent to one.

Now I've made my decision, it's as though a whole hundredweight has been lifted from my shoulders. My mother always nags me not to stoop – I'm used to compensating for Richard's lack of inches – but I'm sure it was the weight of all my worries that made my shoulders bow. Do I stand taller now? I get up rather unsteadily from the bed and, stripping, stand naked in front of my full-length mirror, the one that swivels when you don't want it to and almost concussed Sally when she posed in front of it in her pink bridesmaid's dress.

Pink – yuk! I don't even like pink.

I throw back my shoulders and my head. My long brown hair falls against my shoulder blades. My skin looks darker in the lamplight. Brown hair, brown eyes, brown skin . . . universally brown, like a gypsy. Slightly overweight but not unattractive: full boobs, plump arse, long legs. Not bad at all, I decide, pissed and in a low light.

I draw myself up, inducing the mirror to reflect not only myself but my new resolve.

Yes, I'm sure I'm a full inch taller now. I shall walk tall when I meet Mother tomorrow. I shall look her straight in her ice-blue eyes and tell her that the wedding is off. She will see a new Fliss, a strong Fliss, a Fliss who knows what she wants and grabs it with both hands, a Fliss who doesn't give a damn whether her mother approves of what she does . . . a Fliss who is kidding herself and is at this very moment contemplating a quick hike back to Richard's place to retrieve the hastily scribbled missive that will rocket her life on to a very different course.

The wonderful drunken abandon is beginning to wear off, and a horrible feeling of panic starts to set in. I'm torn between hiding away in sleep or opening another bottle of wine. Oh, sod it, I won't be able to sleep now anyway. I head for the kitchen, and open a bottle of rather nice Australian Shiraz that I'd been saving for a special occasion.

Hastings the cat (so named because life with her is one long battle of wills), who is already disgusted that I got in late and could only offer a week-old tin of pilchards in tomato sauce for dinner, looks at me out of the corner of one sleepy green eye.

If she had eyebrows she'd raise them to heaven. If she had a voice, she'd chide 'drunk again'. Instead, disturbed from her resting place between the wine rack and the toaster, she stalks off and takes revenge by throwing up said pilchards in my slippers, and then wiping her face on my bed linen.

Chapter Two

I'm woken at seven-thirty by the sound of the telephone. There is only one person who would call me this early on a Saturday morning. One person who, instead of his usual Saturday morning ritual of a hot breakfast and lukewarm sex, has found an empty bed.

'Fliss, is that you?'

I have a throbbing head, a raging hangover, cat sick in my hair, and a very vague recollection that I've done something outrageous.

'No, it's the Chinese laundry.'

I cringe as I pull the offending section of my hair well away from my face and, clutching the hands-free to the relatively clean side of my head, stagger into the bathroom.

'Don't be flip.' He sounds annoyed. 'What on earth's going on?'

'Well, I was asleep, how about you?'

'Felicity!'

Ooh, my full name, now I know he's annoyed.

'What the hell's going on? Why aren't you here, and what on earth is the meaning of this note?'

Note? *Oh, yes*. My memory wakes up five minutes after the rest of my brain. I left a note, didn't I? I remember that much, but I can't for the life of me remember what exactly I wrote, or to be more precise what exactly the two bottles of excellent Burgundy wrote for me.

Sticking the left side of my head under the shower nozzle, I begin to babble.

'Note? Well, yes, er . . . I know, I'm a coward leaving a note, but somehow I'm much more eloquent when I write things down . . . hang on a mo', just swapping over.'

I clamp the phone to my other ear and begin to wash the side of my head.

21

'Felicity!' Richard roars as the line goes quiet for a moment.

'Sorry, all done now . . . what was I saying? Oh, yes . . . well, yes . . . as I was saying . . . I actually look at a person, and try to say something important, and my mind goes a complete blank. All of those well-rehearsed speeches leg it like manic lemmings over the cliff edge of my mind . . .'

'I'd hardly call this eloquent,' he snaps. 'Stop talking nonsense. I asked you a question, and I want an answer. What exactly is the meaning of this note?'

His annoyance is turning to anger, I can hear the tone of his voice getting harder.

'Well, I think it's pretty self-explanatory, don't you?' I offer lamely, hazily aware of the contents but still unable to recall the exact wording.

'Felicity!' His voice rises an octave in indignation. 'I demand to know what is the meaning of this note?'

He's like a persistently annoying parrot that can only speak one sentence.

I think hard. Oh, yes, it's coming back to me now. My hangover-befuddled mind suddenly stops shrouding me in ignorance, and flashes last night's missive across my mind in big red neon letters.

I'm quite surprised at myself actually.

Did I really write that?

I'm also rather surprised to find that instead of being horrified, I'm more than a little pleased with myself.

'Felicity!' He's roaring down the line now, like a large unfed feline. I'm sure if it were possible he would put his hands down the receiver and either shake or throttle me.

'Well, Richard,' I begin, speaking very slowly so that he can fully understand me as I have no intention of repeating the next line, and so that I can control the tremor in my voice. 'Roughly translated I should say it means "Piss off, you boring little fart".'

'That is what it *says*!' he shouts. 'I'm asking you what it *means*.'

I waiver for a moment, but the moment's very brief.

It's now or never, the point of no return. I take a deep breath.

'It means that we're through, Richard, kaput, finito, end of story, finished. Is that clear enough for you?'

'What?'

'I've had enough, I don't want to marry you.'

22

I'm getting to the point now, thank goodness, it's taken me long enough.

'What?' he repeats incredulously.

'The wedding's off. I'm not going to marry you. The whole thing is bloody well cancelled . . .'

Thank heavens for the telephone, I'm sure I wouldn't be this direct in person.

'This is utter madness. You're ill, aren't you?' he cuts in. 'That must be it. I'm coming round.'

'No! I don't think that's such a good idea . . .' I begin to protest, knowing a face-to-face onslaught to be beyond my capabilities at the moment. But it's too late, I'm talking to the buzz of a hung-up receiver.

Richard's coming round!

Help!

I run round the flat in a panic, like a wasp trapped inside a lemonade bottle. As you know, last night's raging bravado has been replaced by this morning's raging hangover, which is not exactly conducive to rational thinking.

I can't face Richard.

If I could have faced dumping Richard, I wouldn't have left a bloody note, I'd have done it to his face, and achieved great satisfaction in seeing the smug expression actually slip for a moment.

I grab the phone and dial Caro's number. She will reassure me, tell me that I've done the right thing, and then hopefully tell me what to do now. And then I remember that she has made the most of the early end of drama lessons due to end-of-term exams, and sodded off to the South of France.

Perhaps that's what I should do. Perhaps I should just go away for a while, until everything cools down. Outer Mongolia is supposed to be nice at this time of year. How long will it take me to pack?

He arrives after I've had twenty minutes of sheer panic. In this time I have packed and unpacked a suitcase twice. Decided to make a run for it twice, and to stay and fight it out twice. I'm currently on the stay and fight it out phase, but my courage falters alarmingly when I see Richard pull up outside.

Never one to fight solo, he has summoned the troops. To my utter horror I see that his large iron grey BMW is full to capacity.

My mother glowers in the front seat, like a small malevolent bird, her feathers well and truly ruffled. My sister, who as an *EastEnders* addict has always enjoyed a good melodrama, sits behind Richard, her cheeks flushed in excited and concerned agitation.

Even poor Dad has been dragged away from the breakfast table. He's still wearing his tartan slippers. I half expect to see Roger, Dad's fat but eager black Labrador, leering at me out of the window.

I watch their arrival from the sitting-room window of my flat. I can't believe Richard brought them with him. I also can't believe how petrified I am to see my mother. It's a sad feeling to know that I'm twenty-eight, that I left home nine years ago, and yet I'm still scared of her. I'm very tempted not to let them in. I could pretend to be out. I could attempt an escape via the hazardous wrought-iron fire stairs that lead out into the back garden, and sanctuary beyond.

Alternatively I could just pretend to be out.

I decide this is by far the best option and scurry to the rear of the flat to hide out in my bedroom.

After leaning on the main building door buzzer for five minutes, Richard remembers he's got a key and lets himself in. I hear them ascending the wooden staircase towards the first floor, like an advancing militia, each crack of shoe on oak floorboard like a rifle shot to my poor aching head.

I decide to make a run for it for the third time.

Sprinting fast enough to outstrip several Olympic hopefuls, I dash over to one of the bedroom windows and tug desperately at the painted lock of the sash, a stubborn obstacle between me and the fire escape and freedom.

They've reached the front door now. I can hear them struggling with the stiff lock. If only I'd thought to put the latch on, but then that would have made it obvious I was here although I've been pretending not to be.

The front door surrenders and in full flight, the ominous descent of the circling vulture, Mother marches into the flat calling my name in a harsh contralto voice that holds more than a hint of Margaret Thatcher and now an equal amount of menace. At last the window sash releases.

As Richard and company troop into the bedroom, I greet them with a weak smile, precariously balanced astride the window ledge. I've got a pink trainer on my left foot, a slipper

24

that looks uncannily like Jimi Hendrix smoking a cigar on the other, I'm still wearing my dressing gown, which is gaping most revealingly, and I'm not wearing any knickers. Jimi Hendrix parts company with my foot and, plummeting earthward, lands upside down in a puddle of dirty water in the rain-sodden garden below. I watch him fall with a sinking feeling that I might follow shortly as Mother looks at me with murder in her eyes. Her acid glare says more than a thousand abusive words ever could.

It's a long session.

Richard is patronising and totally disbelieving.

Sally is tearful, tender-hearted and totally disbelieving, torn between a desire to comfort me, and what appears to be a slightly stronger desire to comfort Richard, who is acting every bit the severely injured party.

Mother is initially gob-smacked and speechless, which is a definite first, and Dad's surreptitiously watching the Wimbledon highlights on the portable in the kitchen while making us an umpteenth cup of tea.

For some reason my mother has got hold of the offending note and has it balled and crumpled in her left fist, which is clenched as though ready to swing.

I'm trying very hard to convince them all that this is not a moment of temporary insanity, and that I really don't want to marry Richard, but at least two members of my family, and of course Richard himself, are finding this very difficult to come to terms with.

I should have known that Mother and Sally would take his side in this. Richard has insinuated himself into their affections with the ease of a tapeworm into an intestine, and now feeds off of their mutual admiration. Mother, who unfortunately regained her power of speech at a disappointingly speedy rate, is banging on about calling a doctor because I'm obviously suffering from a bout of temporary insanity, so I turn to Sally-Anne who will hopefully be slightly more receptive.

'Honestly, Sal, you've got to believe me, I really don't want to get married.' I plead with her to grasp what appears to be an ungraspable concept.

'But why ever not?' Her fine eyebrows are arched like question marks on her smooth pale forehead.

'Well, to be perfectly blunt, I don't love Richard.'

'But why ever not?'

'Well . . .' I'm trying to be polite here. 'I just don't think we're compatible.'

'But why ever not?'

She's starting to annoy me now.

'Do you want a list?' I snap.

Sally sees the manic glint in my eyes, and beats a hasty retreat.

'Er, I think I'll give Dad a hand with the tea.' She escapes to the kitchen.

This leaves me, Mother and Richard.

Whose turn is it next?

They both decide to speak at once.

'Well, I think this is absolutely insane!' they blurt out at the same time.

How clever, synchronised barracking, they are word for word in perfect harmony. They even have the same mixed expression of mingled disbelief and annoyance on their faces. Now I know why I can't marry Richard: he reminds me of my mother. That's probably why she likes him so much, he's a mini Miriam Blakeney. Where she left off dominating my life, and making it a general misery, he will take over.

My resolve deepens. As Dad and Sally come back into the room bearing tea and biscuits, I take a deep breath and make my stand.

'Look, I really am sorry. I know I'm causing a lot of upset and inconvenience. You've all worked so hard on the wedding plans and everything, but I really do think it would be a big mistake for both of us to go ahead with it.'

Dad puts the tray down on the coffee table, and lays a reassuring hand on my shoulder.

'It's all right, darling, we understand.'

'No, we do not!' storms Mother. 'We do *not* understand at all! The wedding is in seven weeks' time, you can't call it all off now. I really can't believe you're even contemplating such stupidity!'

'But I don't want to get married,' I repeat for the hundredth time. 'Surely the stupidity would be to go through with it, when I really don't want to?'

'But why ever not?' says Sally again.

26

Honestly, as much as I love my sweet-natured little sister, I'll swing for her if she doesn't change the record.

'Because, I'm sorry, but I'm not in love with the man I'm supposed to be marrying.'

'Don't be preposterous,' says Richard, as though not to be in love with him is an inconceivable idea.

I try to explain.

'There's no passion, no poetry, no romance.'

'There's more to marriage than *romance*, my girl,' Mother says contemptuously.

'Mother's right,' says Sally, smiling far too brightly, first at me and then at Richard.

'I know that, I'm not totally stupid, but . . .'

'Well, I find *that* hard to believe at this moment,' snorts my mother.

I choose to ignore this particular barb, and turning to Richard himself plough on regardless.

'Look, I'm sorry, Richard. If it was just a case of missing romance, perhaps I could have carried on, but there are so many other things missing as well.'

'Such as?' he asks indignantly, completely unaware of any personal shortcomings.

'Well . . .' I look down at his crotch, home to exhibit 'A', and then look at my mother, who is sourly crunching one of my chocolate digestives like it could poison her.

This is ridiculous.

'Look, do we have to do this in front of an audience? Honestly, I can't believe you actually brought them here with you.'

'Quite right, quite right,' says Dad in relief, and hauls his long frame from the sofa. 'I think we should go and leave them to it, don't you?'

As he heads for the door, I decide the last thing I want is to be alone with Richard, and wish I'd kept my mouth shut. But there's no need to worry, Mother has absolutely no intention of leaving.

'Sit down, Drew, Richard wanted us to be here.'

She manages simultaneously to smile encouragingly at Richard, and scowl at me.

Dad sits down.

'Look, I really am sorry,' I say for the hundredth time,

'honestly I am, but isn't it better for me to realise now rather than six months into married life? I know is seems appalling of me but it's the right thing to do, really it is.'

Richard has tried indignation and anger already. He adopts a different tactic.

'Well, really, Felicity, I just don't understand,' he purrs, using the little-boy-lost look he adopts to charm clients, hoary old judges and indecisive juries. The look he used to first charm me into bed, gazing up at me with big brown eyes from under thick black lashes. It used to make my knees, and various other parts of my anatomy, melt. Now it just annoys the hell out of me.

'Neither do I, *neither* do I,' agrees Mother vehemently. 'Take a look at what you're throwing away, my girl, take a good long look, and then you tell me why you think you're doing the right thing!'

'I don't respect you, Richard. How can I marry someone I don't respect?'

'But he's a barrister,' says Mother as if this fact alone commands that missing factor instantly, and then as I shake my head in disbelief, 'My goodness, girl, what's wrong with you? Don't you realise what you're throwing away?' She's beginning to sound hysterical. 'Richard is a brilliant, wonderful, talented man. He's also a perfect gentleman. You obviously don't know how lucky you are to have found him.'

Sally nods in agreement. I've had enough.

'And he's a perfect wimp! The perfect gentleman is able to fight his own battles, not come in hiding behind the skirts of his future mother-in-law. Sorry, former future mother-in-law.'

'How dare you speak to me like that?' she storms, turning an ugly puce. I flinch away from the murderous impulse in her eyes.

Rescue comes from a very unexpected quarter.

'It's all right, Miriam.' To my surprise, Richard, who has so far been stuck fast to my sofa as if by Superglue, gets to his feet. 'Thank you for defending me, but I think Felicity has made her feelings perfectly obvious. The futility of continuing this conversation is blatantly clear.'

I gape at him in surprise.

That must be the fastest U-turn in history!

He is oddly dignified, and I catch a glimpse of the man I thought he was when I first met him. He holds out a hand.

'I can respect Felicity's decision even if I cannot for one moment understand it. Goodbye, Felicity.'

I take it meekly. His grip is firm, his hand is warm, his gaze is steady. For a second I wonder if I'm doing the right thing, but then he reverts to true Richard form.

'Just don't expect to come crawling back when you realise what a horrendous mistake you've made.'

He strides towards the door. I'm finally seeing the back of him in every sense of the word, and can't resist throwing a very childish yet ecstatically liberated V-sign after him. With a look of pure disgust, my mother, closely followed by Sally, rushes after him.

'Well . . .' I look sideways, at Dad, seeking approval I suppose from the one person whose opinion really matters, because he is the one person whose opinion will be based on concern for my welfare, and completely unbiased towards his own personal preferences.

He raises bushy eyebrows at me.

'What have you done, Fliss?' He doesn't sound reproachful.

'Something I should have done a long time ago,' I reply, and am relieved to see a wide smile spread across my father's face.

'As long as you're happy, eh? Never did like the man much anyway.' He envelops me in a long-armed hug, drops an affectionate kiss on the top of my head, and then, with an almost imperceptible wink, follows after my mother (who I can hear clattering wildly down the stairs calling Richard's name), muttering 'boring little fart' and chuckling to himself.

God bless my father.

Richard departs rapidly, expressing his indignation by loudly squealing his tyres all the way up the avenue. Although he brought my family here, he obviously has no intention of taking them away again.

I almost expected Mother to throw herself on the bonnet of his car when he drove off without her. Instead, Dad comes back in to call a taxi. Mother refuses to let me drive them home, and won't come back up to the flat. She doesn't wish to speak to me at the moment. I can see her glaring angrily up at my window. As she waits for the taxi to arrive it begins to rain. No doubt I shall take the blame for that as well.

The flat seems strangely quiet after they've gone. Sort of like the moment after a party when the last guest has just left, and you don't know whether to start clearing up the mess or go to bed. I certainly don't feel like clearing up the mess I've just apparently made of my life (according to Mother) so I concentrate on the tangible mess in the mirror, and run a bath.

I usually sing in the bath, an embarrassing thing to do, I know, particularly as I have a voice like an asthmatic cow being battered to death by the digger section of a JCB. Today I'm as quiet as a mouse. I feel sort of drained, empty. I try to concentrate on my exciting new future, and then realise I spent so long planning the end of the old life, I haven't even contemplated the new. I suppose if I'm honest with myself, I never thought I'd have the guts to go through with it.

The phone is ringing. I haul myself out of my bath, chocolate foam bubbles sliding soapily down my wet body, and slip out to the hall.

I stand and look at the telephone for a moment, hand out to pick it up. I'm not sure if I want to answer it. It could be Richard or worse still my mother – then the doorbell begins to ring. I take the lesser of two evils and force myself to pick up the phone. To my surprise it's Sally.

'Hi, Fliss.' She's almost whispering. 'Look, I'm really sorry about earlier. I just wanted to say I think you've done the right thing, you and Richard were never suited. Don't worry about Mum, she'll get over it.'

'Oh, Sal, I'm so glad you said that,' I sigh in relief. 'You really think I've done the right thing?'

'Absolutely,' she replies firmly. 'In fact, the more I think about it, the more I realise that what's happened is definitely for the best.'

'You wouldn't believe how much better it makes me feel to hear you say that, Sal. I thought I'd lost one of my biggest allies . . .'

'Don't be silly, I'll always be there for you, Fliss, you know that. No matter what . . .'

I'm so relieved, I open the door without thinking, and give the milkman a big surprise. He takes in my wet naked soapy form, and a huge grin spreads from ear to ear over his weathered old face.

'That'll be £4.20, please, darlin',' he cackles. 'Cash'll do, I'm getting a bit too old for payment in kind.'

30

★ ★ ★

Come Monday I'm back at school for the last week of the summer term. It drags by. Despite the fact that we finish on Thursday, it feels like I've been in that school for four years, not just four days. My news quickly spreads around the staff room, but fortunately and unusually not around the girls themselves. My closest colleagues are not surprised that Richard and I have split up. Reaction to the news differs. Some think I'm totally mad, others very sane, but all, whatever their opinion, remain commendably discreet.

My two closest friends apart from Caroline, who never rated Richard at all and never made any particular effort to hide this fact, are also united in their opinion.

Wiggy (Wilhelmina – she hated her parents for that one) the Wanderer, a compulsive backpacker, sends me a congratulations card from Australia which when I open it sings 'I believe in Miracles' at me over and over again. 'So glad you've finally seen the light' is scrawled across the inside in her large bold hand-writing.

Sensible Sasha leaves me a message on my answer machine.

'Fliss, it's Sash. I've heard a funny rumour on the old girls' grapevine that you've finally seen sense and ditched the vile Trevelyan. Give me a call and let me know if it's true, I don't want to waste an expensive bottle of champagne celebrating something that might not have happened. If it is true then well done. And call me, you old tart, so I can talk a bit more sense into you before you get the chance to change your mind.'

I always knew Wiggy wasn't that enamoured of my ex-fiancé, but I'd believed Sasha liked Richard which was why I hadn't already called her to break the news of my broken engagement.

If I'd known he wasn't as high as I'd thought in her ratings, I might just have been bold enough to make my escape a little sooner. It's great to know there's one less person who'll hate me for what I've done. Isn't it sad how many restrictions you put on yourself when you fear the wrath of others?

In fact, thinking about it, there are only two people at the moment who are still very anti-me: Richard, of course, who has quite typically announced to the world that he dumped me rather than the other way round, and my mother.

While I've tried very hard to push Richard to the back of my

31

mind, telling myself that my life is now a Richard-free zone, it's harder to ignore the fact that my own mother is still refusing to speak to me.

I've tried being conciliatory, but it's hard when the person you want to be conciliatory to refuses to acknowledge your existence. My mother is the Pope and I have been excommunicated.

As Henry VIII would have been the first to point out, this does have its advantages, like total autonomy in his case, and in my case the freedom to do whatever I want without fear of reprisal or in-your-face disapproval.

I, however, am fairly realistic in recognising that it's not an ideal state of affairs, and have offered a tentative olive branch on several occasions only for it to be whittled by the sharpness of her rebuff into an olive *arrow* to be fired straight back at me.

Still, the fact that no one can say I haven't tried does a lot to ease my conscience on this score, and I have therefore been pretty much able to concentrate on getting through the last week of school.

On the very last day of term, congratulating myself on what I feel has been fairly smooth progress through what could have been quite a bumpy week, I prepare to make a swift and silent exit from the huge old Victorian house which makes up the main body of the school. Unfortunately, as I am attempting to sidle out of my classroom, heading for the car park with a box of papers, I am accosted by a deputation of smiling fifteen and sixteen year olds. My girls, Upper Five B, have bought me a wedding present, carefully wrapped in ribbons and presented with a well-rehearsed speech about having to remember to call me Mrs Trevelyan when we reconvene for the autumn term.

I could die.

They are insistent that I open their gift straight away, they want to see my face and share my pleasure. Unfortunately my face is currently expressing a rather different emotion. I think the word horror is more apt. I open my mouth to explain but Mrs Monkton the headmistress, who is witness to the occasion, shakes her head so I just mumble a tearful 'thank you'.

They observe my choked expression, and thankfully decide it's because I'm touched and overwhelmed by their kindness. Full of the joy of giving, and of finally reaching the summer holidays, they depart with much banter and backward calls of good luck, voices heavy with insinuation, shouting laughing comments about honeymoons and the three S's one should enjoy on a really good one.

Still Single, Sorry.

Mrs Monkton and I are left alone in the classroom.

She is a little queen bee of a woman, with steely grey hair, matching eyes, and personality. But she is kind and wise. She puts a small, wizened hand on my arm, a conspicuous display of affection on her part.

'Now is not the time for explanations, Felicity,' she says quietly. 'We have reached the summer holidays so relax and enjoy the break, see if you can get away for a while. Come autumn everything will seem so much better. The start of a new term – out with the old, in with the new.' She smiles encouragingly at me.

Out in the car park that borders the hockey field, where a few determined, disciplined individuals are still at practice, the sun is spreading weak warm fingers through a spattering of mashed potato cloud in the pale blue sky.

I load the box full of papers and books I'll need over the summer holidays to set the next term's work into the boot of my car. As I climb in and grip the steering wheel to stop my hands from shaking, the sun catches the stones embedded in the platinum band on my wedding finger and I realise I'm still wearing my engagement ring.

The Beeches, Clayton Avenue, is an old and sturdy house built in the reign of the old and similarly sturdy Queen Victoria. I was born here, twenty-eight years ago – a painful birth that lasted a phenomenal three days according to my mother. She has since made me pay for that pain threefold. We've never got on, and after I so thoughtlessly and callously rejected Richard, her far from quiet dissatisfaction with the way I have led my life so far, rebelling, against everything she values, has turned to vengeful hatred. It has taken me all weekend to pluck up the courage to come round. I'm supposed to have left for Caroline's an hour ago, but I haven't even packed yet. I know if I don't do this now, I'll lose my nerve and never will.

I knock timidly on the warped and peeling wood of the front door. Fortunately, as I'd hoped, Sally-Anne has got the day off to Mother sit. I see the heavy lace curtains lift as she looks out of the front window, then hurries to let me in.

33

'Is she in?' I whisper quite unnecessarily.

My mother is always in at this time of day. She has never worked, although she has run an ordered and immaculate household with the efficiency of a military sergeant. My father, who started his career in the RAF, took early retirement from a civil engineering job two years ago. They don't have much of a social life. Well, not with each other anyway. Dad is rarely in the house. He still has his gardening and his fishing and the odd weekend away playing golf, and Roger seems to get taken on an awful lot of exceptionally long hikes in the country. Mother has the local branch of the Women's Institute where she is the most efficient secretary Oxfordshire has ever seen.

Sally puts a finger to her lips, and points upstairs. Since the previous Saturday afternoon Mother has been threatening us with a nervous breakdown, and has taken to her bed like Jane Austen's Mrs Bennet, refusing to come downstairs, taking all of her meals on a tray, and generally berating life and decrying me.

Sally squeezes my hand, an affectionate, much-appreciated gesture.

'Come into the sitting-room,' she says in hushed tones. 'It's best if we don't disturb her, she's still in the most awful mood.'

We go through to the sitting-room. It's ominously quiet except for the ticking of the grandmother clock in the alcove by the door. Going into my parents' house is like stepping back a century or so. The house has been in my father's family since the first stone was laid over one hundred years ago. I sit down on the 1950s chintz sofa, which is the most modern item in the room. Sally, who has been making afternoon tea, pours into bone china cups so thin they're almost transparent.

'I've just called round to let you know I'm going away for a while,' I tell her, accepting a steaming cup gratefully. 'Caro's back, she called me earlier and asked me to go and stay so I'm going down to Angels Court for a few weeks. Give everything and everybody a chance to settle down, get back to normal.'

'What's your definition of normal?' Sally laughs wryly.

'Mother being just plain horrible to me, rather than completely and utterly obnoxious,' I say sarcastically. 'Then again I could quite happily get used to her not speaking to me, as long as I know it's going to last.'

Sally looks fearfully above her head as though Mother could be listening in at this very moment.

34

Putting my teacup down on the coffee table, I delve into my handbag and locate a small black leather box. I hold it out towards Sally-Anne.

'I need a favour, Sal. I'll understand if you say no, but you'd really be helping me out.'

I pause but she merely smiles at me encouragingly.

'Would you give this back to Richard for me . . . please?' I falter. 'I can't face him at the moment – not that I think he'd want to see me anyway. He was absolutely furious, wasn't he?'

'He wasn't too happy, no, but he seems all right now,' Sally murmurs, taking the box. Opening it she removes the ring and holds it in the palm of her hand.

'You've seen him?' I ask in surprise.

'Mmm,' she nods, casually sliding the ring on to her finger, watching the diamonds catch the light that filters like a kaleido-scope through the lace curtains. 'He came round last night.'

He came round?

'What on earth was Richard doing here?'

'I think he wanted someone to talk to.'

Sally looks back at me, smiles in a slightly embarrassed fashion, and slips the ring from her finger. She puts it back in the little leather box which snaps shut with a sharp crack.

'About what?'

'Well, about what happened, of course,' Sally replies, raising her eyebrows at me, 'amongst other things . . .'

She is obviously surprised by the fact that *I'm* surprised Richard felt the need for a heart to heart. I think in a way I expected him to be as relieved as I was that our relationship was finally over. He never really gave me any cause to believe he would be overly upset not to have me around. I think I saw myself as as much of a habit to him as I felt he was to me, and believed I would be doing him a favour by calling the wedding off.

I'd always secretly thought that his proposal was the result of his getting carried away in the heat of the moment. It wasn't as if he even had a ring hidden in his pocket when he popped the question, and I don't know who looked more surprised that he'd actually asked, him or me.

It was totally out of the blue for me anyway. As far as I was concerned, Richard and I weren't getting on too well at the time. He'd been coming up with some pretty dodgy excuses for

35

breaking dates, and I hadn't really seen that much of him until the night he hit the carpet on his knees.

For the first time in ages we'd had a pretty good evening together.

I think this might have had something to do with the fact that we'd both had quite a bit to drink before meeting up. I'd been boozing because we were due at a family dinner, and a little glass of something alcoholic always makes the evening more pleasant. I don't know why Richard was half-bombed, but we both got stuck into Mother's lukewarm Leibfraumilch with a lot more relish than normal.

So we'd had a laugh, but to be honest, when he moved in close and said he'd got something to say to me, I was expecting a push off rather than a proposal.

It was also kind of unfortunate that we were with my family at the time. Before you could say 'Forget it, I was pissed', my mother had announced it to the world in the local papers, and organised a family party complete with champagne toasts, speeches and engagement presents. Steamrollered into formalising a relationship I already thought had hit the rocks, we set sail again under a barrage of streamers and popping corks.

I really hadn't thought that once the break was made Richard would be that reluctant to move on with his life.

'What did he say?' I ask uneasily.

'He seemed really sad, Fliss.' Sally smiles sympathetically.

'Of course,' I reply bitterly, 'I can just imagine it now, the wounded dog act, guaranteed sympathy puller. Make me look even more horrible than everybody already thinks I am.'

'No, it wasn't like that, Fliss, honestly. Far from it really. He seemed to be blaming himself more than you. Wanted some assurance it wasn't all his fault.'

'Oh, yes, and what did you tell him? I suppose Mother laid the blame entirely at my feet?'

Sally shrugs, embarrassed.

'Well, you know what she's like.'

'All too well,' I sigh. 'So he came round to cry on your shoulder. Is that all he said?'

'Well, he did say that just because he wasn't with you anymore, didn't mean we should lose touch.'

'He said that?'

'Yes, he said that!' snaps a familiar voice.

36

I look up with a start, an embarrassing lurch of fear hitting my stomach. Mother is standing in the doorway.

'I don't know why you find it so surprising.'

I really wish I could conquer the sick feeling of panic and apprehension she always induces in me. I am after all an adult, in charge of my own life, so why does she have this infallible ability to make me feel like I'm ten years old and due for a severe telling off?

She leans against the frame of the door as though her legs are too weak to support her. She looks pale, and is resting the back of her hand against her forehead, drama-queen style. It's four in the afternoon, and yet she is still in her dressing gown.

Funereal black. Very appropriate.

She stalks across the room, an ominous crow come to pick the bones of a dead subject.

'He cares about us, Felicity. He hasn't got a family of his own – he'd come to look upon us as his family, and then you took it all away from him,' she croaks hoarsely.

She stops and glares at me, then leaning heavily against the sideboard and ignoring the tea on the table, pours herself a large brandy.

'I'm surprised you dare to show your face around here.'

'You're *my* family,' I breathe indignantly, 'I can't believe you'd side against me. I need your support at the moment. This has been traumatic for me too, you know.'

'Don't expect any sympathy from me.' She takes a sip from her drink and pulls a face. She's never been a drinker. I imagine I'm supposed to have driven her to it.

'You've made your bed . . .'

'And now you're going to suffocate me with one of the pillows! I think I better leave.' I get up from the sofa. 'I can see it was a mistake coming here.'

'You've made rather a lot of mistakes recently haven't you, Felicity?' she says nastily. 'But then, what more should I expect from you? I suppose it was only a matter of time before you and Richard split up. You were never good enough for him. In fact, I'm surprised your relationship lasted so long, especially after what he said to Sally-Anne last night!' Downing the rest of her brandy in one go, she glares at me challengingly.

'Oh, yes, and what exactly did he say last night? What are you talking about?'

Mother sneers at me but says nothing, simply turns and pours herself another drink.

'What did Richard say?' I turn to Sally.

'Nothing,' she whispers, shaking her head. 'She's upset, that's all.'

'Sally!'

She takes my arm and starts to usher me out of the room.

'Just ignore her, Fliss, you know what she's like, she's upset, it's best to leave it for now.'

'Yes, leave it for now, Fliss,' Mother calls after me mockingly. 'Run away. Run away from this like you do from everything else.'

I pull away from Sally and face Mother.

'I am not running away! I'm trying to do the right thing for me, can't you understand that?' I plead, searching her face for one iota of compassion, of understanding. It is as cold, hard and closed as the lid on a chest freezer.

'Don't you want me to be happy?' I persist, but she doesn't reply. She doesn't need to; I already know the answer to that one. Happiness is not a state of mind necessary for satisfactory living. Duty, social standing, financial security; all are far more conducive to a good life than actual happiness.

'You're my mother, you're supposed to be on my side. Would you rather I made the biggest mistake of my life, married Richard, no doubt divorced Richard, and end up a lonely embittered old bitch like you?'

She walks up to me, eyes blazing angrily. Jerking her arm back, she hurls the brandy at me. I feel the sting as it hits my eyes and runs down my face to mingle with the steady stream of salt water already flowing.

Chapter Three

Evening is falling as I finally reach Angels Court. The crumbling old stone farm house looks familiar and reassuring. A huge yellow sun is gradually disappearing below the line of ridge tiles at the summit of the roof, casting pointed fingers of light against my windscreen and temporarily blinding me.

I'm on the proverbial emotional roller-coaster. On the drive down, I have been alternately singing and sighing, ecstatic and sobbing. The recent confrontation has thrown me. My life is on a totally different course. This is what I wanted, so why do I suddenly feel so empty inside?

Caroline is waiting at the drawing-room window, looking out for me, no doubt worried that I wouldn't get this far. She is frantic following my pretty incoherent phone call telling her I am finally on my way. The drive, which should only have taken an hour, has taken me two. I kept missing turnings due to lack of concentration, and had to backtrack several times, driving dangerously fast in reverse, threatening seriously to shorten the life of any rabbit that dared to hop in my way.

'Fliss, where the hell have you been?' Caro hurries out of the front door toward me, first scolding and then hugging me, enveloping me in affection and the warm waft of Chanel and clean blonde hair.

'My goodness, you're a wreck! Look at the state of you.'

She pulls away, holding me at arm's length for inspection.

'You're all sticky!'

She sniffs my hair and clothes.

'You smell like a brewery. You haven't been drinking, have you? Oh, Fliss, you know never to drink and drive.'

I shake my head.

'Of course not. I may be an idiot, but I'm not that stupid. I made the mistake of going round to see Mother before I came down here. She'd been hitting the medicinal brandy, but thought it would be far more effective chucked over me than down her throat.'

'Why, the old cow!' Caro's eyes are wide with outrage, her soft pink lips drawn into a hard line of disgust.

I sense sympathy, and sniff dejectedly.

'For someone who's not talking to me, she had plenty to say.'

'What exactly?' Caro's beautiful face looks angry on my behalf.

'Oh, I don't know. Richard had been round dishing the dirt, looking for sympathy, campaigning for new recruits to the Richard Trevelyan party. She hinted heavily that if I hadn't dumped him it would only have been a matter of time before he dumped me, and then she threw a full glass of Remy Martin in my face and walked out of the room.'

Caroline shakes her head in disgust, and takes my arm.

'Well, you're amongst friends now. The only alcohol we'll be throwing is down your neck. You come along inside, we'll send David out to fetch your cases.'

'Oh, yes, cases,' I muse. 'I knew I meant to pick something up before I left.'

Caro leads me into the house and takes me upstairs to one of the guest rooms which has unofficially become my room.

Sanctuary.

The room is comforting and welcoming with its warm terra-cotta walls turned honey-gold by the last rays of the sun streaming in through windows set either side of the bed, antique pine furniture and a jungle of house plants.

As it is summer, the open fireplace is filled with flowers in place of a fire, a heavy copper pot brimming over with pretty pastel-coloured sweet peas, their delicious scent hanging lightly on the warm air. White gauze curtains flutter at the open windows in the slightest of breezes, I can hear birds' evensong from the orchard just beyond the garden. In the village just over a mile away loyal parishioners are at bell practice in the ancient spire of the Saxon church. Angels Court is so beautiful, so peaceful, Paradise found, a little corner of Eden in which to rest and recuperate.

I collapse heavily on to the wrought-iron bed, and it creaks in gentle protest. Caro disappears into the bathroom. I can hear the thunder of water filling the old cast-iron bath, and the smell of lavender as she shakes salts into the foaming water. I curl into a ball, knees to my chest, like a baby in the womb.

This house is a home, so warm, so alive, you can almost hear its heartbeat. For the first time since my confrontation with my mother I feel my hands cease to tremble.

I emerge from my bath feeling decidedly more human. Caro has left me one of her sweaters and some clean jeans on the bed. The jeans are a touch too tight, she has always been enviably slim.

The sweater's dark blue angora. Despite the mildness of the evening, I'm glad of its warmth, and its length covering my midriff which doesn't exactly hang but protrudes a little too much over the tight waist band of the jeans. I bet they're her largest pair as well. I sigh. Perhaps my new life could incorporate a new figure. Then again I'm still on official comfort eating time. It's going to be hard to give up junk food, especially when it's justified junk food.

Making my way down the twisting narrow back stairs, I find Caroline and David in the kitchen. They are listening to Radio Four and sharing a bottle of wine. Caro is hovering over huge black pans on the Aga. David is seated at the kitchen table, shelling peas, dark head bent, half-moon glasses perched on the end of his long nose, reading yesterday's *Sunday Times*. He looks up as I enter and smiles warmly, then looks across at Caroline.

I slip into one of the seats at the long scrubbed kitchen table. Darius, David's Labrador, rises from his basket and, plumy tail wagging so hard it shakes his whole backside, pads across the red flagstone floor to me. I stroke his silken head. He scrapes my thigh with his paw when I stop, and thrusts a wet nose under my hand, urging me to stroke him again.

'At least someone loves me,' I whisper.

I can feel my bottom lip begin to tremble again.

David the diplomat, no doubt primed by Caroline, makes his excuses and heads toward the study, his paper folded bulkily beneath his arm. Caroline waits till he's out of the room, then turns to me with a wide smile.

'Feeling more human?'

I nod slowly.

She hands me a glass of wine.

'This really ought to be champagne, then we could have a celebration.' She raises her own full glass to me. 'Well, congratulations, you did it, you did it. You're finally free.'

She sounds pleased.

I obviously don't look too ecstatic.

She peers more closely at me.

Fliss . . . earth calling Fliss, are you all right, dear? You're not regretting it, are you? Thinking about the wedding?'

I leap out of my wine glass like a salmon jumping upstream.

'Oh, my goodness, the wedding!'

Somehow in the whole drama of everything I'd forgotten it. I hadn't forgotten the marriage – I mean, that's what the whole damn' argument was about – but the actual mechanics of getting married, the church, the flowers, the reception for two hundred people. The empty paranoid lethargic feeling turns to blind panic.

'I must start cancelling things or people will turn up expecting a marriage!'

'Calm down, Fliss.' Caro sloshes another litre of red into my bulbous gallon-sized glass. 'It's not for another six weeks. Besides, I'm sure Miriam will be taking care of all that. Why don't you give her a call just to put your mind at rest? Have a little chat.'

I lay my poor aching head down on the kitchen table. The old wood is smooth and warm. Comforting.

'We can't have a *little chat*,' I groan. 'You know she's not talking to me. You know how much she idolised Richard. She's in mourning as we speak. I can just see her retiring to a darkened room, complaining bitterly about her errant and ungrateful elder daughter, and being waited upon hand and foot by poor old Sally-Anne. You know, that girl's got the patience of a saint . . .'

'More likely making wax effigies, calling them Fliss, and doing unspeakable things to them with pins and stuff,' says Caro with far too much relish. 'Oh, and you forgot stupid.'

'What?' I lift my head from the table and look at her in confusion.

'Her errant, ungrateful, and unspeakably *stupid* daughter. You forgot the stupid.'

'You don't think I'm stupid, do you, Caroline?' I wail in concern. 'Please tell me you don't think I've made a huge mistake?'

'Certainly not!' she replies adamantly. 'That's not what you think, is it, Fliss? You don't think you've made a mistake by calling it all off?'

'I don't know,' I wail, 'I'm soooo confuuuused.'

The tears that have been switching on and off all evening like the stop and go sign on a pedestrian crossing begin to slide down my face again. It must be all the alcohol I've drunk over the past few days, I need to lose some liquid from somewhere. Caro abandons the Aga and comes to put a comforting arm around my shoulders. The scent of Chanel is overpowered by tarragon.

'There, there . . .' She has her teacher's voice on. 'Let it all out.'

'I'm not crying for him,' I sniff, 'I'm crying for me. I'm nearly thirty, and look what I've gone and done . . . I've just turned my whole life upside down. I'm too old to change everything, I shall become an ancient lonely spinster . . .'

'That's the Château Neuf-du-Pape talking, not you, and you're twenty-eight – I'd hardly call that ancient now, would you? If you're old, what does that make me? I'm nearly thirty-three'.

Caro sits down in the chair next to me, and takes my hand.

'Now look, Fliss, do you love Richard?'

I stop crying, and look up at her.

'No. No, I don't.'

'There now, wasn't that easy? You didn't even hesitate. And if I were going to marry somebody I didn't love, and I had these massive doubts and came to you for advice, what would you say to me?'

'I'd tell you not to go through with it,' I answer slowly, registering my own words. How come Caroline can always put everything back into perspective so easily?

'So, tell me, do you really think you've made a mistake by calling the whole thing off, or do you want to spend the rest of your life being married to some pompous twit who only wants a woman to stroke his ego?'

'Well, his ego is the largest thing he's got. I'd rather stroke that than certain other parts of him.' I begin to giggle.

Caro smiles brightly at me.

'See? At least you've got your sense of humour back now.'

David sticks his head round the door, and raises his eyebrows questioningly at his wife.

'Is it safe to come in?'

43

'I think the patient is well on the road to recovery.' Caro indicates me, still slumped, but giggling. 'She seems cheerful enough now.'

'I thought she'd dumped Richard the Rat, not had a personality transplant?'

'Why, you cheeky . . .' I lob a bread roll in his direction.

'Pax, pax!' David holds up large farm-callused hands. 'Well, I'm glad you're feeling better, Felicity dear. You are feeling better, aren't you?' He peers at my reddened eyes. 'More fortified?'

I nod.

'Good, 'cause your mother's on the phone for you.'

I'm shaking as I pick up the receiver. The last thing I need right now is another torrent of abuse.

'Hello?' My voice is a whisper.

'Fliss, is that you?'

My heart does a yo-yo action, dips to my boots and then boings back up again as I realise it's not Mother after all, it's Sally.

'Oh, Sally,' I sigh in relief. 'Thank goodness it's only you.'

'Fliss, are you OK?'

'I think so. David just said you were Mother. How is she?'

'She's gone to bed . . . she didn't mean to be so awful, Fliss, not really, she was just very upset.'

'I'd never have guessed,' I say sarcastically.

Sally pauses for a moment.

'About the wedding . . .' she offers tentatively.

'The wedding that was but isn't anymore? I was just saying to Caro that I ran off without even thinking about the wedding, I'll have to contact all the guests, return the presents, cancel the caterers . . .'

My voice begins to rise in panic at the enormity of the task in hand.

'Look, Fliss, that's one of the reasons I'm calling. I know how upset you are at the moment – the last thing you need is to have to run around like an idiot cancelling a wedding. I don't want you to worry about a thing, I want you to leave it all to me. I'll sort everything out. I'll do whatever has to be done, OK?'

Such a tempting offer, to be able just to forget the whole fiasco. Unfortunately, I'd feel far too guilty to offload the burden

44

on to Sal, especially when she has everything else to cope with as well. I ran away from the flak, she's still slap-bang in the middle of it. Well, slap-bang in the middle of Mother and Richard.

'Are you absolutely sure?' I ask her. 'It's such a burden to put on you, and there's so much to cancel . . .'

'Now, no quibbling, Fliss. I mean it, leave it all to me. I want you just to relax and forget about everything, do you hear me?'

I'm suddenly desperately grateful to my little sister.

'Well, if you're sure . . .'

'Positive, I don't want you to worry about a thing. Leave it all to me.'

I return to the kitchen in better mood.

Sally-Anne has lifted a big weight from my shoulders. I'm surprised at her really. We've always got on well but we've never been what you would call close.

I was seven when Sally was born. I wasn't into dolls, so this sweet-scented gurgling cherub didn't really interest me. In fact, I think I was disappointed. When Dad told me there was going to be a new addition to the family, I was hoping it would have four legs and eat hay.

Give me the child until he's seven – and then I'll give up and have another that's hopefully more trainable, was my mother's philosophy.

Sally got off to a good start with me. Thanks to her, Mother spent her first night ever away from home, and I got to spend the evening alone with Dad, who although required at the conception was not apparently necessary at the birth. We had an excellent night eating junk food and staying up late to watch inappropriate television programmes.

The obvious difference in my mother's attitude to Sally perhaps made me a little jealous to start off with, but I soon came to realise that instead of a rival I had an ally. Sally's always been able to handle Mother's moods far better than I. Probably because I always seem to be the one to cause them, whereas Sally has fitted happily into my mother's image of the perfect child right from pink dresses through to becoming an assistant bank manager. Mother's idea of the perfect career.

Sally also models part-time. She's one of those wholesome healthy pretty girls with perfect teeth who you see smiling happily out at you from the front cover of *Woman's Weekly*, or cuddling angelic children in the knitting section of *People's Friend*. She's the human equivalent of a kitten on a chocolate box. Totally adorable.

Come to think of it, I always thought if Richard had met her first he wouldn't have given me a second glance.

'Well?' Caro is curious. 'What did Mater say? You look surprisingly cheerful for somebody who's just had a conversation with their Nemesis.'

'It wasn't Mother, it was Sally.'

'David!' Caro chastises her husband. 'That wasn't a nice thing to do. Did you see poor Fliss's face when you said it was Miriam on the phone? Honestly, darling, your sense of humour has no sense of timing!'

He holds up his hands and backs away.

'But it sounded like Miriam, honestly,' he defends himself, 'I wouldn't be so cruel . . .'

'It's an easy mistake to make,' I come to his defence. 'They sound alike.'

'They act alike,' says Caro, returning to her stew and stirring it gently. She holds out the huge wooden spoon for David to taste some. 'More salt? What do you think?'

He shakes his head. 'Perfect as always, darling,' he replies, kissing her forehead. 'Just like you.'

Here most people would reach for the sick bag, but David's not being nauseating, he's just being nice. The sincerity saves the sentiment.

'I think I ought to watch and learn,' I say enviously. 'Tell me, what is the secret of such an idyllic marriage?'

'Idyllic!' Caro laughs, as does David. They share a look.

'Come on, I want to know, I wouldn't mind a shot at happy families myself someday. With the right man of course,' I add hastily. 'Don't want to make another mistake like last time.'

'You want some lessons in family life?' Caro asks.

'I suppose so, yeah.'

'Good, the kids are arriving at the end of next week, you can entertain them. Maura's going to some retreat in Scotland or something, so we've got them for five days.'

I walked right into that one.

Maura is David's ex-wife, the bane of Caro's life, an aging hippy who believes in alternative medicine, alternative religion, and alternative ways of bringing up children. Hannah, just sixteen, and Charlie, nearly eighteen, are good kids but rather wild. Used to a total lack of discipline from their mother, they find even the relaxed regime of Angels Court restricting. The only time I've ever seen David and Caro argue was over the kids' behaviour. David tries to over-compensate for Maura's lax attitude and tends to lay down the law with them, but just ends up wound-up. Perhaps I didn't pick the right time to visit. Out of the frying pan and into the fire?

'A retreat?' I laugh half-heartedly. 'Any spare places? I could do with retreating somewhere nice and peaceful myself, I need to recharge my batteries.'

'I thought that's why you'd come to us?' says Caro indignantly. 'Don't worry, David has promised to be relaxed and laid-back, just to let everything float over his head, haven't you, darling? Besides, you don't want peace and quiet, you want life and action. You need to see what you've been missing out on so you don't look back with regret. It's very easy to paint the past with a rosy glow, you know.'

'Nothing could make me recall Richard as a glowing memory. You know, that's a lovely thing to be able to call him.'

'What's that?'

I raise my glass.

'A memory.'

I spend the majority of the next week sleeping.

I wake only to eat and play the odd game of chess with David which, gallant as always, he usually lets me win despite being a far superior player. I soak indulgently for hours in lavender-scented baths, and wander gently through the beautiful country-side with Darius, wearing a pair of David's green wellies that are far too big for me.

Total recuperation.

Caro is waiting on me hand and foot, and I am unashamedly and unadulteratedly making the most of it all.

I know I've got to think about my future, but even thinking is too much of an effort for me at the moment. The forward-planning, practical thinking part of my brain has gone on a long holiday.

I realise I'm vegetating. It's very enjoyable.

I decide to go with the flow. Whatever life throws at me, I shall conquer. A very easy philosophy to adopt at Angels Court, where the only decision to make is red, white or both at dinner.

It's wonderful too be with people who totally laud my decision to leave Richard. Even when you're sure that you've done the right thing, there are always the 'what ifs' to contend with. Caro washes these away with bitchy, wonderfully witty comments about him and his irritating foibles, his endless egocentricism.

Unlike my mother and Sally-Anne, Caro never took to Richard; she saw through the façade to the shallow man he really is even before I did. If I start to view the past with rose-tinted glasses she quickly swaps them for a microscope under which Richard the Toad can be easily dissected and seen for what he really is.

Everybody is being terribly kind. Caro and David are nurturing me with more care than they nurture the crops on the farm, spoiling me more than an overindulged child. Even the sun is smiling down on me, caressing me with her warmth. Angels Court is aptly named, it's truly a corner of Eden, I begin to think I might stay here forever.

Oh, the danger of beginning to enjoy oneself too much, of doing comparatively nothing, because this is always the time when my overdeveloped sense of guilt kicks in to ruin everything.

Just over a week into my stay, and Caro and I are enjoying another idyllic summer's day stretched out on rickety old wooden sun loungers in the garden.

Darius is chasing the small rosy apples which fall from the trees and roll across the grass, the ring doves which congregate on the roof of the house are cooing softly to each other, the air is tinged with the smell of warm grass, lavender, lilac and old roses – and typically, where most normal people would surrender their mind to the near Nirvana surrounding us, I begin to think of the chaos I left behind me.

The tears, the tantrums, the clutter and confusion that Sally-Anne has been left to clear up. I breathe in the fresh sweet flower-filled air, warm with the scent of the fallen apples sweating in the sun, and sigh heavily.

Guilt wins over self-indulgence, as usual.

'It's no good. No matter how much I don't want to, I really must go home,' I announce to Caro who is sun worshipping beside me. 'I know Sally said to leave everything to her, but it just isn't fair. It's my mess, I ought to be there to clean it up.'

'I wouldn't worry.' Caro stretches and turns over to get the sun on her back. 'I'm sure Miriam's doing a wonderful job of sweeping the whole thing under the carpet. Besides you can't go yet, you promised to help me with the kids. They arrive at the end of the week.'

'I know, but I'm running away from my responsibilities, Caro. I can't leave it all to poor old Sal, not with Mother to cope with as well.'

'Sally-Anne wouldn't have offered if she didn't feel she could cope,' Caro replies matter-of-factly.

'I suppose so, but I still feel like I should . . .'

'Fliss!' She holds up one elegant hand, like a traffic policeman stopping cars. 'Stop right there! I'm not going to let you ruin such a beautiful day by going on a guilt trip.'

'Sorry, but I can't help it. Every time I close my eyes I get visions of wedding cakes and flower arrangements arriving at The Beeches. Something like that would give Mother a heart attack.'

'Every cloud has a silver lining!' Caro laughs. 'No, seriously, forget about your mother and the wedding and Richard and Sal. Try and think about something else for a change.'

'Such as?'

'Well, I certainly have different fantasies when I close *my* eyes.' Caro smirks. 'I don't know, think about what we can do with the kids for six days. You know how bored they get down here. It's far too rural for them after the bright lights and excitement of London.'

'I thought all kids loved the countryside, especially farms?'

'Well, they used to love it, but I suppose they're not really kids anymore. They get bored so quickly, Charlie especially. He used to like helping out Mr Macready the farm manager, but I suppose even trawling round the fields on a tractor will have lost its charm now he's got his car licence.'

'We could organise something – a trip down to the sea or a treasure hunt perhaps?'

'Would they appreciate organised events? Rather too reminiscent of school, I should think. You know what they're like if they think they've got to do something someone else wants them to, rather than something they chose themselves. And you know what Hannah's like at the moment. Everything you suggest is "so juvenile".' She lapses into a fair impression of

Hannah's bored drawl. 'The only thing she likes down here are all of the horses and some of the farm hands.'

'How about a treasure hunt on horseback?'

'Juvenile.'

'I'd enjoy it, does that mean I'm juvenile?'

'Very.' Caro looks at me through eyes narrowed against the sun, and laughs at my sulky expression. 'Face it, Fliss, the next six days are going to be teenage hell on earth. They row all the time at the moment too. They've got to that age where they cease to be friends, and become enemies for the next couple of years, before settling back into cosy companionship when they're suddenly old enough to appreciate each other again . . . oil my back for me, darling.' Too lazy to move, she points to the suntan oil with her foot. 'At least the weather's bloody wonderful. We won't have them stuck indoors all the time. You know, it's so hot, it's almost like being in the Med.'

'Apart from no beach, no cheese and wine, and no tasty bronzed French men?'

'Well, we can supply the cheese and wine, no problem. We might even run to some men, if you like? Not French, of course, but tasty all the same. In fact, I think that's probably what you need to keep you amused.'

'I thought we were discussing entertainment for the kids, not me?'

'Well, we could turn your horseback treasure hunt into a horseback man hunt, and keep you and Hannah happy at the same time.'

'Eighteen-year-old farm hands are hardly my scene.'

'Have you actually seen the eighteen-year-old farm hands that run around this place?' Caro props her golden head on an elbow and looks mischievously at me. 'Young, tanned and bulging with bronzed muscles. Perhaps that's actually what you need. Come to think of it, perhaps that's what I need too . . .'

I try to get excited about young, tanned, bronzed and muscled, but find that I can't.

'I think I'll give Hannah first choice,' I say dryly.

'Well, we could always find you something older and more sophisticated, if that's what you want?'

'Caro, at the moment I don't want anything. I've had my fill of men.'

'Are you sure?' she asks wistfully. 'I love playing Cupid.'

Stupid Cupid, who needs him? I'm too tired for men at the moment. No, rephrase that. I'm too tired *of* men at the moment.

'No, Caro,' I plead, knowing full well how much she would enjoy fixing me up. 'Promise me, no playing Cupid? Please.'

'Not just a teensy bit?'

'Not at all, promise me? No men, OK?'

She sighs.

'Well, I think it's just what you need.'

'No, Caroline,' I tell her as firmly as I can, 'it's just what I don't need. I'd rather get a dog, they're less demanding and far more loyal and affectionate. Please, no matchmaking. Promise me?'

She rolls her eyes to heaven.

'OK. No men.'

The next Sunday I return from one of my self-indulgent solitary sojourns, my arms full of flowers stolen from the nearby gardens of some dilapidated stately home as a small thank you to Caro for putting up with me, to find that Hannah and Charlie have arrived.

David, who had to go to town to pick them up from the station, has thoughtfully retrieved my suitcase from the hallway of my flat so – bliss – I now have some clothes of my own to wear. He has also brought my mail. There's a fistful. My credit card bill, which is horrendous, a letter telling me I've won a free carpet shampoo, an insurance renewal notification, and three wedding invitation acceptances which I promptly bin in a fit of carefree abandon. So what if they turn up for a wedding that isn't taking place? Serves them right for not replying by the RSVP date.

I haven't seen Hannah and Charlie for over six months. Since Christmas actually. They always prefer to spend Christmas with Caro and David who see it as a time for traditional celebration. Maura, their mother, with her weird and not at all wonderful ideas about alternative religion, refuses to celebrate the birth of Christ and spends the entire Christmas holiday fasting and chanting. Caro says that it's nothing to do with religious beliefs and is simply because she's too tight to buy presents, and also doesn't want to end the festive season with the traditional spare tyre hanging round her waist.

Charlie has grown about a foot since I last saw him. He is the

51

image of his father, tall and dark with hooded sleepy eyes that never betray too much emotion. I'm told Hannah looks like her mother. Never having had the dubious privilege of meeting Maura, I couldn't say. She is the complete opposite of Charlie, small and lithe, with amazing hair the colour of the sun setting over a field of ripe corn, strange but very beautiful.

Caro calls her orange-blonde which she does not appreciate. Unlike Charlie, Hannah bears little physical resemblance to David. He swears that if she didn't have his very evident stubborn streak, and the unusual gull-grey of his eyes, he wouldn't believe she was his.

David has obviously filled the kids in about Fliss and her recent cock-up on the way back to Angels Court as they are initially far too polite to me, making me endless cups of coffee, and offering me first choice of which radio station we tune in to while making Sunday lunch, even though they are both obviously dying to listen to the charts.

This solicitude doesn't last very long, however.

'What you need is another man,' announces Hannah out of the blue when we finally sit down to dinner.

'That's the last thing I need!' I choke over my glass of iced water. 'You've been talking to Caroline, haven't you?'

'Not at all,' she replies. 'But if Caro's said that too then she's right. Take it from me, Fliss, the best way to get over one man is to find yourself another.'

'Such words of wisdom from one so young,' mocks David.

'Oh, shut up, Daddy. Just because you're far too old to know about these sort of things.'

'Too old?' roars David. 'Too old, cheeky madam? You're not too old to go over my knee . . .'

'See what I mean, Fliss?' Hannah yawns purposely to annoy her father. 'Such outdated attitudes. We're living in the twenty-first century now, Daddy. Lay one finger on me and I'll sue, you know.'

'I don't need to get over Richard,' I state adamantly, ignoring their squabbling, 'I was over him a long time ago.'

'Then why are you hiding out here?' she challenges, toying with her carrots disdainfully.

'I need to get over the consequences of getting over Richard.'

'She's avoiding her mother,' adds Caroline.

'Mad Miriam? Honestly, Fliss, it's so pathetic to be frightened of one's mother!'

52

'Hannah, don't be rude!' snaps David.

'Well, I'm only sixteen, and I'm not frightened of Maura, and she's even stranger than Mad Miriam.'

'You're not frightened of Maura because you've got her wrapped around your little finger. She lets you get away with murder.' Caro gets up and starts to clear away the dishes.

'Mum believes in freedom of expression.' Charlie grins as he tells us this.

'Is that what you call it?' The sarcasm in David's voice is heavy.

'She doesn't want us to stifle our true selves, believes our personalities should be free to grow and develop without harmful parental interference,' Hannah explains.

David shudders.

'How horrible. If I close my eyes it could almost be Maura, here in the room with us. Please don't take after your mother, Hannah. If there's one ambition I have for you, it's that you shouldn't take after your mother.'

'Why not? Mother is a free spirit.' Hannah's eyes are wide with feigned innocence. 'Don't you want me to be a free spirit?'

'Your mother may be a free spirit but she is also a free-loader, and that I do not want you to be, Hannah dear.'

'That's not a very nice thing to say about the woman who bore your children.'

David turns pink with indignation.

'Don't deliberately provoke your father,' Caro chastises gently. 'Think of his blood pressure. These old wrinkles have to kept stress-free.'

Hannah laughs. 'Yes, I keep forgetting that Dad's past it,' she says with relish. 'When are you going to have children, Caro? You'd better hurry up or Dad won't be able to manage it anymore . . .'

David opens his mouth to argue, looks at Caroline, shakes his head and then closes his mouth again.

'I'm not having any children,' states Caro firmly, stacking pots in the large white enamel butler's sink.

'Why ever not? I want at least six.'

'Six!' splutters Charlie, scraping mashed potato into Darius's bowl. 'I don't think so. You can't look after yourself, let alone six kids.'

'I don't want them yet, silly, I'm going to wait till I'm a lot older, at least twenty-eight. That's old, don't you think?' She looks at me slyly. 'Do you want children, Fliss?'

'Not if they're going to turn out like you, she doesn't.' Charlie flicks a pea at his sister.

David gives them both a warning look. 'Just drop it, OK?'

Caro suddenly looks pale and tired.

David looks pointedly at his children again and they lapse into silence. Caro finishes clearing the table.

'Sit down, Caro, Hannah and Charlie can do the dishes,' David tells her.

'But we're taking Fliss out for a walk, aren't we, Fliss?' Hannah protests.

'Dishes first,' says David emphatically.

'Caro doesn't mind, do you, Caro darling? She's not a wicked stepmother, are you? Besides, you said we'd got to look after Fliss.'

'Hannah!' David gives her a warning look.

Charlie the peacemaker steps in.

'I'll do the dishes. It doesn't take two of us to stack the machine.'

David shakes his head, but shrugs in reluctant submission.

Hannah takes my arm as we step out into the warmth of the evening. The sun is sinking slowly over the edge of the dark green woods that lie beyond the fields surrounding the house. We follow the sun and walk towards them.

As we reach the edge of the field beyond the orchard, where the beech trees begin to grow in a tangled mass of thick brown and mossy green roots, Hannah lets go of my arm and dives ecstatically into the smoke-scented gloom of the wood, drawn by the deep pink sea of wild rhododendron growing densely before us.

She runs and dances through the trees, gathering flowers, like a maenead, her web of hair fluffed about her face like a halo of golden flax.

She makes me feel so old, yet it feels like only yesterday I was a teenager. Was I that self-confident at her age? I don't think so. But look at the world teenagers have to live in now, they must learn to cope from a very young age. When I was a girl every summer was hot and every Christmas it snowed. Life was more simple, easier somehow. Oh, dear, I sound like my deceased grandfather whose every sentence used to begin 'When I was a lad . . .'

Hannah dances back to me, her arms full of already wilting petals, which she proceeds to scatter like confetti along the narrow woodland path before our feet.

'Did you know Caroline's arranging a party on your behalf?' she laughs, skipping backwards so that she can see me as she talks. 'Daddy let it slip on the way back from the station. I think they've got some man lined up as a prospective boyfriend. I'd be careful if I were you, Caro has suspect taste. After all, she married *him*, didn't she? Do you know, he's nearly sixteen years older than her? That means that when he was my age, Caro was only just being born or something. Talk about cradle snatching! Your bloke's probably sixty, with a receding hairline and a fat belly. Then again he might have a fat bank balance as well. I want a rich man, someone who can keep me in the lifestyle to which my parents are determined I won't become accustomed. If I get a rich and old man then I can kill him off with lots of sex and be a very merry widow.'

'Hannah!' I shriek, amused but slightly shocked. 'There's more to life and love than a full wallet. Believe me, I'm speaking from experience.'

'I know that,' she says wearily. 'I may be *young*,' she stresses that as though it's an insult, 'but I'm not stupid. An older man has a lot of other things going for him as well. He would be more experienced sexually for one thing.'

'I thought sex was your secret weapon for premature but ecstatically happy widowhood?' I mock her.

'Oh, sex can be for enjoyment too,' she says airily, with all the conviction of a seasoned duvet diver. 'I want to be initiated by someone who knows what they're doing. Was Richard good in bed?'

'Hannah!'

'Well, if I don't ask I won't learn, and the best way to learn is from other people's mistakes.'

'Well, Richard was certainly one of those. As far as I was concerned anyway.'

'Mmm,' agrees Hannah. 'It was my sixteenth birthday last month. You could introduce me to Richard, couldn't you, Fliss? He may need some consoling now you've dumped him. He was sort of stuffy, but I'm sure I could coax him into unbending a little. From what I can remember, he was rather good-looking in a Tom Cruise kind of way.'

'Richard looks nothing like Tom Cruise!'

'Well, they're both short, dark and rather handsome.'

'Yes, and that's where the similarity ends.'

'You still haven't answered my question.' She looks at me slyly. 'Was he good in bed?'

She's not going to give in, I decide on honesty being the best policy.

'Frankly? He was bloody useless. Not that I've got much to compare him with, but he didn't do a lot for me.'

Then, feeling a touch guilty, I add, 'I don't suppose that's totally fair. Just because he didn't rock my boat doesn't mean he can't make the right moves on someone else. One word of advice, though, Hannah. Whatever you do, avoid selfish men.'

'Well, that goes without saying,' she replies, snapping a slim branch from our path, 'I'm far too selfish myself to put up with that. I want a man who puts me before anything else, and a selfish man wouldn't do that, now would he? Besides if Richard's useless in bed then I don't want to know. Was that why you got shot of him then, 'cause he was a failure in the sex department?'

'That was one reason, not the most important,' I answer truthfully. 'I just decided it wouldn't be a good idea to spend the rest of my life with someone I didn't particularly like.'

'Well, that certainly makes sense,' she agrees.

'And I realised I was justified in wanting more, that I didn't have to settle for second best. Actually, no, Richard wasn't even second best, that's too generous to him, he was lousy last.'

'Was he really that awful? I know Caro didn't like him, but you must have liked him at some point. I mean to . . . you know . . .' She giggles. 'To go to bed with him.' Despite her previous frankness, she almost whispers this last, as though the trees are listening in and will be shocked.

'You don't have to like someone to love them,' I answer carefully.

She digests this for a moment, and then nods her head slowly in agreement. 'I suppose so. I mean, I absolutely detest Charlie at the moment, but I suppose I do love him really.' She rounds on me, wagging a long finger. 'But you must promise me never to repeat that to him, OK? He'll only throw it back in my face.'

'I think he probably knows already.' I smile. 'But you can count on me not to remind him.'

We walk in silence for a while as the path dips down a bank, concentrating on our footing for the descent. At the bottom of the bank lies the river which waters David's fields, narrowing here as it runs through the wood, little more than a stream, clogged thickly with bulrushes and green algae fed by the sun.

'I wonder what your next lover will be like?' Hannah muses, smiling mysteriously at me. 'That's if you can bag yourself another one,' she teases. 'I mean, you're getting on a bit now, aren't you?' She takes the rest of the bank at a run as I throw a handful of leaves at her and collapses in a fit of giggles, flopping down on the long grass at the edge of the stream.

'Perhaps Caro's man will be your dream man,' she murmurs, eyes shining excitedly. 'Wouldn't that be romantic? Your eyes meet across a crowded room, he's drawn to your side, he offers you a drink . . .'

'Please!' I hold up my hands, pleading for her to stop. 'I made Caro promise me that there would be no matchmaking.'

I take the steep ground at a steadier pace, relieved when I'm back on even footing. I sit down next to Hannah, who is stripping a reed.

'She was probably crossing her fingers,' she replies without looking at me, face screwed up in concentration.

'Sorry?'

'Could you see her hands when she promised?'

'Well, no, I suppose not, I had my eyes closed against the sun actually.'

'Then she was probably crossing her fingers.'

'Lying, you mean?'

'Not at all. It's perfectly legitimate to cross your fingers when making a promise under duress, it just means you don't have to carry it through.'

'Well, she'd better not have been,' I state crossly. 'I meant it when I said no men.'

'But why?'

'Well, they're a complication I really can't cope with at the moment.'

'I've never heard them called that before.' Hannah laughs. 'Numerous other things, far *far* worse, but never a complication.'

'Give it another few years and you'll understand what I mean,' I promise her.

Hannah places her stripped reed between her thumbs, and blows. A little black moorhen shoots away from us, startled by the high-pitched noise. Hannah laughs.

'Sounds like Charlie after one of Maura's curries!' She turns back to me. 'What's the secret to a good relationship, Fliss?'

'You're asking me?' I say incredulously.

'Uh-huh.' Hannah nods enthusiastically.

'Haven't got a clue.' I lie back against the bank, feel the sun warming my face and hair, the soft curl of the long grass tickling my bare legs. 'I'm the last person to ask, I'm still searching for an answer to that question myself. Why don't you ask your father or Caro? They have a really good relationship.'

'Dad must be getting better second time round then. Still, they do say practice makes perfect. Mum said he was a lousy husband.'

Well, I've heard that it was your mother who was hell to be married to, I think, but don't say.

'Oh, I think they do pretty well, it wouldn't hurt to observe and learn,' I tell her instead.

'Watching one's own father trying to be romantic? Yuk!' Hannah shudders. 'It's unnatural.'

We make our way back to the house via the stable yard. The sun has fallen beyond the horizon yet still spreads a warm glow up through the sky, blazing orange, pink, and red like a raging field fire.

' "Red sky at night, shepherd's delight",' I quote.

'Red sky at night, shepherd's house on fire.' Hannah grins.

Jake, the son of Angus Macready the farm manager, is wielding a pitchfork in the end stable. He is stripped to the waist, his muscular torso brown from the sun and gleaming with fresh sweat. As we clatter noisily across the cobbled yard, he pauses in his toil and looks up. His eyes flick over me, he smiles in greeting, and then he looks over at Hannah.

They haven't met before. Jake has recently come down from a three-year degree course at Oxford, started before his divorced father came to Angels Court. His brief visits have somehow never yet coincided with Hannah's.

I think this may have been fortuitous. His large dark eyes

register extreme interest now. She smiles coquettishly, looking at him with her strange grey eyes, blinking slowly as he incredulously takes in her willowy body, pretty face, and amazing silken cornfield hair. When she is sure she has his full interest, she turns away and, completely ignoring him, walks over to one of the boxes, swinging her hips seductively.

Mac, David's handsome chestnut hunter, sticks his thoroughbred head out of his loose box and, recognising a friend, blows affectionately in Hannah's hair. She reaches in the pocket of her bleached denim cut-offs, and pulls out a half-eaten packet of Polos. His thick whiskered lips mumble against the palm of her hand as he delicately consumes the half-dozen she proffers.

The other horses watch her impatiently, hungrily, as does Jake. I have a feeling she could have him eating out of her hand just as easily as Mac.

Caroline and David are in the kitchen, slumped together on the faded old sofa in the corner by the pottery-heavy dresser. They've finished the bottle of wine we started with dinner and are now more than halfway down a second. Caro's head is on David's shoulder and they are whispering together, Caro smiling as David takes the opportunity to whisper in her ear, to move his lips downward and softly kiss her just behind it – the sensitive part of the neck that makes your body tingle with anticipation when a lover caresses it the right way.

It's nice to see Caro smiling again. There was an exchange going on earlier at dinner that wasn't purely verbal. I make a mental note to quiz her when the opportunity arises. I'm not being nosy, I'm just concerned. Caro's my friend and something Hannah said struck a painful chord, I could see it in her face. I also decide I must have another solo chat with Hannah. She has a reckless curiosity at the moment that could lead her into trouble. I know she's not my responsibility but the fact that she chose to confide in me makes it feel that way.

Hannah herself chooses to continue our conversation two evenings later. Caro and David have gone to a dinner party that was arranged some months ago. I'm kid sitting.

It's one of those slow quiet nights, where boredom prowls around the perimeter of the room like a fox around a chicken coop. Hannah is fractious. Charlie is bringing new meaning to

59

the word apathy. The video I got from the local shop is rejected as rubbish, seen it before. There's nothing interesting on television, and a game of cards soon broke down into a screaming match between siblings.

I've given up being entertainment's manager and referee rolled into one, and retired behind the latest issue of *Cosmo*. Charlie is trying to shunt a cigarette straight from the packet into his mouth, but keeps missing. Hannah is pacing restlessly about the room, having exhausted the remote control batteries, and my eyes, with her endless channel hopping.

'It's really not fair to go out and leave us,' she complains about her parents, breaking the silence, raking a hand agitatedly through her long golden hair. 'We're only here once in a blue moon. You'd think they'd want to spend the time we're here actually with us, wouldn't you?'

'They can't spend every waking moment pandering to you,' mumbles Charlie, as he finally manages to chuck a B & H into his mouth. He now switches his attention to lighting the damn thing, attempting to do this in one movement, like a sharp-shooter going for his gun.

Swoop, click. Swoop, click. An irritating noise.

I'm just about to snap at him to stop when lighter, flame and cigarette finally connect. He inhales deeply, and exhales in a sigh of self satisfaction. Hannah looks at him in disgust.

'There's nothing very clever about smoking,' she sneers at him.

Charlie makes a discreet but very obvious V-sign at her. She throws him a black look in return.

Pacing back across the room, she comes to rest upon the faded gold chaise-longue next to me, tucking her feet under her and peering at the front cover of my magazine.

'What are you reading?' she asks, staring at the feature headlines on the front. 'Sex Fabulous Sex? The Perfect Summer Diet? Have they got an article on combating extreme boredom?'

'I'm reading an article on how to find the perfect man,' I answer her without thinking.

'I thought you didn't want one of those at the moment?' She makes it sound like craving a bar of chocolate.

'Not especially,' I put down the magazine, 'but it's really only one imperfect man I want to avoid. I thought I might pick up a few tips for when I'm ready to go back into circulation.'

'Circulation! Sounds like a vulture on the wing,' snorts Charlie.

'Describe your perfect man, Fliss,' Hannah urges, ignoring her brother.

'Well, I'm still not sure that the words "perfect" and "man" are really compatible,' I reply.

'Thanks a lot,' says Charlie indignantly. 'Women!' he strikes his forehead with the palm of his hand, in pretend exasperation.

'Very true,' Hannah agrees with me, looking pointedly at her brother. 'OK then, what sort of qualities would you want in a man for him to be perfect for you?'

'Well . . .' I muse. '. . . I want someone with a sense of humour. Richard didn't have a sense of humour. Or, not a normal one anyway.'

'Oh, so do I,' agrees Hannah. 'A sense of humour is very important.'

'Yeah,' drawls Charlie, inhaling a cloud of smoke which he then blows out of his nose. 'A bloke would have to have a bloody good sense of humour to go out with you in the first place.'

'I'm going to ignore that remark,' Hannah looks haughtily at him, 'because I know you're too stupid to make sensible comments.' She turns back to me. 'Go on.'

'I suppose it would be nice to have someone who's interested in what I do. Richard only ever thought about himself. Our life revolved around him. If something didn't affect him, it didn't interest him. I'd like someone I can talk to. You know, not just trivialities like, what do you want for dinner, or, did you have a nice day at the office, dear, but a proper, interesting conversation.'

'Mac has all the qualities I'd want in a man.' Hannah smiles thoughtfully.

'How so?' I smile.

'Well, he's well bred, good looking, a real gentleman, and terribly clever and funny. You talk to him and you can tell he's really listening to you, but best of all he never answers back.' She laughs.

'He's a horse,' shrieks Charlie derisively. 'My sister the mad-woman wants to marry a bloody horse!'

He gets to his size ten feet and starts to mock her.

'I always thought you were weird, and boy was I right!' he taunts.

'That's not what I meant and you know it!' Hannah screams back at him. 'But if all men are like you then I'd rather marry a horse, a pig, or even a bloody fat stinking hippopotamus!'

'Wouldn't you prefer Mac's groom?' I tease her, trying to defuse yet another row.

Hannah looks coy.

'Perhaps . . . perhaps not.'

'Women!' snaps Charlie more derisively this time. 'The things you talk about! I'm bored out of my *skull*, I'm going down the pub.' He shrugs on his leather James Dean-style jacket. 'Lend us a tenner, Fliss?'

'You're not old enough to go to the pub, Charlie.'

'Oh, come on, my birthday's in three weeks. What's the difference? Mum lets me drink anyway.'

I turn to Hannah. 'Is that true?'

She nods reluctantly.

'Oh, go on then, but I don't know you're there if your father asks, OK?'

'I've gone round to a friend's,' he replies, grinning. 'You're a doll, Fliss.'

He pockets my proffered ten-pound note.

'See ya later!'

I can hear his DMs clattering noisily across the flagstones in the hall, the bang of the front door, and the slow crunch of gravel as he walks up the drive.

Hannah watches him go from the window, and then turns petulantly to me.

'Well, if he gets to go to the pub, I'm going to have a drink too,' she announces, making her way to the rosewood cabinet that houses David's collection of malt whiskies.

'Hannah, you're *definitely* not old enough!'

'I told you, Mum lets us.'

'Perhaps, but I'm not your mother.'

'But you let Charlie go to the pub!' she cries in outrage.

So I did. The case of the old double standard.

'He's nearly eighteen,' I protest weakly.

'You said it.' Hannah stares accusingly at me. '*Nearly* eighteen.'

'Yes, but it's very different from being only just sixteen.'

'Why does everybody treat me like a child?' she wails. 'I detest being treated like a child!'

'But, Hannah . . .'

'I also detest hypocrites,' she accuses me with a glare, and stamps noisily out of the room.

I hear the back door slam. Darius, who has been slumped on his own personal clapped-out chintz-covered chair for the entire evening, opens one eye and looks at me accusingly.

'Don't you start,' I snap unjustly at him. 'I wasn't being unfair, was I?'

Double standards, he answers with his eyes, or are they simply reflecting my own thoughts, little dark mirrors that they are?

I go outside in search of Hannah, taking a bottle of low-alcohol wine, two glasses, and an apology. She's not in the garden, but I have a good idea where she'll be.

I walk around the side of the house, through the small kitchen garden which smells of mint and warm chives, and under the stone archway into the stable block. The old clock above my head strikes once for nine-thirty. It's beginning to get dark.

In the dim light I can see Hannah leaning over the edge of the half-open door into Mac's loose box. I can hear the low sound of her voice as she whispers to him. Mac's breath is casting curling vaporous pools above her head; I can hear the restless grind of his hooves upon the stable floor.

I'm just about to call after her when a figure slips out of the shadows opposite me.

It's Jake.

Hannah turns quickly, alarmed at his footsteps, then, recognising him, smiles softly. I'm torn between friendly discretion and surrogate parental concern. Discretion wins, as I'm still in the mood to make amends, so I slip back through the archway and return to the house.

Big Ben is just striking for *News at Ten* when I hear the back door again. Hannah sticks her head round the drawing-room door, and grins sheepishly at me.

'Hi, Fliss, sorry I was such a brat earlier. It's no excuse, I know, but I'm really tired and that always makes me ratty, so I think I'll just go to bed, OK?'

Charlie arrives home just over an hour later, also in a better mood. We take a cross-legged Darius for a quick walk in the moonlight and then he helps me to lock up.

I hear Caro and David return. It's about two o'clock in the morning. They are obviously very drunk. Caro is singing softly, David is shushing her loudly. There is a thud and then muffled laughter as someone trips up the stairs, and then the sound of their bedroom door. More laughter, the creak of protesting bed springs, some frantic giggling and then ten minutes on the soft growl of David snoring quietly.

I lie in the darkness for about half an hour. I always find it difficult to get back to sleep if I'm woken during the night. After counting endless sheep, I'm just drifting towards blissful uncon-sciousness when I hear the faint click of the back door being opened and shut very quietly. Immediately I'm as alert as a hound on the scent of a fox.

I sit upright, listening, as footsteps softly ascend the bare wooden staircase. Sliding out of bed, I grab a poker from the fireplace and edge towards the door. Feeling carefully for the round wooden handle, I turn it, slowly, quietly, and pull the door open towards me, raising the poker above my head so that I can easily bash any burglar before he can bash me. There is a figure at the head of the stairs paused in mid-step, like a trembling whippet listening for its master's whistle.

I'm trembling slightly too. Angels Court is reputed to be haunted; although I refute this as ridiculous, it always seems more plausible after midnight. Ghosts, however, don't creep around the house carrying a pair of worn red Kickers in their right hand.

'Hannah!' I hiss, relief turning to outrage. 'I thought you'd gone to bed hours ago.'

She looks at me, and then at the closed door of Caro and David's bedroom which is next door to mine. Bed springs creak again as someone stirs inside. We both shoot like conspirators into my room.

'Where have you been?' I whisper crossly, closing the door softly behind me.

She sits on the end of my bed.

'What would you say if I told you I was in love?'

'I'd say you still haven't answered my question.'

'I've been up at Woodsman's Cottage.' Her eyes are bright,

pupils dilated, she looks like she's been drinking.

'With Jake?'

'With Jake,' she confirms, trying to look sheepish but failing dismally, a broad grin on her pretty face.

'And I suppose that's who you think you're in love with?'

'I don't *think* I'm in love with him, I *am* in love with him,' she states emphatically.

Oh, the certainty of youth.

'You've only known him five minutes!'

'Nearly three days actually.'

'Oh, and that's a really long time, isn't it?'

'I didn't realise time was a prerequisite for falling in love with someone,' she answers indignantly. ' "Oh, I'm sorry, Jake, I can't love you, I haven't known you for the mandatory six months or whatever it is yet!" Honestly, Fliss, I thought you of all people would understand. You usually treat me like an adult, talk to me like one. I thought you'd be able to give me some advice about . . . well, you know . . . sex and stuff.'

I swallow hard. The only advice I could happily give Hannah at the moment is *don't*.

'I'm probably not the best person to ask about this sort of thing,' I mutter, 'you know me, an embittered old cynic. Shouldn't you really be talking to Caroline about this?'

'Why? She's not my mother.'

'Well, what about your father then?'

'Oh, I know what *he'll* say. That I'm far too young to form any sort of relationship, and that Jake is too old for me.'

'Don't you think that might be right?'

'I believe age is irrelevant when it comes to love,' she sighs, hugging her knees to her chest.

'How old is he, Hannah?'

'Oh, he's getting on,' she replies. 'He'll be twenty-three at Christmas. But as you know I think I prefer older men.'

'Oh, and Jake's absolutely ancient.' I mock.

'He's seven years older than me,' she says wide-eyed.

'Well, David can hardly say anything when he's sixteen years older than Caroline, now can he?' I say without thinking.

A smile slowly spreads across her face.

'No, of course, I hadn't thought of it like that. Thanks, Fliss, you've been a big help.'

She yawns loudly, slides off my bed, and mouthing 'Thanks'

again, slips silently out of the room before I can say anything to redeem the last statement.

Oh, dear. She may think I've been a big help, but I don't think Caro and David would look at it that way. She's taken the gun, and I've just handed her the ammunition.

Breakfast next morning is a sombre affair. Hannah is quiet, pleading with me using her black-shadowed eyes not to mention last night's escapade.

Fortunately Caro and David are far too hung over themselves to notice Hannah's state. Caro is slumped at the kitchen table nursing a mug of black coffee; David is struggling to pull on and strap up his boots, and complaining that he's desperately late to meet Angus Macready down in Far Meadow.

Charlie, still in excellent spirits from his trip to the local, whistles while he fries spitting bacon, fat black-bellied mushrooms and runny golden-yellow eggs in a huge black pan the size of a small satellite dish.

I'm fighting yet another battle of conscience. I'm worried about Hannah. Worried she might do something silly – sixteen is a good age for that. I remember when I was sixteen, I was old enough to get into mischief and too young to worry about the consequences.

A dangerous age.

Charlie slides the greasy mess from the pan to his plate, and slaps the whole lot down on the table.

David visibly gags and shoots out of the kitchen door, towing a reluctant drooling Darius after him.

Caro takes one look and sprints off to the downstairs loo. She comes back five minutes later looking decidedly ill. Her skin has the pallor of a corpse, and her hands are visibly trembling.

'You look like the Angels Court ghost,' I tell her, trying not to laugh. She darts me a black look through red eyes.

'I'm going to go back to bed,' she just about manages to utter, 'I think I've got a touch of food poisoning . . .'

'Don't you mean alcohol poisoning?' says Charlie politely.

'I don't know what you mean,' she replies indignantly, but flatly refuses to meet his mocking eyes.

'Come off it, Caro.' He grins. 'We all heard you come in last night. You were making enough noise to wake up the neighbours, if we had any.'

He bursts into a tuneless chorus of the song Caro was singing as she staggered up the stairs the night or rather morning before, and starts to dance about the table.

Hannah and I start laughing as he whisks a protesting Caro into his arms and begins to spin her round the room, until she turns a most unbecoming shade of green.

'Must have been a good party,' he taunts her, finally letting go.

'I hope it was worth it!' Hannah adds her voice to the proceedings as Caro beats a hasty retreat.

Laughing, Hannah puts down the piece of toast she's been staring at but not actually attempting to eat for the last ten minutes.

'Well, I'm off out, see you later.'

And with that she's gone. I don't have to ask where.

'Are you OK, Fliss? You look a bit down.'

Charlie moves around the table to the seat next to mine.

'You're not still brooding about Richard the Turd, are you?'

Just taking a sip from a cup of coffee, I choke over the new nickname, trying very hard to look disapproving and suppress the smile that's blossoming instead.

'Actually I'm a bit worried about your sister,' I confess to him.

'Aren't we all?' he sighs. 'Still, the doctors said she'd never be normal.'

'No, seriously, Charlie,' I elbow him gently in the ribs, 'I need your advice.'

'I'm all ears.' He grins. 'Although that's not what my girl-friends tell me . . .'

'Can't you be serious for one moment?' I groan in exasperation, setting my cup down on the table. 'I really am worried.'

'About her and Jake?'

'You know?'

'Of course. I may look innocuous, but I see all and hear all,' he jokes.

'Charlie . . .'

'Don't worry, it's only a stupid crush, she's had tons of those before and lived to tell the tale.'

'Maybe. But this one worries me. It feels different . . . she's so intense about the whole thing, so serious, it's quite frightening really.'

'Maybe, but you need to let her work it out, Fliss, she's not stupid.'

67

'I know, but she is *totally* infatuated with him.'

'Hannah's not your responsibility.'

'No, she's your father's and Caroline's, which is why I think I should tell them what's going on.'

'And have her fall out with you big time? What's the problem? Why interfere? Why not just let her get on with it if she's keen on him? She's had boyfriends before.'

'But she's *too* keen on him, Charlie, I'm frightened she'll do something stupid.'

He pushes his floppy black fringe out of his eyes and grins easily at me.

'You worry too much. She'll be all right, let her work it out for herself. Do yourself a favour and forget about it, Fliss. Hannah won't thank you for interfering, and Dad's got eyes in the back of his head, I bet he knows already. Anyway, we're only here for another three days. We'll go back to London on Friday and she'll forget all about him. Besides that she's far too young for him. If Jake's got any sense he'll tell her to back off, and if he's got any scruples, he won't take advantage of the fact she's totally dotty about him.'

'Twenty-three-year-old men don't have any scruples when it comes to sex.'

'Don't they?' says Charlie, his eyes brightening perceptibly. 'In that case, sod desperately waiting for eighteen, and roll on twenty-three!'

All seems quiet on the Jake front over the next few days. Hannah is quiet and miserable, and finally admits to me that he seems to be avoiding her. I guiltily heave a sigh of relief. I hate to see her unhappy, but I think seeing Jake is a bit like overindulging in alcohol. It may make you feel bloody wonderful at the time, but you'll wake up with one hell of a hangover. With things a little more settled on that front I have time to analyse why I was so concerned about him, and decide that possibly one of the reasons I've thrown myself wholeheartedly into sorting out Hannah's life is so I don't have to think about my own.

When Sally phones again it almost feels like an intrusion. This is wrong, I know, but I've managed to push all thoughts of Richard and Mother and the cancelled wedding quite out of my mind, and I like it that way. Speaking with my sister only brings it all back into too-sharp focus.

She sounds rather odd, but when questioned puts it down to stress.

My guilt increases tenfold as I'm pretty certain any stress Sally is under has one direct cause – me.

When pushed she tells me that my name is still pretty much taboo in the Blakeney household, but that Mother seems to be surfacing from her me-induced misery incredibly well. What precisely has caused this miraculous recovery escapes me, and Sally seems almost reluctant to offer an explanation, simply pointing out that I should be grateful she's no longer blaming an imminent early demise on my thoughtless incomprehensible actions.

I don't know whether to be sad or relieved when Sally says with a slight laugh that she imagines that at this rate I'll be allowed back into my mother's life in say . . . five years time instead of maybe on her death bed, and that only so she can have the chance to swear at me before she pops her clogs.

Ten years would have been a more realistic time for me to psyche myself up into seeing Miriam again, but grateful I suppose for small mercies, I manage a smile when Sal then informs me that my poor put-upon father has moved into the potting shed on a pretty much permanent basis, when he's not off night fishing with Roger.

Although Sally is adamant that she's coping pretty well, I decide for her sake and my father's that I've been self-indulgently hiding out for too long and I really must go home. When I announce this intention to Caro, however, she goes to great lengths to persuade me to stay till the end of the week.

She apparently has a surprise for me.

I remember Hannah's warnings about men and parties, and this only deepens my resolve to go. I'm feeling one hundred per cent better but I don't think I'm up to surprises just yet, especially not one of Caroline's who does tend to go somewhat over the top.

However, I owe her far more than tolerance and, after much good-natured grovelling on her part, agree to stay.

The night before Hannah and Charlie are due to return to London, Caro has arranged a trip to the local theatre.

Charlie, who has been forced out of his usual uniform of jeans, white T-shirt and leather jacket, and into a suit, is making rude comments about local culture or rather lack of it and pulling agitatedly at his tie and collar as though they are actively trying to asphyxiate him.

'I don't know why you made me get all topped and tailed,' he complains. 'Market Atherton is hardly West End. Besides Oscar Wilde is definitely not my scene.'

'Stop moaning, you heathen,' David replies, grinning broadly, his strong straight teeth unnaturally white in the hall light. 'A bit of culture instead of Culture Club will do you good.'

'Culture Club!' groans Charlie. 'Honestly, Dad, what century are you living in?'

'Flisssss,' hisses a voice. I turn my attention away from the others. Hannah, who has spent the past two hours in the bathroom, is standing in the shadows by the doorway, beckoning to me in a conspiratorial fashion. I sidle over.

'Guess what!' she whispers, excitedly grasping hold of my wrist. 'Jake wants me to meet him.'

She's beaming broadly, obviously delighted by this change of heart.

'But you can't,' I protest. 'We're all supposed to be going out, it's your last night here.'

'Exactly, my last night, the last chance I'll get to spend some time with Jake.'

Her eyes are shining brighter than Charlie's polished leather shoes.

'Will you cover for me, Fliss?'

'I really don't know that I should . . .'

'Please,' she begs, anguished. 'Would you stand in the way of true love?'

Her grip on my arm tightens desperately.

'I may never see him again, Fliss, this could be our last evening together. Pleeease, I'm begging you . . .'

'Oh, OK,' I sigh. 'What do you want me to do?'

'Fliss, you're an absolute angel!' The grin returns as quickly as it left, and she stretches up and kisses me warmly on the cheek.

'I'm not an angel, I'm a fool.' I shake my head. 'I can't believe I'm doing this.'

'Just tell them I feel ill and I've gone to bed. I'll be back before you get home, I promise.'

'But . . .' I start. Hannah cuts in quickly.

'You won't let me down, will you, Fliss? You're my friend.'

70

I crumble.

'OK, OK, but Hannah . . .'

'I know, I know, don't do anything you wouldn't do!' she laughs, letting go of my arm and skipping away from me. She turns as she reaches the back door and calls mockingly, 'Which means I can do just about anything I want to, doesn't it?'

She winks lasciviously, blows me a kiss and is gone.

Caro, David and Charlie have made their way out to David's Range Rover. Caro is trying and failing to step up into the high front passenger seat in a long fitted skirt. Charlie has just sat on a bridle, and is muttering about cheap thrills.

'At last,' says Caro as I walk out of the front door. 'Now all we need is Hannah. Where is she? Don't tell me she's still in the bathroom?'

'Er . . . she's not coming.' I can feel my face going red. I hate lying, especially to Caro. 'She said she doesn't feel too good.'

'Oh, dear! Really! I'd better go and make sure she's all right,' says Caro in concern, turning back towards the house.

'Oh, she's fine,' I blurt out quickly, practically rugby tackling her away from the door. 'Just a bad headache, thought sitting in a stuffy theatre all night might make it worse.'

'Well, I'd better make sure she's not coming down with something.' Caro steps round me.

'She said she wanted to be left on her own . . . You know, a couple of hours in a dark room.'

Caro stops.

'Typical Hannah. She's probably in a bad mood because she's got to go home tomorrow.'

'Oh, yes? Why should that upset her?'

For a panicky moment I think Caro knows more than she's letting on.

'Well, she'll miss the party tomorrow night, she's quite put out about that. Never mind, if she wants to cut off her nose to spite her face and miss out on tonight as well, then so be it.'

'That was total crap,' moans Charlie as we pull back into the drive, nearly three hours later. 'I've never yawned so much in my life. If it had gone on for even one more milli-second, my jaw would have stuck or I'd have died of complete and utter boredom.'

'Heathen,' mutters David, but he's still smiling.

'Actually it finished a lot earlier than I thought it would.' Caro looks at her Cartier watch, an anniversary gift from David.

Me too, I add silently to myself, a lot earlier. Let's hope Hannah's here.

'You've just got to learn to appreciate the finer things in life, my boy,' David calls back to his son. 'There's more to life than fast food, fast movies, and fast music.'

'Yeah,' Charlie leers. 'Fast women!'

David raises his eyebrows to heaven.

'Hannah knew what she was doing welching out.' Charlie is still moaning as we enter the house, which is in darkness.

'Actually, I'd just better go and make sure she's OK,' says Caro. 'David, be an angel and get me a large G & T while I check on your drama queen of a daughter.'

I follow her upstairs, praying that Hannah has kept her promise and got home before us.

Sure enough, she's in bed, duvet pulled up to her neck. I send up a silent prayer of thanks. She opens her eyes as the landing light illuminates her room.

'Feeling better?' Caro glides across the room, and flicks on the bedside lamp. 'Actually you do look flushed. Are you running a temperature?'

She puts a cool hand on Hannah's forehead.

'You know, I really thought you were faking it,' she laughs, 'but don't worry, I feel quite guilty now. Would you like anything? Some aspirin, or a hot drink perhaps?'

Hannah shakes her head. She's trembling, she actually does look ill, but I know she's not, so why does she look so awful?

It's then that I notice the reason.

A pair of boxer shorts lies on the floor just behind Caroline, who is sitting of the edge of Hannah's bed.

Hannah's eyes keep darting from them, to Caroline, to me.

Rescue me! they plead.

I surreptitiously slide down the wall and, picking up the offending article, hold it behind my back.

'Well, if you're sure you're OK?' Caro stands up.

Hannah nods again, not trusting herself to speak. I can see relief flood her elfin face as Caro leaves the room, closing the door softly behind her.

'Well?' I demand, bringing my hand from behind my back and waving the boxer shorts at Hannah.

In response her cupboard door creaks open three inches, a hand slides out of the gap, takes the shorts and slides back in again. Hannah, who has been shaking throughout with suppressed laughter, and no other emotion or illness, can contain herself no longer. Silent laughter explodes from her mouth like Coca-Cola fizzing from a shaken bottle.

Hannah and Charlie's last day. As the farm cock crows and I awake, I experience this wonderful feeling of relief. I mean, I've enjoyed having them here, but I don't think my nerves could cope for much longer. Jake must have managed to escape from the wardrobe last night without incident. I heard nothing. I lay awake with my ears on elastic, waiting for an explosion of some kind, but nothing came. I finally dozed off in the early hours of the morning and, sleeping fitfully, have woken up with large bags under my eyes, and what I am certain, as I peer blearily into the bathroom mirror, are at least five new wrinkles. Stress fractures to my skin. I decide I'm not even going to mention last night to Hannah, who grins disturbingly at me all through breakfast. Lectures are futile. The horse has already bolted.

Hannah and Charlie's last day is also the day of the previously threatened party which as it turns out is Caro's not very surprising surprise. She expects me to be amazed at her announcement despite the fact that she has let it slip on several occasions that she has a party planned for this evening. I think the fact that I'm still here and haven't bolted back to Oxford makes her think I haven't sussed yet. She also expects me to be pleased about it, so I do try to be, but I'm not. I've never been party hearty, all that small talk and polite conversation, I'm not really very good at it.

One and all are gathered in the kitchen. Hannah is shelling peas for our final lunch together, Charlie is lovingly cleaning a gun which he's threatened to take back to London with him, and David has threatened to shoot him with it if he so much as carries it across the threshold. David is doing amazing things with a blender whilst watching Charlie out of the corner of one wary grey eye, and Caro is polishing wine glasses.

Feeling unemployed, I have embarked on the ambitious construction of a rich chocolate torte for this evening's soirée.

'We're only having a light meal,' David protested, when I announced my intentions. 'Soufflé, seafood, that sort of thing.'

73

'Are you saying my torte will turn out like a brick?' I ask indignantly.

Hannah seems much happier, much brighter. I notice she's wearing Jake's signet ring – an object she had previously dismissed as vulgar – on a chain about her neck. Her only gripe at the moment is that she will miss the party.

I'd happily offer her my place.

'I really don't think it's fair that you hold a party *after* we leave,' she complains. 'Typical really. Get us to do all the hard work, clean the house, prepare the guest rooms, peel the veggies, go grocery shopping, and then when the whole thing culminates to form the good part, the *party* part, ship us back to Mother's.'

'It's an adults only dinner party,' states Caroline firmly. 'Strictly no kids allowed.'

'I'm not a kid!' Hannah gives her usual disclaimer, but this time instead of throwing Charlie the usual accompanying look of indignation, she is serenely smug.

'Then why do you always act like one?' goads her brother, throwing an empty pea pod at her.

'Just following your example,' she snaps back at him.

'See, now you're squabbling like children,' laughs Caro. 'I'm sorry, Hannah, but your mother's coming to collect you.'

'You could phone and put her off.'

'She'll already have left, it's a long drive from Scotland.'

Hannah's face falls in disappointment but I know it's not really the party she wants to stay for. I sigh heavily. I really hope they were careful. I suppress the flutter of concern that is winging round my stomach like a moth bashing against a light bulb.

'Maura's coming to collect them?' I ask David, who nods and rolls his eyeballs in response. This will be interesting. I have never actually met the much-maligned Maura although I've built up this picture in my head, from everything that's been said about her, but people never normally look how you imagine them to.

'It will be great finally to meet her,' I tell Caroline in hushed tones, 'I'll be able to see if she's as potty as you say she is.'

Maura arrives trailing wafts of Patchouli oil and tie-dyed Indian silk.

To my surprise, she is just as I imagined, David's and Caroline's description being so vivid; what they failed to mention, however, is how beautiful she is. Glorious red hair tumbles in waves down her back, falling almost to her waist, her skin is the colour of double cream, and despite the baggy, totally unflattering clothes, she still looks slim and elegant.

'Darlings!' She swoops down upon Charlie and Hannah like a brightly coloured parrot in full flight, her fuchsia pink and emperor purple caftan, which clashes amazingly with her flame hair, flapping in the breeze behind her.

'Charlie, my darling handsome son!' she exclaims, kissing him first on both cheeks and then on his forehead.

'Mother!' he exclaims in embarrassment, blushing deep crimson and pulling away.

'Hannah, my little girl, I swear you've grown another inch!'

'You've only been away for five days, Maura.' Hannah rolls her eyes. 'Not five years! I hardly think I've grown in five days. And I'm not a little girl, I'm a woman!'

After hugging her children for almost five minutes apiece, she finally turns to Caroline, David and me waiting quietly in the background. She floats over and ignoring Caro and me, stands in front of David, silent and appraising.

'David, you're far too pale. I sense tension in you.'

'I'm fine, Maura, and how are you?' he says dryly.

'How was your journey?' Caro asks. 'I expect the roads were packed as usual.'

'I always find physical travel exhausting.' Maura sighs dramatically. 'Craignathie was wonderful, so enlightening and enriching, but I shall be glad to get back to London, as I'm sure will you, my darlings.' She turns back to Hannah and Charlie. 'I do hope you haven't been too desperate without me? The country can be so stifling. You must have been bored in this quiet little backwater.'

Caro raises her eyebrows and looks over at me.

'This is a friend of ours, Fliss, she's been helping us entertain the kids. Trying to help me stop them dying of tedium in this boring backwater anyway.' The obvious sarcasm in her voice is lost on the visitor.

Maura turns and looks at me. Her eyes are unnerving: huge, doe-like, the colour of a ripe avocado pear, they seem to look into you rather than at you.

75

'Your aura is cracked,' announces Maura.

'That's not the only thing that's cracked,' mutters Caro. I try to suppress a nervous giggle and fail.

'You know, they had the most marvellous healing sessions at Craignathie. I'm thinking of starting my own healing workshop. You should come, I sense you need some spiritual guidance. Do you have a spiritual guide?'

'Er, I used to be a Girl Guide,' I offer, 'does that count?'

'That woman drives me round the bend!' Caro clenches her fists in exasperation. 'I thought she'd never leave! It's all your fault, Fliss, you and your bloody cracked aura, she was banging on about it for over half an hour.'

Maura has finally carried Charlie and Hannah back to the civilised capital in her Mercedes convertible. Very bourgeois for a self-proclaimed communist. I thought hippies drove VW campers crammed full with other hippies.

'A healing workshop!' David collapses into a chair and shakes his head in amusement. 'Whatever next?'

'She could call it Maura's Auras,' I suggest, laughing. 'Cracked auras and crackpots a speciality.'

'Well, I don't think it's very funny,' Caro snaps, beginning to panic. 'We've got a dinner party to organise, and the guests will start arriving in an hour.'

'Don't worry, darling, everything's just about ready anyway,' David says soothingly. 'The food's prepared, I've chosen the wine . . .'

'I've made a chocolate torte,' I announce with pride.

'Hannah cut the flowers for the table from the garden earlier and put them in the sink in the boot room. All you have left to do is make the table look beautiful and then work the same magic on yourself . . .'

'You haven't forgotten we're eating earlier than usual tonight, David?'

They exchange a look. Caro's passing eyeball messages, tapping out Morse code with the lifting of her eyebrows. David deciphers.

'Oh, yes, of course. Don't worry, it's all in hand.'

I wish *I* could decipher that little exchange. Perhaps Hannah's right, perhaps tonight is a set up and I shall find myself besieged by some pot-bellied businessman or pink-faced farmer. I feel the first stirring of nerves, butterflies drifting to and fro in my stomach.

By seven, I'm dressed, coiffured, and seated at the dressing table, painting my face. Such is the freedom here at Angels Court, the blissful isolation, I haven't worn make-up for three weeks. There's been no need. Caro, David and Darius don't care if my eyes look like two shrunken raisins in the head of a gingerbread man, and my lips are paler than a ghost's. I've almost forgotten how to apply it. It takes three attempts to get my lip-liner straight, not just through lack of recent practice but from my nervously trembling hand.

I can hear people arriving. Cars pulling slowly down the long gravel drive. Doors slamming, voices calling and laughing, David playing genial host-cum-butler in the hallway, gathering coats and distributing drinks. Puccini drifting up the stairs.

There seem to be an awful lot of people arriving. The long table in the dining-room seats at least twenty, but surely they haven't invited that many? I don't want my first foray into society as a newly single person to be that nerve-racking. It's very easy to take for granted the ease another person creates in your social life, a cushion to social interaction.

Can I remember how to socialise? Do I *want* to remember? I think what I really want to do is curl up in bed with a bottle of wine all to myself and watch *Blind Date*. Unfortunately that option is not available to me this evening.

I force myself to make my way downstairs, reluctant to leave the sanctuary of my room. I have become rather introverted in the past weeks. It's very easy not to socialise. I am more than ever aware of how people can become monks and lock themselves away in cloisters for years. They say solitude is hard to cope with, but really it's much more of an effort to be gregarious.

I look through the double doors that open into the lemon-coloured drawing-room. Glamorous people are standing in groups, talking. The combined noise sounds like the babble of geese in a field.

I balk at the numbers. There *are* over twenty people in the room. Perhaps I should feign a headache and return to the safe haven that is my bedroom. Then again I'm so tense I don't need to pretend I have a headache, I can already feel one coming.

I'm just backing out of the doorway when David appears at my side, whispers encouragingly that I look 'Bloody marvellous' and guides me across the room.

I recognise some of the group he's introducing me to from previous forays to Angels Court. Caro and David are sociable people, always throwing dinner parties, yet I've never attended one on this scale before. I think they're rather cruel. I would have preferred to be eased back into society gently rather than thrown in at the deep end with a full-scale party.

I have already met the oh-so-glam blonde bombshell Eloise who is talking to Caroline in her perfectly pitched Sloane Ranger voice. We've never really hit it off. She's a bit of an ice queen, you know the type, and also weirdly possessive of Caroline. Like she's not allowed to have any other friends. I therefore am not Eloise's favourite person. She raises eyebrows plucked to the point of extinction in just about civil greeting, but continues with her conversation in a manner that pointedly excludes me.

David introduces me next to an incredibly pretty and petite woman. She's like a little doll with enchanting eyes, wide and fawn-like and thickly fringed with long black lashes, a little rosebud mouth, which is painted a glossy cherry red, and a tiny tip-tilted nose. I'm a little taller than the average woman, a fact I've always rather enjoyed, but next to this dainty doll I feel like a giantess.

As far as her figure is concerned, God may have stinted in the height department, but he more than compensated in other areas. She has the largest chest I have ever seen outside of *Treasure Island*. My eyes are drawn to it as shiny metal dust to a pyramid magnet. How can such a small person carry such a large front without overbalancing, and with such great aplomb too? Then again they appear to defy gravity. Perhaps they're weightless, like balloons filled with helium, and it's only the material of her low-cut bodice that is actually stopping them from floating right up to the ceiling.

She catches me staring. I blush as crimson as her mouth, but she simply smiles. I suppose she's used to a lot of attention. She must be the epitome of many a male fantasy, the object of much female envy.

'This is Sukey.' David smirks at my fascinated expression. 'She breeds horses.'

'No?' My surprise is genuine. I can't imagine her doing anything more manual than filing her finger nails, let alone getting down and dirty in a loose box.

Sukey laughs lightly. She has the original sound that the hideous Kat Christian was trying to achieve, the tinkling bell effect, but with Sukey it's natural and therefore nice.

'This is my husband Bob,' she says, putting a small, perfectly manicured hand on the arm of the man standing next to her. Husband Bob is thin, plain, straight-faced and unprepossessing. The boring but necessary bamboo cane supporting the wonderfully exotic bloom, I suppose.

'Bob's a chef,' says David, 'so my soufflés will have to rise to the occasion tonight.'

'Amongst other things!' Sukey giggles.

They all laugh as though this is some kind of 'in' joke.

Bob doesn't look creative enough to be a chef, although his face does have the quality of an unrisen loaf.

A tall rangy blond man who has been standing quietly at the edge of the group, elbow resting casually on the mantelpiece, glass of wine in hand, steps forward and raises his eyebrows at David.

'Aren't you going to introduce me then?' His voice is low and soft.

'Fliss darling, I'd like you to meet Gwillem Davies.'

Gwillem takes the hand I offer him but doesn't shake it, preferring instead simply to squeeze it gently while holding it for a fraction of a second too long.

'Gwillem's a very old friend of ours from London,' David continues, laughing at my flustered expression. 'He's an artist, you know. He painted the portrait of Caroline you like so much, the one that hangs over the fireplace in the sitting-room.'

'Oh, but that's wonderful.' I'm genuinely impressed. 'It's such a good likeness.'

'Unfortunately he is now far too popular and well known ever to paint for us again. He would never find the time, and we could never afford him!' Caro, angelically beautiful in cream silk, leaves the side of a disgruntled Eloise to join in our conversation.

She squeezes Gwillem's arm affectionately.

'Caro is an unadulterated flatterer!' he laughs. His voice is low, with just the softest trace of a Welsh accent.

Reaching out, he takes my hand again. I notice that his fingers are very long, and his nails perfectly manicured.

'So pleased to meet you. I keep telling Caro that we could do with some new blood in the group.'

He holds my hand and my gaze for longer this time. I don't know whether to feel flattered or uncomfortable.

I find myself seated next to Gwillem at dinner. I wonder if this is the potential date that Hannah warned me about. I don't normally go for blond men. I don't know why, but I just don't find them attractive. I have to admit though that Gwillem is very good-looking.

I estimate that he's either in his late-thirties or early-forties. Tall and golden, he's like a rangy lion, far removed from Hannah's balding, fat fifty year old. He can also hold an intelligent conversation, a rare trait, much appreciated after the barren wasteland of unused intellect I previously shared with Richard the Turd.

He also seems flatteringly interested in me. There is a stunning redhead to his other side, Amber Dixon, a friend of Caro's I've met before who is absolutely gorgeous in every way, face, body, and personality, but apart from a polite hello when we first sat down to eat, he has almost completely ignored her in favour of me.

The food as usual is superb, a combined effort between the gourmet David and the artist Caroline. Caro's artistic skills have come into play with the table. They consider the setting for a meal to be as important as the food. The lobster bisque is served against a backdrop of white and palest pink roses on white linen. Candles flicker in silver Art Deco candlesticks that twist and turn like entwined lovers, casting golden flickers of light across the room. The room is all flesh pink and white like a luscious Rubens lady, sensuous, flirtatious, yet at the same time pure and virginal.

'How long have you known Caroline?' asks Gwillem, passing me a bread roll.

'Since I was a child.'

'Really? Very old friends then. I'm surprised we haven't met before.'

'We lost touch,' I reply. 'Only found each other again last year when Caro started to work at the same school.'

'A happy coincidence . . . so you're a teacher?'

I nod unenthusiastically. Teacher sounds so boring, so worthy. I want to be exciting and unconventional like the rest of them. Gwillem as you know is a painter. Eloise is an actress. The man beyond her, who looks a little like an aged Laurence Olivier, is apparently a rather well-known poet. His name is Blakesley Hardington – sounds like some new suburb of Milton Keynes. Sukey breeds her horses, Bob cooks for the rich and famous, and Amber Dixon, a record company PR, is being flirted with by an opera singer even I, a self-confessed musical Philistine, have heard of.

'You don't look like a teacher,' muses Gwillem, narrowing his eyes as he assesses me.

'Oh, yes, and what are teachers supposed to look like?'

He laughs quietly.

'I don't know. I suppose I always have this rather clichéd picture of Maggie Smith as Miss Jean Brodie, but you're nothing like that. Nothing like that at all.'

I begin to feel awkward again under such close scrutiny and look around the table for rescue. Angus Macready is sitting opposite me. He is a handsome man, with dark hair greying elegantly at the temples. His face and hands, tanned from the outdoor life, are exaggerated by his pure white shirt. This is the first time I've seen him without a tweed jacket and a flat cap. He always wears a tie, even when the weather's at its hottest, although tonight the usual brown knit has been replaced by a far more flamboyant multi-coloured silk.

'Is Jake as devastated as Hannah at their enforced separation?' I ask him.

Angus smiles to show incredibly large even teeth, but shakes his head.

'He liked her well enough, but he's a young lad. I'm afraid they don't take things so much to heart as girls, do they? He'll be moving on soon.'

Moving on? Physically or emotionally? Another day, another woman. Bastard.

'I see,' I answer, smiling through clenched teeth. Poor Hannah. What price love?

'We're not all as fickle.'

'I'm sorry?' I turn back to Gwillem who is leaning towards me, his elbow resting on the table, his chin resting in his hand, gazing at me rather unnervingly.

'Men. We're not all as fickle in our affections.'

I smile nervously, unsure of what to say. He's like headlights on full beam, approaching well over the usual speed limit.

'Try this, it's wonderful.' He holds out his fork to me.

I decide that I haven't known him long enough to share his cutlery, which is odd as I will happily share lips – but only lips, thank you – with someone after just one evening. I can only conclude I don't really fancy him.

I lie to him that I'm so full I couldn't swallow another morsel, which is unfortunate as in order to keep up the pretence I have to refuse dessert. I always hate to refuse dessert, especially as no one else seems remotely interested in the chocolate torte I made and I'd be more than happy to lay into a massive piece.

To my surprise, there is no lingering over coffee at the end of the meal. I'm disappointed, I like that part best of all. It's not just the chocolate mints and the brandy that appeal, it's the relaxed atmosphere where conversation tends to sparkle at new heights.

But everyone is getting up and adjourning to the sitting-room. There's a hurried scraping of chairs, an air of excited anticipation. A buzz almost.

'What's going on?' I ask Caro.

'Party games,' she replies.

I look confused.

'It's a tradition at Angels Court,' says Gwillem, smiling at me.

'Is it?' It's a tradition I've never been party to before when I've visited with Richard. Perhaps he wasn't favoured enough for this sort of thing.

'When *we* all get together, yes,' he replies.

'Why don't you take Fliss for a stroll around the garden while we set up in here?' says Caro, a mischievous gleam in her blue eyes.

Hannah was right, I do believe Caro is matchmaking.

'I've seen the garden before!' I protest. Gwillem seems very nice, intense and unnerving, but nice all the same, but I'm not at all sure I want to be set up.

She raises her eyebrows at me, warning me not to be obstructive. I suppose the least I can do after all she's done for me is play along. I follow Gwillem out into the garden. The air is still warm, and scented with night stock, lilac and old roses.

Billie Holiday starts to sing on the old gramophone David

treasures so much. He believes that all old records should be played on an old gramophone. His philosophy is that as they were made to complement each other, you will never get a better sound.

I find myself singing along to the music until a frog at the bottom of the garden starts croaking in tuneless harmony and I realise it sounds more in tune than I do.

'Would you like to dance?' Gwillem holds out a perfectly manicured hand.

I think he's been primed in the right seduction techniques by Caro. Without waiting for an answer, he takes my hand and pulls me on to the lawn. The grass is damp with evening dew. I stand awkwardly in front of him for a moment until he pulls me close and begins to waltz across the dew-strewn grass.

I finally get to dance in the moonlight.

It's nice but I'm not comfortable. I'm not a good dancer, stiff as a board from sheer nerves. I try to follow his feet without actually treading on them, which is rather difficult. I finally get the rhythm and look up. He is gazing down at me. His eyes are the colour of amber, bright shining stones amidst that mane of golden hair. He's so dangerously like an animal, I almost expect to hear him begin to roar at the moon above us.

He's attractive, but unattractive. Appealing, and yet invidious. Like the lion, whose beauty captivates and whose savagery repels. Hypnotic almost.

'What are you thinking?'

I realise with embarrassment that I have been staring at him, and quickly look back down at the short damp grass we are slowly trampling underfoot.

'You looked so deep in thought,' he continues, 'I know you must be thinking something interesting. I'd love to be able to paint people's thoughts. Now *that* would be fascinating. What would yours be, I wonder? Do you have a twisted mind? Would you be a Chagal? A Breughel? Or perhaps something a little more erotic, a Schiele maybe?'

'More like a Rubens with their plump thighs and dimpled bottoms,' I say without thinking.

He smiles lasciviously at me. I flush pink.

'You have a lovely skin tone,' he whispers into my hair. 'Perhaps one day you would let me paint you.'

My heart skips a beat.

Fantasy Island.

The Svengali syndrome.

You are a beautiful girl, let me paint you.

Not normally spoken in a Welsh accent, a French accent carries the right tone, but exciting none the less.

I'd forgotten how enjoyable it is to be chatted up. I relax a little. Gwillem notes that I am no longer stiff and poker-like, and takes his chance to pull me a little closer. His arms around me are warm and strong. He smells nice of some clear as crystal and obviously very expensive aftershave. He begins to whisper very flattering things in my ear.

I suppose I *could* get used to this.

I think I'm beginning to warm to him a little. Maybe even enjoy myself.

'I can feel your heart beating,' he murmurs. 'Boom, beboom, beboom.'

I try hard to suppress a laugh and fail dismally.

I'm instantly reminded of that cartoon where the skunk falls in love with the black cat whose tail is somehow painted with a white stripe.

Gwillem's murmurings cease to be romantic. The whole thing – the moonlight, the music, the dancing – simply reminds me of some bad film *d'amour*.

The music slowly winds to a halt. We can hear shrieking and laughter coming from the house.

'The games have commenced,' says Gwillem, smiling, obviously completely unaware that his rating, which was rising, has just sunk to an all-time low. 'Shall we go back in and join in the fun?'

I agree enthusiastically, trying to hide my relief that I have a chance to escape being alone with him. I've been twitchy all evening, struggling to overcome the faint feelings of dislike, distaste even, that he arouses in me. I'm faintly embarrassed that I dropped my guard even to let him in a few millimetres.

I've learned one thing on my search for happiness, though. The romance in a relationship isn't necessarily missing, it just doesn't work properly if you're with the wrong person.

Gwillem's all wrong.

The lights have been dimmed back in the sitting-room. It takes a few moments for my eyes to adapt. Even when they've adjusted to the low light, I still spend several seconds blinking as though I'm trying to focus properly.

I close my eyes and then open them again. Close and then open, close and then open, open wide, very wide, until they almost pop out on to the carpet.

Am I imagining things or are there naked people on the floor?

It takes a few moments for my shell-shocked mind to acknowledge that we have walked back into the house and into a full-scale orgy.

Blakesley Hardington's little white bottom rises like the full moon from a pile of maroon cushions in the corner, and then sinks below the horizon of Sukey Aimes's legs as he buries a prick the size of a small French stick between said legs, and his face between the plump pink cushions of her plentiful bosom, gnawing on her left nipple with far more enthusiasm than he showed for any of the delicious things presented to him at dinner.

Her husband Bob, no longer sporting a face the consistency of dough, and certain parts of his anatomy fully risen like a yeast-fed loaf, frolics happily with two half-naked girls upon the chaise-longue where in recent weeks I have happily reclined with a good book from David's well-stocked library.

A slim black girl who was lasciviously sucking her fiancé's dessert spoon at the dinner table has now got her full sloe-coloured lips wrapped around something far more interesting.

Angus Macready, his weathered face and brown arms a strange contrast to the lily-white hue of the rest of his body, is running a weathered hand along the creamy white flank of the local MFH's wife, as he does with Mac and the other horses to test that they're sound enough to ride.

Open-mouthed, I look round for Caro and wish I hadn't.

She is kissing Eloise. Slow, open-mouthed, tongue-entwined kissing. Her left hand is clasped firmly around the flesh of Eloise's right breast, thumb strumming across the hard pink nipple; her right hand is travelling down the soft curve of her friend's belly where the fingers gently tangle in the blonde pubic hair before dipping in between the hollow of her thighs. Eloise, who is already completely naked, is struggling with the buttons of Caroline's blouse.

David, the only person in the room apart from myself and Gwillem still fully clothed, is seated in an armchair, like a king indulgently surveying his subjects. He is watching them in fascination, smiling his usual lazy smile. All around them people are abandoning clothes and inhibitions.

I look incredulously at Gwillem, but he doesn't seem at all fazed.

He looks back at me, eyes bright from drink and arousal. He smiles and begins to unbutton his shirt.

Party games!

I was expecting charades.

This must be a group re-enactment of *Caligula*.

I start to giggle hysterically until Gwillem, divested of his clothes, begins to try to divest me of mine, and then the hysterical giggle turns into a rather loud scream.

Pulling away from his expertly undoing hands, I stampede across the room, trampling bodies as I go. The rather well-known opera singer hits the highest note of his career as my high heel engages with the flabby cushion of his backside.

My handbag and car keys are on the dresser in the hall. Without really thinking, I grab them and head for the door, passing the dining-room and the unpleasant sight of a skinny eager stockbroker spreading my untouched chocolate torte over the trembling thighs of his plump girlfriend. She is spread-eagled on the dining-room table like a large suckling pig served up for the main course, a gloriously naked Amber Dixon poised between her thighs, ready to devour my torte from such an unusual plate without the aid of a spoon.

As I leap in my car, fire up the ignition and speed up the drive, pedal to the floor, I see Caro in my rear-view mirror, chasing after me out of the house, her boobs, which Eloise obviously succeeded in freeing from her blouse, bouncing elegantly in the moonlight.

Chapter Four

I shall never view that chaise-longue with quite the same affection again. After nearly three weeks, I drive home from Angels Court in pretty much the same state as I drove down to it, one minute down and disillusioned, the next laughing like a drain at the thought of it all. Oh, my poor chocolate torte to come to such an end after hours of love and toil! I just hope Amber thought it tasted good. I never meant it to be eaten with that type of cream after all!

I'm on autopilot all the way home. Looking back I'm not quite sure how I managed to get there because I certainly wasn't taking much notice of where I was going. I somehow manage to make it back to the flat without ending up in a ditch or flattening any wildlife that dares to sprint kamikaze-style in front of the car.

The phone's ringing as I insert my key in the lock of my own front door. Fortunately it stops before I've managed to get the door open, therefore saving me from the dilemma or whether to answer it or not. When it starts to ring two minutes later, however, I yet again take the emotional coward's way out and unplug both my handsets.

Home doesn't really seem very homely. It smells cold, damp and empty.

I turn up the central heating, and run around the flat switching on lights and lamps until the place has a rosier glow. Then, raiding the fridge for my supply of comfort Mars Bars, I retire to my duvet with the huge pile of post that was waiting on my front door mat, nearly jamming the door as I pushed my way inside.

I sort the post into three piles, junk, bills and personal, then deciding that I can't really face opening any of them, shove them all inside the top drawer of my bedside cabinet, trying to ignore the nagging voice that's telling me I should really deal with all the ominously red-etched envelopes that look like they could possibly be final demands.

I'm also trying to ignore another nagging voice that's telling me what a washout I am, hiding away from the world under my duvet.

I tell this particular nagging voice that it's nearly one in the morning and where the hell else should I be at this time of night anyway, stuff another Mars Bar in my mouth, and try to find something trashy on the TV to take my mind away from the pretty pornographic scenes that are filling it at the moment.

It doesn't work.

I may as well tune into the Fantasy channel, all I can see are pictures of Caroline and David. Well, Caroline and Eloise to be more precise.

Who'd have thought it?

Certainly not me!

I mean, I know they have a pretty healthy sex life. Girls chat, don't they, and Caro and I are no exception. I thought I'd heard all of the gory details, but she's somehow managed to forget to mention the fact that their pretty healthy sex life is so sociable it includes half of the local neighbourhood as well.

A brand-new meaning to the Chiltern five hundred!

Totally knackered, I try to sleep but my mind's too full for rest. I feel very alone. I really need to talk to someone at the moment, but the one person I really want to talk to is the one person I really want to talk about so I'm at a bit of a stalemate, aren't I?

Of course I have other friends, I'm not a total Billy No Mates, thank heavens, but Caro's the one I'd usually call at three in the morning when I'm feeling like hell. I wouldn't want to phone Sash in case I woke the children, and I can't phone Wiggy because nobody ever really knows where the hell she is exactly.

Lucky her.

I wish nobody knew where I was. Unfortunately you can pretty much guarantee that if you search for me, you'll find me. Not difficult considering I've been in pretty much the same place for the whole of my life.

All my friends seem to have gone somewhere. Well, further than me anyway. Caro's been all over – ooh, dear, that's a double entendre if ever I heard one. No, I'm not going to think about her at the moment. I can't think about Caro at the moment because instead of my usual picture of her, smiling and *fully clothed*, she now pops into my head chasing me down the road with her boobs bouncing like tennis balls in Wimbledon week.

Wiggy is currently having the time of her life tramping her way round the world. Take the 'tramping' in whatever sense you want. You'd be right on both counts. When she said she wanted to work her way round the world, she didn't mean in a succession of low-paid bar jobs. She has made it her mission to sample as many international 'dishes' as she possibly can.

Sash, well, I think she's the bravest of us all. She's a working mother.

Do you have to move on to feel like you've actually achieved something in your life? I've moved on from Richard. I think that should count, BIG time.

I finally emerge from my bedroom after dark the following evening. I feel like a vampire venturing out of the crypt. It's only my stomach that's managed to force me from my self-inflicted purdah, insisting that if I force feed it another Mars Bar it will explode rather messily all over the duvet. As my fridge is pitifully empty, at this time of the evening I have a choice of traipsing around a late-night Sainsbury's or heading for yet more junk food that, while still fat and calorie-laden, at least isn't sweet and covered in chocolate.

However, halfway towards the drive-through, I suddenly find myself bypassing the route to McDonald's, and heading for Clayton Avenue, The Beeches, and my father. A sort of homing instinct that tells me I need a kind of sustenance other than food. I look at the car clock, glowing digitally green in the darkness. It's nearly ten o'clock, Dad will be in the potting shed at the bottom of the garden, avoiding Mother.

I'm in desperate need of his calming influence and reassuring normality, but I'm not keen to face her. Still, I can't avoid her forever. It's been nearly three weeks, she may have calmed down a bit by now. Nevertheless, I give in to my cowardice and take the bumpy track that runs along the back of the avenue, entering the long rear garden through the back gate. As the rusty latch clicks up, and I slip through, Roger appears out of a clump of heavily overgrown delphiniums, his gums exposed in a

89

doggy grin, his stumpy tail wagging enthusiastically.

I bend to pat his head, which is sticky with sap from the limes which mark the end of the garden. He licks my hand and then tries to lick my face with a rough warm tongue. His breath smells of Beef Chum. If Roger is wandering loose in the garden, then where's Dad? They're normally tucked up in the shed together, Roger KO'd on a smelly old horse blanket in one corner and Dad sucking his pipe on some ratty old deckchair in the other, Radio Two crackling out of the old pre-war wireless he spent many a happy winter's evening restoring to health.

There's no tell-tale glow of a gas lamp from the shed so I head up the garden path towards the house. It's a beautiful evening, but I'm still shaking like a leaf.

The dining-room and kitchen face on to the back patio. The lights are on in the kitchen. The heavy blue velvet drapes that usually cover the stained glass of the French doors into the dining-room are still tied back.

I can see the incandescent flickering of candlelight, and can just make out through the green and red of the glass fleur de lys the outline of my father sitting at the head of the table. My mother is seated to his left, and to his right is Sally-Anne. At the end of the table, with his back towards me, sits a man.

His outline looks vaguely familiar.

I stumble up the three steps that lead on to the patio, trip over a violent pink fuchsia in a very hard terracotta pot, and press my nose up against the window to get a better view.

Bloody hell!

I don't believe it!

It's Richard!

Just my bloody luck, a most unwelcoming committee.

I'm about to beat a very hasty retreat when suddenly someone starts to scream. This time I know it's not me.

'There's someone in the garden! There's someone out there! I can see them staring in at us!' It's Sally, shrieking at the top of her voice.

Dad drops his dessert spoon, which was halfway to his mouth bearing sherry trifle, and rushes to the doors brandishing the carving knife. His face is so red he looks like a Native American on the warpath.

He cautiously pushes open the door and steps out into the night.

'We know you're out there!' he bellows gruffly, the blade flashing ominously in the moonlight, 'Come out, you swine . . . show yourself!'

Roger joins in the foray by beginning to bark.

At Sally's scream I had instinctively stepped back into the shadows.

'Felicity?' Dad stops brandishing the knife, and peers through the darkness.

I smile sheepishly.

'Fliss!' He puts a hand on his chest. 'Oh, my goodness, you nearly gave me a heart attack!'

'Drew! Drew!' my mother calls out to him. 'What's going on?'

'It's OK, everybody,' he calls back. 'It's only Fliss! Goodness, girl, what are you doing lurking out here?'

'Dad, what's going on?' I echo my mother, indicating Richard who is still seated at the table; trust him to let my father face intruders alone, even if it is only me that's intruding. Dad follows my gaze as I take in the best china, the silver cutlery, the candles, the delicate pink roses so carefully arranged in Grandmother Blakeney's precious silver vases.

'Look, Fliss, I think we'd better have a private chat,' he says, biting his bottom lip. Dad takes my arm, and starts to lead me away from the house, but is pre-empted by Mother who, composure fully regained, sails out of the dining-room and grabs my other arm.

'Felicity, how nice to see you.'

I've got Dad pulling me in one direction, Mother pulling me in the other.

I'm still in shock from earlier events and it takes a while for these words of welcome to register.

'It is?' I ask warily.

Mother smiles at me.

'Of course. I was just saying that all we needed to complete the evening was Felicity, wasn't I, Sally-Anne dear?'

I was expecting another screaming match; this unexpected pleasantness is far more disturbing.

I look back at Dad who looks at the floor, and then at Sally-Anne, who also looks away as Mother leads me into the candlelit room. Richard is leaning back in his chair, looking far too relaxed and happy for my liking.

'Hello, Felicity.' He smiles at me, sweetness and light, a world away from the glowering angry man I last saw almost a month ago.

'What's going on?' I ask cautiously, not at all sure that I want to hear the answer.

Mother and Sally return to their seats. Dad draws up another chair and gestures for me to sit down.

'We're having a little celebration.' Mother is also smiling far too much for my liking.

'Celebration?'

'Yes.' Her eyes are shining, and it's not just the reflection of the candles on her contacts. 'A celebration.'

She pronounces the word almost phonetically, she's so precise, and I realise that she's slightly drunk.

'In fact, we were just about to propose a toast. Drew, give Felicity a glass of champagne.'

'Miriam, this really isn't . . .' Dad begins to object, looking thoroughly uncomfortable.

'Champagne, Drew!'

She waits while Dad goes to the cabinet and pours me a drink. I send him a silent look of thanks as I realise he's actually handed me a glass of brandy. I've got a horrible feeling I'm going to need it.

'Does everybody have a full glass? Lovely. A toast.' Mother gets rather unsteadily to her feet. 'To Richard and Sally-Anne . . .'

The pause is long, drawn out, for me agonising, yet I recognise, for my mother, triumphant.

'To Richard and Sally-Anne,' she repeats unnecessarily. 'On the *wonderful* occasion of their engagement. Congratulations!'

I've got the glass halfway to my mouth before the words actually register.

'This is a joke, right? You're winding me up.'

I put my glass down on the table with a thud, spilling brandy on the heavy linen cloth.

Sally and Richard?

.It can't be true.

I just about resist the urge to pinch myself to test if I'm asleep and having a nightmare. That's what it is, you know. I'm still in bed, and this is all some terrible Freudian dream. It was the Mars bars. Nobody can consume that amount of serious glucose and get away with it, especially someone in my current state of mind.

I'm going to wake up any minute now and laugh about the whole thing.

Roger, sensing my unease, thrusts a warm wet reassuring nose into the palm of my hand and licks, in a doggy attempt to comfort.

The touch is very soggy, and very, *very* real.

I look at the faces surrounding me.

Mother, smiling orgasmically.

Richard, smiling smugly as usual.

Sally looking pained and not quite meeting my eye.

Dad silently oozing sympathy and helplessness from every pore, still clutching the brandy decanter, ready to top me up should I look any more faint and shocked than I already do.

I look over to Richard and Sally-Anne again and notice for the first time that they are actually holding hands.

'Oh, my god, you're totally serious, aren't you?'

'This is no joke, Felicity.' Mother smiles benignly at Sally-Anne who is still looking at the floor.

'Sally, how could you!' I stare incredulously at my sister.

To her credit she looks highly embarrassed.

'I'm s-sorry, Fliss . . .' she begins stuttering wildly.

'Don't be ridiculous! You've got absolutely nothing to be sorry for. Felicity has made her bed and she must lie in it.'

Mother is crowing like a cockerel, not even I can put a damper on this occasion.

'You shouldn't let petty jealousy spoil your sister's good news, Felicity. You had your chance, now it's Sally's turn.'

She makes Richard sound like a fairground ride. I've just got off, now it's Sally's turn to take a spin.

'I'm not jealous,' I snap. 'Just completely and utterly . . .'

I struggle for a word that will describe how I'm feeling at the moment. I'm still struggling with major disbelief. This wasn't exactly what I thought Sally-Anne meant when she said she'd take care of everything.

I look from face to face. We are all silent.

Finally I look quizzically at my sister, choosing my words carefully.

'Sally, are you sure this is what you want? Richard isn't exactly a hand-me-down pullover that you're obliged to wear because I've grown out of it.'

He opens his mouth to protest.

'It's what I want, Fliss,' Sally cuts in, but she won't quite meet my eye.

'Honestly? This is really what you want?'

'I don't know why you find this so hard to believe,' Richard says indignantly. 'In fact, when you think about it, my marrying Sally-Anne is a far more plausible prospect than my ever marrying you was. We're much more compatible, aren't we, darling?'

He squeezes my sister's hand, and smiles warmly at her.

Darling?

I think I'm going to throw up.

Sally returns his smile with equal warmth.

'In fact I should be thanking you, Fliss. It was you walking out that threw Sally and me together, gave us a chance to realise our true feelings for each other.'

This can't be real. I'm asleep and having a nightmare. Either that or I've just walked on to the set of a very scary remake of *The Stepford Wives*.

'This is madness. I've been away for three weeks! How can you decide you want to spend the rest of your life with someone after only three weeks?'

'We've known each other for as long as you and Richard have been together. If that was long enough for you to marry him, then I'm sure it's long enough for me.'

Sally sounds more determined now.

'Besides, I've always carried a torch for him.'

Richard smiles conceitedly at this.

'Of course, I would never have acted on my feelings if you'd gone ahead with the wedding, Fliss, but when you ran out . . . well, Richard needed someone to talk to. It's just grown from there really . . .' she tails off lamely, totally flustered, and then adds for justification, 'You'd made it pretty clear you didn't want to marry him.'

Well, I can't deny that. So this is what Mother was hinting at the night she christened me 'Bitch' with a glass of Remy Martin. Richard getting together with Sally-Anne. My brain, which has been struggling to fit the concept of my sister marrying him into the compartment called reality, gives up the fight and surrenders unreservedly. It's really had far too much to cope with in the past few weeks. A fight is definitely beyond its current capabilities. I wave a verbal white flag.

'Well, if this is really what you want . . .'

'Oh, it is!' chorus Sally-Anne and Mother in unison, Sally smiling at me hopefully.

'In that case,' I pause, searching for something to say, 'congratulations.'

If I'm being honest, I certainly don't mean that, it wasn't the first word that popped into my head by any means, but a toast is a good excuse to knock back my brandy. The trembling has now turned to major shakes. I hand Dad my empty glass for a refill.

The decanter looks pretty empty, first aiding Mother's recovery at the loss of the old wedding, and then no doubt stopping Dad from having a heart attack at the discovery of the new one.

'So when are you actually going to get married then?' I sink back into my seat, completely exhausted mentally.

This time Sally definitely can't look at me. It's left to Richard to answer, and he does so with a noticeable amount of pleasure.

'At the end of the month, the twenty-fifth.'

'But that was when we were . . . the date that . . .'

Dad hands me another brandy.

'Well, everything was already booked, it seemed such a shame to have to cancel it all and then rearrange everything,' Mother says cheerfully.

I decide I *am* asleep and having a nightmare after all.

'It was jolly convenient really,' she continues, 'all we've had to do is notify Reverend Parsifal, reissue the invites, and change the wedding stationery. Oh, and get the dress altered, of course. Sally is a tad more slender than you are, Felicity dear.'

'She's wearing my dress!'

'Well, Sally-Anne did help to choose it, didn't she? In fact, I think it suits her better, Felicity. She looks so lovely in it . . . I always thought it was a touch too fussy for someone of your stature, and since you're not going to need it after all . . .'

I'm completely outraged. I hated that dress, and when Mother says that Sally-Anne helped to choose it she actually means that Sally-Anne helped *her* to choose it.

I'd found this marvellously simple dress in old ivory silk, and they manhandled me out of it and into the meringue concoction, but it was still *my* dress, for *my* wedding. I feel like the female lead in a play. I bow out and the understudy steps straight into my shoes to rounds of rapturous applause.

Mother is talking again.

'You don't look too happy, Felicity. Surely you don't begrudge your own sister . . .'

She's fishing now. There's nothing that would make her happier at this moment than for me to express regret, jealousy, then she could do the I-told-you-so routine and really rub my face in it. Richard would like that too. He's playing from a superior position now, and he knows it. I hope to God he's not just doing this to get back at me.

I force the widest smile I think I can get away with, and raise my glass.

'If Sally is happy, then of course I'm happy too. Congratulations to you both.'

I must have been taking note of Caro's drama lessons.

Caro . . . oh, dear, that's another problem I'll have to face at some point.

Dad gives me an approving look.

'That's the spirit!' he whispers so that only I can hear. 'Don't let her think that you're upset.'

Richard looks disappointed. I think he was hoping for some display of desperate passion from me.

A fight for his love between the two sisters?

I bet that would have been a major turn on for him.

I'm forced to endure another hour of lingering over coffee and brandy. My timing is so lousy. Why couldn't I have turned up after dinner instead of during? Either that or not turned up at all. I could just have stayed under my duvet for the rest of the summer holiday. Hell, the rest of my life maybe. As it is I can't just get up and leave, that would look too much like sour grapes, and if there's one thing I'm determined to do, it's to show Richard I don't give a fig that he's not marrying me.

I don't you know. All this has proved to me that I don't love Richard and I really did do the right thing in calling off *our* wedding. I feel absolutely no pangs of regret that he suddenly belongs to someone else. The only regret I do have is that it's this sudden, and it's my sister.

The only consolation I have is that this new shock has taken my mind off the earlier one. I don't even want to think about that at the moment. I eventually manage to escape to the kitchen by offering to wash up.

Mother's gone the whole hog with this meal. Dirty pots and pans litter the side; a roasting dish swimming with grease is floating in the sink. This must be the only occasion in my life I've been pleased to see so much washing up. I wash everything, slowly, meticulously, scrubbing, scrubbing and scrubbing.

I pretend one particularly virulent food stain is Richard, and take great satisfaction in obliterating it with Vim and a scourer. I never thought I would find washing up therapeutic. I just wish I could wash all my current problems down the plug hole, along with the dirty soapy water.

The others have gone out on to the patio with more brandy. I can hear Richard talking. He still likes the sound of his own voice then. I can hear Mother laughing at appropriate intervals. Sally seems very quiet. Dad and Roger join me in the kitchen. Dad silently takes a tea towel and begins to dry the dishes.

'I'm sorry, Fliss,' he finally says, 'I only found out myself tonight. I knew something was going on, they've been secretive for a few weeks now, but I had no idea that this was what they were planning. I tried to phone you earlier as soon as they told me, but Caroline said you'd left yesterday.'

'You spoke to her? What did she say?'

Dad looks at me sideways.

'So there *is* something going on in that quarter then? I thought Caroline sounded rather odd. She asked me to get you to call her, sounded quite insistent about it. Is everything OK, Fliss?'

I think back and am assailed by a vision of Blakesley Hardington's little white bottom. Ugh! I concentrate on scrubbing a saucepan and thankfully the vision goes away.

'Not really,' I answer carefully, 'but never mind that now . . . what on earth are we going to do about Sally-Anne?'

'What can we do?' Dad shrugs. 'She seems determined to marry the chap.'

'It just seems so surreal, I keep expecting to wake up and find out the whole thing's some strange dream.'

'I hate to say this,' Dad bends to feed a piece of leftover lamb to a slavering Roger, 'but it wasn't totally out of the blue. I mean, I had no idea, but when they told me I wasn't completely surprised. Sally's always had a soft spot for Richard, a pretty obvious soft spot – I would have thought you'd have noticed before.' Straightening, he resumes his slow wiping, stacking another rose-patterned plate on top of the others in the cupboard.

I shake my head.

'Too wrapped up in my own feelings, I suppose. As usual.'

I can feel the tears welling up again. I tell myself it's the stress. I hate weepy women.

'Why so sad?' Dad's the picture of concern. 'You don't still love Richard, do you?'

'No.' I wipe my eyes on the tea towel, and blow my nose on a piece of kitchen roll. 'But I do love Sally. I want her to be happy.'

'Sally loves Richard, she is happy.'

'Do you really believe that?'

'I've got to believe it.' He shrugs, hanging up his tea towel and looking out on to the patio at Richard. 'It's the only thing that stopped me from carving him up instead of the roast.'

I finally arrive back home at midnight, remembering at last to collect my struggling angry cat who really does not want to come back home, thank you very much, from the girl upstairs who never seems to go to bed, and fall back into my own in a daze.

Life is so confusing. I think I've finally got Richard out of my hair once and for all, and now the bastard has made sure he's there to stay.

I suppose brother-in-law is better than husband, but I'd still rather there was no connection whatsoever.

I'm really very concerned about Sal.

What's got into her? I know there is such a thing as a whirlwind romance, but this is ridiculous! I'm just so worried for her. I can't believe Richard's motives for this are purely romantic.

I'm not trying to make myself the centre of this whole thing out of some sad form of ego trip, but if you think about it, this is the ultimate revenge.

If he'd spent the rest of his life trying to think of something that would really piss me off, he couldn't have come up with anything better than this.

I feel so guilty.

Sally is about to throw herself away on the egotistical, self-centred scum-bag and it's probably all my fault.

The last couple of days have been completely awful. I was supposed to be at Caroline's recuperating. Now I need another break to get over the recuperation!

Perhaps I should just have stayed at Caro's and joined in the orgy. Flung off my clothes and my inhibitions and sampled some carefree, strip, smile and simply shag swinging. Even a grope with the man who put smarm into charm, the greasy quick change artist Gwillem, would have been preferable to finding out about Richard and Sally!

Chapter Five

The shock of hearing about my sister and my ex-fiancé has really knocked me for six. Good old guilt has now become a permanent fixture in my life, 'If only I'd done everything differently' becoming my new catchphrase of the moment. For example, instead of leaving Richard in bed when I walked out on him, I should just have smothered him with one of his pillows.

Problem solved.

A long stay in Holloway would have been a small price to pay, wouldn't it?

I feel like I'm in prison at the moment anyway. Maybe without the dodgy food, drug abuse, lesbianism and lock-up time, but I'm definitely becoming a recluse. My own form of solitary confinement.

I leave the flat once in the next few days to buy cat food and the Sunday papers. I spend the rest of the time holed up in the sitting room with the curtains drawn and the phone off the hook, watching mindless television and eating junk food, trying to work and failing, and struggling not to think too much.

If I think, I get depressed. Mainly because I know I'm being a totally sad git who should really pull herself together and get on with what she had promised herself would be a wonderful new life if only she could get up the guts to make a break for it.

Well, I made that break and I knew I'd have to suffer whatever consequences arose from it. Unfortunately in all of the imagined post-Richard scenarios the one about him marrying Sally-Anne never actually came up!

On the Thursday morning Richard and Judy do a slot about people who spend their lives holed up on their own watching television and eating junk food, and I decide that enough is enough. Life is a bitch, but I'm not going to let it get the better of me.

I try to think of happy things.

I go shopping.

I return home three hours later feeling decidedly better. Why is splurging on one's credit card so incredibly therapeutic – at least until the bill comes in?

As I push the key into the lock I can hear the phone making up for its enforced silence by ringing itself off the hook.

I dump my six million carrier bags on the hall floor and force myself to answer it.

'Hello?'

'Fliss, it's me, I've been trying to get you for days. Is there something wrong with your phone?'

'No, my phone's fine. In fact it's rather happy really, it's just got engaged.'

'That's not funny, Fliss. Look, will you meet me? I think we need to talk.'

'Really there's no need, Sally.' I'm still on a shopping high. 'Just as long as you're happy that you're doing the right thing, then everything's fine by me.'

This is what I managed to convince myself halfway round John Lewis anyway. My new mantra, quoted twenty times in each department, so that I looked like a madwoman muttering to myself constantly.

Although I've almost managed to convince myself that I mean it, I don't think Sally-Anne's very impressed by my sincerity.

'I wish I knew that you really meant that, Fliss . . . I really do think we should meet up. Please, I'd like a chance to explain what's happened, I think it would help put your mind at rest.'

The two key words, mind and rest.

'OK,' I sigh, 'when?'

'How about tonight? We could go for something to eat, if you like, have a proper talk.'

'Where?'

'Eduardo's is supposed to be nice.'

Eduardo's? Oh, dear, Richard's favourite haunt. Do I really want to spend any evening there? Still, I suppose there's no point in harbouring ghosts.

It's a good restaurant, I just need to disassociate it from miserable memories.

'OK, if you think you can get a table.'

'Richard said it wouldn't be a problem if I mention his name.'

'If you mention his name, we'll probably be barred for life.'

'Fliss!'

'OK, OK, what time?'

'About eight-thirty.'

I arrive at the restaurant early.

It's sod's law that when you allow yourself plenty of time to park in what is usually a car-parking battleground, you find a space straight away.

I have a choice: sit in the car for twenty minutes, or sit in the bar for twenty minutes. It's no contest really. I head for the restaurant. As usual it's incredibly busy. I manage to find a dark corner at the end of the bar, and try to blend into the décor.

A thin-faced barman with a lazy eye that turns permanently inwards towards his nose sombrely informs me it's happy hour as I settle down on a stool in the corner with a gin and tonic. I didn't think a place like Eduardo's would indulge in a happy hour, the staff are all so po-faced.

Not so the group of dark-suited businessmen at the other end of the bar. They are taking advantage of the wait for their table to down as many doubles as possible. I can hear lots of hearty 'Richard' laughing coming from their general direction as they gulp their drinks.

Why is a bar man's natural domain? I've always envied men their ability to be completely at ease when on their own in a bar or pub. It's so hard to escape the myth that a woman on her own is just waiting to be picked up.

I'm obviously giving that impression right now. I can see out of the corner of my eye that one of the not quite so raucous suits keeps looking over at me. I gaze at my reflection in the mirror behind the rows of bottles, determined not to look back, but the next minute he's heading in my direction.

'Excuse me, but I know you, don't I?'

Oh, dear, corny chat-up line number one.

I turn to face him, semi-polite rebuff at the ready, but the face *is* actually quite familiar. The man's eyes narrow in thought, and then widen in friendly recognition.

'It's Fliss, isn't it? Richard's fia— I mean, we met here, when you were with Richard Trevelyan. You don't remember me, do you? Alex . . . Alex Christian.'

Ah, the nice husband of the horrible ex-girlfriend. I thought I knew him from somewhere.

'Of course. How nice to see you again.'

He runs a hand through his short brown hair and smiles. I remember that smile, warm and open. He holds out his hand. That's warm too. We shake rather self-consciously.

'I take it you're waiting for someone?'

'My sister actually.'

'Ah, yes, Sally-Anne. We met last week.'

'You did?'

He looks slightly uncomfortable.

'An evening Kat, my wife, arranged. Sally's a lovely girl. Look, can I buy you a drink while you're waiting for her?'

I'm just wondering whether to accept when I hear my name being called. It's Sally-Anne.

I turn to Alex.

'Thanks. That would have been nice.'

'Perhaps some other time then?'

He returns to his party, stopping briefly to say hello to Sally on the way. I watch him leave, thinking of the first time I met him. It was only five weeks, but it seems like a lifetime ago.

'Fliss!' Sally pushes her way over to me, hugs me, kisses me gently on one cheek and then steps back a little awkwardly.

'Have you been waiting long?'

'Only about five minutes.'

'I didn't know you knew Alex?'

'I've only met him once before. Apparently he and his wife are old friends of Richard's, but I gather you know that already.'

'That's right. We met up with them last week at the Sandpiper Hotel for a meal.'

'Oh, yeah? Whose idea was that then?'

'Oh, I think Richard arranged it. He's really nice, isn't he?' she says enthusiastically, smiling at Alex as he glances over at us again.

'Yeah, he seems to be.' I look at him. He is talking to a tall, distinguished-looking man in a sombre grey suit, slightly apart from the more raucous members of the crowd.

He catches my gaze, and his smile broadens.

'Have you met his wife?'

'Sorry?'

I drag my eyes away from Alex and back to my sister.

'Have you met his wife?' she repeats. 'Katherine . . . Kat.'

'Unfortunately, yes.'

'Unfortunately? You didn't take to her then?'

'Not really, no. She seemed a bit false if I'm being honest.'

'And I thought it was just me,' muses Sally. 'I thought I was being a bit bitchy because she's an ex of Richard's.'

Oh, so either he or Kat's got that piece of information into play already.

'You couldn't be a bitch, Sal, it's not in you.'

'Okay then, a bit twitchy maybe. She's very . . . um . . .'

'In your face?' I offer. 'Or perhaps I should say in Richard's face?'

'You noticed that too?' She smiles wryly at me.

'It was hard not to.'

Sally catches the barman's good eye and orders a white wine, and another G & T for me. 'You didn't like her much either then?' I ask as Sally hands me my second drink and takes a big gulp of her own.

'Not especially. She's a bit over the top, isn't she? She spent the whole of the evening fluttering her eyelashes at Richard. They were batting so hard she could have turned out for the England cricket team.'

'Oh, yes? And was he encouraging this sickening display of affection?'

'Of course he wasn't,' says Sally indignantly. 'He only had eyes for me. Come on, our table's ready.'

She slips into the seat opposite me, and puts her bag by her feet. She looks across at me, and smiles nervously.

'You know, I'm really glad you agreed to come tonight. I wasn't sure if you'd still be speaking to me.'

'Of course I'm still speaking to you, why shouldn't I be?'

'Because of what's happened.'

'Yes, well, it was rather a shock to arrive home in the middle of your engagement party, especially when your fiancé turns out to be Richard,' I reply, unable to keep the sarcastic note out of my voice.,

'I'm sorry.' Sally nervously knocks back half her glass of wine in one go. 'It was rather bad timing, I know, but Mother insisted on a family celebration. She was so ecstatic.'

'I bet she was. I'm surprised she wasn't swinging from the chandeliers when I arrived.'

I twist my napkin agitatedly.

'Look, I'm sorry, but I've got to ask this – she's not forcing you into this wedding, is she?'

Sally snorts with laughter.

'Of course she's not! The British don't believe in arranged marriages, Fliss.'

'Mother does.'

'Don't be silly, of course she's *happy* but this was very much our decision, not hers.'

'You do love him, don't you?'

'I think so.'

'Only think? That doesn't sound too promising considering you're supposed to be marrying him in three weeks' time!'

'I only said "think" because I've never been in love before. I'm not quite sure how it should feel.' She looses her linen napkin from its ring and begins to twist it, looking at this rather than me as she speaks.

'Do you believe in love at first sight, Fliss?'

'Well . . .' I muse, exhaling into my fringe '. . . that's a tricky one. I suppose I believe in *lust* at first sight,' I answer matter-of-factly.

Sally looks up and giggles.

'No, I'm serious, what do you think? Is it possible?'

'I suppose it is possible, yes, but I think it takes a bit longer than thirty seconds to really, *truly* fall in love with someone. I mean, how can you profess to love someone when you couldn't possibly know anything about them?'

'Well, I think I fell in love with Richard the first time I saw him.'

'Really?' I ask in astonishment.

'Really.' Sally smiles nervously. 'I used to be so jealous of you, Fliss.'

I'm genuinely surprised, I must have been thick not to notice.

'Well, you never let it show,' I tell her slightly accusingly.

'How could I have done? You're my sister. I'd never have deliberately done anything to hurt you.'

She pauses as the waiter appears and hands us each a menu, and then leans towards me and whispers confidentially, 'You know, I couldn't believe it when you said you didn't want to marry him.'

'So I noticed,' I say, recalling Sally's rather obvious and annoying disbelief at that time.

She laughs.

'And then when he started showing an interest in me . . . Don't get me wrong, nothing went on before you two split up, I promise you. I mean, he was always really lovely to me but . . .'

'Creepy,' I butt in, thinking back to how Richard always used to smarm – er, I mean charm – the female members of my family.

'No, *lovely*,' she insists. 'It may look a bit suspicious, everything happening so quickly, but honestly, nothing really happened between Richard and me until after you two split up. I thought it was important I should make that clear.'

'Nothing *really* happened?' I pick her up. 'When people say nothing *really* happened, that usually means something did.'

'Well, we always had a rapport . . .'

'That's a good start,' I cut in. 'It's more than Richard and I ever had!'

She pulls a face at me, finishes the rest of her wine, and then looks at me coyly from under her long lashes.

'I remember the first time he kissed me,' she muses happily.

'You threw up?' I smile evilly.

'Fliss!'

'Sorry. Do go on.'

'As I was saying, I remember the first time he kissed me.'

'So you should, it can't have been that long ago.'

'Fliss, stop interrupting, I'm trying to convince you here.'

'You shouldn't have to *try* to convince me, I should be convinced already,' I say huffily.

'Yes, but you're not, are you? So just shut up and listen.'

I sigh heavily.

'OK, the first time he kissed you, go on.'

'It made my tummy go all funny . . .'

'Yes, it usually had that effect on me as well.' I grimace.

'I mean in a nice way!' she says indignantly. 'You know, butterflies in the stomach, going weak at the knees, feeling dizzy?'

'That doesn't mean you're in love. You could just have been going down with a bout of 'flu or something.'

'Oh, Fliss, do stop being flip, please.'

'I'm sorry.' I smile weakly. 'I've had a rather stressful few weeks, that's all.'

I pause and look at my sister. She's so young. She's only twenty-one, she doesn't need to get married yet.

'Please, Sal, just tell me you're doing the right thing.'

'I'm doing the right thing,' she answers easily.

'And that Richard loves you?'

'Of course he does. Do you think he'd be marrying me otherwise?'

'Ah, that is the question – *that* is the question.' I shake my head slowly. 'I can't help thinking he's only doing this to get back at me, Sally-Anne. I'm sorry, but it's got to be said.'

'Well, thank you very much!' she spits. For the first time this evening her pretty face is actually clouded with anger. 'It's not possible he could love me, is it? It has to be for revenge! Life doesn't revolve around you, Fliss. Can't you just accept that Richard and I are in love?' She stops and puts down her fork, which she had been angrily jabbing in mid-air as she spoke, and takes a deep breath.

'Look, I'm sorry, I shouldn't get angry with you. I really don't want Richard to come between us, Fliss.'

'Well, don't marry him then!'

'Yes, but I am marrying him, aren't I?' She looks beseechingly at me. 'I'm not asking for your blessing . . . well, I suppose I am really.'

'I don't know if I can give it,' I state miserably, snapping open my menu, ostensibly to choose my meal but in reality so that I can hide behind it.

'Fliss, please . . .' Sally begins, but is pre-empted by the return of the waiter to take our order. I suddenly find that I'm far from hungry. I take another look at the menu, unsure of what to order. One thing's for sure, I definitely won't be having a peppered steak.

Sally orders tomato salad followed by salmon. I take the easy option and ask for the same. She also orders a bottle of Chablis. I'm tempted to ask for one of those too.

The waiter leaves. Sally looks at me with puppy dog eyes.

'Please don't be horrible, Fliss.'

'Horrible?' I mutter. 'I'm not being horrible. If I really wanted to be "horrible" I could say that you said to leave all the wedding cancellations to you because you had absolutely no intention of cancelling anything. I mean, why bother? Everything was all arranged, Richard just needed to find a replacement bride and you conveniently offered to fill the vacant position!'

I know I sound like a petulant accusing child but I can't help it, this has been preying on my mind since the weekend.

'It wasn't like that, Fliss, you know it wasn't!'

'Wasn't it? You and Richard were already seeing each other when you phoned me at Caro's, weren't you?'

Sally hangs her head.

'Weren't you?' I demand. 'That's what Mother was hinting at when I came round and asked you to give him back the engagement ring, wasn't it?'

'Yes,' she admits quietly, still not looking up. 'But we'd only just admitted how we felt. Honestly, Fliss, I really wanted to help – I could see how upset Mother made you, that's why I offered to help, to cancel everything for you. I didn't know what was going to happen, believe me. I mean, nobody could anticipate that we would decide to get married so quickly.'

'You said it.'

There's a long silence. Sally can't look me in the face. She's tapping her long finger nails agitatedly against her empty wine glass. The waiter returns with our starters. My appetite has now gone completely, but I don't object when he fills my glass.

Sally leans back in her chair, and looks at me through narrowed eyes.

'I know you don't approve, but do you really mind me marrying Richard, Fliss? I want the truth now.'

I know what she's implying, the same thing that's on everyone else's lips and minds: do I still want him for myself? Is that where my objections to this whole bloody farce stem from? How am I supposed to answer? I choose my words carefully.

'Well, you're both free agents . . . it just seems really *odd*, that's all.'

'How exactly?'

'Well, it will take some getting used to, seeing you together, you know, as a couple. It's hard to imagine, I suppose, you and Richard. And it all seems so rushed. Do you have to get married? Why don't you just try being together for a while, see how things work out?'

'It's all settled now, Fliss, it's a bit too late to back out.'

'Believe me, it's never too late to back out! As you know, I'm speaking from experience.'

'Honestly, I'm happy with the way things are, I want to get married.'

'Are you sure?'

Silence.

'Look, I'm not saying don't be with him. If that's what you want then there's nothing to stand in your way, I certainly won't. Richard and I . . . well, there is no Richard and I. Trust me, I don't regret for one minute that I'm not marrying the man. What I am saying is that it took me nearly two years to decide that Richard and I weren't right for each other. Why don't you give yourself a bit more time to get to know each other first before you actually get married?'

'I've known Richard for almost as long as you have.'

'Yes, but not in the same way. He's a completely different person as a lover. He's very selfish, Sally. He made me so miserable sometimes. Actually, no, he made me miserable most of the time.'

'Please don't use your relationship with Richard as a measure for my relationship with him.' She pushes her untouched plate to one side. 'You've got to understand that they're two separate things entirely.'

'Do you really think he can make you happy? Believe it or not, I do want you to be happy.' I plead with her to see sense.

'Are you telling me that you will never have another successful relationship because your relationship with Richard didn't work out?'

'No, of course not,' I reply indignantly.

'So why are you saying that he can never make another woman happy because he couldn't make you happy? How would you feel if he said that about you?'

I digest the logic in this.

'I suppose you're right,' I say slowly.

I could labour the point, and try to make Sally see that Richard can only make one person happy.

Himself.

But what's the point? I can see that she is determined to

marry him, and I'm only going to make things much worse by taking a stand against that decision. Besides, like Sally said, I wouldn't want people to write me off because of one failed relationship, so it's hardly fair to do the same to Richard. Maybe he can make her happy. I know it's hard for me to contemplate that he would, but it is possible, and seeing as this is really my only legitimate objection to the whole thing . . .

I admit defeat. I don't have a white flag so I wave my napkin instead.

'Peace?' I offer sheepishly.

Sally laughs in delight. One of her many good qualities is that she can never stay cross for long. Really my sister is a beautiful person, not just externally but inwardly too. This is the reason I want to protect her, she can see no evil in anybody.

She has the nature of a saint to cope with our cantankerous mother as admirably as she does. Why would I find it hard to believe that Richard would want to marry her simply because she is so lovely, and not to get back at me? Perhaps I am jealous. Perhaps I don't want her to succeed where I have indeed failed quite dismally. Perhaps I've always been jealous of Sally and her easy ability to find good and love in those around her.

I must be more magnanimous, less egocentric.

'If it's what you really want, then I wish you nothing but the best.'

'Oh, Fliss, do you really mean it?' Sally's eyes are wide and hopeful, a smile playing cautiously about her pretty lips. 'Can we stop fighting about this? Will you give me your blessing?'

I nod slowly, not quite trusting myself to speak.

'Oh, that's so wonderful!' The smile blooms fully. 'This is definitely a cause for celebration, and for a celebration we need one thing . . . champagne!'

She calls to a nearby waiter, who hurries away and returns with a dusty bottle. Picking up on Sally's excitement, he opens it with all the dash of a grand prix driver celebrating a victory. The cork shoots towards the ceiling, dangerously skimming a delicate light fitting. Fortunately he doesn't spray us Damon Hill-style, but manages to find our glasses before losing any of the precious liquid.

'Cheers!' Sally raises her glass.

'To a happy future,' I offer, and drain mine in one go. I put my hand over it as the waiter hovers nearby with the bottle, waiting to refill. 'No more for me, thank you.'

'But, Fliss, we're celebrating!'

I still think that's debatable.

'I can't,' I excuse myself, 'I'm driving.'

'Haven't you had too much already? Oh, come on, you can pick your car up in the morning, we'll give you a lift home.'

'We?'

'Richard's picking me up.' She smiles happily.

I take my hand away from the glass.

'On second thoughts, I think I will have another drink. But I don't need a lift, OK? I'll get a cab.'

'Don't be like that, Fliss, we've all got to learn to get on.'

'I know,' I sigh, 'but I don't have to start learning tonight, do I?'

We slowly work our way through the rest of the bottle, and the rest of our food. Sally, who has fully recovered her appetite, is happily talking wedding plans.

I pretend to listen, nodding and smiling at what I hope are appropriate moments. She is so carried away with excitement she doesn't notice that I may be with her in body but not in spirit. Suddenly I feel this overwhelming weariness, like a knight at the end of a long and bloody battle who finds he must submit to defeat after all. I just want to lie down and go to sleep for the next century.

After Sally has eaten all of her main course and most of mine, consumed a pudding that is far too large and fattening for someone so slim and svelte, and insisted that we continue the 'celebration' by having brandy with our coffee, she finally looks at her watch.

'Oh, my goodness!' she trills. 'It's gone eleven, Richard will be waiting for me. I'd better get the bill. No,' she waves away my money, 'I told you, this is on me. Well, on Richard really.'

I look on incredulously as she reaches into her bag and pulls out a credit card.

'He gave you a platinum card?' I breathe in surprise. 'Maybe things *will* be different for you.'

Sally smiles at me, and reaches out to take my hand and squeeze it gently.

'Trust me. I know how difficult this must be for you, Fliss, but I honestly think things will be different for Richard and me. Vastly different . . . *amazingly* different!' The smile broadens and her eyes begin to glow with happiness.

'OK, OK, you've made your point,' I reply with raised eyebrows, but my smile is less grudging.

Letting go of my hand with one final squeeze, Sally calls over our waiter and hands him the card with a flourish. The waiter waves his arms in the air, and hands the card back to her. That would be more like the Richard I know: giving Sally a platinum card that isn't actually accepted anywhere. It's a few moments before we realise that it isn't the card he won't accept, it's actual payment of our bill.

'No, no, Mademoiselle, ees not necessary.'

'Sorry?'

'The bill ees already paid, Mademoiselle. Mr Alex Christian, ee take care of eet. Ee ees very insistent.'

Sally goes pink with pleasure.

'How terribly kind. Where is he? I must thank him.'

'Ee just leave, Mademoiselle. You miss him only by five minutes.'

Richard is waiting outside when we leave. I'm surprised he's not revving the engine of his car, he used to do that purposely to infuriate me if I ever dared to keep him waiting.

'Hello, darling, did you have a good evening?'

He gets out of the car and presses his lips to Sally's cheek, all the time looking smugly in my direction as though he's thumbing his nose at me.

'Fliss, are you well?' He turns to me, peering through the darkness. 'You're looking rather run down. Don't you think so, darling? Felicity looks tired, doesn't she?'

'Do you think so?' Sally turns to me in concern. 'You do look tired actually, Fliss. Are you sure we can't take you home?'

'I'll make my own way, honestly, I'll be fine.'

'But . . .' Sally begins to protest. Richard interrupts her.

'Fliss said no, Sally-Anne.' This time he looks at me with badly disguised animosity.

'Well, if you're sure?'

'Positive,' I state firmly.

'Thank you for coming.' Sally touches my arm. 'I'm so glad we've had a chance to talk and sort things out.'

I watch them drive away together. We haven't really sorted anything out. I still loathe Richard with a passion. Loathe the idea of Sally marrying him with a passion. I suppose I have just come to accept the inevitable, like a prisoner on death row without appeal, there is no chance of escaping this sentence.

I'm just about to go back into the restaurant to phone for a taxi when a long dark blue Aston Martin pulls up next to me. The driver's window winds down with an electrical whirring sound. A tousled brown head appears. Through the gloom I recognise Alex Christian.

He smiles.

'Are you OK? Can I give you a lift somewhere?'

'No, thank you, I'm fine. I'm just going back in to call a cab.'

'You don't need to do that, let me take you home.'

'Thank you, but I'm OK, honestly.'

'I can't leave you here alone in a darkened street.' He grins. 'Anything could happen to you.'

'And I can't accept lifts from strange men.' I smile back at him. 'Anything could happen to me.'

'I'm not strange,' he laughs, 'just mildly psychotic. Why don't you hop in?'

'Thanks,' I gesture to the busy restaurant behind me, 'but I'd hardly call this place isolated.'

He gets out of the car, and walking round towards me, opens the passenger door.

'Look, if I promise not to butcher you horribly down some darkened alley, will you get in?'

He's more likely to get butchered than I am, I'm in rather a murderous mood.

'I'm completely out of your way,' I mutter a touch ungraciously.

'I really don't mind.' He's still holding open the door, obviously not to be deterred.

'OK, thank you.' I give in and clamber rather ungracefully into the low-slung car, settling back against the cream leather as he shuts my door gently then climbs back into the driver's seat.

'Where to?'

'Laurel Road,' I say somewhat apologetically. 'I told you I was out of your way.'

'I really don't mind.'

As he restarts the car and pulls away Mahler begins to play softly on the CD player. His car's so quiet you can't even hear the engine running. It makes the silence between us seem even more noticeable.

114

Finally I think of something sensible to say to him.

'It was really very kind of you to pay our bill.'

'Think nothing of it.'

'Sally wanted to say thank you as well, but we just missed you. It was very kind . . .' I repeat a touch nervously, the situation, being in a car with someone I don't really know that well, making me feel a little awkward.

'Well, it was a celebration, wasn't it? Of Sally and Richard's wedding?'

'Sort of.'

'And I just wanted to congratulate her.'

It's more usual to send a card than pick up a tab for a £200 meal. What sort of man is Alex Christian? A wealthy one very obviously. I'm too cynical to accept that such a generous gesture could be borne of kindness rather than self-interest, but I don't know him very well yet. I remind myself again that I mustn't go through life holding Richard as my standard for the male sex.

'We've received an invitation to the wedding,' he says conversationally.

'Are you going?'

He shrugs.

'I'm not sure, Kat hasn't quite made up her mind . . . are you?'

'Is there any question that I wouldn't?'

He glances across at me.

'Well, that would depend, now wouldn't it?'

'On the circumstances,' I finish for him. 'Wouldn't miss it for the world,' I add dryly.

We travel in a more companionable silence for a while.

I watch him, his face alternately light then dark in the intermittent beam of the street lamps. When the light falls upon him I study him curiously. He has slanting eyes, exotically opalescent blue-green, with thick dark lashes that most girls would commit murder to possess. He also has a beautifully shaped mouth. To my infinite surprise I find myself wondering fleetingly what it would be like to kiss, and turn and look out of the window, embarrassed.

I can still smell him, though, even if I'm not looking directly at him. He smells of some wonderfully expensive aftershave, warm and heady, they type that makes you turn your head in the street to see the wearer, or inhale so deeply you're almost

115

eating the air, like going past the open door of a baker's shop or walking into Harrods food hall for the very first time.

I find my eyes drawn back to him again, curiosity getting the better of me. Unfortunately, he chooses this moment to look across at me, and catches me staring. I look away in embarrassment.

'You hear of people changing the venue or the dress at the last minute, but never the bride,' he says quietly after another moment's silence.

'Oh, the dress and the venue are the same all right,' I mutter.

He looks sideways at me, smiles slowly.

'I'd be lying if I told you I wasn't curious.'

'Most people are, but they're too polite to ask what happened.'

'So I'm rude?'

'No, just refreshingly honest. Turn right here.'

The sweep of the headlights picks up the trees on either side of the road as he moves off the main Oxford bypass and heads towards my little corner of suburbia.

'So that's why you offered to give me a lift, so you could assuage your burning curiosity?'

'Of course,' he replies.

I look across at him again. He's smiling.

'Didn't Richard give you the details? He's not usually backwards in coming forwards, especially when it comes to safeguarding his own reputation.'

'Oh, yes, I heard *Richard's* version of events,' he says. 'But somehow I got the feeling they wouldn't be exactly the same as yours?'

'How perceptive of you.'

'Well, I don't know Richard that well, so I shouldn't really comment, but I get the feeling you should often take the things he says with a small pinch of salt.'

'How long have you known him?'

'About three years. For as long as I've known my wife really.'

'I'm surprised we never met before.'

'Well, Kat and Richard had been . . . er . . . friends for some time, but I think they kind of fell out when she met me.'

'Friends?' I raise my eyebrows at him.

'Very good ones. Yeah,' he admits. 'On and off. They were on a big off when I met her. I think I made it a more permanent off

116

than Richard actually wanted it to be.'

We pull up outside my building. He gets out of the car and walks round to open the door for me, offering me his hand as I step from the low seat on to the pavement. Briefly his thumb brushes softly over the back of my hand, as he helps me to stand. We're face to face.

He looks at me; I look back at him, suddenly feeling kind of awkward again.

'Thank you for the lift.' I break the silence.

'Any time.'

'Well, I'll see you at the wedding then.'

'I hope so.'

I've bought myself one of those phones that displays the number of whoever is calling you.

It's The Beeches.

My mother hardly ever calls me, so it's a pretty even bet that it's either Dad or Sal. I feel safe enough answering.

It's Sal. She sounds excited.

'Fliss, are you free on Saturday night?' she bursts straight in without even a hello.

'I think so,' I reply cautiously, 'why?'

'Because we're going out.'

'We?'

'Everybody. It's my hen night!' she cries enthusiastically.

'Oh, right.'

'You're going to come, aren't you? Don't tell me you'll turn down a night of drunken debauchery and general bad behaviour? It's tradition, you know.'

I only hesitate for a moment.

'Of course I'll come,' I tell her determinedly.

'You will?'

She sounds kind of surprised.

'Yeah, if you're sure that you want me to? You sound like you were expecting me to say no.'

'Well, I was, sort of,' she replies honestly, 'but of *course* I want you to come, it wouldn't be the same without you.'

'No, you'd probably have a better time!' I joke.

I'm not surprised Sally was a touch shocked by my immediate acceptance of her invitation, I was a bit surprised myself. Still, it's a step in the right direction.

117

I keep telling myself I should get out more, even if it is for my sister's hen night for a wedding I wish wasn't happening.

Joking and self-indulgent pessimism apart, things don't seem as bad as they did. The proof of the pudding, as they say, is in the eating, and the times that I have seen Richard and Sally-Anne together, I've actually been impressed by the way they seem to be so comfortable and happy with each other.

Even Dad says that he doesn't find Richard as obnoxious as he used to, that he's far easier to get on with than he ever was when we were together. Maybe it was just me, maybe I brought out the worst in him. Perhaps with Sally he's a better person.

They seem to be far better for each other than Richard and I ever could have been. Perhaps my reasons for opposing this marriage are more selfish than I'd admit to. I did want Richard out of my life for good, I felt that this was the only way I could move forward properly, and I've been allowing the fact that he's now in it permanently by no choice of my own to overshadow all my plans for the future.

Knowing there is after all a strong possibility that Richard and Sally will be happy together makes me feel that perhaps, once the wedding itself is out of the way, things could start to move on in my own life.

I'd be lying if I said that I was looking forward to the actual day.

I wish I was. I mean, it's my little sister's wedding day, and it should be something I can't wait for, a major celebration, a happy day, but unfortunately I just know it's going to be overshadowed by the fact that as the song goes 'It Should Have Been Me'.

Not that I want it to be me, but you know what people are like. It's going to be the main topic of the day, isn't it, and by rights it bloody well shouldn't be.

It should be Sally's day. Her BIG day.

A little part of me thinks that maybe it would be better if I didn't go, but I'm not sure which would make it worse for her – my being there or not being there.

Mother has made sure that all of my friends have been uninvited to make way for Sally's. I can see why this has happened, it makes perfect sense logically, but I could have done with some allies.

There's no way I'm going to miss the hen night, though, and

absolutely no reason why I should, although this time I definitely think some back up would be a good idea. A family-sized box of Cadbury's Roses and a quick phone call should do it.

I pick up the phone and dial.

''Lo.'

It's Jack, Sasha's toddler, who is slap-bang in the middle of the terrible twos.

'Hello, Jack, is Mummy there?'

There's a long pause while I can hear him ignoring the telephone and giggling at something on television.

'Jack . . . Jack, is Mummy there?'

'Mummy's head down toilet . . .'

'Oh, dear, is Mummy sick, Jack?'

Fortunately I can hear Sasha's voice in the background.

'Give Mummy the phone, Jack . . . hello?'

'Sash? Are you OK?'

'Fliss! Mummy was just cleaning the bathroom actually. Kids, honestly! Do you know, he told my boss that Daddy and Mummy were playing Doctors and Nurses in the bedroom the other day!'

'And were you?'

'Chance'd be a fine thing! Niall was in bed with 'flu, which he caught from the childminder who was therefore off sick, and I had to take the day off to play nursemaid to the kids and my husband who, by the way, had the only ever strain of 'flu that could kill a grown man. My boss thought I was skiving for a day of nookie. Fortunately he saw the funny side after I'd explained it to him. Anyway, enough of my troubles. It's about bloody time you called me, you old trout. Where the hell have you been? One badly spelt text message to say you're going down to Caroline's for a while is definitely not enough! I've been ringing and ringing and you never answer the bloody phone. Your mobile's always switched off. You never respond to my messages. I'd nearly given you up as a waste of energy and struck you off my Christmas list.'

'You'd never do that,' I interrupt the flow of recriminations.

'Yeah, and don't you know it? That's why you take advantage of my good nature and keep me waiting for a month before you contact me. Wiggy's worried about you as well. She's tried to phone you about eight times and that's a record for her as we

119

normally consider ourselves privileged if she contacts us more than once a month.'

'I know, Sash, I'm really sorry, honestly I am.'

Sash sniffs, but any pretence at being cross with me never really lasts for very long.

'Well, I suppose you have had a lot on your plate recently, haven't you, what with cancelling the wedding and everything? I just wish you'd phoned me. I could have helped, you know, that's what friends are for.'

'I know,' I repeat. 'But everything's been a bit strange recently . . .'

'I can imagine,' Sash replies dryly.

She pauses for a moment. I can almost hear the radar working overtime down the telephone line.

'Something else has happened, hasn't it, Fliss?'

'How can you tell?'

'Come on, how long have I known you? I recognise your tone of voice.'

'Well, yeah, there is something I need to tell you. But first, I don't suppose you fancy a night out?'

'A night out! Do I fancy a night out? What's one of those then? Oh, yes, I remember, it's what people do when they don't have children, isn't it?'

'Does that mean you'll come?'

'With bells on. When?'

'Next Saturday.'

'That's good timing. Niall's been offered tickets to go and watch Arsenal play on Saturday morning and he's already promised on his own life to take me and the kids shoe shopping. You would not believe how hard that is with two children under two. He'd do anything to get out of that one – babysitting Saturday night will be letting him off lightly. Where are we going?'

'Sally's hen night,' I reply slowly.

'Sally? Your sister's getting married? Since when?'

'Well, it's all been kind of whirlwind . . .'

'You're telling me! I didn't even know she was dating. Well, who's the lucky man then?'

'Er . . .' I pause long enough to stuff another couple of strawberry creams into my mouth, 'Well, you know I said that there was something else I needed to tell you . . .'

★ ★ ★

As an apology, and as part of the activity trade-off we need to do to get Sash out for the evening, I end up taking Niall's place on the dreaded shoe-shopping trip. I also feel a touch guilty, as Sash is right and I really don't see enough of her. She may joke with me but it's true that I'm pretty confident of the fact that when I do see her, there won't be any real recriminations about my neglect of our friendship. This doesn't make it right for me to take it for granted, though.

That was one of the things I promised myself I'd do when I split up with Richard – see more of my mates. Hell, I'd even got it into my head that I might take some time out and go and join Wiggy on an exotic beach somewhere. So far I've done nothing, wasting most of the summer holiday slouching round my flat like a bored teenager instead.

The shoe-shopping trip is a big success in different ways. We not only manage to find two pairs of shoes for Jack without any major tears or tantrums, but we also manage to squeeze in a few clothes shops on our rounds by bribing the kids with a trip to the cookie shop, which I'm ashamed to confess is as much of a treat for me as it is for them.

I could give up sex for their caramel swirls. That's if I had any sex to give up.

We do a running handover of the kids to Niall, like a tag team in the Olympics passing the baton, and then head back to my house to parade round in our new clothes before getting primped, preened and pampered for our big night out.

An ecstatic Sash spends more than half an hour in the bath.

'This is absolute bliss!' she sighs, wiggling her toes happily in the bubbles. 'I don't think I've had a shower or a shit, pardon my language, on my own for the past two years.'

Taking pity on her, I complete the idyll by taking her a glass of wine and what's left of my family-sized box of Roses – which is now no-appetite pygmy size – and offering to scrub her back for her.

Sash is almost purring as I attack her shoulders with my loofah.

'Careful,' she laughs, 'you're the first person over eighteen to touch me for at least a month. If you turn me on I might have to jump you.'

'Are things really that bad?'

'Worse. What about you? Have you had any offers since you dumped Richard the Turd?'

'Well, only if you count Caro's party,' I reply without really thinking.

'Oh, yes? What party was this then? Tell all.'

'Nothing much to tell really,' I bluster, wishing I'd kept my mouth shut.

'Why do I find that hard to believe? Come on, Felicity, spill the beans.'

Under Sash's gentle yet enquiring gaze, I suddenly find myself confessing all about that night at Caro's. If I'm totally honest I've been dying to talk to somebody about it anyway.

To my surprise Sash bursts into peals of laughter.

'Oh, my goodness, how wonderful! And you just walked out? Well, you didn't walk, did you, you ran. I wish I'd have been there.' She stops as she realises that I'm staring at her open-mouthed.

'You've got to see the funny side, Fliss.'

'I have?'

'Yeah, and think how fortunate you were.'

'What, to escape?'

'No, actually to be there in the first place.'

'You what?' I exclaim.

'Well, it's not everybody who gets the opportunity to go to an orgy, is it? I certainly never have. Do you think you could get me an invite to the next one?'

'Honestly, Sash!'

'Well, I'm not getting any at home.' She pulls a face at me, and I finally break into a smile.

'I suppose I should laugh about it,' I say slowly. 'I mean, looking back it's kind of funny, but the hard part is how am I ever going to face Caroline again? I'm too embarrassed.'

'For running out, or for seeing her half-naked and in the arms of another woman?'

'Well, I've seen her half-naked before, but certainly not in those circumstances . . . I feel really bad, Sash, she keeps calling and leaving messages but I haven't got back to her.'

'I know the feeling.' Sash smiles wryly.

'I know, I know, I'm sorry . . .'

'Stop apologising, babe, and pass me a towel. I suppose I

should get out, I'm not going to pull if I go out looking like a sun-dried raisin, am I?'

'Oh, so you're out on the pull tonight then?' I tease her. 'Does Niall know this?'

'I don't think Niall would notice if I took Jared Leto home and shagged him on the living-room carpet right in front of Niall's face. As long as I wasn't blocking his view of the football on TV, that is.'

'Are things really that bad at the moment, Sash?' I ask her for the second time.

She looks up at me from under long dark eyelashes, her equally dark brown eyes narrowed.

'I'm bored out of my skull, Fliss,' she finally admits. 'I've been pregnant for two years out of the past three. Now I'm either working, potty training, or watching *Postman Pat*. I mean, what sort of life is that?'

I shake my head in sympathy.

'All Niall and I talk about is the kids. We're too tired for sex. Either that or we've just got to the point where we can't be bothered. It shouldn't be like this, I'm not even thirty yet. I should be standing in the middle of the bedroom in my thigh-length boots with a whip in one hand and a King Dong vibro in the other, with Niall tied to the bed head, spread-eagled and helpless . . . not curled up under my duvet by nine-thirty with a cup of hot chocolate and a trashy novel I'm too tired to read.'

'Do you still fancy him?'

'I don't know.'

'Really, it's gone that far?'

'Well, it's so hard to see him as a love object when he's fast asleep and snoring on the sofa, dressed in an old sweatshirt with baby sick on one shoulder and sweatpants with no knees left in them, three days growth on his chin, in dire need of a haircut and breath worse than the dog's. I know he scrubs up well, I just about remember that he looks more than half decent in a suit, but I can't remember the last time I saw him looking anything other than knackered. In all senses of the word.'

'So now you're tempted to go out and find someone else?'

'Is it better to do something that you regret, or to regret something that you haven't done? I really don't know the answer to that one, Fliss. I suppose it would be nice to see if I

123

can still pull. I feel a lot older than I am at the moment. I think I'm having a mid-life crisis, only it's come a couple of years too early. Although of course that does have its advantages in the fact that my bod's still in semi-decent shape, despite my off-spring's attempts at sabotage, so my chances of pulling are marginally better than they might have been. It does make it harder to pick myself a toy boy, though, doesn't it? I mean, when you're hitting your forties, you can choose yourself a nice twenty-seven year old. When you're twenty-seven yourself, you might just have to opt for a schoolboy.'

'Or a boy scout.' I giggle.

Sash rolls her eyeballs at me.

'You've got to see the funny side.' I echo her words of earlier.

'Tripped up by my own tongue,' she jokes. 'Tell you what, let's just relax, forget about our woes and have a really good night, yeah? Come on, get your kit on, we've got a party to go to.'

Half an hour later, I'm squeezed into the new outrageously sexy dress that Sash persuaded me to buy in town. It's a cobalt blue sequinned tube that holds me in and pushes me out in all the right places. I wouldn't even have picked it up if I'd been on my own. It's from Miss Selfridge. I haven't shopped in Miss Selfridge since I was nineteen.

'Wow!' Sash says as I head back into the bedroom to put the finishing touches to my make-up.

'Is that a good wow or a bad wow?' I ask, nervously tugging at the hem which seems to be at least three inches shorter than I remember it being in the shop.

'Oh, a good wow.' Sash nods. 'Definitely a good wow.'

'You haven't scrubbed up too badly yourself.'

'You would not believe how wonderful it is to get all glammed up.'

'You look a total babe,' I tell her. 'Really hot.'

Sash pushes at her gorgeously glossy short-cropped curls before applying another liberal does of hair-shine spray.

'Really? Thanks, Fliss. At home I'm always a mummy, never anything else.'

I detect a wistful note in her voice.

'I wonder if Sally-Anne and Richard will have kids?'

'Oh, my goodness!' I cross my eyes in horror at the thought of the world being populated by mini-Richards. 'I hadn't even thought of that.'

'Don't worry, darling.' Sash puts a reassuring hand on my arm. 'It'll be OK as long as they take after their mother.'

The plan is that we're to meet Sally and the others in a local wine bar then go on to Dune, one of Oxford's newest night-clubs, which neither Sash or I has ever been to, as we feel ourselves to be teetering on the edge of too old.

Sad, isn't it? But even if you feel like you're in your prime in your late-twenties, when you're surrounded by a horde of size eight nineteen year olds who think the tender age of twenty-three is positively geriatric then you forget prime and start to think mutton instead.

However, we're determined to have a good time tonight, despite the fact that due to Sasha's prolonged soak, we're running late and have to skip the wine bar and go straight to the club. Nine o'clock may seem ridiculously early to head into a nightclub, but it's one of those places where they have a fairly decent restaurant, and Sally has arranged a table for twenty.

Sash and I hit the bar first and knock back a couple of quick doubles before heading into the restaurant. We feel that we'll need to catch up with the others before we sit down to eat. There's no point having food if we haven't got any alcohol inside us for it to soak up. I'm glad I did knock back a couple of quickies when I see who's seated to Sally's left.

Mother.

I don't know which surprises me more, the fact that she's actually there, my mother, dressed up, made up, sitting in a night club, or the fact that when I walk in she gestures for me to go and sit next to her, and then stands up to greet me, taking my hand and pressing her lips against my cheek, before I collapse in to my chair in shock.

Even Sash looks wide-eyed and surprised at this unexpected show of affection and has to grab a glass of wine very quickly.

'I've bought Sally a little pressie,' she tells me, knocking back her wine and eyeing my mother nervously.

'So have I, what did you get her?'

'You'll see when she opens it. The only problem is I'm not sure that I can give it to her in front of your mother.'

'Me neither.'

125

It seems, however, that everyone else has had the same idea. Mother starts the gift giving with an exquisitely beautiful gold locket, then looks expectantly at me.

'Er, just got to get mine out of the bag . . .' I prevaricate, pretending to struggle with my carrier bag, 'Why don't you move on to Sash first?'

Mouthing 'Rat' at me, Sash gets up and walks round me and Mother to Sal's chair, and places a long thin parcel in front of her.

'You might want to wait until you get home before you open this one.' She smiles.

'No way!' roar Sally's mates.

Laughing nervously, Sal tears the bright pink paper from the box. Opening it gingerly, she gives a shriek of laughter and pulls out an eight-inch, flesh pink, throbbingly veined dildo.

'Don't assume that just because you're getting married, you'll get a constant supply of the real thing,' Sash tells her, throwing an arm around Sally's shoulders and squeezing. 'In fact, expect your rations to be significantly reduced.'

Sally blushes such a bright shade of pink you can see her glowing, even in the gloom of our corner table.

Feeling slightly more emboldened now that Sash's present has been greeted by my mother with laughter instead of the expected horror, I lean over and hand Sal my gift.

'What did you get her?' Sash asks me, sliding back into her seat as Sally carefully unties the ribbon around the box.

'Well, let's just say we obviously think along the same lines.' I wink at Sash. 'In fact, I think we may have gone to the same shop.'

Everyone watches as Sally unties my parcel, carefully placing the gold ribbon to the side of her bread plate before pulling out a pair of black velvet-covered handcuffs, a bull whip, and a blindfold.

Eyes and cheeks still glowing, she reads out my card.

' "Just so you can let him know who's the boss!" ' she giggles. 'Thanks, Fliss.'

'Well, it's always best to start out as you mean to go on,' I reply.

'Hopefully that'll be on an even footing.' Sally smiles.

'In that case you take it in turns to use them on each other.'

'Can I borrow them?' Sash asks, reaching over to pick up the whip and caressing the plaited leather affectionately. 'I could do with something like this to liven Niall up a bit.'

It seems like some of the other girls in our party have done an Anne Summers run too. As well as my and Sash's little offerings, or not so little in the case of Sash's gift, Sal ends up with edible panties and lickable body lotion, a full colour photographic *Kama Sutra*, several sets of rather racy undies, a mini handbag vibrator that looks like a lipstick, and a large chocolate willy.

It seems that nearly everyone's bought her sex-related gifts, apart from Mother of course, and Sally's best friend the ever-practical Erica who's bought her the latest Jamie Oliver and a pair of oven gloves, although Sash points out that you could count Jamie Oliver as a sex toy if you wanted to.

The *Kama Sutra* is currently doing the rounds to many gasps of amazement and amusement. Even my mother's laughing and exclaiming over the photographs. She's been an entirely different person tonight, happy and chatty all the way through dinner, and then straight out on the dance floor when we head into the club afterwards.

I've never, ever been in a nightclub with my mother before.

She's giddy. Like a little girl on her first outing to the fair ground. Her eyes are bright, her face is shining, she's dancing, and drinking, and laughing, and, well, she's actually being affectionate. If I didn't know her better I'd say she's popped something illegal.

She's definitely drunk.

She's even hugged me several times in the space of an hour. I don't quite know how to handle this.

It must be happy pills.

If so could she put me on to her supplier?

Not that I'm having too bad a time myself this evening. Sally's friends are a really great bunch, like Sal really, easy to get on with, all out for a good time, especially the ones from the bank. Boy, do they know how to party. I suppose it comes with having to be strait-laced and disciplined during the day, they let their hair down with a vengeance at night. They're currently having a competition to see who can deep throat Sally's new Mega Throbba the farthest, the winner getting the honour of devouring the large smooth bell end of the chocolate willy.

The club is pretty packed as well, and I've even had a few eye meets with some pretty tasty men. I'd also forgotten how much

I enjoy dancing. I used to embarrass Richard with my enthusiasm for a good boogie. It's lovely to be able to strut my funky stuff without someone looking on in disapproval whenever I get too carried away by the music.

Unfortunately, my enthusiasm is pretty short-lived. In fact it dies a death at about eleven-thirty when I realise that there was one aspect of this evening's festivities that Sally neglected to mention to me.

The stag party.

Or to be more precise the location of the stag party.

Having spent the past three hours on an extended pub crawl, it has now just staggered en masse into our night club.

Of all the bars in all the towns . . .

Why didn't Sal tell me they'd arranged to meet up later on? Well, I know why Sal didn't tell me.

As Richard and his cronies walk in one door, I just about manage to restrain myself from walking out of another.

I look around for backup, but Sash has disappeared, and as a temporary escape measure I head for the loos instead.

I find her inside, perched on the Formica work top that surrounds the cigarette and loo roll-stuffed wash basins, trying to hold a mobile phone conversation with her husband over the muted noise of the club music, and the not so muted squawking of the girls fighting to redo their make-up in the limited mirror space.

'Well, I'm not surprised Jack's been sick if that's what you let him eat this evening, he's a two year old, not a waste disposal unit . . .'

She catches sight of me and rolls her eyes.

'No, I can't come home yet! Honestly, Niall, can't you cope with them for one evening on your own? I've managed it a million times, and you keep telling me you're the brains of the family . . . well, he's a baby, that's what babies do . . . it's either nappy, food or Bonjela, one of the three normally does the trick . . . if you get absolutely desperate you could always call my mother . . . What was that, darling? Shhhhhhhhk . . . I can't hear you . . . sorry, I think my signals going to f—'

She presses the end button on the phone and sighs heavily, smiling and shrugging her shoulders at me in exasperation.

'Honestly, you leave them alone for one evening!'

'Guess who's here?' I cut in agitatedly.

'Er . . . don't tell me, Tom Cruise, and he wants us to go back to his bachelor pad for a threesome? Tell him I'm on my way!'

'I wish. Think of something less appealing.'

'Richard.'

'Bang on.'

'You're joking, aren't you? What's he doing here? There's more than one night club in Oxford, isn't there?'

'I think it was all pre-arranged. You know, go out separately and then meet up later. Only for some reason Sal forgot to mention that part to me.'

'Odd that, yeah,' Sash agrees sarcastically. 'What do you want to do, go home?'

'That'd look a bit off, wouldn't it? Besides I don't want to go, we were having a good time.'

'We still can.' Sash links her arm through mine. 'This is a big place, we can avoid him if we want to.'

When we go back out my mother is dancing with Richard.

The two groups have intermingled. Some of Sally's friends' other halves are out on Richard's stag do, and vice versa. They've all taken over a group of chairs and sofas in one darkened corner of the huge room on the edge of the dance floor.

Sally spots Sash and me emerging from the loos and waves for us to go over, probably thinking that if she doesn't collar me straight away I'll be heading for my coat and home. I just about manage to comply, safe in the knowledge that my mother will monopolise Richard for as long as she possibly can. Besides, determined to stay till the end, Sash has a firm hold on my arm, thwarting any ideas I may have of bolting to the taxi rank, and heading home to my duvet and another Mars Bar-swallowing session.

Sal smiles sheepishly at me.

'Surprise!' she mumbles weakly, as I raise my eyebrows at her.

Determined to be magnanimous, it is Sally's night after all, I return her sheepish smile with a half-hearted 'Don't worry about it' one of my own.

Someone has ordered a dozen or so bottles of champagne, which is now flowing freely. Sally hands us a glass.

'Sorry, Sis, but I thought you wouldn't come if I mentioned that we were meeting up, and I really wanted everyone here.'

'And here we all are,' I murmur, taking a long swig from my glass.

'Well, apart from Dad, yes,' Sally agrees, missing the irony in my voice, 'which is a shame, but night clubs aren't really his scene, are they? And apparently he and Roger had a prior appointment with a rod and some cod somewhere off Kent. He probably would have come if they let Labradors on the dance floor, though.' She trails off, laughing nervously. Poor old Sal. She should be relaxed and enjoying herself but instead she's worried about my reaction to what in normal circumstances would be nothing out of the norm.

'It's not a problem, Sal.' I shrug. 'Honestly.'

Sash winks at me and mouths, 'That's the spirit.'

Amidst the large group of men is a woman, smiling happily like a lone cow that's just stumbled away from the herd and into the bull's enclosure.

Despite the fact that I've only met her once before, I recognise her instantly.

The immaculate make-up, glossy hair and expensive clothes are the unmistakable trademark of just one person I know.

Katherine Christian.

She wasn't with us, so she must have come in with Richard's party. What on earth is she up to?

I notice that Sally is watching her as well.

'I thought stag nights were men only? Well, apart from the stripper that is,' I murmur.

Sally sighs heavily.

'So did I. Richard suggested I should invite her to the hen night, but I couldn't bring myself to. It wasn't too horrible of me not to, was it, Fliss? After all I don't really know the woman, do I?'

'You didn't want her here tonight, I take it?' I ask in concern.

'No.' Sal shakes her head and, refilling our glasses, takes another sip of champagne. 'Awful, aren't I? But for some reason she makes me feel uncomfortable. Oh, well, I got my just deserts for being horrible, didn't I? It backfired because she just tagged along with Alex and went to the stag party instead,' Sal says a touch sourly.

'Who's that then?' Sash asks, narrowing her eyes as she looks over to where Kat is holding court among a group of semi-pissed men, mesmerised by the way she keeps crossing and uncrossing her long legs, like Cupid Stunt on repeat play.

'An ex of Richard's.'

'Really?'

Sash looks from me to Sal and then back again.

'You two look so alike sometimes,' she laughs, taking in the identical way we're both gazing sourly at Kat Christian. 'What's she done to upset you then?'

'It's not what she's done . . .' Sally murmurs.

'It's what she might do,' I finish for her.

'You get that impression too?' Sal turns to me.

'It's hard not to. Maybe that's just the way she is though,' I try to reassure my sister. 'Anyone can see she's a big fat flirt, and not just with Richard. Besides, this time next week you'll be dancing at your wedding reception . . .'

'You're right.' Sally relaxes, the frown replaced by a smile. 'Of course you're right. I'm being ridiculous, aren't I? The jealous little wife.' She giggles with pleasure as she awards this title to herself. 'Oh, my goodness, I'm getting married next week!' The giggle broadens into a wide happy grin.

'Yeah, well, I suggest you go and rescue your husband-to-be from the clutches of his future mother-in-law, before he changes his mind about marrying into a family where madness is so obviously in the genes,' I warn her, watching as Mother attempts an enthusiastic, if somewhat ungainly, reggae grind against a worried-looking Richard.

'You don't think Kat's after him, do you?' Sash asks me as Sally rescues a relieved Richard from my mother.

'I don't know. Like I said, she's probably just a bit of a flirt. But I was with Richard for nearly two years and the woman never figured in our lives. Now that she's returned, she seems to have returned with a vengeance.'

After the strange, almost hypnotically odd scene of my mother dancing to trance, garage and jungle, you'd think it would be easier watching Richard smooching with my sister. Well, it is easier on the eye, but it's also really strange.

'This is so weird,' Sash muses, echoing my thoughts, as Richard wraps his arms around Sally-Anne's waist and pulls her to him, leaning down to rest his forehead against hers.

'You're telling me.'

'Seeing them together, Sal with Richard instead of you. It's ever so odd.'

'I know.'

'I really don't believe this . . .' she says yet again.

'Well, believe it, honey, 'cause it's real,' I reply, taking a swig of my drink and letting my heavy head loll on to her shoulder as I watch Sally and Richard begin to kiss.

'Do you think they look good together?'

Sash raises her eyebrows at me.

'No, I mean it, if you didn't know that Richard was, well, Richard, and Sally was my sister, say you'd never met them and you were just like watching them together or something . . . would you think they made a good couple?'

'Well, unlike you she's actually shorter than him which is good, for him anyway . . .' Sash finally ventures after careful consideration.

'No! Well, yeah, you're right, but that's not what I meant. I mean, do you think they look happy? What would you pick up from the body language, do you know what I'm trying to say?'

'I suppose so.'

'You mean, you know what I mean or you think they look happy?'

'Well, both, I suppose.' Sash shrugs.

'Good.'

We're silent for a moment as we watch Richard lean down and whisper something in Sally's ear.

'I wish you could come to the wedding, Sash, to hold my hand.'

'Well, I *was* invited.'

'Until the change of bride, yeah.'

'Maybe we could persuade Sal to reinstate me.'

'There's no maybe about that. Sally didn't want to upset anybody on my original list by uninviting them, but unfortunately it's not down to her. Mother is self-elected censor. She blew off all my mates the minute it ceased to become my wedding and became Sally's instead.'

'I know younger siblings quite often get hand-me-downs, but this is pushing it a bit,' Sash jokes. 'Tell you what, why don't we hit the bar? This champers is nice, but it's not really hitting the spot.'

We skirt around the dance floor, away from the mingled stag and hen parties, and manage to find ourselves a couple of vacant stools right at the far end of the long stretch of oak. Sash manages to attract the attention of the barman.

'Another vod?'

'Absolutely.'

'Double?'

'Is there any other way to drink it at the moment?'

'Yeah,' Sash grins, 'straight from the bottle.'

'I don't think I'm feeling that desperate.'

'Glad to hear it.' She passes me my drink. 'But you are pissed off, aren't you?'

'Well, yes, I am a bit fed up. I dumped Richard because I wanted him out of my life. But he's still going to be in it. Permanently. I'm still going to be related to him.'

'I know, but surely brother-in-law has to be better than husband?'

'For me, yeah, but what about Sal? I know I've done the right thing for myself in calling off the wedding, but I'm really worried Sally's not doing the right thing for her.'

'Maybe, but you have to let her make her own decisions, don't you?'

'I suppose you're right.'

'I'm always right,' Sash jokes. 'Anyway, enough of this, we agreed tonight was a night to party.'

'We did, didn't we?' I smile.

'Yeah. Now what do you want first? Booze, boogie, or how about a good old flirt with a bonkable bloke?'

'And where are we going to find one of those then?'

'Heavens, Fliss, we're in a night club. That's like asking "Haven't you got any chocolate?" in a sweet shop. We're surrounded by men.' She waves an arm around expansively. 'In fact,' the arm stops mid-wave and she peers over my shoulder, her eyes lighting up as she does so, 'there's a pretty tasty one heading right for you at this very moment!'

I follow the inclination of Sash's head to see a good-looking man with short brown hair and smiling blue-green eyes approaching me.

It's Alex Christian.

I'd caught a glimpse of him in the distance earlier, when Richard first came into the club, but to be honest I was more concerned with watching his wife than anything else.

'Hi, Fliss. How are you doing?'

His greeting is as usual relaxed and friendly, but suddenly I feel a little nervous and only manage a very-high pitched squeaky hello.

'I was going to say that I'm surprised to see you here, but actually I'm not.'

'I know,' I trill, coughing in the hope that my voice might go back down to its usual level. 'Wherever there's a bar . . .'

'That's not what I meant and you know it.' He smiles good-naturedly. He's standing between Sasha and me, turned slightly more towards me so that I can see Sasha's face but he can't without turning his head to the right.

She takes advantage of this temporary blind spot by pursing her lips together in a kissy movement and mouthing 'Phwoar!' at me, whilst making squidgy movements with her hands in the vicinity of his very tasty backside, as though she's going to reach in and squeeze it, like testing melons for ripeness.

Throwing her a 'Will you behave?' look, I introduce him to my drooling friend.

'Alex, this is my friend Sasha.'

As he turns to say hello, Sash hastily rearranges her features into something that doesn't resemble a leer, and holds out her hand.

'Sash, this is Alex.'

She takes his hand and smiles seductively.

'Alex Christian, Katherine Christian's husband,' I add.

Sasha's immaculately plucked eyebrows shoot straight up her forehead.

'Really?' she breathes, glancing significantly at me. 'How *nice* to meet you.'

'Likewise.'

Sash and I have been watching Kat Christian with a mixture of amusement and consternation. She appears to be following Richard everywhere he goes, like a little tugboat bobbing after a docking cruise liner, anxious to shepherd it in precisely the direction she wants it to go.

And I thought my mother was bad.

Even the sweet-natured Sally was driven to come out with the comment, 'I thought Richard was having a stag night, not a moose night.'

Sash was therefore very keen to meet the husband of the aforementioned moose. However, when I look back over at her, expecting her still to be drooling over Alex, I find that she's actually gazing over at the dance floor, eyes wide with astonishment. I follow her gaze. She's looking at Richard. He's still on the dance floor, smooching away to a slow romantic ballad, but the woman he's got his short arms wrapped around is most definitely not my sister.

It's Kat Christian.

So he's dancing with an old friend? Big deal. At least it would be nothing if she didn't have her head resting tenderly on his shoulder, and her hands resting under his shirt and inside the waist band of his trousers, fingers down out of view but easily far enough to be touching a great deal of his arse.

To Richard's credit he does look a little uncomfortable. Good job too or I'd probably end up grabbing the empty Bud bottle sitting on the bar next to me and crowning him with it. He's certainly not hanging on to Kat with the same intensity or intimacy, in fact he looks a bit rigid. You know how stiff you go when you suddenly discover something with more legs than you crawling up your arm?

I peer across the room looking for Sally. She's spotted them, and is watching this strange display of affection with an equally strange expression.

Alex is watching them too, the usual ready smile replaced by a heavy frown, but he doesn't make a move until he too spots Sally-Anne's concerned expression.

'Would you excuse me a moment?'

''Ere we go,' Sash nods, nudging me as Alex leaves the bar and goes down towards the dance floor. I watch Alex make his way to Sal. After a moment's conversation he pulls her out on to the dance floor. I can see him now, whispering in her ear and making her laugh. He dances with her for one record, the smile which had slipped when his wife dragged Richard out on to the dance floor getting broader every moment, lips moving constantly as he and Sally sway to the music.

Then when the next record starts he moves so that they are closer to Kat and Richard, and engineers a swift excuse-me so that the right partners are back together again.

Very smoothly done.

Sash starts to applaud her appreciation of the manoeuvre. Fortunately the music's too loud for anyone relevant to hear, but the barman's looking confused. While I'm equally impressed

I find myself wondering if Alex did it for himself or for Sal. Both probably.

Richard wasn't really doing anything to merit an outburst of jealousy, and Alex didn't make a move until he spotted Sally's miserable face, but it can't be that much fun watching your wife run around after another man.

To my surprise, however, instead of staying on the dance floor with Kat, he immediately leads her back to the group lounging and drinking in a corner, deposits her in an empty chair, and despite the fact that there are still plenty of bottles of champagne at the table, leaves her there and heads back to where Sash and I are standing at the bar.

'Mind if I join you?' he says with a lopsided smile.

'Not at all,' Sash smiles, licking her lips and winking surreptitiously at me.

'Large brandy, please.' He waves a twenty at the bartender. 'Are you ready for another one?'

'Man or drink?' Sash whispers to me.

'Don't tell me, you want both. Poor old Niall!'

'Poor old Niall, my arse!' she hisses.

'Thanks, but we'll get that.' I grin at the barman. 'Add two large vodkas on to that as well, please, will you?' I turn back to Alex. 'I think I owe you a large drink for what you just did.'

'I think I need a large drink for the fact that I had to do what I just did.'

'The Kat's in the dog house then, is she?' Sash grins at him. She is too pissed to be subtle. I elbow her swiftly in the ribs.

'Ouch, Fliss, you big meany – what did you do that for?'

'Because Sensible Sash is now Sozzled-can't-keep-my-mouth-shut Sash, that's why!' I hiss at her.

Alex laughs.

'It's OK, I hardly think subtlety is the key word for anybody this evening, do you?'

'Well then, if we don't have to be subtle can I ask you something?'

'Sure,' he replies, looking at me cautiously.

'What the hell is your wife up to, running around after Richard like that, in front of everybody?'

He hesitates for a while, and I start to regret the fact that I slightly overstepped the mark with that particular question.

'Sorry, I shouldn't have said that.'

'No, it's OK.' He holds up his hands. 'I think she's like most women.' Alex's mouth twists into a wry smile. 'Always wants something that much more when she thinks she can't have it.'

'I'm like that with chocolate,' I sigh.

'Well, I don't think it's fair to lump us all into that category . . .' Sash starts.

'I did say most, not all.'

'True.' Sash reflects for a moment. 'Then again I can't deny that I'm probably a sex maniac at the moment because I'm not actually getting any. In fact I'd be more than happy to turn the tables for you and help make your wife jealous?'

She winks heavily at Alex, who I can see is unsure whether to laugh or run away very quickly.

'It's all right,' I tell him reassuringly. 'She's only joking.'

'No, I'm not!' Sash cuts in indignantly.

'She's just had a bit too much to drink, I think,' Alex replies.

'Well, I might have had a few . . .'

'I meant my wife, not you.'

He leans in and kisses Sash gently on the cheek.

'Thanks for the offer, it's the nicest one I've had all night, but I think I should probably take Kat home.'

He drains his glass and smiles a little grimly at us.

'Well, it was lovely to see you again, Fliss, and very nice to meet you too,' he adds as Sash, fuelled by the compliment and the vodka, leans in and drunkenly lands a wet kiss on *his* cheek. The smile gets a little warmer as I hastily wipe away the lipstick mark she left with the little paper coaster from under my drink.

'Why can't he take me home instead?' Sash asks wistfully as she hungrily watches Alex's retreating backside. 'What a lovely bloke. How on earth did that woman get her claws into someone like him?'

'Well, maybe she's not so bad. All we've taken into account is the fact that she's flirty, especially to Richard. We don't really know her, do we?'

'True,' Sash replies, a little shame-facedly. 'Take me as a case in point. I'm a nice person, aren't I?'

'Of course you are!' I exclaim, throwing an arm around her swaying shoulders to hug her. 'You're the best.'

'Yeah, and sod feeling his buns – if that Alex had just turned his face a fraction more I'd have had my tongue down his throat like a whippet after a rabbit.' She grins lasciviously.

'Well, I'd say Kat Christian was restrained compared with you then,' I say dryly.

'Oh, come on, darling, you've got to agree that Alex Christian is a bit of all right?'

'I hadn't really thought about it,' I lie.

'Yeah, and I'm a virgin.' She raises her eyebrows in disbelief.

'OK,' I admit, 'yes, he's lovely, but he's married, isn't he?'

'Trust me, babe, that means bugger all to some men.'

'Yeah, but if that's what Alex is like, then I wouldn't be interested anyway.'

'Not into the thought of some extra-marital sex then? You know, a nice bit of no-strings nookie?'

'Not really.'

'Does that mean I can have him then?'

'No, you can't!' I howl.

'Ah, so you *do* want him for yourself,' she teases me.

'It's not that and you know it. It's just that with my sister's wedding only a week away, I really want to believe in the sanctity of marriage at the moment and nobody's helping me do that really, are they? Especially not you, you old tart,' I tell her affectionately. 'Banging on about banging someone else.'

'Well, I didn't know that sanctity meant total chastity.' Sash's big eyes make her resemble a puppy sitting by a door, desperate to be let into the garden. 'I may not be a virgin, but I could easily be one of those born-again ones. They say if you leave it alone for long enough your hymen grows back, don't they? And, boy, has mine been left alone for long enough. Fidelity I could cope with as long as it didn't mean living like a nun. I didn't think marital rights meant a cup of cocoa and the re-run of *EastEnders* at bedtime.'

She follows my gaze to where Alex has collected Kat and, with a firm grip on her arm, is saying goodnight to everyone.

'Don't worry about your sister, they stand as good a chance as any of us at getting it right.'

'With a few other detrimental factors thrown into the equation,' I sigh, watching as Kat makes a point of saying a prolonged goodnight to Richard before they leave.

'Well, he'll be a married man this time next week.' Sash smiles encouragingly at me. 'Hopefully that'll be the end of it.'

'Yeah,' I sigh uncertainly, recalling Alex's words of wisdom about the wayward wants of women. 'Either that or the start of something worse.'

Chapter Six

The day of the wedding dawns bright and clear. Rain would have suited my mood better. I lie in bed for far too long, hoping that some miracle will occur that excuses me from going, or better still results in the permanent cancellation of the whole thing.

Earthquake, flood, hurricane . . . I don't mind which, the problem would be containing the phenomenon to Richard's apartment only.

The last three weeks have been a nightmare of the first degree. I thought it would be nice to see Mother happy for a change, her usual air of long-suffering misery can be very wearing. What I didn't realise was that a happy Miriam Blakeney is even more intolerable than a miserable and martyred Miriam Blakeney.

She has gone into wedding overdrive.

I have had to see far too much of her recently. I had hoped that due to the rather unusual circumstances, I might be spared the usual rigours of the pre-wedding party, but Mother is determined I'm not going to miss a thing.

I have my orders to be at The Beeches for 10 a.m. sharp to supervise the arrival of the bridesmaids, the flowers, and enough booze to float the *Titanic*. I suppose things could be worse: Sally-Anne had tentatively suggested that I might like to be a bridesmaid. Fortunately she didn't push the point.

I finally drag myself out of bed, and end up arriving at The Beeches an hour late, but fortunately Mother is on too much of a wedding high to notice. Sally-Anne has six bridesmaids, one of the reasons why she wasn't too bothered about my reluctance to add myself to the number.

Two friends, two cousins and two of Richard's nieces make up the motley crew. They range from age six to twenty-six. The six year old is the only one who is treating me normally.

Nobody else knows what to say.

Of course rumours have been rife, ranging from the sublime to the ridiculous, the most amusing being that Richard was of a religion where he could take more than one wife, and is due to marry us both, and the most common being that he left me for Sally-Anne. I can just about cope with people thinking this. What I can't handle is the quiet sympathy, the looks, the whispers when they think I'm not listening.

The house is full of relatives I haven't seen for at least ten years, and wish I didn't have to see for at least another ten.

Up in Sally's large bedroom all is mad activity. Mother is arguing with the hairdresser, who is valiantly attempting to pin, curl, and coiffure eight people within two hours. The younger bridesmaids are being chastised by the beautician for stealing her lipsticks. Mother's swooping around the room interfering with everything, like an excited budgie let out of its cage after a long period of imprisonment.

Seated at her dressing table, clad in a pretty floral silk dressing gown, long brown hair in papers, Sally-Anne smiles happily, serene amidst the chaos.

I escape to the comparative solitude of the kitchen where I valiantly make enough sandwiches for fifty people in half an hour. Somehow I feel more comfortable brandishing a huge carving knife. I hack my way through fourteen loaves with great gusto. It's a brilliant way of relieving tension.

There is one particularly awkward moment when Dad's dotty sister, Aunt Vera, arrives. She obviously hadn't received an amended invite, and proceeds to make a great show of congratulating me and giving me her wedding gift.

Dad, God bless him, manages to steer her quietly away and explain the new turn of events. She strides back to me, not in the least embarrassed, and says in her booming voice, 'Drew says you're not marrying the man. Glad to hear it, never liked him. Don't know why Sally-Anne has to step in, though, just as you've seen the light and escaped, but then again you've always had more sense than her.'

She thrusts the present at me again.

'Bought this specifically for you so you may as well have it. I'm sure Sally-Anne won't mind, she'll be getting plenty.

Besides, now you're young, free and single again, you need it more than her.'

Blushing crimson, I open the beautifully gift-wrapped box. It contains the most wonderfully luxurious, racy-lacy set of Janet Reger.

'Find yourself a man who'll appreciate it.' She winks one heavily blue-shadowed eyelid.

'I'd rather find a man who appreciated me,' I say wistfully.

She ponders on this for a moment.

'Impossible. All men are pigs,' she snorts, and strides off into the garden dragging my father with her. I can hear her bullying him from the other end of the hundred-foot lawn.

'You know, you really ought to tie those delphiniums back, Drew, they're running amok . . .'

Upstairs the bridesmaids are too.

The little ones, bored with waiting around in their underwear and hooped underskirts for the appropriate moment to be dressed in their frilly pink outfits, descend on the kitchen like a flock of hungry young vultures and start to make mincemeat of my platefuls of sandwiches stacked like high-rise buildings.

They look at me in my blue-striped apron worn to cover my Ungaro suit – an extravagance that ironically should have been my going-away outfit – a whispering little clique, in their own way more unnerving than the adults.

Eleven-year-old Lucy, my cousin's eldest daughter, her mouth full of baked ham and wheatgerm, is elected spokesperson.

'Auntie Fliss?'

I turn away from the cake I'm slicing. She sidles up to me and, being a child, takes the opportunity of my distraction to slide a large piece of chocolate gâteau into her mouth alongside the ham.

'Is it true . . .' She's finding it difficult to talk with so much food in her mouth.

'Is what true?' I'm trying to sound bright and unaffected.

'. . . that you were supposed to marry Uncle Richard?'

'Well . . . yes, that was what was going to happen.'

'So why is Auntie Sally marrying him instead?'

That's a good question, but what would be a good answer to give an eleven year old?

'Um, because I don't want to,' I offer.

'My mummy always makes me do things I don't want to,' she

143

replies. 'Like have a bath when Disney's on, or eat liver. I hate liver but I can't give it to Emma,' she gestures towards her younger sister, 'because she doesn't like liver either.'

'Well, I didn't exactly give Sally-Anne Richard because I don't like him . . .' I start to say, but am saved by the appearance of Glenys the Menace, mother's so-called best friend, staunchly single, chairwoman of the parish council, local Tory councillor, branch leader of the WI, and raging snob, she is of the era of Maharajahs and Memsahibs. Her father was a Colonel in the colonies. She still runs her life like a military operation, a fact that I'm actually grateful for now as she rounds up the youngest stragglers with a metaphorical crack of the whip and, thankfully, bears them away for final preparation and dress fixing.

More close friends arrive. I busy myself handing round drinks and canapés, and trying to look pleased to see everyone.

My sandwiches are beginning to curl at the edges in the dry heat of the day. I feel like I'm beginning to curl at the edges too. The false bright smile I've been wearing all morning is beginning to slip, and if one more person touches my arm and smiles sympathetically I'm sure I shall crack and hit them.

The bridesmaids finally descend, all dressed, coiffured, and those allowed to wear it, made up. They are laughing and chattering like a flock of bright pink parrots.

Dad, looking handsome yet somewhat funereal in a grey morning suit, with grey silk cravat and a grey mourning face, appears at my side.

He hugs me.

'You're a real trooper, Fliss, the way you've handled this. I'm really proud of you.'

'The worst is yet to come,' I mutter gloomily.

I've elected to drive myself to the church, that way I can arrive unannounced and slip away if desperate. Threading my way through the throngs waiting to greet the long black line of cars that are carrying the main wedding party, I slide in as inconspicuously as possible, and ignoring a frantically signalling usher, slip into one of the rear pews, just behind a well-placed pillar.

I chose my lampshade-style hat specifically to hide my face. If I could have got away with it I would have worn a veil as well, not through some misplaced desire actually to be the bride but so that I could remain anonymous throughout.

Huge arrangements of pink and white carnations, white roses, pink roses and cloudy gypsophila flank the altar. Smaller posies are throwing sweet scents from the end of each pew. Garlands of dark ivy are wound around each pillar like serpents climbing to the vaulted roof.

Richard emerges from the vestry with his best man James, who's actually a really decent guy, and Reverend Parsifal. I'm almost surprised to see Richard. I suppose right up to this moment I still thought that the whole thing was just a ruse to piss me off, but there he is in his grey morning suit actually looking like the nervous husband-to-be.

He looks very handsome too. Suits suit him, make him look taller. He would never admit to it but he has been known to have his shoes made with a slightly stacked heel. Stacking the odds in his own favour, you could say. He's highly delighted at the recent seventies clothes revival, he was just waiting for stacked shoes to come back into fashion. He keeps looking around, seems agitated. Perhaps he's worried that Sally-Anne might actually come to her senses and stand him up.

Mother sails in with Aunt Vera and Glenys. She's wearing a hideous pink creation with a wide-brimmed hat trimmed with flowers to match the ones in the church and Sally's bouquet. She fortunately doesn't notice me, she's too busy nodding regally to the friends and relatives already beginning to fill the small church as she makes her way up the aisle and into the front pew, waving graciously to either side of the aisle like the Queen from her royal carriage. The few people who notice me don't know what to do. A few smile nervously or sympathetically; some look away quickly, pretend they haven't seen me.

None of them dares to sit in the same pew as me. Is this an indication of what the rest of the day will be like, being treated as though I have some frighteningly contagious disease? Unfortunately I think it is, although there are a few people I'm glad I don't have to sit with.

Ollie Barton-Davis, Richard's hideously oily head of chambers comes in.

I call him Ollie the Octopus. He's short, fat and stumpy but you'd think his arms were eight feet long, the places his hands always manage to end up. He has been harassing me since the first day we met; inane comments, sexual innuendo that's

145

always accompanied by the laughter and 'it's only a joke, darling' exterior that protects him against rejection or particularly nasty harassment cases.

For one horrible moment I think he's going to come and sit next to me, until he's accosted by an usher and made to sit on Richard's side of the church.

The click of high Russell & Bromley heels on the stone floor heralds the arrival of Kat the predator, ex-fiancée, the clothes horse in the closet. So she decided to come to the wedding after all. Probably dying of curiosity like all the rest of them. She is looking decidedly chic but positively bridal in a very expensive off-white Chanel suit. Give her a bouquet and she's ready to march straight up the aisle instead of my sister.

She and Alex edge into the pew opposite me on Richard's side of the church. Alex looks over, tilts his head sideways as though he has to look under my hat to recognise me, and mouths 'Hello'. Kat, who has been staring up the aisle like the watchman on the *Titanic* looking for icebergs, looks over too. She doesn't recognise me. I can see her asking Alex who I am. At his reply, she looks over with renewed interest, and smiles. It's not a particularly nice smile.

The choir slow-step like bridesmaids down the aisle to the sweet strains of 'Jesu, Joy of Man's Desiring', which is being played not by the vicar's wife, whose skills as an organist are somewhat limited, but over the recently installed Tannoy system. Cassocks immaculately white, faces scrubbed and cherubic they file into their designated pews and sit down. One choir-boy promptly spoils the angelic tableau by pulling a Game Boy from under his cassock.

Two minutes later the piped music stops abruptly and the organ revs up with noisy farts from the ancient bellows as, following a cue from one of the ushers positioned by the door, Alice Parsifal begins to play the 'Wedding March'.

There are gasps as Sally enters the church and floats up the aisle on Dad's arm. She really does look beautiful, ethereal even. Whereas I looked like a dessert in that dress, she looks like a fairy princess.

Richard turns to greet her. I strain to see his face. Does he look proud? He should. I send a fervent prayer to God that he really, truly loves her.

Dad hands his younger daughter to her future husband.

'Dearly beloved . . .' Reverend Parsifal intones. Looking not unlike a large magpie in his flowing black gown and white collar, he speaks slowly, clearly, his voice reverberating around the building.

Sally almost whispers her vows, I have to strain to hear her.

'I call upon these persons here present to witness that I, Sally-Anne Louise Blakeney, do take thee, Richard Edward Trevelyan . . .'

Richard's voice sounds clear, confident. He is hidden from my view partly by the pillar, and partly by a huge arrangement of flowers which is almost indistinguishable from Mother's hat. I'm not complaining.

'. . . speak now or forever hold your peace.'

Am I imagining it or do all eyes turn to me at this point? I tell myself I'm imagining it. The moment passes.

James the clown pretends to have lost the rings. Oh, that he had for real. Like a magician, he produces them with a flourish from his silk handkerchief. A bubble of laughter rises around the church, and breaks against the vaulted ceiling.

The rings are exchanged.

The vows are complete.

Richard and Sally-Anne are married.

How do I feel about this? I ask myself? Bloody awful comes the answer.

Mother is dabbing her eyes with a small lace handkerchief. I glance over at Kat. She is biting her bottom lip so hard, it's white through lack of blood. Dad blows his nose noisily on a man-size tissue. I think it's time to go.

Ducking under a blizzard of pink confetti and white rice, I'm just about to slip down the gravel path to the car park when I'm collared by Erica, Sal's best friend and Chief Bridesmaid. She was head girl at the school we both attended, and is awfully nice and jolly and terribly bossy to boot. She's helping James do his best man duties by rounding up people for the photographer – I think she secretly harbours the hope of continuing the tradition of best man and chief bridesmaid getting together, flashing her large coltish teeth at him at every possible opportunity.

'Smile time,' she announces happily. 'Family shots first. Fliss, you go over. James, you come and stand with me until they need us.'

Oh, hell. I start to stutter an excuse.

'Er, well, I really ought to be heading off to the reception, make sure everything is ready, no last-minute hiccups . . .'

'Nonsense! That's what we paid the caterers for,' she says, beaming in what is supposed to be a reassuring fashion. 'They really are first class, Fliss, I'm sure they're coping admirably.' I know they're first class, I want to shout at her, I'm the one that booked them in the first place. Now, please, I've got to get out of here! Instead I submit and am led away to where the photographer from hell is attempting to pose Sally and Richard.

'Say "Naughty knickers"!' he intones at every shot when we've joined the happy couple, in a voice that could rival Joe Pasquale for irritation factor.

I'm finding it incredibly difficult to smile. Every time he says 'Naughty knickers', I just about manage a grimace. Hopefully the only things you'll be able to see on the photographs are my hat and my chin.

Chapter Seven

Adesley Hall is a long honey-coloured stone building that basks like a golden sleeping cat at the bottom of the Whystone Valley. As the procession of cars winds its way up the long tree-lined drive, the cat opens an eye, stretches and awakes. A buzz of activity emerges from within. The wedding reception begins.

I chose Adesley Hall for the reception because it is so romantic. It automatically assails one with visions of heroes climbing the rambling vines that clutch its crumbling walls, to rescue some fair maiden stuck in one of the two towers which flank the porticoed main entrance. Ironic, really, that the same romantic beauty I once craved now mocks me silently.

There was no reason for Sally-Anne to change the venue, indeed she wouldn't have found anywhere so good at such short notice, so I am to be faced not only with sympathetic, curious, gossiping relatives, but not-so-sympathetic but equally as curious and even more gossipy hotel staff as well.

I've driven like the devil to get here before everyone else so that I don't have to walk in through a sea of wedding guests.

It's a very strange feeling to walk into the reception room.

The great oak-panelled hall is empty of people as yet. The tables are set with pink and white flowers, and pink and white linen, and pink and white place cards with gold writing, and a little gold cherub is drawn in the top right-hand corner of each menu (not my touch, I can assure you).

'Richard and Sally welcome you' announces the board that displays the seating plan, more argued about, thought out and prevaricated over than the Magna Carta.

The room is all pink, fluffy and cosily romantic, my original ideas transformed by Sally's very feminine touch. I'm a romantic too, definitely, but more of a Heathcliff and Cathy type romance, wild and breathtaking, not the chocolate box, Valentine card

149

kitsch this room now resembles.

I shudder.

Somehow it reminds me of Caro's dining room on the night of the orgy – not quite so tasteful but not quite so lascivious either.

The manager with whom I spent many a fraught hour discussing seating plans, menus, and the merits of various wines, greets me with a half-smile as he hurries to the main doors to welcome the wedding party. He looks at me, lips twitching nervously, and then looks away quickly. Two young waitresses lined up with trays of champagne by the front door also look over at me, look at each other and giggle.

I manage to get out of the official greetings line up by hiding in the loo. This was one ritual my mother was not prepared to spare me. She wanted me tortured by thirty minutes of hand-shaking, cheek brushing and general conviviality, of questioning looks, silent appraisal and, worse still, silent sympathy.

As it is I manage to hole up for long enough to sneak to the end of the line just as the last few people are coming through the foyer, and therefore only end up having to kiss some dotty old Great-great-aunt thingummybody who doesn't know me from Adam, second cousin Muriel from Australia, who always used to get Sally and me confused anyway, and horror of horrors, no doubt queen of the late entrances, Kat Christian.

Just my luck.

Kat seems to have perfected the lips hitting the air to either side of your face style of greeting. I can see her waving her crimson-painted mouth in the vague direction of Sally's cheeks. She lingers over Richard. Her lips somehow manage to hit flesh this time.

It will probably take him half an hour and a bottle of Vim to scrape off the crimson marks she's left behind. Her lipstick's so thick and glossy it looks like her lips are moulded out of clay, painted, hard-glazed and baked till they set.

Alex, who seems embarrassed by their tardiness, continues rapidly ahead of her down the line, charming my decrepit relatives with his easy manner. He reaches me and stops.

'Hello again.'

He gently takes my automatically outstretched hand.

'I won't shake, I should imagine your arm will drop off if one more person tries that manoeuvre.'

'Actually,' I confess, suppressing a small smile, 'I cheated.'

I tell him about hiding in the loo, and he bursts out laughing, earning me a reproving glare from Mother for daring to hold up the line, despite the fact that Kat is still hovering by Richard and hasn't caught her husband up yet.

Casting a backward glance at his wife that is hard to read, Alex squeezes my hand gently and walks on.

Richard's speech is smug and self-congratulatory.

Dad's is very brief. He looks remarkably uncomfortable in his morning suit, and the way he keeps tugging at his cravat makes me think he's convinced it's trying to strangle him.

Sally, I'm happy to report, is smiling and radiant.

Mother is also grinning like a gargoyle, her smile so wide she could swallow the whole of the garlanded top table and its occupants.

Richard, despite the fact that he is the world's most natural bastard, actually has two parents. They are divorced. They haven't spoken for eight years. They clearly want to kill each other. They are currently attempting this with looks, and strange cutlery gestures.

One of my major problems with the seating plan was how to keep them at least arm's length apart. Richard says they had an amicable divorce. At least, they were delighted to divorce one another. Apparently they fell out over who should keep the family silver. I think the truth of the matter is each blames the other for producing a child like Richard.

I'm seated at a table reserved for antique and distant relatives. Fliss the embarrassment, they really didn't know where to put me. I'm relieved that I'm here, though, tucked out of the way with a bunch of people who aren't really sure who I am. Rumours are circulating as expected, however, and so I've been speaking in a fake Australian accent all through lunch, which has really helped to confuse them.

After the speeches the huge four-tiered cake is wheeled in to further gasps of astonishment. The cake is indeed a marvel of modern cake engineering. It has more flowers than the church, and is so delicately balanced you'd imagine one touch from the knife Sally and Richard will wield would send it crashing to the ground.

Richard stands up and takes Sally's hand. They walk regally round to the front of the table, smiling, happy. Sally's eyes are

151

shining. They take the long silver knife trailing pink ribbons, Richard's hand protectively over Sally-Anne's.

Cameras begin to flash again as the blade slices cleanly through the white icing. Sally-Anne gazes up at Richard in adoration. He looks over to where Kat Christian is sitting and raises his eyebrows. This one's for you, he seems to mock her silently.

As the tables are wheeled away and the disco is wheeled in, and people begin to circulate, I adjourn to a chair in a dimly lit corner. I feel like a charity collector waving her tin. People are taking obvious alternative routes to avoid me. You certainly find out who your friends are at a time like this. Most of mine were struck off the amended guest list. They could at least have left me one crony for moral support. I think of Caroline. She was going to be my Matron of Honour.

Or Matron of Dishonour maybe.

Perhaps another drink would be a good idea.

'It must be so weird being a guest at your own wedding.'

I look up in surprise as a waft of Poison assails my nostrils and find that Katherine Christian is standing next to me.

'I'm sorry?'

'Are you?' she replies quizzically.

She is trembling, like the taut string of a bow preparing to launch an arrow. Why do I get the feeling I'm her target? She grabs a glass of champagne from a passing waiter and, totally uninvited, sits down next to me.

'Lovely dress,' she says unconvincingly, looking over at Sally-Anne.

'If you like that sort of thing,' I murmur cautiously.

She turns to me, her blue eyes brazen.

'I must say, it's very brave of you to be here. It must have been so difficult for you, being dumped by Richard. You must be a very forgiving person. Of course, don't take this the wrong way, darling, I wasn't surprised when I heard he'd called the whole thing off. I knew you couldn't hold on to him the moment I saw you. I think I know Ricky better than any woman and I could see straightaway you weren't the one. "Now that couple," I said to Alex – you remember my husband Alex, don't you? – "Now that couple," I said, "are not happy together." '

The front of the woman! I'm torn between being rude back or

reluctantly tolerant. I decide that I'm still coping just about well enough to be tolerant.

'Well, you're right about one thing, we weren't happy together. But Richard did not dump me for Sally-Anne, I simply decided that I couldn't marry him. His relationship with Sally developed after we split up.'

Kat looks at me incredulously. She obviously finds it hard to believe that lowly old me could ever decide I didn't want glamorous, wonderful Richard. As if to emphasise this point she looks over at him, surrounded by a group of fluttering women, headed of course by my mother, and sighs.

'He has such charisma. Look at them, like moths around a flame.'

'More like flies around shit,' I blurt. Whoops, Fliss, wash your mouth out!

Fortunately, Kat is obviously one of those people who talks but rarely listens. She toys with her champagne, running a heavily jewelled finger around the rim of the glass until it begins to sing.

I can see her thinking. The slow mechanics of her brain are so obvious, they're almost audible. She obviously feels the need to dump, and I'm the lucky person she's going to dump on.

'You know he wanted to marry me? Was desperate to, actually, but I turned him down. I felt I was too young to settle down then. He was devastated when I left him.'

A similar but noticeably different version of the story I heard from him. Somebody's telling fibs. I wonder who?

'Oh, yes?' I tell her, looking sideways to gauge her reaction. 'That's funny, in all the time we were together, he never mentioned you.'

This is true, I'm not being malicious – well, perhaps I am just a little as she seems to have this knack of rubbing me up the wrong way, but clashing personalities apart Katharine Christian was a very well-hidden skeleton in Richard's walk-in closet.

I thought Richard was too egotistical to be secretive.

Now I think Kat Christian is too egotistical to be dismissed from Richard's life so easily. I wait for her reaction.

I get a lot more than I bargained for.

'I know that Richard didn't dump you for Sally-Anne,' she says slowly, still not looking at me, 'because he left you for me.'

She pauses and finally turns to look at me, obviously expecting some dramatic reaction. My mind shrieks in outrage, but I manage to control the rest of me.

'I'm sorry, Felicity. I wasn't going to say anything, but I think you deserve to know the truth. It was that chance meeting in the restaurant, you see. It just awoke all the old feelings he had for me.'

Well, this is a turn up for the books. The woman's obviously completely mad, or totally deluded.

'Richard did not dump me for anybody,' I repeat slowly, hoping that this time it will register, 'I decided I didn't want to marry him. *I* called off the wedding.'

She looks at me calmly without blinking. It's pretty obvious she's thinking exactly the same about me as I've just thought about her: mad or deluded?

'He wrote to me last year when he heard that I was getting married, begged me not to go through with it, and to come back to him,' she says slowly so that it will register fully. She waits for my reaction again, but I'm not going to give her the satisfaction of betraying my surprise by even a flicker of my eyelids, so she continues.

'Last June to be precise. I still have the letter. It's quite touching really, he offered to give up everything to be with me . . .' She looks sideways at me, a flash of triumph in her pale blue eyes.

A year ago? Last June?

Richard asked me to marry him last June.

Kat can see she has struck home, and smirks happily.

'I very nearly gave in to him, he was so insistent and so obviously desperate to be with me again. And the flame between us, of course, can never be extinguished. You know, that special kind of love that's bigger than both of you . . .' She glances at me again from under her curling black eyelashes – I'm sure they're false – looks me up and down appraisingly. 'But then again, perhaps you don't . . . I very nearly gave up everything to be with him, but I was due to marry Alex in only two weeks, and I'm not the sort of person to run away from my responsibilities.'

'Or a very large bank account,' I snap.

She doesn't rise to this. 'Certainly Alex is a very wealthy man, but I didn't marry him purely for his money, although a sensible

154

woman always values financial security. He has other attributes.'

He certainly has.

I may have momentarily shoved his wife to the back of that dusty closet I call a mind, but if I'm totally honest with myself Alex Christian's face has returned to haunt a few of my dreams.

'Of course, you had a lucky escape really.'

I realise she's talking again, and snap out of fantasy mode.

'It's Sally-Anne I feel sorry for.'

'Richard has married Sally because he loves her,' I snap back.

Who am I trying to convince, her or me?

'He's only done it to get back at me.'

'That's funny,' I say quietly, 'for a while I thought he was doing it to get back at *me*. I would have been worried apart from the fact it's so screamingly obvious he's crazy about my sister.'

'He called me the following day.'

'Sorry?'

'The day after we met in the restaurant . . . he called me. The very next evening, said that he'd call it all off with you if I went back to him.'

Why, the sneaky rotten . . . No wonder he was so quick to concede defeat that day I told him it was all over. He thought he could walk out of our relationship straight into the arms of Katherine the not so Great!

'We had a huge row. I don't like it when people try to manipulate me,' she continues, pouting. 'He was trying to pressurise me into making a decision, into leaving Alex. He was using his marriage to you as a threat. For leverage. Of course, I knew he wouldn't go through with the wedding. You can hardly demand a ransom from someone when you have no intention of taking a hostage.'

Or when the hostage has escaped in the nick of time, I think crossly.

'You're right.' I smile at her, but my smile is about as sweet as a lemon.

'Sorry?'

She will be.

'I said, you're right, Kat. When he phoned you, Richard knew he wouldn't marry me. He knew he wouldn't marry me because I'd told him so that very morning.'

She starts to protest.

155

'I have witnesses,' I add quickly.

Her glossed mouth opens slightly. Is this a sign that her brain's working? I think what I've been saying is finally sinking in. I hope so, it's taken long enough to get the message home.

'You mean, you really did finish with him?' she asks weakly.

I nod.

'He didn't finish with you? He told me he'd finish with you . . . for my sake.'

'Well, he would, wouldn't he? Hardly good for his ego or his image, is it, being dumped by someone like me. It must have been quite convenient for him, bumping into you the night before, softened the blow really. He thought he had someone to fall back on.'

'Fall back on! He doesn't want to fall back on me. It's me Ricky loves . . . do you hear me? ME!'

'Oh, yes, that's obviously why he's just married someone else! I hardly think even Richard is fool enough to marry one woman simply to get back at another.'

This is what I've been telling myself the past few weeks anyway, and now I say it out loud it actually rings pretty true.

'He threatened he'd do something drastic if I didn't take him back. He left you for me, and when I turned him down your sister was just waiting to snap him up. He's only married her to get back at me,' Kat snaps viciously.

'Oh, really? Thank you so much for putting my mind at rest,' I add sarcastically. 'You've made me feel so much better. I *was* feeling horrendously guilty, thought Richard was totally messing up my sister's life because of me, but now I know it's all your fault.'

'I tell you, he loves *me*, not your sister,' she whispers angrily.

Her eyes are ablaze as she scrapes back her chair and starts to back away, repeating insistently, 'You'll see, he only married her to get back at me . . .'

'Oh, yes? I thought you married someone because you loved them!' I shout after her. 'But I was obviously totally wrong, wasn't I?'

Everybody turns to look, and then realising it's me yelling they quickly turn away. Of course it's just the jilted fiancée having a tantrum, they all knew her calm and placid acceptance wouldn't last forever.

I rest my head in my hands.

Kat has finally drained the last of my strength, renewed my myriad doubts over Richard's intentions towards Sal. I'm having a bad day. Come to think of it, I'm having a bad year. I reach for my glass but it's empty.

Typical!

'I do hope my wife wasn't being too obnoxious?' says a low calm voice amidst the babble.

I look up to see Alex Christian smiling down at me. He hands me a glass of champagne, and gestures to the empty seat next to me.

'Do you mind if I join you?'

'Are you sure you want to?' I gaze unhappily at the bubbles rising in my glass, suddenly feeling too flat to drink champagne. 'I seem to be something of a social leper today. Everybody's avoiding me. They don't know what to say to me, you see. The rumour is circulating that Richard dumped me for Sally, and everyone's too embarrassed to speak to me. Everyone except your wife, who by the way *was* completely obnoxious but I gather that's her usual style.'

'I'm sorry,' he replies uncomfortably.

'No.' I shake my head. 'It's I who should be apologising, I didn't mean to take it out on you, it's just been a very stressful day.'

'I can imagine. I should think you're having a pretty lousy time, aren't you?'

I look at him. He's got such a kind face, you can tell he'd be a good listener. I've got this incredible urge to tell him everything. The only problem is he's married to Kat so how can I?

'I do know about Richard and my wife,' he says as though he can read my mind.

He does? The question is, does he know everything about Richard and his wife?

'Kat likes to tell me about it,' he continues. 'ALL about it.'

This is uncanny, he *can* read my mind.

'Well, she's just told me all about it too. Not very discreet, is she?' I complain, and proceed to be completely indiscreet myself.

The whole story comes pouring out. Words flow well on champagne. He sits with his elbow on the table and his head resting in his hand, gaze steady, listening quietly. He doesn't interrupt and his eyes don't glaze over. When I finally stumble to a halt, he actually reaches over and squeezes my hand.

'You poor old thing.' He's laughing at my tragi-comedy, but he's not taking the piss, and I can tell that he's not being patronising either. 'I'm sorry she had a go. I'm not making excuses for her, but she's finding this very hard.'

How can he be so understanding about this?

'I think she thought she'd have Richard twined round her little finger forever,' he continues.

'I'm really surprised you're so calm about all of this. If I were in your situation I'd be fuming.'

'Why make a crisis out of a drama?' He shrugs. 'Kat is the queen of melodrama, her whole life's one long play with her centre-stage. It's all an act, her and Richard, it's not about real life, so I don't let it bother me that much. It's pure *Romeo and Juliet* syndrome. Do you think their romance would be quite so intense if they were allowed free access to each other?'

'If they were so *madly* in love,' I say sarcastically, 'then why did they split up in the first place?'

He shrugs. 'I don't really know, I got a different story from each of them.'

'Me too.'

'I think it's the sort of relationship where they can't live with each other and can't live without each other.'

'So they have to go off and make other people miserable instead?' I mutter angrily, glaring over at Richard who is holding court amidst his legal cronies at the bar. Alex catches me staring, and like everybody else misinterprets my unhappiness.

'Fliss, you never did tell me your side of things. Did you love him?'

Oh, dear, the note of sympathy, I can hear it stealthily creeping in again.

'You know, I feel like wrestling the microphone off the DJ and announcing I wasn't dumped by Richard, that in fact I'm absolutely ecstatic we're no longer together. The only reason I'm miserable today is that I'm worried he doesn't really love my sister . . . and would everybody please stop spreading gossip about me!'

He smiles.

'Sorry. Point taken. But what makes you so sure he doesn't love Sally-Anne?'

'Well, it was a bit of a whirlwind courtship, wasn't it? And what with Kat's claims about their relationship . . . oh, the whole thing's such a mess, and I feel like it's all my fault!'

Alex reaches across and to my surprise takes my hand, squeezing it reassuringly.

'Sally's a lovely girl, any sane man would be over the moon to find someone as patient and understanding and beautiful as her.'

'That's true,' I agree, gazing affectionately at my sister who with typical unselfishness is dancing with a rather old and smelly relative everyone else has been avoiding.

'Can you honestly see Richard marrying Sally if he doesn't have any feelings for her?'

'If it benefits him, then yes I can. Richard's motives for doing anything are always purely selfish. I mean, what a spectacular way to try to get Katherine back. If the only thing that turns her on is his unavailability, then getting married was one clever move.'

'Are you always this cynical?'

'Where Richard and my sister are concerned, can you blame me?'

'You don't want her to get hurt obviously, but who's to say she will be?'

'But you've just agreed that Kat and Richard are playing games.'

'Exactly, it's all a game. Richard's devotion makes Kat feel good, and she likes to think she makes me jealous which makes her feel good too.'

'Does she?'

'Does she what?'

'Make you jealous.'

He bites his bottom lip and exhales.

'Not really. Kat's an egotist and a narcissist. She loves herself, and wants to be loved by everyone, to feel infinitely desirable to all men. Richard feeds her ego. She wants me to feel insecure, and she wants Richard to feel the same. She feels her indifference is the only thing that keeps us hanging on. The irony of it all is that she's fuelled by her *own* insecurity. Now Richard has married your sister, she wants him. It's Richard's indifference that spurs her into winning him back. Kat's in it for the kill. She's *like* a cat really, will toy with a mouse till the poor thing pops its clogs, and then suddenly find she's completely lost her appetite.'

159

'She's a bitch then,' I say without thinking. 'Whoops, sorry, that's your wife I'm slagging off, isn't it?'

'That's OK,' he replied, mouth curling into an almost imperceptible smile. 'She *is* a bitch.'

We smile slowly at each other.

'Why did you marry her?' Suddenly I'm very curious. The more time I spend with Alex, the more I like him. 'How did someone as nice as you marry someone as horrible as her?'

He goes quiet.

'Oh, dear, I'm really sorry, that was such an impertinent question considering I've only really known you for a little while. It's just . . . er . . . I feel like I've known you longer. I wouldn't normally ask things like that . . .' I'm digging myself deeper.

I blush then realise that he's looking at me with an amused expression on his face, indulgent almost, like he's chaperoning a naughty child he should be terribly cross with for misbehaving but can't be because they're being rather entertaining at the same time.

'You know, that's a question I frequently ask myself.' He smiles wryly. 'I think it was one of the few things in life I've ever rushed into.'

'Marry in haste, repent at leisure,' I muse, looking over at my sister.

'When you first meet somebody it's really hard to tell whether what you're seeing is the true person. Everybody puts on an act, don't they? I just didn't realise how different . . .' He stops talking, looking at the floor instead. It's my turn to squeeze his hand, which is for some reason still holding mine, feeling so comfortable I'd almost forgotten it was there.

'You really shouldn't stay in a relationship if it makes you unhappy,' I announce with all the conviction of the newly and thankfully separated. 'Why do you put up with her?'

He shrugs.

'Marriage is a big commitment, and even though I was brave or stupid enough to make that commitment to someone like Kat, I feel I should work at it. Why did you put up with Richard for so long?'

'Oh, I can answer that one quite easily – cowardice. Too scared to make the change. Almost convinced I didn't deserve any better.'

160

'Well, I can tell you, you definitely deserve better than Richard,' he states.

'Anybody deserves better than Richard.' I shrug.

'Don't put yourself down, Fliss, a lot of men would give their right arm for a girl like you.'

I look at him in surprise. No, he's not taking the piss. I was uncertain about Alex Christian's character and motivation before, but I think he's just a genuinely nice guy.

I tell him so.

'I know,' he replies. 'And nice guys always finish last, don't they?' He turns and looks at me. The laughter lines around those amazing aquamarine eyes deepen as he smiles. It suddenly hits me like a fist in my face. This man is gorgeous! I must need glasses not to have noticed sooner. I get this almost irresistible urge to run my fingers through his short dark hair. I manage to resist, but only just. Alcohol has a terrible habit of breaking down one's inhibitions and smashing straight through the usual social barriers, such as not molesting someone else's husband in public. I must be blushing because he asks me if I'm hot and heads across to the bar to find us another bottle of champagne.

On the darkened dance floor, Richard is dancing with Mother while Sally-Anne is dancing with Dad. As the music changes to a slower number I watch Kat march across and tap Mother on the shoulder. She must think this is a ladies' excuse me. For a moment I think they're going to fight for him, and then Mother concedes and stalks indignantly back to her seat.

Alex returns with a full bottle. We watch as they float round the dance floor. Their feet are in perfect sync but their expressions are far from harmonious. You can see them talking heatedly through pursed lips, like a couple of ventriloquists. It's obvious they are arguing. Fortunately Sally-Anne is too preoccupied to notice.

'Just look at them,' I murmur bitterly. 'Poor Sally-Anne. I thought I'd managed to overcome my doubts, but now I know he won't make her happy.'

'How can you be so sure?'

'The only happiness Richard is concerned with is his own,' I state emphatically.

'Aren't we all like that, though? Don't you think every person, no matter how altruistic they claim to be, is essentially preoccupied with their own happiness?'

'True, but Richard is the ultimate narcissist. Life revolves around him, he is the centre of his own universe. Sally is just a satellite orbiting the great solar system known as Richard Edward Trevelyan. You know, I always wished his middle name was Andrew or Adrian or something. It would be sooo appropriate . . . Your wife,' I waggle the same finger in the general direction of Kat, 'is the moon preparing to eclipse that little satellite.' I take another swig of my champagne.

'I wonder if Richard was the first man on the moon?' I muse thoughtfully.

He laughs.

'She doesn't look very happy, he's probably fending her off.'

'Yeah, sure,' I say belligerently, totally unconvinced.

'No, seriously, the guy's just got married, Fliss, to a fantastic girl. Take a good look at your sister, she's seriously beautiful and seems like a really great person too . . .'

'Yes, she is, really great. Too good for him.'

'Perhaps, but don't write them off before they've even got started. I know it's hard, but you have to give them a chance.'

'Oh, I'll give them a chance, no problem, but do you think your wife will? Look at her!' I round on him angrily. 'You know, perhaps if you were dancing with your wife, Richard might be dancing with his.'

He stares at me. I'm surprised to see a small smile play across his lips.

'In other words, if I tried to control my wife's actions, perhaps she wouldn't be running around after Richard. That is what you meant, isn't it?'

'I suppose so,' I reply sheepishly, suddenly ashamed of my outburst. 'I'm sorry, I'm about as subtle as a brick, aren't I?'

He shrugs his shoulders, both to accept my apology and as a prelim to his reply.

'I'm afraid it doesn't work like that. The more interest I take in her little games, the worse she gets. She'd love it if I stormed over there and dragged her away. She feeds off the attention. Therefore I shall remain perfectly calm and controlled . . .' the smile flickers back again '. . . because I know it irritates the hell out of her.'

He leans forward and slowly wipes a smudge of mascara away from my cheek with his thumb. 'Don't look so sad, I'll go and drag her away if you want me to.'

162

'I wouldn't if I were you. She's like a leech – pull her away and she'll draw blood,' I mutter, though my concentration is no longer on Kat but centred purely on his thumb gently rubbing my cheekbone.

I get a sudden urge to replenish my make-up.

It's only when I stand up that I realise how much I've had to drink.

Too much as usual.

'Must just go to the loo.' I indicate with my thumb over my shoulder toward the Ladies'.

I gaze at my face in the brightly lit mirror that dominates an entire wall of the Ladies'. I'm paler than the lilies in Sally-Anne's bouquet, the one I ducked to avoid when she so charmingly and obviously hurled it in my direction earlier.

My eyes look huge. They are glowing like hot coals dropped in the cold snow. I try to replenish my lipstick and find I can't draw straight. My already full lips appear engorged and swollen as I trace way beyond my natural lip line. I look like someone's hit me in the mouth. I feel like someone's punched me in the stomach.

What a bloody, bloody day!

When I stagger back from the loos, Alex is waiting for me.

'Would you like to dance?' He gestures to the dance floor.

'I'm not sure that I can,' I reply, surprised at how legless I actually feel. 'My legs seem to have divorced themselves from the rest of my nervous system. I'm finding it difficult to stand, let alone move to music.'

'Well, you can just lean on me then.' He smiles that lovely slow lazy smile, and my legs go even weaker.

He leads me on to the dance floor. We're being watched from all sides. My behaviour this evening has been under the microscope. Everybody's been waiting for me to crack.

'You're very brave dancing with me. Everybody's watching us,' I murmur, resting my head against his collarbone.

'Let them,' he says. 'They obviously haven't got anything better to do.'

'I can just hear the gossip now,' I whisper into his ear. 'Awful old Fliss, jilted by what should have been *her* husband so now she's out to nab somebody else's. Lock up your hubby, Fliss Blakeney's on the loose!' I giggle, amused by the me-as-man-eater image this conjures up in my head.

'Shall we give them something to really gossip about?' Alex laughs and pulls me closer, putting his hands firmly on my backside.

Kat catches sight of us over Richard's shoulder, and her eyes narrow.

'Your wife is glaring at me,' I murmur in his ear.

'She's probably jealous.'

'Of us?'

'Yep.'

Psychology never was my best subject, I struggle to find the logic of this one.

'So, let me see if I've got this right. Basically she wants Richard, yes?'

'Correct, but only if she thinks she can't have him.'

'But she also gets jealous of you?'

'Correct, but only when she thinks I'm losing interest.'

'So really if you and Richard were both totally devoted one hundred per cent of the time, she wouldn't want either of you?'

He laughs. 'I suppose it might work like that, yes, I hadn't really thought of it before.'

'So if you were both being indifferent she'd probably want you both at the same time. Therefore, because Richard has just got married and you have spent the past half an hour giving your undivided attention to lucky old me, we have one unhappy shitty Kitty, sharpening her claws as we speak, who doesn't know quite whose flesh to stick them into first. This could get complicated.'

'I think it already is complicated,' says Alex. 'She wants to have her cake and eat it too.'

'No, no, no,' I slur. 'She wants to have her cake, eat her cake, and then have somebody else's cake and eat *that* too. With all that cake she should by rights be a very sick person. I think she *is* a sick person. She must have something up here . . .' I twist my finger against my temple. 'You know, a screw loose or her knickers or something, even to *think* about old Dickhead over there when she's got you.'

I flush as I suddenly realise what I've just said, but when I dare to look up into his face again he's laughing softly.

When I start to laugh too, I realise that I'm very drunk. I'm actually at that awful point of drunkenness where you're still lucid enough to know you'll end up doing something stupid if

164

you carry on drinking, but where you're also drunk enough not to give a damn.

Dangerous.

Especially as I'm finding Alex more attractive by the moment, and I don't think it's the effect of the alcohol at all. Holding him close, feeling his flesh under his clothes, under my touch, being able to bury my head in his chest and breathe in the scent of him.

Dizzy, and not just from champagne.

I try to drag myself back to reality.

Kat is still dancing with Richard so I look around for my sister. She's sitting at the side of the floor with my father, both of them watching Richard and Katherine dancing together, Sally looking unhappy, Dad fingering his unused butter knife.

Sally looks very unhappy actually.

She shouldn't look unhappy on her wedding day.

Alex sees me frowning, and turns to look at Sally-Anne as well.

'I'm going to ask you to do something that might be a bit difficult for you,' he murmurs in my ear. 'Feel free to say no if you want to.'

'It's OK,' I tell him, 'I think I'd already had the same idea. Go for it.'

Overcome by a feeling of total revulsion at what lies ahead, I close my eyes and think of Sally-Anne as we manoeuvre our way across the dance floor towards Richard and Kat. A swift excuse me, and suddenly she is safely back with her husband, and *I* am dancing with Richard.

I never thought this would happen again, especially not today.

I think Richard is as stunned as I am.

He opens his mouth to say something, then for once just shuts it again without speaking. The fact that I'm having to dance with him for Sal's sake is suddenly made worthwhile for me too, just to see him speechless for once.

Everybody's staring, so I force a smile on to my face.

'Congratulations,' I tell him.

Richard's eyes open even wider in surprise.

'I hope you'll both be very happy together. No!' I cut in as he opens his mouth to protest. 'I really do mean that. You're a lucky man, Richard Trevelyan. Sally-Anne is one of the best people I know, and I really do hope you have a good life together.'

'Well, thank you.' Richard is obviously taken aback. 'It's nice to know that you can be so . . . er . . . magnanimous.'

I nod in as gracious a manner as I can and, taking the lead, rather inelegantly dance him back over towards my sister.

'Oh, and just one more thing . . .' I whisper as I hand him over to Sally-Anne. 'If you *ever*, I repeat *ever*, hurt her, I will personally make certain that you have to keep *little* Richard,' I waggle a finger in the direction of his crotch, 'in your inside jacket pocket instead of in your Y-fronts.'

Pausing long enough to see Sal and Richard safely out on to the floor together, I head back to my darkened corner, rescue the remainder of the champagne and head towards the French doors which lead out of the state room and on to the long stone terrace. I'm suddenly in desperate need of some fresh air.

I slip across the spotlit terrace, which is dotted with couples enjoying the gorgeous velvet warmth of the evening, and disappear into the warm damp darkness of the gardens, flitting across the lawn like an escaped convict and skidding to a halt as I reach the lake at the end of the bottom lawn. It's a very cultivated lake, not allowed to grow wild and free and dramatically beautiful. Too obviously man-made. Do all men want to control beauty? I want to be wild and free and dramatically beautiful.

Parting the reeds, I plonk myself down at the water's edge and kick off my shoes, dangling my feet in the dark inky water. Ripples spread outwards. I try to count them.

'He loves me, he loves me not, he loves me, he loves me not . . . damn!' I can't see to count any further. I suppose that means he loves me not, but I don't care 'cause I love him not as well, it's just a shame that my sister does.

So that's it.

Sally-Anne has married Richard.

I meant what I said to him. I do wish them well. In fact, as well as wishing I will probably do an awful lot of praying that things will work out for them.

I may not love Richard, but I do love Sal.

I look up at the clear dark sky and try to find the biggest star I can wish on. My head spins as I throw it back and gaze into the heavens, so much so that I find I simply have to lie down, feet and ankles still dangling in the water, head resting on the grass, which while slightly damp is also still warm from the very last rays of the sun, like clothes pulled out of the tumble dryer before they're quite ready.

Suddenly I feel a shadow fall across my face, and then a dark figure blocks my view of the Plough and Orion's Belt.

'What on earth are you doing?' a familiar voice asks in amusement.

'Counting ripples instead of petals,' I murmur. 'At least, I was. Now I'm wishing on a star.'

'And what are you wishing for?'

'True love and happiness,' I reply, thinking of Sally-Anne.

'Is that what you want?'

'Don't we all?' I murmur. 'But no, for once I wasn't wishing for myself.'

I look up at Alex who is gazing across the water like a beautifully carved figurehead on the prow of a ship.

'Think I see a frown,' I murmur, lazy with alcohol. 'Did your ripples come out evens as well?'

'Sorry?'

'Don't be, we all make mistakes. Is getting married always a mistake?'

'It is when you marry someone you don't love.'

'True.' I nod.

'Or someone who doesn't love you,' he adds quietly.

'If Kat didn't love you, then why would she marry you?'

'Perhaps she was on the rebound from Richard.' He is not being self-pitying, he's not a self-pitying kind of person, he is merely stating what he believes.

'She's an idiot then,' I exclaim. 'You don't rebound on to someone like you from a prat like Richard. You rebound on to someone like Richard when someone like you dumps you!'

How much have I had to drink?

'I think there was a compliment in there somewhere,' he says dryly. 'I'd need an interpreter to verify it, but thanks . . . I think.'

A frog, no doubt disturbed by my feet, chirrups noisily as it breaststrokes over to a quieter part of the water.

I don't know why I drink, I end up saying such stupid things. It's like my mouth goes on automatic pilot while my brain falls into a drunken stupor in a corner somewhere. Speech completely independent of any known brain function.

167

Is this a rare phenomenon? Remind me to donate my body to science when I finally shake off this mortal coil.

I look up at the man standing quietly next to me. Damn, he's attractive.

'For someone who doesn't really love you, she looked awfully jealous when you danced with me.'

'Kat's a possessive person. Just 'cause she doesn't want me, doesn't mean anyone else can have me.'

I could understand those feelings quite easily.

'Do you love her?'

'That's an impertinent question.'

'I know, but I'm in an impertinent mood. Besides, you asked me the same thing earlier. Well, do you?'

He shoves his hands deeper into his trouser pockets and looks up at the still star-lit sky.

'Oh, look, I can see the Great Bear.'

'DO you?' I insist.

I'm not going to let him change the subject.

He thinks for a moment.

'I suppose so.'

Oh, boy, I didn't want him to say that. Did I really expect him to say 'No, I don't love her'? I suppose I did, he seems so indifferent to Kat's flirtation, if that's the right word, with Richard. If I loved someone, and they behaved the way she did, I'd be spitting nails.

If I loved someone.

Isn't it funny how emotions can creep up on you? Why did it hurt so much to hear Alex say he loved his wife?

'She's been acting like a complete bitch, though,' he adds after some thought, which makes me feel a bit better. 'I don't know what I see in her.'

'She's very beautiful,' I say wistfully.

'You know, you're very beautiful too.'

I look at him through narrowed eyes.

'I may be drunk,' I slur, waving the champagne bottle around as if I need evidence to prove this fact, 'but I am *not* stupid.'

'No, I mean it,' he insists, slumping down on the grass next to me.

'In that case, *you* must be drunk.' I offer him the bottle. 'Blind drunk.'

'Perhaps I am,' he agrees, taking the proffered Krug and

168

raising it to his lips with the careful precision of someone who *has* had a good few too many. 'But you're still beautiful. Inside and out, and that's a rare quality.'

He smiles at me with his wonderful mouth, and with his glittering blue-green eyes. They're as liquid as the champagne, like an aquamarine swimming pool, inviting me to strip off and dive in. I'm gazing so hard, my own eyes begin to blur.

'You know, I can see two of you now,' I murmur. 'Which is quite good really. One for Kat . . .' I pause and then add quietly, 'And one for me.'

We both fall silent.

The desire I've gradually recognised I feel for this man suddenly hits me full strength. I've dived in, and now I think I'm drowning. He's so close I can feel him breathing. I reach forward with one hand and, taking hold of the material of his shirt, pull him towards me.

Our lips meet.

My eyes involuntarily close.

I think I'm going to pass out. Is it through passion or alcohol? I'm not quite sure, I just wish I was sober enough to enjoy the moment properly, and sober enough to be able to remember it clearly afterwards. It's a moment that should be brought out like best china, to enjoy, savour and revel in on special occasions, but I'm concentrating too hard on remaining conscious throughout the length of the kiss actually to register the kiss itself.

Then I have the most sobering thought possible.

He's married. Somewhere inside that beautiful house behind us is a beautiful wife. She's a mega-bitch of the first degree, but she's still his wife.

Thou shalt not commit adultery.

A burst of sound as the doors on to the terrace are opened. Voices, laughter, people coming out of the heat of the disco into the gentle, beautiful warmth of the night. The moment fades, reality reasserts itself.

We break apart. He looks away guiltily and gets hastily to his feet to head for the house.

He looks back once, I think, but I'm blinded by the hot wet tears that are brimming in my eyes. Tears of frustration, anger, helplessness. Why did I do that? I'm such a bloody fool. The whole damn' day has suddenly jumped upon my back like a demon, its hands slowly closing around my throat and squeezing the life out of me until I can't breathe.

I have to get out of here. Lurching unsteadily across the lawn, I make my way to the front of the hotel and fall into a taxi that was waiting for someone else, swearing blind that, yes, I am definitely the Mrs Hayes who ordered the cab, and just happened to give them the wrong address.

Having spilt the remainder of the Krug on to the poor taxi driver, who judges from my conduct that I am in fact drunk enough to forget where I live, we finally arrive home. I hand him a twenty-pound note for an eight-pound fare, and stagger blindly up the stairs to my flat.

Once the front door is locked and bolted behind me, there is only one thing left for me to do, and if I do say so myself I think I do it with great aplomb – I pass out.

Chapter Eight

I can hear music and laughter coming from the dining room. I wander back in from the garden, pushing open the French doors and walking through gauzy curtains so light they feel like spider's webs on my face. Caro lies draped along the table illuminated erotically pink in the candlelight. A sylph-like blonde girl is painting her naked flesh, dipping her brush into a glass of champagne and slowly trailing it along Caroline's body. Mother is seated at the head of the table, Richard to her left. They are talking quietly, apparently oblivious to the fact that the main course is a naked female. They look across at me, then at each other and laugh. Mother leans across and kisses Richard full on the mouth, all the time her eyes never leaving mine. Caro looks up, sees me standing in the doorway and beckons slowly. I stumble across the room, trying to escape. My limbs are so heavy I can barely move. She is so close behind me I can feel the warmth of her breath on the back of my neck. I run into a room, bare but for a tall mirror. Standing in front of it is a bride. She is wearing my wedding dress. I call out Sally's name. She turns round slowly and pushes back her veil, only the face looking out at me is not Sally's it's mine. My own image smiles at me, and as if in slow motion throws my bouquet. I can see a waterfall of flowers tumbling through the air towards me. I reach out to catch them, trip and begin to fall, on and endlessly on. Any minute I'll feel the solid floor rush up to meet my falling body, knocking the breath and the life out of me completely, and then I'm caught by a pair of strong arms. I look up, expecting to see the face of the unknown stranger who usually haunts my dreams, only this time Alex Christian is smiling down at me.

I wake up with a start. I'm on the floor in the kitchen, still fully dressed apart from the fact that I've lost my shoes, and hugging

171

the empty Krug bottle to me like a comforter. The cat, who has a foot fetish, is licking my toes. The kitchen clock is ticking louder than a bomb. It tells me that it's 11.30 a.m. Where the hell am I? slides briefly through my mind, followed swiftly by the thought, Alex.

It keeps repeating, like the ticking of the clock, and hurts more than my hangover. There's a blinding ache behind my eyes, and this awful ringing in my ears which I eventually realise is the telephone.

Clutching the reassuringly solid kitchen table for support, I clamber up, stiff and cold from the floor, and stagger out into the hall, shoeless, and from the waves of instability that are flooding through my body, still legless. I practically knock the receiver off the phone, and haul it to my ear with trembling hand.

'Fliss, it's Dad. Are you all right?'

I think hard, and decide that, no, I'm not really OK.

'Define all right?' I growl.

'You left so suddenly last night, I was worried.'

'I was tired . . .' I say, not altogether untruthfully.

'You missed Sally's departure. She and Richard left half an hour ago. Your mother went with them to the airport. You know, I think she'd be going on the actual honeymoon if they'd let her.'

'She'd have worn the wedding dress and taken the vows if they'd let her,' I snap.

'You're not all right, are you?' says Dad. I can hear genuine concern in his voice, but I'm in too evil a mood to be pleasant.

'How perceptive of you to realise.'

'You don't regret it, do you, Fliss? Not marrying him?'

'Heavens, no. Honestly, Dad, if one more person asks me that question, I'll . . . I'll . . .'

'You'll what?' he probes gently, obviously convinced I've finally cracked.

I try to think of something suitably heinous.

'I don't know, spit in their eye, murder them most horribly, er . . .' I look at the cat who is hovering dangerously close to my feet again. 'Feed them stewed cat.'

She looks at me in disgust and stalks off into the kitchen.

'Honestly, I do NOT regret not marrying Dickhead. My only regret is that my poor little sister ended up lumbered with him. No, I've got other problems, I'm afraid.'

172

I think back to last night, and physically feel this little pain, deep in my stomach. What is it? Longing? Guilt? I'm not sure, but it hurts.

'Anything I can help with?'

I soften. Dad's always there for me when I need him, I shouldn't be taking my lousy love life and my hangover out on him.

'Thanks, but I think I've got to work this one out for myself,' I murmur.

'Look, darling,' Dad's voice is hesitant, 'I know this is probably lousy timing but I really need to talk to you.'

He sounds strange. I've been so wrapped up in my own warped thoughts that I didn't notice at first. Guilt and concern flood through me, adding to the nausea.

'Dad, what's wrong?'

'Well, I'd rather not talk about it over the phone. Can I come round and see you? Is that all right?'

Now I'm worried.

I pace the floor until he finally arrives. It's a fifteen-minute drive at Dad's usual pace, but it takes him over half an hour today by the end of which I have no nails left.

I go to open the door and catch sight of myself in the hall mirror. My face is as pale and haunted as a ghost's, my eyes more vacant than the *Mary Celeste* ever was.

Dad staggers up the stairs to my front door. He looks tired. He's always been tall and gangly, now he looks gaunt.

I feel guilty for not noticing before. He carries an air of doom about him, as though he's about to tell me something really awful. I feel like a priest in the confessional. This is definitely the time for a stiff drink, but I've had far too many of those recently.

'Coffee?'

I sod the instant, and go for the strong stuff with the percolator. I try to grind some beans; the buzz of the grinder makes me feel sick. Leaving the percolator bubbling and spitting like a little glass geyser, I edge back into the sitting room.

Dad's sprawled on the sofa, like an Irish Wolfhound trying to relax in a smaller dog's basket. He's fidgeting like mad, and won't look me in the eye. Finally he stops pulling at his shirt collar and speaks.

'Well, what a day yesterday turned out to be, eh?' He starts to pull his chin instead of his collar.

173

'Mmm, you could say that.'

'Fliss, I've got something to tell you.' He stops fidgeting again and studies his feet, looking at his reflection in his highly polished black shoes.

'Don't tell me, you've finally snapped and murdered Mother?' I laugh half-heartedly. The state he's in, I almost expect him to look up and say yes.

He sort of smiles. His face is too unhappy for it to be a proper smile.

'If only it were that simple,' he says quietly.

He looks so sad, I sit down at his feet and rest my chin on his knees, like I used to do as a child.

'Dad, you're scaring me, what's wrong?'

He doesn't answer.

'Come on,' I wheedle, 'it can't be that bad, surely?'

'Fliss, I'm in love with someone else.'

It comes out in a rush, so garbled that he's forced to repeat it. 'What?'

'I'm in love with someone else . . . I've been seeing someone else.'

The words take a moment to sink in, and then they hit the part of my nervous system that controls my jawbone. It drops to the floor like a broken lift, you can almost hear it clang as it hits the carpet.

'You're seeing someone else?'

I don't know whether to cheer or cry. I thought I knew him like the back of my hand. What a strange expression that is. Do I ever really study the back of my hand? I thought I knew him like the inside of my fridge would be far more appropriate. Completely in shock, I manage to realign my mouth and move into speech mode.

'How long?'

'Seven years.' He looks at me sideways, trying to gauge my reaction.

'Seven years?' I repeat incredulously.

'It started not long after you moved out. I'd never have got away with it if you'd still been there, Fliss, you'd have noticed. You'd have caught me out.'

Now the dam gates have opened the words are flooding out.

'I've wanted to tell you for so long. Your mother never loved me, Fliss, our marriage was a sham. I stayed for your sake and

174

for Sally-Anne's. I can't do it any more. As soon as Sally walked out of that front door this morning, I just knew I couldn't spend the rest of my life alone with your mother. Florence is so sweet and kind and loving . . .'

'Florence?' I query.

'Sweet, sweet Florrie . . .' His face softens for a moment, the tension slips away fleetingly. 'You'd like her, Fliss. She gives me everything your mother never could or would. You don't know how hard it is to continue in a relationship that's totally barren, devoid of any real affection.'

'Do you love her?'

He nods.

'Then I'd like her,' I decide. 'It's all right, Dad, I understand.'

'You do?' There's a spark of hope in his weary grey eyes.

'Of course I do, better than anybody. My only wonder is that you managed to stick it out for this long. Oh, Dad, I always knew you were unhappy, but not to that extent. Why didn't you ever tell me?'

'I wanted to be the perfect father, God knows I owed you that much. I tried to make up for the way your mother treated you, Fliss. I should have stood up for you, stopped her bullying you and manipulating Sally-Anne, but I never did, did I? Old fool that I am, I never stood up to her . . .' He trails off, voice too choked to speak. He rests his head in his hands, and his shoulders begin to shake.

Gently I pull his hands away from his face. His eyes are glazed with unshed tears.

'You *are* the perfect father,' I say soothingly. 'To me you always will be.'

I squeeze his hands and he hangs on tight, role reversal, the child becoming the parent, the comforter, the parent the child, dependent, desperate for approval.

'I thought you'd hate me.'

'Why should I hate you for trying to find some happiness? Isn't that what we're all searching for?'

He looks up and smiles hesitantly.

'I think I've finally found my happiness, Fliss. Do you think I'm selfish for not wanting to let it go?'

I shake my head.

'Not at all.'

'Do you think I'm doing the right thing?'

175

'What *are* you going to do, Dad?'

He takes a deep breath.

'I'm going to go and live with Florrie. I'm leaving your mother . . . leaving her,' he repeats as though finding it hard to believe himself.

'OK.' I chew thoughtfully on my bottom lip. 'So what happens next?'

'Well, I'll wait till Sally comes back from Mauritius and then . . .'

'And then you're going,' I finish the sentence for him.

'And then I'm going,' he agrees. 'I know it will be such an awful homecoming for poor Sally, but I really can't go on.'

I spend the next four days holed up in my flat, pretending to work on assignments for next term. My heart's not really into *A Winter's Tale*, and Chaucer is driving me potty. I decide to go out for a walk. I really should get a dog the amount of walking I've been doing in the past few days. Why is walking conducive to thinking? Is the pace of one's brain connected to the pace of one's feet? I don't think so. Outside, summer has taken a breather after a lengthy debate on whether it should make way for autumn, who is currently on a trial run.

The weather has changed more quickly than someone in a communal changing room wearing their greyest undies. The intense heat has given way to long bouts of rain and grey cold skies. Leaves brown from sunburn are falling prematurely at my feet, swept along in front of me by the wind.

This summer has certainly been memorable. Sally is due back in just over a week, and then Dad will be dropping his bombshell on an unsuspecting nation. I'm still reeling from this new revelation. I wasn't surprised but I was, if you know what I mean.

I know how unhappy my father has been – I mean, Mother makes my life absolute hell, and I don't even live with her any more – but even though I always expected Dad eventually to find someone else, it was still a shock when it actually happened.

Life is so confusing. I suppose what I'm trying to say is that no matter how much you expect something to happen, you're still never as prepared as you think you are for the reality. I received a postcard from Mauritius this morning. Beautiful crystal blue

176

sea, white beach, waving palm trees, a perfect Paradise. Sally tells me the weather is wonderful, the hotel is amazing and she's thinking of me, whatever that means.

I think of Alex all the time although I know I really shouldn't. When I think of what I did I could almost die of embarrassment, but underneath that emotion is something else. That first faint thrill of excitement, of knowing that you've found someone, a person who really could make a difference to your life.

I try to tell myself very sternly that I'm not interested in him, but I don't believe me. I try to tell myself very sternly that he's probably not interested in me, and I unfortunately find that far more believable. What shared ground do we have? One evening of confessions, and one wonderful if rather drunken kiss. Hardly the basis for the all-consuming, undying love I'm ready to declare.

You see, that's the emotion that crept up and hit me in the face with all the subtlety of Barbara Cartland's wardrobe.

Love.

If Sally asked me 'Do you believe in love at first sight?' now, I'd have to reply, 'Well, almost.' Will love at third sight do? Why does Cupid always strike when he really shouldn't? I think I'm falling for Alex. Alex is married to Katherine. Katherine is in love with Richard. Richard is married to my sister. Why is life so complicated?

Do I really need to add further confusion to the *ménage à* twat that is Richard, Sally-Anne and Katherine?

I tell myself it's not love, I'm obsessed, either that or completely stupid. Best just to forget about everything and get on with the rest of my life. I am not in love. Although they do say love is a drug and I'm getting terrible withdrawal symptoms.

Back to school next week. Time to face another trauma: Caroline. When I get back home there's another message on my answer phone from her. She's been desperately trying to contact me since that night. In a way I feel really awful about it, but I won't phone her back. I don't know what to say to her. I'm still in shock from the sight of her sprawled on the floor, her hands full of Eloise Gray.

So that was the secret to their happy marriage.

Free love.

And they used to take the piss out of Maura for being so seventies!

I'm beginning to wonder if the words 'happy' and 'marriage' are at all compatible, what with Caro and David, Mother and Dad, Sasha and Niall, Sally-Anne and Richard, Kat and Alex . . . Alex.

Every time I think of him I feel so sad. If this is love, who needs it?

Being a perverse sort of person, the apparent onset of autumn makes me feel like spring cleaning. Depression makes me feel like redecorating. My flat doesn't stand a chance.

It's the Saturday after the wedding. This time last week I was drinking my way towards making a tit of myself with someone whose opinion I really care about, someone I don't want to think of me as being a drunken moron.

Tonight I am blitzing. Unable to control my life so efficiently, I have decided that I will control my surroundings. I am determined that my untidy home will become my tidy home. Anything movable has been bin-bagged: clothes I was determined to slim into, magazines I was keeping to cut recipes out of and never have, ornaments that I must have liked at some point in my life – all destined for black plastic bin bags, and the rubbish tip.

Having denuded and scrubbed my flat to within the last inch of its life, I start on the washing.

What clothes I have here – Caro still has my suitcase.

I have a running battle with my washing machine. If I'm desperate for it to work properly it won't. I have to load it casually, appear nonchalant, make it think that I don't care if it won't work. Just sidle up to it and chuck things in. If it so much as gets a hint of the fact that I need my best blouse for the next day, or I've run out of knickers entirely, then it will seize up on me instantaneously.

The washing machine from hell.

It's just managed to turn my best white undies the dingiest blue-grey when I hear the doorbell and stop in mid-swear word.

I'm not expecting anybody.

It must be the milkman. He always collects the milk money on a Friday or a Saturday night. At least this time he's caught me with my clothes on. I grab my purse from the kitchen table

178

and head for the hall. I struggle with the lock as usual, and finally manage to pull the door open.

'Sorry about that, blasted lock stuck . . .'

I start, and then stop. Standing on my doorstep is Alex Christian. He smiles at me. I just stand there, my bottom lip detached from the top by about half an inch. Does desire always immobilise one's brain?

'You don't do anything by halves, do you?' he finally ventures.

I look confused. He holds out a pair of shoes.

'Cinderella managed with one, you had to leave a pair.'

'My shoes,' I say stupidly.

'Well, I don't think they're mine.' He smiles gently. 'I rescued them from the hotel garden.'

'Thanks.'

That means he came back to look for me. I manage my first smile in a week.

'My pleasure.' He looks at my purse. 'You don't have to reward me, at least not with money anyway.' He laughs wryly.

I blush.

We're at that stage again, conversation running dry. We just stand there gazing at each other. I remember what happened last time we just stood there gazing at each other, and my blush deepens.

'Look, I'm really sorry about . . .' we both say at the same time.

We both start to laugh as well, and the ice is, well, not entirely broken but fractured. I stand back and pull the door wider.

'Do you want to come in?'

I know if I ask and he says no I'll feel stupid, but if I don't ask I'll kick myself very severely later.

He follows me into the sitting room, and looks about him, assessing an unfamiliar place. Thank goodness I've just had a major clear out. The flat actually looks really good. Minimalist chic.

Shame I don't, though. Scrubber style.

He's wearing faded Levis and a loose collarless white shirt. His hair is tousled and he has dark circles under his eyes, but he still looks amazing and disgustingly desirable.

I'm suddenly acutely conscious of my old ripped jeans and faded blue t-shirt, my clearing-out gear, of my dirty bare feet and unmade-up face.

179

We stand facing each other for a moment, awkward, silent, then he asks after Sally and Richard. I show him their postcard. He says they must have cheated and posted it from the airport for it to reach me so quickly.

We fall silent again.

I remember my manners and ask him to sit down.

I can't look at him, keep darting surreptitious sideways glances at him, like looking at the last cream cake on the plate, pretending you don't want it really but fighting the saliva that's gathering in full flood on your tongue.

He starts talking about the wedding, but I'm concentrating too hard on fighting my own discomfiture really to listen. The atmosphere's so charged I can almost hear it buzzing.

'Coffee?' I suddenly blurt, my mind finally fixing on something normal.

I leave him sitting uncomfortably on the sofa in mid-meaningless sentence and escape to the kitchen. I attempt to refill the percolator, but my hands are shaking. I surreptitiously check my face in the round reflective sides of the stainless steel kettle. My eyes are wide, pupils dominant. They say that your pupils dilate when you look at someone you find attractive.

'Fliss?'

I jump at the sound of his voice.

'I'll be with you in a minute . . .'

'Fliss.'

'I'm just making some coffee.'

'I don't want any coffee.'

I turn around. He's standing in the doorway.

'Look, it's no good, we've got to talk about what happened on Saturday night.'

I'm very tempted to deny all knowledge, pretend the whole evening has disappeared in a drunken haze, that I don't remember what happened at all, but he looks so concerned that wouldn't be fair.

'Don't worry about it.' I try to smile brightly at him. 'It was just a kiss.'

'That's the problem, it was more than just a kiss and we both know it.' He falters, looks away and then back at me again.

'This is going to sound completely insane. I mean, I hardly know you, but I don't know what it is, I've never felt this way about anybody before. There's just something . . .' He shrugs, at a loss for words to describe what has happened. 'It's just there, a feeling, a very strong feeling that I've got to be with you. Don't you feel it too?'

I look at the floor. Talk about inner conflict!

'Dear Auntie Ruth, I met the man I want to marry at what should have been my wedding, the problem is he's married. I've tried to forget him, but I can't get him out of my head. I dream about him, I fantasise about him, in fact every time I see him, I just want to cut the crap and rip off all of his clothes. What do I do?'

I decide the best form of defence is attack.

'Why did you run away from me then?' I accuse him. 'I kiss you, you bolt. Hardly good for my ego . . .'

'Infidelity isn't exactly my forte.'

'No, you leave that to your wife,' I quip without thinking.

He's silent.

I kick myself mentally. Very hard.

'Besides I'd hardly call one kiss a major infidelity,' I bluster, trying to cover up my embarrassment.

'No,' he agreed. 'It's what followed the kiss.'

'Nothing followed the kiss. You ran away, remember?'

'And when I came back you'd done exactly the same thing.'

He walks over to me.

I back away.

I can feel the table top jutting into the small of my back. I suddenly find the floor tiles very interesting.

'Maybe that should tell us something.'

I'm whispering, but he's close enough to hear me easily.

'You normally run and hide from people you dislike.'

'Or people you like too much,' he answers softly.

His face is so close. I can see the soft down on his full upper lip. My senses are so heightened, I can feel the warmth of his skin even though he's not quite touching me.

'Fliss?' His voice is quiet, uncertain, questioning.

He reaches out and pushes a stray tendril of hair away from my downturned face. As he touches me I realise that it's just no good. No matter how much I want to fight this I can't. Just the sensation of his fingertips against my face carries pure electricity. His face is so close, my senses suddenly so heightened . . .

He's gorgeous.

I want him. Oh, *boy*, do I want him.

He's married.

How can something so wrong feel so right?

His kiss is as soft as thistledown. This time my eyes stay open. I want to remember every single minute detail.

I trace his face with my fingers like a blind man reading Braille, desperate to burn the image into my mind. He follows the contour of my neck with his lips. The warmth of his breath against my skin makes me shiver. As his lips return to my mouth and he kisses me again, my stomach begins to churn like the washing machine which is now stuck on spin.

My hands slide under his shirt, feel the warmth of his skin, the smooth firm curve of his back. He pulls me closer, fingers tracing the length of my spine, tangling with my hair. I revel in the weight of his gloriously fit, lean body pressing against me. The kiss gets harder, less tentative, more passionate, and this little voice in my head begins to nag.

It's just no good, I can't do this. It's like indulging in too much of your favourite ice cream. No matter how good it tastes at the time, the guilt afterwards takes away the majority of the pleasure.

Reluctantly, very reluctantly, I pull away.

'Fliss, what's wrong?'

'This is wrong.'

He looks at the floor, then back at me.

'It doesn't feel wrong.'

'I know, but the situation. Katherine, Richard, you, my sister . . . it's all too much, too complicated. And at the end of the day, you're married. I don't want to break up a marriage.'

'Even if that marriage is turning out to be a total farce?'

'You said yourself, it's a commitment you have to work at.'

He backs away and leans against the kitchen table, arms crossed, suddenly defensive.

'If you don't feel the same then just say so, don't hide behind false guilt.'

Oh, that it were. Guilt is an emotion I can rely on to be with me all my life, never to leave my side. I should have been Catholic I'm so good at it.

He's upset. His face is drawn, and he won't look me in the face. All I can think is how much I long to kiss that angry mouth again.

'I think I'd better go,' he mutters.

If he doesn't I'm going to do something I'll regret.

'It's for the best,' I force myself to say.

How trite those words sound.

'I suppose so.'

As he leaves, he looks back. I have to look away and cram my fist into my mouth to stop myself calling after him.

Love is supposed to make you feel on top of the world. I feel like I'm at the bottom of a pit. So I can't love Alex. If I really loved him, I'd be happy. One part of me keeps saying if I really loved him, I wouldn't have sent him away. The other tells me that it's *because* I love him that I turned him away.

'He's married,' says my head rather bluntly.

My heart keeps telling me not to get hung up on technicalities. Kat is hardly keeping to her marriage vows, now is she?

'But,' says my head, 'that doesn't mean I should sink to her level. Somebody's got to have some standards around here.'

'Why, oh, why, does that somebody have to be me?' answers heart despondently.

'It's that guilt thing again,' sighs head sympathetically.

'Hello again, guilt, you old bastard,' sighs heart.

It's been three days now since I sent Alex away. Three whole days of thinking of nothing but him. Nothing but him and what could have happened if I'd let him stay.

I decide that if I'm not in love with Alex, then I was right before and I am obsessed with him. Obsession is a destructive form of love/lust. I know this, I've seen *Fatal Attraction*. Glenn Close wasn't exactly full of the joys of spring. She was suicidal and homicidal.

Well, I'm not going to murder his pets or pour acid over his car – I'd rather do that to Richard – but I can't switch my brain to any other channel.

I think of Alex constantly.

I must pick up the phone about ten times in one day and then put it back down again. I am desperate to talk to him. Desperation . . . what a sad state. Even if I could pluck up the courage to call, what the hell would I say to him? Besides we keep coming back to the inescapable, unshakeable truth – he's married.

And look who he's married to as well.

The *ménage à* twat becomes the kinky quintet?

I don't think so. A whole bloody chain reaction could be set off if I give in to the feelings I have for this man. Besides, I'm not a home wrecker and I've never cast myself in the role of mistress. Mistress of the Rolls . . . Mistress of the rolls in the hay. I've just got out of one destructive relationship, I don't want to go chasing after another.

No, I can't call him.

I keep telling myself this as I sit by the phone hour after hour. I'm not going to ring him, I want to but I can't. Perhaps he'll call me.

As the days drag by with no contact, I get more and more depressed, mooning around, staring at the walls, climbing the walls, staring out of windows, contemplating throwing myself out of said windows. A momentary high every time the phone rings, then sadness when I answer and it's not him.

The telephone has become my enemy. Sitting there, mocking me with its silence. I can't work, I can't settle to anything. I prowl around the flat at night, unable to sleep. I keep having hot flushes, getting agitated and bursting into tears for no apparent reason. I'm right, I'm obsessed. Either that or I'm undergoing a very early menopause.

The sensible little voice that keeps nagging me just to forget about Alex and get back to reality, and therefore back to relative normality, is gradually getting more and more subdued. The longer I go without seeing him the worse it gets. One day very soon reason may pack its bags and bugger off completely on an extended holiday, and then what do I do? I wish my conscience would pack its bags and run away with reason, and then the path forward would be far easier.

Far easier perhaps, but would it be the right path?

Nowadays I just don't know what I'm doing, but whatever it is, I must be doing it wrong. In the past few months I've lost my husband-to-be (no *great* loss, I know), my best friend, soon my father will be packing his bags and shipping out, and now I'm losing my mind. Even the cat has abandoned me. She's practically moved in with the girl upstairs who provides Whiskas on tap, always has the central heating on, and is not a gibbering emotional wreck all of the time. And when I finally find a man I lust after, a man I could love, a man I really truly *like*, he's married.

Sash doesn't help.

She calls round midweek for a coffee and an update, and to

flick through the wedding photographs my mother insisted on dropping off as soon as she'd done showing them off to her cronies.

Sash is obviously still being denied the pleasure of Niall's libido, which according to her has disappeared somewhere in the middle of the bodily Bermuda triangle known as his brain and is now on a par with Shergar and Lord Lucan.

'You should just go for it, Fliss,' she urges, drooling over a photograph that, oh, cruel fate, actually has Alex in it. 'I know I would if he'd offered himself up on my sacrificial altar. A little of what you fancy and all that.'

'Things still bad at home then, I take it?'

'How did you guess? To be honest it's worse. Niall's just so knackered all the time. I mean I am too, but at least I make an effort, for what it's worth. His cock's got a "No Access" sign on it at the moment. Do you know, I put my hand on it the other night in bed, just to say hello, see if it was still talking to me, and you've never seen anyone jump so high or so fast. It's the biggest display of energy I've seen from him in months. I don't know what to do. Maybe it's not sex he's gone off, maybe it's me.'

'Oh, come on, Sash, I'm sure that's not true. We all know how much Niall loves you and the kids.'

'Well, yes, I know he loves me, Fliss, but does he still fancy me? Some men are funny like that, you know. You have children and suddenly cease to be a sex object. Instead you're a thou-shalt-not-touch mother figure.'

'I'm sure that's not the way it is. You've both got stressful jobs . . .'

'Well, yes, he does work long hours, I'll grant him that, and Jack's being a total daddy's boy at the moment, wants Niall with him constantly when he's at home . . . but it's so frustrating, Fliss.'

'Don't talk to me about frustration!' I grin at her.

'I know. What are you going to do?'

'Oh,' I sigh heavily, 'I haven't a clue. I want him sooo much, but it's all wrong. I think the best thing I can do at the moment is nothing.'

'Actually . . .' Sash puts down her coffee cup and looks sideways at me under her eyelashes, a small smile playing about her red lips. 'I've got a confession too.'

'Oh, yes?' Grateful for a diversion from my own thoughts, I offer her another biscuit and curl my feet under me, ready to listen. 'Tell me all.'

'I've been asked out for a drink.'

'You haven't?' I breathe, intrigued. 'Who by?'

'This new guy at work . . .'

'You're not going to go, are you?'

'I don't know, I'm tempted. Boy, am I tempted! He's gorgeous, and he's only twenty-two.'

'Well, he's past his peak then. Don't they say a man's at his best at nineteen?'

'Oh, well, in that case I'll definitely stand him up.'

'Stand him up? Don't tell me you've already agreed to go out with him?'

Sash nods, biting her bottom lip in excitement and contrition. She looks guilty but happy at the same time.

'When?'

'Well, that's the difficult one. Finding an excuse to get out.' She pauses and prods my leg with her finger. 'Fliiiisss . . .' she wheedles.

'You want a favour, don't you?'

'Uh-huh.' She nods. 'Will you be my alibi?'

I hesitate. I really like Niall, but Sash is one of my best mates.

'Please? Can I tell Niall we're going out for a drink or something? I mean, I haven't actually decided whether or not to go ahead with it, but if I do, will you cover for me . . . I know it's a hard thing to ask, what with you and Niall getting on so well, but you could look upon it as helping our relationship . . .'

'Oh yeah, and how do you work that one out?'

She grins.

'Well, if I don't get my leg over soon, I'll probably end up murdering him.'

A slight respite for my sanity is my return to school. Here *I* am in control, a rare feeling lately. I say slight respite however because now I have to face the music as far as my girls are concerned.

They say that curiosity killed the cat.

Hastings is living proof of this theory, having used up quite a few of her nine lives by sticking her furry bits in places where she really oughtn't; falling asleep in the washing machine on laundry day being one example.

Curiosity, however, does not kill fifth formers. It fuels their over-eager minds like dry moss on a camp fire. It's not long before news of my spectacular lack of a wedding ring filters down from the upper echelons of the school hierarchy. Not to mention the pretty obvious point that I still have the same surname as last term.

As at the wedding rumours abound, my personal favourite being that I discovered Richard in an *après* stag night clinch with the male stripper from *my* hen night. Where this particular little beauty came from I don't know, but as a counter to the other rumours flying around like Chinese Whispers at a sore throat convention, it was a moment of exquisite light relief from the heavy burden of being the most talked about person in the whole school community.

I keep reminding myself of the inevitable brevity of my fifteen minutes of fame, and try to keep my mind looking forward to the day when I'll be yesterday's news. The imminent arrival of a new, young, attractive, *male* sports coach gives me hope that this will be sooner rather than later as the girls' attentions are transferred from my failed love life to his potential love life. Unfortunately, there is also something else I have failed to address. Yet another confrontation awaits me, another problem on my long list.

Caroline.

I can't deny it, I've really missed her. I've really missed them both: David's reassurance, Caro's wicked sense of humour and unswerving loyalty. She's always been there for me when I needed her and I feel a git to have avoided her so completely over the last four weeks. I just wish they hadn't tried to involve me in their sex life.

I don't think I'm a prude, not really, but orgies I cannot handle. I mean, it's all very well displaying your flabby bits on a one-to-one basis, but not in front of your friends. I for one certainly wouldn't classify sex as the most obvious choice for a spectator sport. The mystery and allure of a clothed body is so much more fascinating than the reality of the naked body. Clothes are a wonderful camouflage. You can hide those hefty hips under an A-line skirt, but take it off and there they are for all the world to see.

I can just imagine it now . . .

'Ooh, look, don't you think Anna Harrington's put on weight? I'm sure her backside wasn't that large at the last orgy . . . and did you see the state of Jonty's legs? I always thought he was such a hunk – those pins would disgrace a malnourished chicken. No wonder he always wears baggy chinos . . . Oh, and look at Fliss Blakeney's stomach! It's wobbling away like an untamed pink blancmange . . .'

To prepare for one's first orgy must be like getting in training for the Olympics. Don't eat for a month beforehand, and spend every spare moment jogging, cycling or working out at the gym.

No, orgies are definitely not my scene, and not just because I'm slightly shy. I've always been a very giving person, but there are limits to what I'm prepared to share.

I like to think that I'm fairly open-minded. I'm not condemning Caro and David, not really, let he who is without sin and all that, but really what do I say to them? I can't pretend the whole thing never happened, so how do we get back to the lovely easy friendship we shared before?

Can things ever go back to how they were? I really don't know.

I think back to that X-rated scene in the drawing room of Angels Court, and a bubble of laughter escapes. I suppose that's a start on the road to recovery.

I manage to avoid Caroline at first, timing my visits to the staff room with military precision, so that I don't bump into her. I've actually got a copy of her class schedule and skirt round the old buildings like James Bond on a mission. Once I even duck into the gents' loos to avoid her. You'd think with the shortage of men there naturally is at an all girls' school, I'd be fortunate enough to find it empty.

Not so.

Mr Carver, the wrinkled old Latin teacher, is leaning against a stall, pointing an equally wrinkled old John Thomas towards the urinal. He looks over at me, and sighs.

'Nil bastardo carborandum,' he murmurs.

I don't know whether he's talking to me or to himself.

My avoidance tactics can't last forever, though.

Caro eventually corners me in the empty staff room.

'Fliss, we have to talk.' She smiles uncertainly at me.

188

'Can't stop, double English, Upper 5B. Must rush,' I garble with false brightness.

I know, I'm a big fat coward, always running away to avoid the nasty things in life.

'Fliss, pleeease. We have to sort this out.'

'Nothing to sort out really.' I smile inanely at her, and suddenly realise why I have such a hang up about that evening.

Acute embarrassment.

I feel I should be sophisticated enough to cope with one little orgy but I'm not. When I saw my best friend on the floor, in the arms of another woman, I was, well, quite frankly shocked. And, as I said, the feeling that followed was acute embarrassment.

I don't know how to handle the situation. I don't know that I *can* handle the situation. I mean, what do you say to someone you last saw cavorting naked at an orgy?

'Er, did you have a nice break?' I suppose that's a start.

'So you're just going to pretend that nothing happened?' she asks bluntly.

That sounds like a very good option to me. I deliberately drop my file, so that I don't have to look her in the face, and flounder round on the floor after my papers.

'Fliss!' she says exasperatedly. 'Answer me.' I continue to shuffle papers, on my knees. 'I need your friendship, Fliss, please don't shut me out.'

I always thought it was I who needed her. Caro, my friend, my rock, my other sister. I always knew she liked me, loved me even, but needed me? That's a new one.

'Hannah's pregnant.'

That makes me listen. I stop grovelling on the floor and look up.

'You're kidding!'

'Afraid not, we've just found out.'

'How?'

'How do you think?' She smiles wryly.

No, smiles isn't the right word, it's more of a pained grimace.

'Well, I'm an English teacher, not a Biology teacher, but I think I know the basics by now. I suppose what I really meant was, who?'

'Who do you think? Jake.'

Jake?

Oh, dear.

With a rush of guilt, my ever-present companion, I stumble to my feet, clutching my file to my chest.

'Oh, Caro,' I whisper, 'I'm so sorry. It's all my fault, I encouraged her to see him.'

She shakes her head.

'Hannah only does what Hannah wants to do . . . It's not your fault.'

'How is she?'

'Remarkably all right actually, after the first round of hysterics. It's still very early days, but she now seems amazingly calm about the whole thing.'

'I suppose Maura the free spirit is overjoyed? Another soul embarking on the wondrous journey into the universe?'

Caroline shakes her head.

'Actually she's furious.'

'Well, that's a turnaround.'

'She threw Hannah out.'

'You're joking?' I'm outraged. 'Of all the hypocritical . . .'

'Don't worry, we're looking after her now.'

'What will she do?'

'Well, she's adamant she doesn't want to get rid of it. She doesn't believe in that. But she's so young, you never know what will happen . . . but assuming she has the baby, then David and I . . . well, we've offered to look after it for her.' Caroline flushes and looks at the floor. 'We're going to bring him or her up. Hannah's really happy with the idea. She doesn't want to get rid of it but she doesn't want the responsibility either . . . she wants to make something of her life, you know, finish her exams, go to university . . .'

I gaze incredulously at my friend.

'But you don't like children.'

'That's what I'd always tried to convince myself, Fliss, but only because I knew I could never have any.'

'You never told me that . . .'

'I haven't known myself for very long, I don't suppose it had sunk in enough to be able to talk about it.'

'So that's why David got so touchy when the kids were winding you up about babies?'

She nods.

'Now a new child is joining the family . . . well, it's made me

190

realise how desperately I really wanted one. Not that I intend to take him or her away from Hannah,' she adds hurriedly. 'Even though David and I will be bringing the child up, it will always be her son or daughter. And when I'm a surrogate mother that means I'll have to behave . . .' she pauses and looks meaningfully at me '. . . more responsibly.'

I digest this last.

'And you, Fliss, how are you?' she asks quietly. 'I heard about Sally-Anne and Richard. It was a shock for me, so goodness knows how it made you feel. I did try to call . . .'

'I know,' I hang my head in shame, 'I'm sorry.'

'It's all right, I do understand. How do you feel?'

'Confused,' I answer. 'I just hope he makes her happy.'

The bell heralding the start of class begins to ring.

'You know, Hannah would love to see you . . . we all would. We miss you. I miss you.'

'I've missed you too, Caro,' I murmur.

'Then come and see us . . . please?'

I nod slowly.

Sally and Richard arrive back from honeymoon. They are brown, relaxed, and seem very happy. I am summonsed to a celebratory 'returned from honeymoon' sherry and photos session at Mother's where Richard is attentive and loving towards Sal in a manner that even I cannot fault.

The usual smug smile does not appear once.

In fact, for the first time in ages I can react to Richard as if he's a normal human being. It's like he's a different person. Or perhaps I'm just seeing him in a different way now. That's probably what I need to do, give him the same opportunities I would if I were meeting him for the first time, not as my ex-fiancé but as Sally's husband.

I must try to forget the past and embrace Richard as my brother-in-law. He certainly treats me in a very different way, doesn't spend the evening trying to wind me up, focusing more on Sally-Anne than anything else and being, for want of a better word, *polite* to me. I was expecting the usual arrogant, pugnacious attitude, but to some extent my fears are allayed. Or if not allayed they must at least be put aside for there are other things to attend to now.

Dad waits over a week after Sally has moved her final suitcase into Richard's apartment then decides he can stand it no more. He confides in me that things are even more unbearable, alone in the house with my mother and no Sally-Anne the seasoned diplomat to keep the peace. Finally he tells Mother that he's leaving.

She seems strangely unaffected by his decision to go. Not that she would confide in me if she had any feelings on the matter other than the bitter but resolute acceptance that appears to be her current state of mind.

I remember asking my father at a fairly young age his reasons for marrying her. 'Other people's expectations' seemed to rank the highest among a fairly lame list. I never dared to ask my mother the same question, but I think if I had, I probably would have received a surprisingly similar answer.

My mother is someone who always does the correct thing. I'm not saying the right thing, because that isn't always what it is. I'm talking about the socially acceptable path. I think she obediently followed the course she was expected to take, but her life has been tainted by the inevitable disappointments that this entailed when it was never really what she wanted in the first place.

She got married because that's what girls were supposed to do. If it turned out to be a happy marriage then you were lucky, was the belief then. If it didn't you still stuck at it.

I don't think Sally-Anne's surprised at Dad's decision. Like me, she has grown up in a family where only an idiot would fail to notice that the parental unit is far from unified and less than happy. She can't help but be desperately upset, however. The beginning of her marriage has heralded the end of her parents'. She can't help but associate the two events and wonder if this is some sort of omen.

Sally and I help Dad to pack. It's amazing really how few of the things in this house belong to him. Just one small tea chest, filled mainly with bits from the shed, one small suitcase, and one fat Roger. After all these years you'd think they'd have some shared history, some treasured memories.

That's the saddest part of all, that they've lived like this, in an emotional, loveless void for so long. I know now I made the right choice in not marrying Richard. This could have been him and me thirty years from now.

I just hope it isn't the fate that awaits Sally and Richard, but I'm starting to think I could be wrong on this front.

It's Monday evening and Richard is working late but seems to be phoning Sally every half an hour to make sure that she's OK.

Mother is playing St Joan at the stake. She sits on the sofa, glowering like a malevolent old crow, watching with sharp little eyes to make sure that Dad doesn't take anything she feels he shouldn't.

Glenys the Menace has been drafted in as mediator.

She keeps droning on about how strong Miriam is.

She's not being strong about Dad leaving.

She just doesn't care.

She enjoys playing the martyr, it's a role she has perfected over the years. Any opportunity to display her expertise is gratefully accepted. As far as my mother is concerned Dad is an unnecessary part of her life. To her it's rather like having a wart removed. You may have got used to it being there, but you're certainly not going to profess you miss it after it's gone. The only time she shows any emotion is when Dad starts to wrap up a rather valuable painting given to them as a wedding present by his family. Unfortunately the emotion in question is greed.

'Put that back, Drew!' she shrieks. 'It was a present to us both, you must give me half the value if you want to take it.'

We wave goodbye as Dad and Roger drive down the road. When they reach the end, Dad stops the car and turns round to blow us a kiss. It's a relief to see that both he and Roger are smiling.

Sally is crying quietly.

'It's for the best,' I try and reassure her. 'They weren't happy together, Sal. At least now they've got a chance to find some joy.'

'I know they weren't happy together, and I know it's for the best for both of them really, and I know it's a selfish reaction, but things will never be the same for us again, Fliss. Home won't seem like home any more.'

Home never felt particularly homely to me anyway, but I do understand Sal's reaction. She takes my arm as we walk slowly back into the house. We are both silent as we re-enter the drawing room where my mother is rearranging the remaining ornaments with a strangely satisfied expression on her face.

'Well, thank goodness that's all over,' she says, as though

referring to the end of a rather boring television programme.

'Today or your marriage?' I can't help snapping at her. 'How can you just let him leave like that?'

I know it seems an odd question, me being an advocate of their separation, but I've never really understood why my mother has always been so careless of my father's feelings, knowing him to be such a good man.

'I'm not going to beg him to stay,' she replies, staring icily at me.

'Because you're too proud, or because you simply don't care?'

She doesn't reply, merely continues to glare at me, her eyes as cold as her seemingly frozen heart.

'Did you ever love him?' I persist. 'Tell me, why did you marry him?'

'Because he asked me.'

'And that was it? Are you telling me you never loved him?'

'I'm telling you as I've told you a thousand times before though you've never listened to me, there's more to marriage than a foolish ideal of love and romance.'

'Yes, there's trust and respect, but you never had those either, did you?'

'I don't believe you,' she hisses. 'You keep telling me what a sham my marriage was, and then you ask me why I didn't beg your father to stay! You may think you know everything there is to know about life and love, Felicity, but you've got an awful lot to learn, I can tell you. I've tried to teach you, to prepare you, but you never listen to me. You just can't understand the true value of security and stability. Love is a fickle emotion with no substance, you can't build a good life based on love.'

'You call what you've had a good life? You don't care that your husband of thirty years has just left you, and you want me to model myself and my future happiness on your example! Well, you've set me an example I shall never forget! You've made me determined I shall never lead an existence as miserable as yours!'

I run out of the front door. I'm so angry I'm shaking. Sally follows me out, puts her arms around my waist.

'It's a difficult time for us all,' she murmurs, briefly resting her forehead against my shoulder before pulling away and encouraging me to smile again with a resigned smile of her own.

194

'I know, I know, but she just doesn't seem to care about Dad going.'

'She's not like you, Fliss, she has a completely different set of values. Don't hate her for it.'

'Hate her?' I turn to Sally, my eyes damp with tears. 'That's the strangest thing, I don't hate her. Do you know, I actually feel sorry for her.'

Chapter Nine

The one good thing to come of this whole mess, is the fact that Sally-Anne and I have become a lot closer. Although we'd always rubbed along well, we'd pretty much taken each other for granted. With Dad gone we need and appreciate each other a little more.

Mother is driving Sally round the bend. She has moved in with Richard, and it seems that Mother is determined to follow suit. She's practically decamped into their apartment. The spare room has ceased to be a spare room and become Mother's room instead. Every time she goes to stay, which has in the three weeks since they returned from honeymoon been about ninety per cent of the time since my father moved out, she moves something else over.

She's like a backwards kleptomaniac, sneaking in belongings in her overnight bag. It's got to the point where Sally wants to frisk her every time she comes through the door to make sure she's not attempting to smuggle anything else in. It's a slow and devious process of ingratiation.

Sally has started to retreat to my flat just to get away from her.

'I'm sure Richard thinks he married both of us,' she frequently sighs. 'I know Mother must be lonely on her own, but we've only been married five weeks. I really don't think he relishes the idea of turning our guest suite into a granny flat just yet.'

I feel guilty for the fact that I don't get on well enough with Mother to take some of the burden off Sally. I would if I could, but even if I asked her over to stay with me for the weekend, I think she'd probably just laugh in my face. We've never had the kind of relationship where we do things together. Or not by choice anyway.

We've got about as much in common as a chocolate bar and a stick of celery. Both food, but one's far harder to swallow.

It's kind of sad really.

Then again, I've always been so close to Dad, I've never really felt I was missing out that much.

He has been gone for three weeks now. It seems like forever. We speak a lot on the phone, but it's not the same as having him fifteen minutes' drive away. The elusive Florrie lives in Kent, which explains the amount of time Dad spent there 'fishing' over the past years. I know it's only a couple of counties away, but at the moment it feels like it's in another hemisphere.

I haven't heard from Alex at all either. Not that I really expect to. I had my chance and I blew it. I know that's what I *should* have done, I just didn't realise how lousy it would make me feel. What was it Sash said? Is it better to do something you might regret than to regret something you haven't done? She and I are both still undecided on this front.

Apparently she's still being pursued by the gorgeous twenty-two year old. She hasn't succumbed yet, but it's doing her ego the power of good.

Maybe that's what I need, to be unashamedly lusted after by a gorgeously fit, sexily single twenty-two year old. Unfortunately the only thing I want at the moment is to be pursued by a gorgeously fit, maddeningly married thirty-five year old.

Six weeks after their return from honeymoon, Sally calls to invite me to dinner. I decline as graciously as possible. Although I'm still as confused about where I'm going as I've ever been, I do seem to be getting over my self-destruct mode. I don't spend my evenings hiding out under my duvet watching crap on the box, and amazingly the fridge has been empty of Mars Bars for two weeks.

At the moment, however, I don't even want to go out to the supermarket, let alone to a dinner party which, despite being given by my gorgeous sister, will no doubt be graced by the presence of her horrible hubby and several of his equally awful friends. I feel about as sociable as a virgin at a vampire's birthday party.

Apart from missing you-know-who, work is horrible – or should that be my new upper-fifths are horrible? They've latched on to my, shall we say, less than firm attitude at the

198

moment, have re-christened me Wuss, instead of Fliss, and are generally doing everything they can to make me think they should be called Damien and have 666 permanently tattooed on their foreheads.

I know it's my fault, I can normally handle a bunch of hormonal teenagers with whip-cracking and wise-cracking ease, but the fact that it's my fault for being such a miserable wimp at the moment only goes to make me feel worse about it.

I could easily jack it all in.

The prospect of a trip to join Wigs, who is currently in a place that she describes as 'frighteningly beautiful', a tiny island just off the coast of Sri Lanka, is becoming more and more appealing at the moment. Unfortunately my wimpishness extends to being unable to make such a momentous decision.

Also unfortunately Sally is not to be dissuaded, and since she has far more force of mind than me at the moment, which isn't difficult seeing as an oven chip would have far more force of mind than me at the moment, I soon find myself crumbling.

'Oh, Fliss, of course you must come. It's my first dinner party, I want you to be there.' Her voice holds just the right note of pleading.

'Honestly, Sal,' I groan. 'I'd rather not, I'll feel such a gooseberry.'

'Don't worry about that, we'll find you a nice man.'

'In that case I'm definitely not coming,' I reply belligerently.

'Pleeeease, Fliss!' Sally-Anne begs. 'I need you there, I really do.'

She sounds strange.

'Sally, is everything OK?'

She goes quiet for a moment.

'Yes, of course it is, I just want some moral support, that's all.'

'Moral support? For any particular reason?'

'No.' She's not quite convincing enough. 'Just first-night nerves, I suppose. Say you'll come, Fliss, please?'

Curiouser and curiouser, as Alice would say.

I give in.

'OK, but promise me you won't try and fix me up with one of Richard's stupid friends? That would be too humiliating for words.'

'Well, you really ought to have a partner to keep the numbers even.'

'Couldn't you just flout convention for one evening? Does it have to be boy/girl, boy/girl?'

'You're the one who said you'd feel like a gooseberry on your own. Trust me, Fliss.'

Why is it that when people say 'trust me' your instinctive reaction is to do exactly the opposite?

'Fine, just not one of Richard's stupid friends, OK?'

'Richard's friends aren't all awful. You like James, don't you?'

'Everybody likes James.'

'I know, he's gorgeous, isn't he?'

'Yep, but that doesn't mean I want to be fixed up with him.'

'Don't worry,' Sally laughs. 'I've already got him ear-marked for someone else.'

'He will be pleased,' I remark dryly, thinking back to the wedding and Erica's dogged pursuit of him. 'Sal, promise me you won't try and fix me up? I don't mind sitting next to someone and making polite conversation, but no matchmaking, please.'

'Oh, OK,' she sighs. 'Who would be acceptable then? You know, just to sit next to?'

'How about Roger? That would negate the need for polite drivel masquerading as conversation, he won't get drunk and obnoxious, and the only thing he'll try to get his leg over at the end of the evening is a lamp post.'

'I don't think his table manners are quite up to scratch,' Sal laughs, 'but I get the point. You want somebody obedient and affectionate, who'll drool all over you and be permanently pleased to see you.'

'Sounds like the perfect man, as long as I don't have to tickle their tummy and play fetch all evening. Can I bring anything?'

'Just yourself,' she says pointedly.

'Don't worry, I'll be there. What time do you want me?'

'Well, dinner's at eight-thirty, but if you could come a bit earlier I'd be eternally grateful,' she wheedles.

'Oh, yes, you just want me there to answer the door and carry coats while you play the genial hostess, don't you?'

'Well, it would be nice to know you're there if I get desperate, like if the doorbell rings while I'm trying to flambé something.'

'To be on hand to call the fire brigade?'

'Something like that. I'll see you about seven-thirty?'

★ ★ ★

Saturday night. I arrive at Richard's apartment – sorry, Sally and Richard's apartment – at seven-thirty on the dot, resplendent under my coat in obligatory little black dress and fetching blue and white striped butcher's apron. This is the first time I've been round to Richard's apartment since they got married. In fact it's the first time I've been round since that fateful night in July that seems more like three years than three months ago.

When Sally answers the door, I get this urge to say, 'What are you doing here?' It seems so strange to see her in this setting, like we've swapped lives or something.

Sally is similarly attired to me, only she's forgotten the dress. She is wearing pale pink silk undies beneath her pink floral apron, and nothing else. She is flushed, her long dark hair which is curled and pinned is starting to come loose, and she is waving a wooden spoon, burnt black, in her right hand as though she's going to hit me over the head with it.

'Oh, Fliss,' she burbles breathlessly, 'thank goodness you're here, everything's going wrong. It's all a complete disaster . . . I've spilt seafood sauce on my new dress, set fire to the kitchen curtains, burnt the potatoes, and dropped a whole box of silver napkin rings down the waste disposal. And worst of all – oh, Fliss, it's horrible – the first course is still alive!'

'I beg your pardon?'

'The first course,' she wails, 'it's alive and walking round my kitchen! Fliss, you've got to do something!'

I get very strange visions of chasing a manically mooing mad cow around the apartment. I blink hard. They go away.

'Er, what exactly are we having to eat?'

'Oh, Fliss!' she snivels. 'It was all Richard's idea, and of course he's been into work today and he's late home, and I'm left to massacre the little beast. Not that it's very little, it's bloody huge, I've never seen one this big!'

Well, she's definitely not talking about what Richard keeps down his trousers.

'What is it, Sally?'

If she gets any more hysterical, I shall have to slap her.

'It's horrible! It's so scary and vicious, and it's got these mean little eyes . . .'

'Mother's not here, is she?' The sarcasm is lost on Sally.

'No,' she replies, her own eyes wide.

201

'Well, I suppose I should be thankful for small mercies. Now lead the way, McDuff.'

Sally edges towards the kitchen, ushering me in front of her. What horrible fiendish thing lies behind the swing door? I don't see it at first. Then Sally spots it, shrieks and jumps on to a chair.

'It's under there, Fliss, it's under there!'

I crouch down and stare under the kitchen table.

A pair of beady black eyes stares back at me out of a hard brown face. The largest lobster in the universe is squatting under Sally's kitchen table. It waves a threatening pincer at me. I could swear it's scowling.

'It's supposed to be the centrepiece, we're having seafood pancakes. But when I opened the box I got such a shock, I thought the thing would already be . . . well, you know . . .' she runs a finger across her throat in slitting action '. . . dead.'

What a way to end your life, as dressing for a dinner table! No wonder the thing looks so bloody pissed off.

'It looks a bit like Richard,' I comment, staring at its hard little brown face and mean little eyes. 'I shall enjoy boiling it alive!'

I'm joking, of course. I'm not particularly squeamish but even I don't relish the thought of cooking something while it's still moving.

'I'm sorry, Sally.' I admit defeat as, having finally managed to recapture the blasted thing using a pair of salad tongs and a dustpan and brush, I chicken out of dunking it into the boiling cauldron on the stove. We're going to have to think of another way.

'We could drown it in the bath?' she suggests tentatively.

'Drown it? Honestly, Sally, where do you think the thing has lived for the past goodness knows how many years?'

'I don't know,' she wails, 'the box said Portsmouth.'

'I think we need a drink.' I dump the lobster back in its coffin of a wooden crate, and pour us both a very large G & T.

Three further very large G & Ts later we're a lot more relaxed, the lobster's been grandly christened Ethelred the Unready-cooked, and we're still no closer to a solution as to how to humanely kill the bloody thing. Sally suggests shooting it with the pistol Richard keeps in the top drawer of his desk in the study, but serving a starter with a fresh bullet hole through its head wouldn't really be the done thing.

Knowing my luck the bullet would ricochet off the thing's armour-like body, and shoot me instead. After another large gin, we hit on the bright idea of trying to suffocate it, but the sight of a lone Waitrose bag running around the kitchen floor is pretty disturbing after drinking so much. In the end we dunk it in a bucket of whisky and water, and stick it in the oven with the gas on, which amazingly seems to do the trick.

'At least it died happy,' says Sally, waving her glass in the air. '*Salute*, Entrée.'

'Cheers,' I agree, making a mental note to go vegetarian, if I can only beat the bacon sarnie cravings.

I send Sally-Anne off to the bedroom to find something else to wear, and manage to get the meal back on course. By ten to nine, I'm sobering up, there's still no sign of Richard the Turd, but the table is beautifully set, even if I do say so myself, and everything is cooked and waiting. The lobster is resplendent on a silver salver, resting on a bed of lettuce and lemon, and Lollo Rosso.

His beady eyes fell out while being boiled. I'm pleased about this. They tended to follow you round the room like the Mona Lisa's, only he definitely wasn't smiling earlier, enigmatically or otherwise. The scowl has been replaced. I'm sure he's smiling now – he should be, he's just been wallowing in almost a whole bottle of Jack Daniel's.

The doorbell chimes. I'm surprised Richard hasn't got a musical doorbell installed along with the other electronic gadgets that litter his home. 'Mr Vain' would be quite appropriate, or Hot Chocolate singing 'You Sexy Thing' at him every time he opens the front door.

'Fliss!' Sally-Anne calls plaintively from the bedroom.

'Don't worry, I'll get it.'

Trust Richard to be late for his own dinner party.

The first arrival is Sal's best friend Erica who I haven't seen since the wedding. She has obviously made a big effort to look good. At the risk of sounding a total bitch it's a real shame it didn't work.

Her over made-up face can only be the work of one of the more over-enthusiastic local beauty salons. The lines of kohl around her eyes are so precise they must have used a compass, her foundation is not so much pancake as Yorkshire pudding, and her blusher is a hard streak of red across her non-existent cheekbones. With her dark hair slicked back *à la* Jennifer Lopez, she looks not unlike a large jolly Matrioshka doll, with the smile of Julia Roberts.

She is carrying a bottle of Pouilly Fumé and grinning in excited anticipation. As I open the door I'm almost knocked out by the bottle of Je Reviens she has poured down her cavernous cleavage.

She's wearing a killer dress, a little red number that swoops down low like a bird of prey at the front and at the back as well, and her pillar box lipstick matches her outfit exactly. I am therefore not surprised when five minutes later the doorbell goes again, and James is standing there holding a single red rose.

'For Erica?' I ask him. 'How appropriate.'

'Er, no.' His face falls. 'For Sal actually.' He looks nervously past me into the sitting room, and whispers, 'Erica's not here, is she?'

I nod.

He puts a finger to his lips, waggles his fingers at me in a silent goodbye and starts to back away, but it's too late. Sally-Anne emerges from the bedroom.

'James, so glad you could make it!' She takes his hand and kisses his cheek.

'I'm not!' he whispers to me as Sally leads him into the sitting room like a lamb to the slaughter.

If poor old James has been lumbered with Erica against his will, then who am I going to get? Perhaps I should be attempting a swift getaway as well while there's still time.

Sally has dumped James on the sofa next to Erica. It's a long black leather sofa. I can hear him squeaking his way up to the far end as he surreptitiously tries to manoeuvre as far away from her as possible.

I follow Sally over to the drinks cabinet. She is pouring James a very large whisky.

'Er, Sally darling, you know you said you'd find me a nice man? You were only joking, weren't you?'

'Well, we had to get someone to make up the numbers, Fliss,' she murmurs non-commitally.

'And who exactly will be making up the numbers?' I ask.

Sally hands James his drink and grins nervously at me.

'Er, just going to check that the lobster's well and truly

dead . . .' She moves away, but I catch her arm.

'Its eyes have fallen out, Sally,' I hiss through clenched teeth, 'it hasn't moved in the last ten minutes. In fact, I think rigor mortis has set in. If it's not dead then it's a better impressionist than Bobby Davro. And speaking of dead, you will be if you don't answer my question.'

The doorbell rings again.

'Saved by the bell,' mutters Sal. 'That'll probably be him now. Why don't you go and see for yourself?' She whisks away rather quickly.

I make my way somewhat hesitantly to the door. Sally has definitely aroused my suspicions. As I opened it, I have this churlish urge to cover my eyes.

'Feliiiicity . . .' growls a deep voice, tongue running lasciviously over the consonants of my name like a child licking an ice-cream.

I've died and gone to hell. This must be punishment for my part in the murder of an innocent, if irritable, lobster. There, lounging against the door frame, is Ollie Barton-Davis.

Ollie the Octopus. A member of the sea squad come to exact revenge on behalf of Ethelred the Unready-cooked.

Fat, balding and fifty, Ollie is the Head of Chambers at Richard's firm. I say add a 'Dick' to the front and you'd get a better description.

He thinks he's God's gift to women.

I think he's God's reminder to women to appreciate a decent man.

Ollie is not a decent man. He is a lech of the highest order – the sort who as a child would lift your skirt and twang your knicker elastic to get his kicks. Come to think of it, he's the sort who as a man would lift your skirt and twang your knicker elastic to get his kicks.

I can't sit next to him all evening, it's not nice, and it's certainly not safe. Not unless I put a mousetrap in my knickers.

'You're looking par-tic-u-lar-ly lovely, my dear. When Richard said you were in need of a partner for tonight's repast, I leapt on my charger and galloped on down. Haw-haw-haw! Actually I leapt in dear old Richard's BMW really, he's just parking. He dropped me off at the front because I was *panting* to see you . . . now that we're both young, free and single, eh?' He winks heavily.

Forget the lobster, it's me that's been served up on a platter. Trust Richard to toady to the boss by offering me as a company perk. His head is so far up Ollie's backside he might never see daylight again, just the back of a set of perfectly capped teeth.

Ollie leans forward and takes my hand. My arm is as stiff as an one-armed bandit's as he pulls my hand to his mouth and kisses it. I suppress the urge to shudder, but only just. As he bends forward, I can see that sweat is already shining on his bald head.

I have nothing against bald men in particular, just this particular bald man.

He has rubber lips, too. Not Mick Jagger-style rubber lips, more like Planet of the Apes-style rubber lips, all pale and limp and trembling. The feeling of them running slowly across my hand and up my arm is not dissimilar to that of a pair of slugs trailing slimily across your body.

Removing his lips from my shoulder is akin to prising off an over-enthusiastic leech, but I manage it and reluctantly take him through to the sitting room, dumping him on the sofa in the space that James has somehow managed to vacate next to a disgruntled Erica.

Five minutes after Ollie's unwelcome entrance Richard arrives, smiling happily and rubbing his hands in eager anticipation of the evening to come. I shoot him a look that would definitely kill, and doggedly follow him as he scurries off to hide in the kitchen. I corner him against the cooker which is still slowly roasting the beef we're having for the main course.

'You little toad!' I hiss venomously at him. 'How dare you set me up with that slime ball!'

Richard shifts away, takes some ice out of the freezer compartment and turns to grin infuriatingly at me.

'My, my, the worm turns,' he mocks. 'You used to be such a compliant little thing, Felicity.'

He reaches into a cupboard above his head, and takes out a bottle of twelve-year-old malt. James got Bell's. He pours the golden liquid liberally into a cut-glass tumbler, and then adds a fistful of ice.

'Be a dear and take this to Ollie.'

He holds the glass out to me challengingly.

The doorbell rings.

'Sorry,' I smile sweetly, 'I'm on door duty. Water the weed yourself.'

I turn and march away. He'll keep.

Although tighter than a rusted bulldog clip on who was actually attending this evening's do, understandably so I see now, Sally did admit there were eight of us for dinner. This is a bit like an Agatha Christie.

Guess who's coming for dinner?

Whoever it is, I reassure myself with the fact that it can't be any worse than Ollie Barton-Davis. I paste a welcoming smile on to my face and reach for the door handle.

I open the door to find Katherine Christian waiting there, impatiently drumming her pink finger nails against the door frame, immaculate in a shocking pink Escada suit. Just behind her, stands Alex.

The moment I've been alternately dreading and longing for. I knew we'd eventually meet again, it's inevitable, somehow our lives seem to be inextricably entwined. I'd played out the different scenarios in my head so many times. Where we'd meet, when we'd meet. They usually involved me starting out resistant and good, but always seemed to end up with me naked and in bed.

Kat never featured in any of them, though. But here she undeniably is, as egocentric and obnoxious as usual.

'The guest of honour has arrived,' she announces without quite enough light-heartedness to save the statement.

She pushes straight past me towards Richard, who has emerged from the kitchen and now saunters forward and kisses her far too casually on both cheeks.

'Kat darling, so glad you could make it.'

He draws her down the corridor and into the sitting room. I'm left still holding the door handle, Alex standing uncomfortably in the doorway, both of us trying desperately hard not to look at the other. We don't even say hello. Let the games commence.

Richard's apartment is still the same as it always was, Sally has yet to make her mark upon any room except the bathroom where her Dune now sits neatly next to Richard's Safari, and the kitchen, which Richard has always believed is a woman's domain anyway. The other rooms are redolent of Richard's taste, and his taste alone, although the connection between

207

Richard and actual taste is a dubious one, being staunchly Bang & Olufsen, black leather bachelor-style.

Apart from the two long black leather sofas that dominate the sitting room there is little other furniture. The room is sparse in its decoration: no pictures, no plants, not even a framed photograph of the happy couple on their wedding day.

A long window dominates the far wall, looking out over the beauty of the city. I always thought the best thing about this place was the view of Oxford's dreaming spires. In relief against this window is a black and chrome structure which houses Richard's collection of electronic gadgets, hi-fi, speakers, TV, a whole tower block of CDs. One shelf alone is devoted to remote controls, not just for the equipment but for the blinds which slide silently across the window at night.

An archway from this room leads into the dining room. A long table sits in the centre around which are eight chairs made of wrought iron by some blacksmith who deduced that shoeing horses was definitely not the way to riches in the twenty-first century.

Intricate and yet not delicate, they are very beautiful, were very expensive, and wouldn't look amiss in some S & M dungeon in the heart of Soho.

The thick slab of glass which forms the surface of the table is smoked almost black in colour, presumably so that one cannot see underneath and determine which feet are dallying with which, and whose knees are being fondled by whom. The walls, as everywhere throughout the apartment, are painted a soft cream.

In the sitting room, Richard is leaning against the black marble fireplace, playing man of the house. He has an arm draped casually along Sally's shoulders, is rubbing the back of her neck with the ball of his thumb. I think he's doing it to wind Kat up.

If it's not working on Kat, it's working on me.

As far as I'm concerned this totally un-Richardlike behaviour is just confirmation that Sally is being used as a pawn in a game far more complicated than chess. To make matters worse, when she goes back out to the kitchen, Richard tries to introduce me to Alex. Erica and Ollie are talking on the sofa, so this is presumably so that Richard can chat to Kat undisturbed.

'This is my *sister-in-law*.' He laughs, enjoying my discomfort.

'We've met before,' I say quickly. As you bloody well know, I want to shout after him when he and Kat move away from us on the pretext of looking at Richard's hi-fi equipment.

Alex and I have a very stilted conversation.

'It's good to see you again,' I say quietly.

This roughly translates as 'I've missed you like mad', but I'm sure it doesn't come across that way.

'How have you been?' he says, not quite meeting my eyes.

We shoot apart like two magnets with the same polarity.

James sidles back into the room and, skirting around Erica as though she is a plague carrier, comes and stands next to me.

'You don't look very happy,' he says, observing my glum face.

'Well, this isn't exactly my idea of a fun evening.'

'Then why did you come?'

'I promised Sally.'

'Me too.' He toys with his glass, rubbing an imaginary smear from the side. 'She doesn't deserve such loyalty,' he says darkly, casting a fearful glance in Erica's direction.

'I agree.' I follow his gaze. 'But I think your date is a little more acceptable than mine, don't you?'

He nods.

'But only just.'

He starts to edge away again as Erica rises from the sofa and attempts to sashay towards us in her unfamiliar high heels.

'Must go to the bathroom,' he mutters.

'Again?' I mock him. 'Feeling a little weak-bladdered, are we?'

Richard slides on a CD.

He's a Phil Collins man.

'That's our tune,' sigh Sally and Kat in unison as 'A Groovy Kind of Love' begins to pulse out of the speakers. Fortunately, although I hear both, neither hears the other.

It's Richard's tune actually, I want to tell them.

The one who loved him least is the one who knows him best.

The blinkers fell away at the same time as the last vestiges of affection. He just shares this particular record with whoever happens to be in his life at the time. Makes it easier on the few brain cells he possesses, I suppose, I think bitchily.

He used to play it non-stop when I first met him. I hate it with a passion.

Although James is still in hiding, Erica seems to have attracted some interest from another quarter. Ollie is smouldering at her. It's not a pleasant sight.

'I think you have an admirer,' I tell her, indicating his pouting lips and come-hither eyes with an inclination of my head.

'Do I?' She seems surprised but pleased.

'Isn't it obvious? Just look at the way he's looking at you. He's practically drooling.'

'You're making fun of me, aren't you?'

'Not at all! I'm being perfectly serious, take a look for yourself.'

Erica casts a shy glance in Ollie's direction, and is rewarded with what is for him a rather nice smile.

'See, what did I tell you?'

Erica turns pink. She's obviously pleased to be admired.

'Ollie is rather sweet, isn't he?' she murmurs, toying nervously with an earring.

Sweet is not a word I would normally use in association with Ollie Barton-Davis.

'It's just a pity he's not the right person,' she sighs.

'Oh, yes. James,' I say.

'Yes, James,' she repeats, head craning hopefully towards the corridor and the bathroom.

'Are you sure he's the right person for you?' I say tactfully.

'Oh, yes, *he* just doesn't know it yet. Still, the course of true love never did run smooth,' she adds philosophically.

'I've always found it such a waste of time and energy wanting someone who doesn't want you.'

This is the most tactful way I can think of telling her that James is definitely not interested, without actually telling her outright.

'True love stands a better chance when nurtured by both parties. Trust me, I speak from experience.'

Erica follows my gaze.

Richard is showing Alex his 'toys', setting Phil to repeat to play on the hi-fi that looks more streamlined than a racing car.

'Yes, um, I never did say . . . that is . . . I'm sorry about what happened between you and Richard. You must have been very upset,' she blusters, misunderstanding.

'I was,' I reply, but I'm not thinking about Richard.

I want desperately for Alex to acknowledge me, but he doesn't. This makes me so angry I want to scream at him 'Look at me! Speak to me!' but of course I can't say anything. It's so frustrating. We may not be able to have a relationship, but I can still offer him my friendship, can't I?

I must convince myself – as I hope I convinced him – that this is all I want to offer.

Sally sees me frowning and thinks I'm angry because of Ollie which is in fact just one of the causes. Nonetheless she decides to placate me.

'Dinner's ready, everybody, if you want to go through to the dining room . . . You go and sit down.' She touches my arm. 'You've done enough to help already. I want you to relax and enjoy the rest of the evening.'

How the hell am I going to enjoy the rest of the evening sitting opposite Alex and the delightful Katherine?

Kat is of course seated at right angles to Richard.

I get this urge to drop my napkin so I can look under the table and see if they're playing footsie.

I slide into my seat. James, who has been hiding out in the bathroom for the past ten minutes, hurries in, hotly pursued by Erica.

'Do you mind if I sit next to you?' he hisses. 'Sally may be determined that she's going to fix me up with Erica, but I'm determined she's not.'

Poor old Erica. I don't know about the eternal triangle, this table is home to the eternal octagon, everybody wanting the wrong person.

I really should say no to James, for Erica's sake.

As she so eloquently put it, the course of true love never runs smooth, and if it needs a bit of help, I ought to be in there assisting in any way I can.

I am ashamed to say that selfishness gets the better of me. I really cannot stand the idea of sitting next to Ollie all evening, especially not with Kat and Alex sitting opposite. I can just hear Kat now.

'So glad you've finally found someone more your type, darling.'

You never know, I tell myself, determined to assuage the guilt, Oliver and Erica might just hit it off. It's obvious he's already developed a huge crush. I can see him gazing in admiration at her ample cleavage at this very moment, while she shoots daggers at me for monopolising James.

'James!' Sally hisses, nodding her head in the direction of the empty chair at the bottom of the table, which just happens to be next to Erica. 'You're supposed to be sitting there.'

'I want to sit next to the beautiful Fliss,' he announces, and firmly parks his chino-covered bottom in the seat next to mine. The fact that if he had sat at the head of the table he would still be sitting next to me is glaringly obvious.

Everyone glares at James, except for Ollie who is obviously highly delighted at this announcement, sliding into James's unoccupied seat next to Erica and beaming broadly. James, however, takes no notice of the daggers being thrown in his direction and insolently rests his head on my shoulder, looking defiantly round the table.

Kat, who has already suffered the slug treatment from Ollie – 'a very old friend, darling' – has been waiting for James to acknowledge her like the Queen on Deb day. She finally realises she has to make the first move, and flicking her long, dark, far too glossy hair back over her shoulder, smiles seductively at him.

'James darling, how are you?'

'Kat.' He nods curtly in her direction.

'You look surprised to see me here?'

'On the contrary, you always come back, Katherine. Like the proverbial bad penny.'

He turns back to me, cutting dead any chance of further conversation.

'That was rather rude,' I whisper in admiration.

'So is whispering,' he snaps, glaring at Katherine. 'I don't like her. She's a bad influence on Richard.'

'I always thought you were the bad influence on Richard,' I tease him.

'I may encourage him to go out and enjoy himself but never to lie and be deceitful, especially not to Sal.'

The usually laid-back James is rather uptight. Alarm bells start ringing again.

'Oh, yes. Do you know something I don't?' I try to look him in the eye, but he turns away.

'Forget it,' he mutters gloomily, now staring down at his empty glass, 'I shouldn't have said anything.'

'Look, James,' I put my hand on his wrist, forcing him to face me, 'I know their history. If there's something going on I want to know. It's not fair on Sally-Anne.'

He looks at me. I'm obviously not supposed to know Richard and Kat used to be an item. I can see him wondering how I got the information. He decides to confide in me.

'I don't know if there is anything going on . . . yet. I'm just going on past form,' he whispers, eyes darting around the table as he makes sure no one is listening to us.

'Past form?'

'Well, they were always bouncing off each other like a pair of bloody rubber balls once. I'm just worried they're going to collide again.' He shoots a black look at Kat.

I think back to her 'he loves me and only me' speech at the wedding, and a thought which had never really occurred before suddenly hits me.

'He cheated on me with her, didn't he?'

James doesn't reply.

'Didn't he?' I demand in a harsh whisper.

He won't look at me. That's answer enough. How could I have been so blind? I'm too glad to be shot of Richard for it to hurt, though I do feel a fool. He gets an extra point on my bastard rating.

'Look, I don't care about that. I got Richard's number a long time ago, there's nothing he can do to hurt me. It's Sally I'm worried about.'

'Don't worry, Fliss, I'll always look out for Sal,' he says tenderly, gazing over at her, his expression softening from angry to affectionate.

'This lobster has a very unusual flavour,' comments Ollie.

Sally chokes on her wine. We trade a glance. I can see her mouth curling up at the corners as she fights the urge to laugh.

'You'll have to give me the recipe. I hope it's not complicated, I'm an atrocious cook. What I really need is someone to take care of me.' He gazes meaningfully at Erica.

Am I imagining things or is she fluttering her eyelashes back at him?

'I think those two may have hit it off,' I whisper to James.

'Thank you, God,' he replies. 'If she gets it together with Ollie the Wally, she might just leave me alone.'

'They'd make a very odd couple.'

'Stranger things have happened. The most unlikely people form attachments. Love can spring from unexpected quarters.'

213

'You're telling me,' I sigh, looking across at Alex, who immediately looks away.

'You know, I always hoped Sally and I might . . . you know.' James gazes into the bottom of his glass and sighs, then looks back up at me and grins. 'But *que sera sera* and all that.'

'Sally?' Ah, so the quick change in the seating plan had more to it than a desire not to sit next to Erica. I should have guessed from his recent promise to defend and honour.

'Really?'

He nods.

'I'm sorry, I never knew.'

'I kept my feelings well hidden.' He laughs wryly. 'Too well hidden. I had this little fantasy of making my move at the wedding, best man and chief bridesmaid and all that, but obviously that wasn't appropriate in the end, was it, what with the sudden change in roles.'

'Well, you'd certainly be better for her than he is!' I cast a venomous glance in Richard's direction.

I think one of the reasons that I currently feel so bloody angry with Richard is that he nearly had me fooled. I really thought he and Sal could be happy together. The way they've been together since the engagement party, the nice Richard that came out when he was with her, I'd almost started to like him again.

There's been no sign of that Richard this evening.

He is chatting to, or should I say chatting up, Kat, leaning towards her so that no one else can hear what they are saying. He is forking up seafood with his left hand. His right is under the table.

James follows my gaze.

'I wonder what his other hand is doing?' he murmurs quietly in my ear, so that Sally, who is seated on the other side of him, can't hear.

I choke on a piece of squid. I can feel my face going bright red.

'James!' I hiss when I finally regain my composure. 'Behave.'

'Oh, darling, do I have to?' he drawls affectedly, running warm lazy fingers along my arm.

Alex shoots us a black look.

James shoots Richard a black look.

'You know, he may be my best friend but he can be a right arse at times!' growls James, pouring more wine into his glass and then mine.

Lounging next to me at the end of the table, licking those fat escargot lips like a lascivious lizard, sits Ollie, Erica to his left. Never one to dally, he has slipped off his black patent Gucci shoe and is pressing her ankle very firmly with a size seven foot.

'So tell me about yourself?' He smiles cheesily at her. 'What do you do all day, apart from look beautiful?'

'I'm a PA,' Erica giggles.

'I bet that stands for Perfectly Adorable?'

I cringe, but Erica is obviously unused to unadulterated, unappetising flattery. She goes pink, and attempts a coy smile.

'I need a new PA,' he continues, leaning in towards her. 'Perhaps you could come and work for me. I think we'd make a great team, as long as you actively enjoy DICKtation.'

He laughs. It sounds like a small donkey with a large pair of lungs. Hee-haw, hee-haw. He brings a new meaning to the word asinine. In fact, he is the perfect personification of it.

Richard laughs because Ollie is laughing. Alex and I look at each other. He shakes his head in semi-amused consternation, and I relax a little. At least we're not desperately avoiding each other's gaze any more like infatuated teenagers.

Ollie is still leering at Erica.

'You could sit on my lap and take down my particulars.'

Erica giggles. It's a good job she finds this funny, I'd have slapped the little toad in the face by now.

'He is such a prat,' confides James, not quite quietly enough. 'Ollie the Wally.'

Sally gives James a stern look, but I can see that she's suppressing laughter of her own. Ollie picks seafood out of his teeth with the surprisingly long and pointed finger nail on his little finger.

'No, being serious,' he breathes, smiling at Erica with his newly picked teeth, 'I do need a decent PA.'

'I thought he'd already got one in Richard,' I mutter to myself. 'Pathetic Arsehole.'

'So what's it like rejoining the world of work after your nice long summer hols then, Fliss?' Richard leans back in his chair at the head of the table and looks at me. 'How long have you been back? A monumental six weeks or so, isn't it? I don't know why teachers are always complaining about pay when they only have to work for eight months of the year. And let me see now, when's your next holiday? I do believe it's half-term next week.

Isn't that lucky? You must be worn out after working such a long period of time in one go . . .'

I ignore him. I know it's rude, but he only wants a reaction so I'm not going to give him the satisfaction of rising to his pathetic little jibes.

'I've always thought it must be so rewarding to pass on knowledge to eager young minds,' sighs Erica, whose happiest days so far were spent ruling as head girl at the girls' school my sister and I both attended. 'What are you doing at the moment?'

'I'm helping ninety-eight puberty-stricken teenagers murder Shakespeare,' I reply far from enthusiastically. It's not the Shakespeare part I loathe, I rather enjoy that, so much as puberty. It was bad enough going through it myself, let alone reliving its horrors through the upper-fifth.

'Oh, I love Shakespeare!' Erica claps her hands together like a child, a movement which makes her boobs judder like two basketballs hitting the hoop at the same time, and Ollie's eyes nearly pop out of his billiard-ball of a head. 'Which play are you doing?'

'*A Midsummer Night's Dream*, but it's more like a Midsummer Nightmare. Every time you say Bottom or Titania, they all collapse into fits of immature giggles.'

'I used to be a bit of a thespian myself,' announces Ollie.

'Until you had the sex change!' guffaws Richard. They laugh heartily at each other from opposing ends of the table. Honestly, they're worse than my upper-fifths! They've perfected this pathetic non-comic double act over the years.

'Me thinks I was enamoured of an Arsehole,' I murmur to myself, watching Richard turn pink with delight at his own wit.

Alex doesn't look very happy. He's stuck between Kat who is monopolising or being monopolised by Richard, I'm not quite sure which way round yet, and Erica who is being unbelievably attentive to the awful Ollie.

I smile at him.

He raises his eyes to heaven, and smiles back.

The tension's finally broken, but now I can't tear my eyes away. Alex has what Sally and I used to call nuclear eyes. They cause an immediate reaction resulting in total meltdown of your entire body and any living brain cells.

'It's rude to stare,' says James loudly, looking at Alex, looking at me sideways, and then flicking his eyes back to Alex again.

I blush and turn away. Alex takes a sudden interest in the tablecloth.

'How's everything in the world of publishing, Alexander?' Richard asks, dragging himself away from Kat to humour the husband.

'I personally think the standard of literature has deteriorated radically in the last decade . . .' Richard launches into this long diatribe about the merits of the latest books which continues well into the main course.

Alex is politely trying to maintain interest although his eyes are beginning to glaze over. James leans confidentially towards me.

'If looks could thrill . . .' he teases me. 'I saw you, Fliss Blakeney, making eyes at Mr Christian over there. I think I should warn Kathrin' Bligh to watch out, there's mutiny afoot.'

'Don't be so ridiculous!' I snap. 'You're imagining things.'

' "The lady doth protest too much, methinks," ' he quotes. 'Now which Shakespeare special was that from? *Romeo & Juliet* perhaps?'

'You know perfectly well it's from *Hamlet*.'

'I know.' He grins. 'But *Hamlet's* not quite so apt, now is it? So what gives, Fliss? Are you playing a little game of footsie under the table too?'

'Of course not. Absolutely nothing "gives", as you so quaintly put it.' I force a smile, trying to sound as normal as possible.

'Honestly?'

'Honestly,' I say.

Well, it's the truth, isn't it? Alex is married so nothing can happen, right?

'Good, because that means I'm completely at liberty to chat you up.'

He proceeds to do this loudly and unashamedly throughout the main course. James has always drunk like a fish. I think he must be fuelled by alcohol. The more wine he consumes, the farther his hands will wander.

Richard, who finished mutilating the beef about fifteen minutes ago, is still brandishing the carving knife around like Sweeney Todd, as he talks animatedly with Kat and Sally, who is seated to his left. I'm shocked but not surprised to find myself mentally willing the blade to slip. The cutlery did it, Your Honour. I'm not that bitter, am I?

Erica has abandoned Ollie and is talking happily to Alex. Ollie looks put out by this. Alex looks even more put out than Ollie as James's hand slips beneath the table and rather obviously along my thigh. He smiles lecherously as his hand leaves silk and encounters bare flesh.

'Silk stockings,' he murmurs happily, 'my favourite. Owwww!'

The exclamation of delight turns to a scream of pain as I stick my fork in his hand.

'Er, right, has everybody finished?' Sally tries to re-establish some order by starting to remove debris and empty plates from the table.

'What did you do that for?' James grumbles, nursing his pronged hand.

'Do you see "Public Access" printed across my forehead?' I stare haughtily at him.

'No.' He looks at my head intently. 'Nothing there, nothing at all. Perhaps it's printed on your knickers!' He pretends to dive under the table.

Sally comes back in bearing dessert: passion fruit ice cream smothered in a wickedly delicious-looking raspberry and orange coulis.

'Everybody for pudding?'

Kat starts virtuously protesting.

'Oh, no. It looks wonderful but I shouldn't. It must be simply bursting with calories, and I really ought to be thinking of my figure . . .'

'You've got nothing to worry about,' purrs Richard. 'You've always had a wonderful figure.'

She smirks happily. 'Then I might just succumb.'

'Suck what?' says James, deliberately mishearing, then roaring with laughter.

'Have another drink.' He sloshes more wine into my glass. 'Has anybody ever told you how attractive you are?' He puts down the bottle, and with his elbow on the table tries to rest his chin in his hand but misses, so rests his head on my shoulder instead. 'I think I need some coffee. How about you and me cutting out and going back to my place?'

I look across at Alex.

His face is as frozen as the home-made passion fruit ice cream.

I elbow James back into his seat.

'Oh, this looks wonderful, doesn't it?' I say brightly, accepting far too much ice cream.

'Stop changing the subject.' He looks sideways at me, and grins wickedly. 'Now that Sally is no longer available perhaps you'd care to console me on the loss of what could have been a beautiful relationship?'

'Are you propositioning me?'

'Of course.'

I could be tempted. James, despite being a terrible lech at the moment, *is* very attractive, but I don't want to be anybody's consolation prize.

Even I, usually too deeply immersed in Fliss World to spot unhappiness in other people, can tell that he is getting drunk and making advances to me because he's miserable about Sally-Anne. I don't want to try to take my sister's place in his affections. I want to be somebody's first prize. James is good-looking. He is also single, solvent, fun to be with, finds me attractive – with the help of two bottles of wine. What more could I want?

Unfortunately I know what more I want.

Alex.

He is so lovely he makes me salivate more than the passion fruit ice cream, but Alex is a forbidden fruit, that ripe juicy delicious pear dangling just beyond your reach on a tree in someone else's garden.

James is a friend, a good friend, but he's missing that X-factor that turns a man from a friend into an object of desire. Alex has my desired X-factor in overly large quantities.

It's not fair.

I try to think back to our first kiss, but I can't really remember it, I was too drunk. I mean, I can remember it happened, but I can't remember what it felt like. I feel robbed. I ran the risk of a 'dalliance' with somebody else's husband, and I can't even remember the bloody good bits.

I think on a bit to the second kiss, completely sober and standing in my kitchen. My stomach and other bits knot with desire. (It's either desire or the lobster *au* Jack Daniel's doing strange things to my insides.)

I know I did the right thing, but I could kick myself for turning away. I feel a foot rubbing against my leg. There's so much illicit foot-rubbing going on under this table it could be anybody. I calculate leg measurements and hazard a guess that it's James.

Ollie is close enough, but he's far too busy spoon-feeding passion fruit ice cream to a simpering Erica.

Since when did Erica learn to simper?

It's only when I stand up to go to the loo that I realise exactly how much wine I've drunk in the past two hours. It's not my fault. Every time I've put my glass back down on the table, James has refilled it. I head fairly unsteadily for the bathroom. Kat is just coming out, having spent ten minutes completely redoing her make-up.

'Oh, it's you,' she says disappointedly upon bumping into me in the narrow dark corridor. She was definitely hoping I'd be Richard, hovering in the hope that he'd follow her out, but he is playing far too devious a game to be so obvious in this respect.

'Are you having a good evening?' I can't resist the opportunity to dig for dirt, and Kat's usually happy to dish it.

'Oh, it's lovely to see old friends again, isn't it?' She smiles but this too is false. 'And to see the old place. It hasn't changed very much since I was last here.'

Now that is definitely a barb. Richard moved in here two months after he and I first started seeing each other. Again, I tell myself, I shall rise above it. I'm high enough on drink to do so quite easily.

'I'm having a lovely evening reminiscing,' she continues, 'although I don't know what's wrong with Alex, he's in such a foul mood.' She smiles smugly. 'Then again, I suppose it was rather cruel of me to bring him here when he's aware of the history Richard and I share.'

And the present you share as well, I want to add, but don't.

'Alex is well up on history and *current* affairs,' I say idly, but she's off, back down the corridor, spraying on more perfume as she goes.

I lurch into the bathroom and lock the door, peer at my face in the mirror and redo my lipstick. My eyes are bright and my cheeks are flushed. James may be a re-bounder, but it's still very nice to be chatted up by him.

A boost to the ego and libido.

The thing is, what am I going to do about Kat and Richard? I can't just sit back and let Sal take all the flak. After nicking some of her perfume, I walk out of the loo and shriek as someone steps out in front of me in the darkened corridor. As my eyes adjust to the light, I realise that it's Alex.

'Don't do things like that!' I breathe. 'You scared me half to death . . .'

He's leaning against the wall, hands in pockets, eyes glittering dangerously in the dim light.

'What the hell do you think you're playing at, Fliss?' he hisses.

'I beg your pardon?'

A surprise attack?

'With James – what are you playing at?'

'I'm trying to have a good time.'

'Oh, yes, and is your idea of a good time letting some drunk crawl all over you?'

'Well, you should know it is,' I hiss back at him. 'Just think back to the wedding!'

He looks crushed. I put a hand to my mouth in horror.

'Oh, no, Alex, I didn't mean that. I'm sorry, you know I didn't mean that. Especially as it was me who did most of the crawling, and I was far drunker than you were . . .' I tail off lamely, aware that I'm digging myself a deeper hole with each word out of my motor mouth.

He leans back against the wall, rubs his forehead agitatedly.

'You're driving me crazy, Fliss. Do you think I want to sit and watch while you publicly get off with another man?'

'I'd be more concerned about your wife than me. That's exactly what *she's* doing!'

Oh, dear, I really must learn to control my mouth. I take a deep breath and start again.

'Look, James is just a friend, that's all, we've always got on well.'

'Too well by the looks of things!'

'If you must know, he's got a thing for Sally-Anne, not me. And besides, who are you to lecture me? You're married, I'm not, I can do what I bloody well want to.'

'I know, I know.' His voice is strained, his eyes narrowed. 'I can't help it, Fliss, you do things to me . . . I can't stop thinking about you.'

Why did he have to say that? This is so difficult. I just about manage to resist hurling myself bodily into his arms.

'What do you want from me, Alex?' I ask, drawing back a

little just in case my self-control snaps and I make a lunge for his underpants.

He appears to regain some of his composure.

'More than I should,' he replies. 'Look, I'm really sorry, I shouldn't have followed you out here, and I shouldn't have had a go at you. You're right, I've got no claim on you.'

'No, but you've got a hold on me, haven't you?'

Does my voice sound bitter? Well, perhaps I am bitter, I don't need this.

'Have I, Fliss?'

'I don't have to spell it out, do I? Surely you know how I feel about you?' I mutter reluctantly, aware that if I start telling him I may not be able to stop.

'No, I don't know how you feel! That's the bloody problem. One minute you're all over me, the next you're pushing me away.'

'You want to know how I feel? You really want to know! I think about you every day. You're always in my head . . . it's driving me crazy. You know, I really think I'm going mad. There's hardly a moment goes by without me wondering where you are, what you're doing, whether you ever think of me, whether I'll see you. It feels like I haven't seen you for so long, each moment stretches to eternity. And all the time, I know that it's so unbelievably wrong for me to feel this way . . .'

I can hear my voice beginning to rise hysterically. Must get a grip. Self-control is my only salvation. I stop, take a deep breath.

'Look, I'm sorry,' I mutter, shaking my head, hardly able to look at him.

Alex shakes his head too, but he's half smiling.

'How come whenever I see you, you're either drunk or apologising?'

'Or both,' I laugh shame-facedly. 'I'm sorry, I think I'd better stop drinking.'

'No, I'm the one who should say sorry.'

'For what?'

'For this . . .'

He puts two fingers under my chin, gently tilts my face upwards, and kisses me. His eyes are open, studying my face intently, awaiting my reaction.

'You shouldn't have done that,' I murmur.

'I know, that's why I apologised.'

I reach out and run my fingertips gently down his cheek and across the full curve of his lips.

'I think you should apologise again.'

We slide conspicuously out of the corridor and bump straight into Sally-Anne carrying a pile of empty plates towards the kitchen. She looks at my flushed and guilty face, and then at Alex.

'Do you know, you're wearing more of Fliss's lipstick than she is,' she murmurs.

I grin sheepishly. Alex looks at me sideways, then frantically wipes his mouth. We both look back at Sally.

It's her move.

She winks at us almost imperceptibly, and carries on into the kitchen.

I look questioningly at Alex. Sally obviously knows something about Richard and Kat or she wouldn't have just let that go. I follow her into the kitchen.

'Sally?'

She is bending over the open dishwasher, stacking plates. She looks up at my voice, pushes some hair out of her eyes. She looks tired.

'Sal?'

'Don't ask,' she sighs heavily.

'What do you know?'

'Well, you'd have to be blind and stupid not to miss my husband and Kat falling all over each other all evening, and I'm certainly not blind.'

'You're not stupid either.'

'Are you sure? I'm beginning to have my doubts. I don't know if there's anything going on yet,' she echoes James, 'but they're playing games with each other at my expense, and I don't like it.' She slams the door shut on the dishwasher, and turns back to face me. 'You warned me, Fliss, but I wouldn't listen to you, would I?'

'Well, we don't know that there's anything going on between them, do we? They've always been flirty with each other. I suppose the fact they're doing it to your face . . .'

'Means they're not doing it behind my back?' She raises her eyebrows.

223

'As long as you don't get hurt, Sal, that's all I'm worried about.'

'Oh, I'm sure everything will be all right,' she sighs, picks up a cafetière and smiles wryly. 'After all, he can't have grown bored of me this soon after the wedding. Besides he hasn't been anywhere without me yet, apart from work, he wouldn't have had a chance to do anything. This is probably just an ego boost.'

'Well, Richard has such an enormous ego it needs a lot of boosting, believe me,' I offer in an attempt to be light-hearted.

Sally laughs quietly, but she's still not entirely happy.

'And what about you, Fliss?' She puts a hand on my arm. 'What if you get hurt?'

'Me?'

'Don't come the innocent with me, I know what I just saw. What's happening?'

'I'm damned if I know.'

I help her carry the coffee through to the lounge where everyone has adjourned from the dining room. The dimmer switch has been turned to low, Phil Collins on repeat play has now been replaced by Ollie with something even more soulful. He is knee to knee with Erica on the sofa. Alex and Richard are talking. Kat is sulking because Richard isn't talking to her. She is winding the tresses of her impossibly silky hair around her fingers.

Impossibly silky hair, impossibly sulky face.

James is pouring himself another whisky. His hands are far from steady. He tries to lift the glass to his mouth but misses. The cut-glass tumbler slips from his grasp and lands on the floor with a soft thud, spilling its contents in a fine arc across the sitting-room carpet. The carpet is impossibly thick, and like the walls impracticably cream. The golden liquid disappears into its depths, like water being absorbed by a sponge.

James picks up his now empty glass, and then gazes despond-ently at the well of whisky vanishing into the floor.

'Anybody got a straw?' He laughs. 'Fliss, my angel, where have you been?'

Forgetting the lost alcohol, he careers across the room towards me, swaying dangerously like a seasoned drunk.

'Come, my darling, I'm taking you home for some coffee and lick yours. Your car or mine?'

'Don't be so bloody stupid,' Alex glares at him. 'You're in no

224

fit state to drive, and neither is Fliss.'

'Then even better we shall share the back seat of a taxi.' James leers at me and slips an arm around my waist.

'I'll take Fliss home,' Alex says firmly, taking hold of my arm. He stares coldly at James who quickly releases me.

'Well, I'm not ready to go yet,' says Kat petulantly. 'I want to go through some old photographs with Richard.'

'Yeah, I bet she does,' I stage whisper, annoyed that nobody's bothered to ask if *I'm* actually ready to go yet.

Alex's grip on my arm tightens.

'Why don't you take Fliss and I'll run Kat home later?' Richard smiles at Kat, who stops looking put out and smoulders back at him.

I look at Sally who is pale and drawn. James is looking at her too. He turns to me, takes in Alex's hand on my arm, my flushed face, and winks slowly at us.

'Well, if that's the case, I shall stay and help Sal with the washing up,' he announces. 'Come along, my darling, let's see how many plates we can break.'

'But I've got a dishwasher!' she protests weakly as he ushers her into the kitchen.

Richard ushers Kat towards his study, and Alex frog marches me towards the front door. As we leave, we pass Erica and Ollie necking enthusiastically on the sofa. At last Cupid's arrows have hit the right targets. Both single, they are free to share an uncomplicated and wonderful love affair. I suppress the desire to applaud them.

Alex and I stand silently together, his hand still on my arm as though he's afraid I'm going to bolt, while the lift descends to the ground floor. I half expect a little red light to appear on the display panel, below B for Basement. A big H for Hell, 'cause I'm going straight there.

'I'm supposed to be morally supporting Sally,' I murmur as he shepherds me out of the building and down the road towards his car. 'How can I morally support someone when I've got no morals of my own?'

We drive back to my flat in silence.

Despite my protestations, I'm savouring every moment, just gazing at his profile as he easily manoeuvres the large car through the dark silent streets. Other senses are heightened in

225

the dim light. I notice the purr of the engine; the monotonous click of the indicator as he turns without direction down the right road. The sheer scent of him is erotic. Isn't it funny how smell evokes more memories than any other sense? Not sight, not sound, but smell.

When we reach my place, he pulls to a halt and switches off the engine. His hands are still gripping the steering wheel. He stares straight ahead. There is silence for what seems like an eternity, and then he begins to speak.

'Do you know how much self-control I've had to exert to stop myself from contacting you?'

He turns and looks at me with those amazing eyes, liquid, intelligent, and burning with warmth.

'In fact, I've exercised so much self-control, I don't think I have any left.'

His tense expression softens to a smile as he reaches out and pulls me towards him.

I suppose this was inevitable really.

The bedroom curtains are open. The room is illuminated by moonlight. He slowly pulls down the zip at the back of my dress, pushes the material away from my shoulders so that it slides easily from my body and falls in a crumpled heap on the floor.

Silently, slowly, I undo his shirt, button by button, until this too falls in a crumpled heap next to my discarded dress. He is obviously not a seasoned adulterer. Surely on the list of adultering dos and don'ts is the use of a coat hanger to ensure clothes remain crease and evidence-free.

Underwear next, and I'm surprised at how unselfconsciously he discards his, and how shy I suddenly become, but finally, with a little help from Alex, we fall naked together on to the bed.

Laughing, caressing, kissing slowly.

He is lean, firm, brown, well built, well hung. His skin is beautifully smooth, a magnet irresistibly drawing my hands and my mouth.

I've wanted him so much for so long.

His fingers slide over my breasts and down my belly, and I'm convulsed with a desire stronger than anything I've ever experienced before.

'I don't normally go to bed with someone on the first date,' I whisper as his tongue follows the route his fingers have just taken.

'We haven't even had the first date,' he murmurs, mouth and eyelashes fluttering against my flesh.

'Oh. No, we haven't, have we? Although I suppose this is sensible. Get down to the sex straight away, and then if that's totally useless we haven't wasted any time or effort going out with each other first.'

He pauses, draws level with me again and smiles, amused, running a fingertip lightly between my breasts, along the curve of my neck and across my mouth. He caresses my cheek with his hand then brings both of them to cup my face. He stares at me with those brilliant, intense eyes.

'Fliss.'

'What?'

'Shut up.'

He silences me with a kiss.

Chapter Ten

I wake enveloped in a golden haze of well-being. The pillow is still dented where his head lay. I can smell him on my sheets and on my body. If I close my eyes I can still feel the burning imprint of his fingers, the soft touch of his lips.

Gazing hazily at the clock on the bedside table, I'm surprised to see that it's gone ten. To think that only nine hours ago he was still lying beside me. I stretch luxuriously, indulgently, running my hands across my own flesh, the swell of my breasts, the slight curve of my stomach, reliving the feel of his touch. Lazy and hazy with pleasure I feel almost ethereal, like I'm dreaming while I'm still awake.

These pleasant thoughts are unpleasantly disturbed.

The doorbell is sounding frantically. Sighing, but still grinning like an idiot, I slide on my robe and pad barefoot across the room and out into the hall. The varnished wooden floor is cold against the soles of my feet, but I'm still insulated by the burning, caressing warmth that buzzes through my body like a live charge.

Without even checking who it is, I buzz them through from outside, and when I hear the footsteps reach the top of the stairs, pull open my front door. A small shaking figure is standing outside, hair slicked back from the rain, face white, eyes puffy and swollen with tears.

'Oh, Fliss,' Sally sobs, falling through the doorway and burying her stricken face in my shoulder, 'he's going to leave me and I can't bear it.'

I park a shaking, sobbing Sally-Anne on the sofa, and wheel out the brandy.

'What happened?' I probe gently, pouring two fingers for myself because I've got a horrible feeling I'll need it, and a whole hand for Sal.

Sally takes a sip of her drink, pulls a face, blows her nose on one of my tissues, and stops sniffing for long enough to speak.

'Last night, after you went, it was awful, Fliss, really awful. Ollie and Erica shared a taxi home not long after you and Alex left. Richard didn't even say goodbye to them, he was nose to nose with *her* on the sofa. James left at two and they were still reminiscing, laughing and touching all the time, even sharing the same glass of wine. You know, I actually felt like a goose-berry. *I* felt like a gooseberry, *me*, his wife!' She shakes her head in disbelief. 'She stayed for ever after you went. Hours!'

'Hours?' I query, ashamed to feel a certain relief in the knowledge that, having left my flat not long after one, Alex would have got home before Kat.

'Well, of course Richard had to take her home, didn't he?' Sally spits. 'Despite the fact that he'd had far too much to drink. He wouldn't hear of me calling a taxi. It was gone four when he finally came to bed. It doesn't take an hour to drive across town, now does it? And then this morning he made some lame excuse and went out.'

'Where did he say he was going?'

'He said he had to go into work for something. He never works on a Sunday, Fliss, never, but when I challenged him, he got so angry. Said that he had an important case on and he needed to research while the office was quiet, and if I didn't believe him I should phone Ollie.'

'And did you phone Ollie?'

'What was the point?' Sally nurses her brandy glass in shaking hands. 'Ollie would back up whatever Richard says, and I'd just end up looking like the stupid jealous wife. But then again, I suppose that doesn't really matter because that's what I am, isn't it? The stupid, stupid, jealous wife.' Her nostrils are flaring in anger as she speaks. She rubs a hand over her eyes, screwing them up in anguish.

'I know he loves me, Fliss, we just need a chance. If every-body would just leave us alone!'

She knocks back her brandy, and putting the glass on the coffee table begins agitatedly twisting her wedding ring round and round her finger. They have only been married for eight weeks yet it is already far too large for her.

'Bloody, bloody Katherine Christian! I've never hated anyone in my life, Fliss, but I hate her. You don't know how much I loathe that woman. We were fine until she stuck her oar in. Happy, really happy. But now, because of *her*, I'm just waiting for him to go. Any excuse and he'll run to her, Fliss, I know it. If she were free he'd go to her like that.' She clicks her fingers. 'If Alex were to find someone else . . .' She pauses and looks at me.

She doesn't need to go on. I understand what she's trying to say.

As Sally is leaving the phone begins to ring. It's Alex. I'm ashamed of how happy I am to hear his voice, sharply aware of the contrast between my happiness and Sally's misery.

'We need to talk, I'll pick you up in half an hour.'

Just the sound of his voice makes my stomach curl and flutter with desire.

Forbidden fruit. Devour the soft sweet flesh of a ripe peach, feel its juices flow over your lips and tongue, savour the taste and the touch – but mind you don't cut your mouth on the sharp edge of the stone because when the flesh is gone that's all that remains.

He arrives early while I'm still showering. He pulls me against him, kisses me slowly. His hands slide inside my bathrobe, curl around the damp flesh of my arse, pull me closer.

I respond hungrily, but Alex pulls away.

'Get dressed,' he laughs, 'I'm taking you out for lunch.'

'I'd rather stay in,' I murmur in disappointment.

'What about that first date?' He smiles. 'I don't want you to feel like you're missing out.'

Despite a very strong desire to take him back to bed, I smile, touched by the sentiment.

'Where are we going? Somewhere dark, where no one will recognise us?' I joke, rummaging through my wardrobe. 'Where can we hide away in an alcove or duck out of the back door if someone we know comes in?'

We pull up outside an old hotel on the outskirts of the other side of town, The Three Swans. An old coaching inn, still with its high arch leading through to the stables that have now been converted into a very good, very exclusive and very private restaurant. The restaurant consists of a main central area, providing room for about twelve small round tables and a jungle of exotic plants, and several more discreet booths around the walls, divided by the old wooden stalls topped with iron bars where the horses were housed.

We are led across the springy varnished wooden floor to one of these booths. The table has two cane chairs to one side and a wooden bench seat running along the back. It is set for two people.

'This is very secluded for someone who didn't want to hide me away,' I tease Alex.

He smiles and rubs his thumb across the palm of my hand, which he had admittedly been holding quite openly.

'I don't want to hide you away. I want to be alone with you,' he responds. 'Besides I like it here, and I wanted to share it with you.'

I slide on to the bench at the back of the booth. Alex sits opposite me with his back to the room, shielded partly from view by the largest aspidistra ever to emerge from soil. The smiling waiter hands us menus, large blue leather affairs. Mine has no prices. Alex asks for a bottle of Pouilly Fuissé.

The waiter leaves. I watch him walking obsequiously backwards, as though leaving the presence of the Queen. My eyes flick across to Alex, greedily devouring the sight. I long to reach out and touch him. He catches my gaze and holds it. The intensity of my desire for him must be burningly, blatantly obvious. Suddenly embarrassed I look away, study our surroundings. Anything to avoid that penetrating gaze.

Our waiter is returning, carrying a silver ice bucket and two glasses. As he passes one of the other booths the occupant calls out to him. He pauses, and balancing the glasses on top of the ice in the bucket, pulls a tab of matches from his pocket. As the match flares, the girl takes the man's wrist to steady it as she lights her cigarette, and the orange glow illuminates her face.

'I don't believe it!' My mouth falls open. A feeling of panic begins to rise from my stomach to my throat which responds by cutting off all contact with my vocal chords.

'What's the matter?' Alex asks anxiously, laying down his menu. 'You look like you've seen a ghost.'

I can only respond by sliding further down in my seat, putting one hand up to cover my face and pointing with the other to a table in an alcove behind us.

'Fliss, what is it?' Alex presses urgently, worried now.

I put a finger to my lips, urging him to lower his voice and direct his gaze to the object of my concern.

Alex turns. It's dark in the restaurant, but the long shining tresses and slender back of Kat Christian are unmistakable. She is wearing a cherry red jacket belted at the waist and a short skirt which stops halfway down her thighs to expose an expanse of long tanned leg, at the end of which is a Bally court shoe tapping irritably against the floor.

She is sitting with her back to us in the same position as Alex, facing into the booth, but every time the door opens she turns. She is obviously waiting for someone.

My voice returns but sounds thin and strangulated.

'Do you think she saw us come in?' I hiss.

Alex shakes his head.

'Do you think she'd still be sitting over there if she had? She must have come in just after us.'

'What do we do?'

He slides across from his seat on to the bench next to me. I can feel the solid warmth of his leg alongside mine, and get an immediate irresistible urge to run my hand along his inner thigh. Lust has no sense of timing.

'Of all the bars in all the towns.' Alex does a pretty good Bogart impression, and smiles wryly at me. But I'm not laughing, I'm staring at the door, just like Kat, at the person coming in. She stubs out her cigarette and stands up as he reaches her. He takes her hand and kisses her lightly on the cheek, then stops, looks deep into her eyes, and leans forward to kiss her on the lips.

She responds by twining a hand around the back of his neck and pulling him closer. Self-consciously they break apart, and together Kat and Richard slide into the shadows at the back of their booth.

Alex has also seen Richard's entrance. His eyes are narrowed like a cobra ready to strike.

'What the hell is *he* doing here!' he growls, then shakes his head. 'I might have guessed.' The waiter, who has been opening our bottle of wine, pours a little into Alex's glass and waits for approval. He looks somewhat put out when I reach across, grab the glass and knock the whole lot back like it's water.

'It's fine, thank you,' Alex dismisses him, looking back over to where his wife and her lover are seated, entwined in the shadows. Richard and Kat are openly necking now. I watch in horrified fascination as he slides his hands under her blouse and begins to knead her full breasts like dough.

I can't believe what I'm seeing. It may be dark and secluded, but it's still blatantly obvious what they're doing. I don't suppose they thought they'd be under such close scrutiny. I begin to feel like a seedy little voyeur, witnessing a live peep show.

'Do they really think no one can see them?' I breathe incredulously as Richard's hand slips down between Kat's legs.

'I don't think they care.'

'If I'd known he was this adventurous, I might have found him more exciting.' I laugh in embarrassment.

Alex shoots me an incredibly black look.

'Come on, we're leaving.' He stands up and throws a wad of notes down on the table without even counting them.

'We can't! What if they see us?' I panic.

'Do you honestly think they'll notice anything but each other?' he growls.

He grabs my hand and pulls me after him, striding quickly across the crowded room to the fire exit which is closer than the main doors, and partially hidden from view by yet another gigantic aspidistra and a six-foot screen of trellis trailing huge pale purple passion flowers. A true hot house. Even as we leave they're turning up the heat behind us.

The heavy door falls silently to behind us, and we find ourselves in an alleyway at the side of the restaurant. I can hear the crashing of pans and raised voices from the kitchen at one end, the buzz of traffic from the other.

It's raining heavily now. The gash of sky above us, an eight-foot gap between buildings, is smoke-grey and dirty. Alex is still holding tightly on to my hand, his grip so hard it's almost painful.

He pulls me round to face him. It's hard to read the mixture of emotions registering in his eyes and across his face but suddenly I feel desperately unsure of everything. He puts out a hand and pushes my already soaked hair away from my face. I can see fine droplets of water clinging to his eyelashes.

Hesitantly I reach out to him, pull him close, press my lips against his, run my tongue along each plump arch of flesh. He returns the pressure, kissing me softly, slowly. All the time his eyes are looking into mine as if searching for something. Abruptly his kiss gets harder. He backs me up against the wall, hooks his thumbs under the hemline of my skirt and pushes it up over my hips. I can feel the hard pressure of his thigh insinuated between my legs.

The wall against my back is harshly abrasive through the thin material of my shirt which is getting soaked and transparent with the rain. He's kissing me so hard I can't breathe, his fingers pressing into the bare soft flesh at the top of my thighs.

I can't help responding. My mouth falls open under his; my fingers caress the back of his neck. Just as suddenly his touch becomes more gentle, his kiss less urgent. I'm almost collapsing with desire, my legs are trembling, and despite the cold wind which is playing about us and the rain which is falling down on us like a waterfall, I feel an intense heat spreading through my entire body . . . and then I think of Sally-Anne, silently begging me with her huge sad eyes. I think of Alex's face at the sight of Richard with Kat, ablaze with anger . . . or was it jealousy?

I pull away.

'Was that for me or for Kat?' I whisper.

'What?'

I have to ask.

'Do you want me, or do you just want to get back at your wife?'

He steps away and looks at me, shaking his head in disbelief. His eyes are hard with disappointment.

'Grow up, Fliss.'

'I just want you to be honest with me?' I plead, suddenly desperately insecure.

Is this what they do? Is this just one big game to both of them? Am I Alex's revenge on Katherine for her behaviour? Is it tit for tat each time? She makes an outrageously obvious play for Richard, so he retaliates? Well, I don't want to be another victim in a game that could destroy lives.

'Have you any reason to think I never have been?' he asks me, still shaking his head.

'I want to know the truth. I want to know whether you really care about me or whether you're just playing games like Katherine? Is that what I am, Alex, a bit of tit for tat? I saw how angry you were in there when you saw them together.'

'What the hell do you expect – pleasure? You want me to be pleased about what we just saw?' He brushes his hand through his hair, raking away the rain. Why is he so bloody gorgeous?

'A lot of men get turned on by watching their wives get off with another man,' I whisper.

'Not in a crowded restaurant with an illicit lover, they don't!'

'Who are we trying to fool? We're just as bad as them, we were doing exactly the same thing,' I shout at him.

'Is that how you see us, Fliss, as a sordid little affair? You think I'm like Kat or Richard, that I'm only using you? Playing stupid games?'

'I don't know,' I wail plaintively.

'You're the one playing games with me, Fliss. You can't keep pulling me in and then shoving me away, you've got to make up your mind what you want.'

'I know what I want, but . . . but . . .'

'But what? What do you want to do?'

'I want to do the right thing.'

It sounds so bloody trite when I say it.

'And what the hell is the right thing anyway?' he mutters angrily.

'I don't know. I just know you're married so this is wrong.'

'Married!' He almost spits the word. 'After what we just witnessed, you still think my marriage means anything? Come on, Fliss, if you don't want to see me, at least tell me why. Be honest with me, you owe me that much.'

'I am honest with you.'

'Honest with me? I'm not sure you can even be honest with yourself.'

He turns and begins to walk away. I stand rooted to the spot watching him go, soaked to the skin, in a tumult of emotion. He's right. How long has it taken me to admit how I feel about him? And now I'm letting him walk away again. I'm shaking from cold, frustration, helplessness, fear.

He's only gone a few paces when he turns back to me.

'Come on, I'll take you home.'

We drive to my flat in silence.

As he pulls in to the kerb, I reach hurriedly for the door handle, but he leans over and grabs my hand.

'No, don't go.'

I pause.

'Fliss, I need to know how you feel about me? What you want from me? What you want *us* to be?'

I look at him sideways, and feel desperate with wanting him.

236

'All I know is I've never felt this way about anybody before, but everything's just so bloody complicated.' I can feel the tears flooding down my cheeks, like the rain running steadily down the car windscreen, and turn away in embarrassment. The upper-fifth were right, I should change my name to Wuss.

'Please don't cry.' His voice is gentle and full of anguish. He pulls me close, stroking my hair, soothing me like a child.

'I thought, because you were so angry, that you were jealous of Kat and Richard,' I sob.

'No.' He shakes his head. 'I wasn't happy, but I wasn't jealous. It just brought it home to me, that's all. You were right, Fliss, when you said that we were as bad as them. It made it seem so cheap – it made *us* seem cheap. I don't want it to be like that, Fliss, I don't want clandestine meetings in secluded restaurants or soulless hotel rooms. This isn't something wrong and dirty. What I feel for you isn't sordid and sullied, to be hidden away like some dark and disgusting secret.'

He looks at me warily under soft dark lashes, his eyes cloudy and uncertain.

'I know what I want. I'm going to leave Kat, Fliss.' He kisses me with infinite tenderness. My stomach dissolves like Alka-seltzer in a glass of water. Bubbles of lust rise from my groin to my throat, and escape in an involuntary moan of pleasure.

'Do you know what you want, Fliss?'

I know what I want. I want this moment to be frozen so that I can stay here forever, being held by him, so close.

And then I think of Sally-Anne, in tears on my doorstep, silently begging me not to give Kat the push she needs to take Richard away for good.

I draw away from Alex as though distancing myself physically will help me pull away emotionally.

'I want you to go home, Alex, go back to Katherine, make it work if you can.' The words almost choke me, and the pain as I see the surprise and hurt in his eyes is almost unbearable.

'What? But I thought . . .'

I put two fingers to his lips to silence him.

'It will be better for everybody.'

'How can you say that?'

'I know Kat must love you, Alex.' I force a smile. 'How could she not?' I pause. 'And Sally-Anne loves Richard . . .'

He nods slowly, registering this last, and then exhales deeply, audibly, a long sad sigh of resignation.

'I think I understand.'

'Do you, Alex? I really need to know that you do.'

'Sure.' He puts out one hand and tentatively strokes my cheek. I can feel his hand trembling.

The rest of the day is an eternity, stretching beyond the realms of endurance. I just want to sleep but I can't. I'm strangely calm, all cried out, but my spirits are leaden. They lie like a dead weight in the pit of my stomach, physically hurting. Can you understand what it's like wanting someone so badly, needing someone so much that every second spent without them feels like a lifetime?

Outside the sky has turned the most amazing shade of pink, touching the houses with rose-coloured fingers, spreading like a huge soft blanket across the horizon. It's so beautiful, but even as I watch in awe the pink gradually begins to fade to grey and then inky swells of ominous black.

Dangerous and threatening.

But still beautiful.

Only now, when it's too late, do I realise exactly how I feel.

'I love you, Alex,' I whisper to the heavens, and as if in response they begin to cry for me, great sheets of rain thundering down to hit the ground like the lash of a thousand whips.

I wake the next day feeling empty and horrible. The rain has stopped and a pale yellow sun is smiling weakly in a cerulean sky, like a patient on their way to recovery. I throw the sun a rude gesture for looking so happy. I want the black clouds to come back, they suit my black mood. I want the rain to come and weep against my window panes. I want to play Cathy and run wailing indulgently across bleak moorland.

When the phone rings I pounce upon it like a starving man on a crust of bread.

It's Dad.

He's happy, he's relaxed, he's enjoying life. He wants to share this with me, especially when he realises that I am currently wallowing in the exact opposite frame of mind.

'It's half-term this week, isn't it? Why don't you come and stay, Fliss? I miss you, and it will do you good to get away from everything for a few days. Besides, I really do want you to meet Florrie.'

Sure, but does Florrie want to meet me? I finally give in and agree to visit. As usual I'm running away. When the going gets tough, Fliss gets going. I head into town to buy a suitcase – my only decent one's still at Caroline's along with half of my clothes. I think she's holding it to ransom to make me visit.

When I return the light on my answer machine is blinking epileptically. A surge of hope, but it's only Wiggy calling to say hello from some beach shack bar somewhere. I can hear music and laughter in the background, and she sounds happy, relaxed, and more than a little pissed. For a moment I wish I'd followed my plan of heading out to join her.

Half-way through packing the phone rings again. I pounce on it like a fretful dog, waiting for the sound of his master's key in the lock. Am I always going to be this jumpy whenever the phone rings?

Again it's not Alex.

Then again, why should I expect him to call when I was the one who sent him away? Reeling him in and then out like a yo-yo tied to my finger, up and down like the painted wooden horses on a merry-go-round.

This time it's Sash.

'Hiya!' Her cheery voice rings painfully in my miserable ear. 'How are you doing, you old tart?'

Well, of course, it all comes flooding out, doesn't it? Never ask a miserable person how they are unless you want a full run down on whatever affliction it is that happens to be making them miserable.

Of course Sash wasn't aware that I was miserable when she phoned, so she wasn't forewarned and therefore gets to listen to a wailing woman for the fifteen minutes that is her entire coffee break when really she just phoned for a gossip. Running true to form as a bloody good friend, however, she listens until I'm totally whinged out, and then announces that she's coming round.

'But you're at work,' I sniff.

'Well, I've suddenly developed severe PMT. My boss is terrified of PMT, he'll send me home straight away.'

Sure enough Sash is round in half an hour, bearing a bottle of brandy and a box of chocolates.

'I want all the gory details first,' she demands, making us both a coffee and tipping a liberal dose of Napoleon's finest into each mug, ignoring my protests that it's only three in the afternoon.

'You mean the sex, don't you?'

'Of course. Come on, Fliss, neither of us has actually had any for so long, talking about it is almost as good as the real thing.'

I shake my head.

I can't help it, a slightly smug smile spreads slowly over my face.

'Well, let's just say up until Saturday night . . . well, Sunday morning to be precise . . . I might have agreed with you. In fact, I might even have gone so far as to say talking about it is actually *better* than indulging . . .'

'But not any more?' she prompts me.

'Definitely not any more.'

'That good?'

'Better. In a way it would have been better if it hadn't been so good, then it would have been easier to give it up. Oh, Sash, it's all such a mess.'

'You could try and look on the positive side . . .'

'You think there is one?'

'Well, I hate to harp on about one thing, but at least now you know what it's like to have great sex.'

'True, but that definitely makes it worse. I may never have mind-blowing, all-consuming, let's do it straight away, great sex ever again.'

'Well, I can sympathise on that front.' She raises her mug to me.

'Oh, Sash, I'm sorry, I feel really bad. Here I am moaning away about my own sad life when you've got plenty of problems of your own, and I haven't even asked about them once.'

She shakes her head.

'Don't worry about it, babe. I should be thanking you actually.'

'For what?'

'Well, one of the reasons I phoned today was to call you in on that favour I spoke to you about.'

I bite my bottom lip.

'Yeah, right, you wanted me to be your alibi, didn't you?'

'Well, I did, but actually I've changed my mind.'

'I can't say I'm disappointed, I would have hated lying to

240

Niall, but why? What's happened in the past half an hour to make you decide not to go through with it?'

'You've happened.' Sash laughs. 'Or should I say your love life? So really I should thank you for making me realise how lucky I am. Life has seemed so mundane recently. All kids, and work, and mortgages and bills, and a husband that I love but know just a little bit too well at the moment. I've been craving excitement like a serial dieter longing for cake.'

'And now you don't?'

'Well, you've made me see that excitement can sometimes be over-rated. Complicated, in fact. I don't really want to lose what I've got. If I start playing around then there's a very strong chance I will, and just end up being miserable instead of frustrated, or both. Oh, my god, think of that! No, I think if I just spice up my own life a little, I could be very happy.'

'So you've counted your blessings then?'

'Something like that, yeah. Sod the twenty-two year old, I think a trip to Anne Summers and a pay rise for my babysitter will do nicely as a starter.'

'Instead of a raging affair with some young stud?'

'You've hit the nail on the head.'

'Glad I could help.'

'I should think it's nice to know that your own dreadful mistakes can have a good effect on somebody else.'

'You're taking the piss, aren't you?'

'Who, me?'

'Yeah, you're taking the piss, admit it?'

'Just a bit. But, hey, isn't that what friends are for?'

The following morning I set off for Kent to stay with my father, carefully leaving an answer phone message that will give all and sundry my mobile number in case of emergency.

As I carry the cat up the narrow stairs to the flat above, she begins to purr again for the first time in weeks. I hand her over to the girl upstairs and the purr becomes pneumatic.

'I think you'd better keep her, you obviously belong together,' I say ruefully.

They both look highly delighted.

'Never did like cats anyway,' I mutter as I descend the stairs two at a time in a fit of reckless pique. 'I think it's about time I got that dog – a stupid, lovable, cuddly, faithful mutt.'

Half an hour later, still not quite believing that I'm actually doing it, carefully sidetracking all the practicalities of dog ownership like the fact that I live in a flat and work full-time, I'm walking along cell block H of the local dog rehoming centre. Row upon row of unwanted, unloved, sad, excited dogs.

'Can I have them all?' I ask the handler who's showing me round, tears pricking hotly at the back of my eyes.

She smiles indulgently. She's obviously used to mad lonely women looking for a man substitute.

I walk up and down the corridor like an expectant father awaiting the birth of a child, filled to the brim with indecision and compassion.

And then I see him.

He's brown, he's fat, he's completely unrecognisable as a breed. He's sitting right at the back of a large cage on his own while the rest of the pack clamours at the wire for me to notice them, and he looks miserable.

I look at him. He looks at me.

'That's the one.' I don't point, it would be rude.

'Are you sure?' The assistant looks at me as though I'm stupid.

I nod enthusiastically. 'He's mine.'

'He's only a puppy, he'll grow bigger.'

'Bigger than that?' I say incredulously. 'What is he, a dog or a pack horse?'

'I thought you wanted a small dog, madam, due to lack of space?'

'I'll move,' I say adamantly, and mean it.

I recognise something in those doleful, hopeful brown eyes. Myself.

I crouch down so that I'm on a doggy level, and make encouraging noises, and wiggle my fingers through the wire mesh. He looks over at me, looks around as if to say, Surely she can't mean me, she must be wiggling at someone else, and then sort of shrugs and ambles over trying not to look too hopeful. He sniffs my fingers cautiously then looks up at me with the cutest brown eyes, and grins.

I fall in love instantaneously.

I smile soppily back at him.

He sort of slobbers on my hand.

242

'Can I take him now?' I ask the assistant.

'Well, I'm afraid it's not usually possible . . .'

'Pleeease,' I grovel. 'I'm a school teacher – that means I'm reliable, right?'

On my way out of town, with my suitcase in the boot and Eric the dog on a blanket on the back seat, I realise I have taken the route that leads past Alex's office. I can see his car in the car park. I wonder which of the many windows blinking hazily in the morning sun is the window to his office. I wonder where he is at this very moment, what he's doing, what he's thinking. Does he think of me as often as I think of him? Does he feel the same dull pain, born from the futility of wanting someone you can't have, the incessant fear that I might never see him again, the need, the endless unforgiving, soul-destroying need?

I shiver, although it's far from cold, and angrily brush away a tear that's dared to slide from my right eye, determined I will no longer be Fliss the Wuss but Fliss the Fearless, who can stand up to and cope with anything life cares to throw at her.

Eric, who is pretending to sleep, hears me sniff and opens one eye. He squeezes between the two front seats and clambers on to my lap, settling down with a deep contented sigh. He must weigh about three stone, and every time I change gear he almost slides down my leg and jams against the throttle, but he's warm, and solid, and comforting.

He must be bloody uncomfortable with his head in the side pocket and his fat backside hanging over the handbrake, but he shows no inclination to move, and I have absolutely no inclination to make him. It's very nice to be unconditionally adored for a change.

Chapter Eleven

The route to Florence's cottage takes me through the Chilterns, practically straight past Angels Court. I drive one mile further on, before exhausting every argument against it and turning back. When I get to the gates that lead to the house, I hesitate. I can see the roof of the old building above the trees that line the perimeter of the property. Along the ridge balance a flock of delicate grey ring doves calling softly to each other.

It's nine-thirty. David will have gone off at least four or five hours ago to toil away on his beloved farm, so at least I shan't have to face both him and Caro at the same time, which should make things a little easier.

I drive slowly down the gravel driveway, and pull to a halt next to Caro's immaculately clean Golf GTi. It puts my mud-splattered car to shame. I've always wondered how she can keep her car so clean living in the country, but then she's always been more lady of the manor than Farmer Giles's wife.

Or should that be Lady Chatterley? Then again Lady Chatterley restricted her extra-marital bonking to just the gamekeeper, didn't she? I think they should give Angus Macready a new job title. Stud manager would be far more suited than farm manager.

Looking in the rear-view mirror, I'm surprised to catch myself smiling.

The early morning, which amazingly promised sunshine, has fulfilled that promise in spectacular style. As I step from the car the sun beats down upon my bare head. A lone bee is skimming the great clumps of buddlia and roses massed around the front lawn, and a pair of bluetits dart across it to settle in the cool dark green shade of a holly bush. An Indian Summer has crept up on us, drying the damp grass as quickly as blotting paper absorbing a pool of spilt ink.

I hesitate before pushing the doorbell set like a thick brass

245

nipple in the wall. Why does it suddenly seem so bloody phallic? Taking a strong mental grip, I manage to connect with my finger and press.

The old bell echoes melodically through the house. I hear the clatter of feet on the wooden staircase, and then the heavy scrape of metal against metal as the thick bolts are drawn home. Caro swings open the door. She is wearing an old shirt of David's spattered with yellow paint, cut-off jeans and faded espadrilles. Her golden hair is loosely secured at the back of her neck with an old Hermès scarf, and her face is bare of make-up. She looks totally amazing as usual.

'Hi.' I smile tentatively.

The surprise on her face changes instantaneously to delight.

'Fliss! How lovely!'

She reaches out to hug me, hesitates and takes my hand instead, drawing me inside.

'Hannah's out, she'll be so disappointed she missed you.'

'I can't stop long,' I point to where Eric is hanging out of the back window of my car, tongue lolling hotly out of his mouth. 'Can't leave him in there in this weather. I'm just on my way down to visit Dad, so I thought I'd call in and see how everyone here is.'

Eric is already proving useful in the excuse department.

'You've got a dog? When did you get a dog?' Caroline exclaims.

'About an hour ago.'

'Why on earth have you got a dog? What are you going to do with it?'

'Er . . . well, the *usual* things, I suppose, like walks and stuff.'

'That's not what I meant and you know it. You don't even have a garden, Fliss.'

'I know. Don't worry, I'll figure out the practicalities as I go along. I think I'd like to move to somewhere bigger anyway, and Edwin the caretaker at school brings his dog into work every day so perhaps I could too.'

'Sure, but that's a bit different. He spends a lot of his time outside, you're stuck in a classroom.'

'Well, Eric's very good at looking attentive. I can sit him at the front of my class as a good example, and teach him Shakespeare. He'll probably grasp it better than most of my pupils.'

'What about the cat?'

246

'We decided an amicable separation would be best for both of us,' I reply.

Caro laughs loudly, putting a hand to her mouth, her pale cheeks flushing pink with amusement.

'Fliss, you're mad.'

'I know,' I mutter, thinking not of the oh-so-happy-to-be-departed Hastings or of Eric, but of Alex and Sally and Richard and Kat and everyone else involved in my fiasco of a life. 'I'm cracking up, Caro.'

'Absolutely barking!' she jokes.

I hang back, unsure what to do or say, but she has no such reticence.

'Come and see the baby's room, I've been dying to show it off to someone.'

She takes me upstairs to the room beyond theirs.

'I know I'm a bit ahead of myself, it's only been a couple of months and you can't even tell Hannah's pregnant yet, which she's highly delighted about, I can tell you, but I thought I may as well get started.'

'I don't know about get started, it looks like you've nearly finished.'

The spare bedroom has been transformed into a nursery with lemon walls, enough toys to start a crêche, mobiles of amazing mythical creatures dancing lightly in the breeze that blows through the open window, and a lemon-washed wooden cot and matching wardrobe, with a pale blue design of soldiers and dolls and jack-in-the-boxes hand-painted on them.

'Well, you know me, once I get an idea into my head . . . I know it's early days yet with Hannah, anything could happen really.'

She reaches out and superstitiously touches the wooden edge of the cradle, getting more yellow paint on the tips of her fingers where it hasn't quite dried.

'But David and I have made a decision that if this doesn't work out, we're going to try for a baby of our own.'

'But I thought . . .'

'IVF, adoption, whatever it takes. I never realised how much I wanted a child until now,' she says wistfully, then forcing a smile on to her sad face surveys the room with pride.

'It's all my own work, you know. I think I have quite a flair for this sort of thing.'

'It's great,' I agree, 'very professional.'

'Could make a good sideline for when I'm not changing nappies, don't you think? Caroline Hunter Interiors has quite a ring to it, doesn't it?'

'What about school?'

'Well, actually, I wanted to talk to you about that, but you haven't really given me much of a chance, have you?'

I shake my head contritely.

'I've spent the past thirty odd years of my life at school, I think it's time I had a change,' Caro continues bluntly, 'so I've decided to leave.'

'I thought you might,' I reply. 'I shall miss you.'

'Will you?' She looks at me sideways.

'Of course I will.'

'Good,' says Caro. 'But of course you'll come to visit often, won't you?'

She looks at me, her head on one side, eyes hopeful and questioning.

'Of course I will,' I agree, and she smiles in relief.

Apparently Hannah is suffering all the awful symptoms of pregnancy such as morning sickness while a radiant Caroline is the one with the glow and the gloriously shiny hair. She seems so excited, far removed from the Caro who always swore she'd never have children of her own.

'Why did you never tell me you couldn't have them?' I ask curiously, leaning on the window ledge to look out into the garden before realising that the paint is still wet there too.

'I suppose I didn't even want to admit it to myself, let alone anyone else.' She smiles now, and hands me a cloth. 'But then again, there are quite a few things you don't know about me,' she teases.

'I thought I knew everything now,' I say in mock horror. 'What other terrible secrets are lurking in your lemon-washed closets?'

She grins.

'Don't worry, there's nothing else. You know me totally, warts and all.'

There's a moment's silence.

'You look great,' I venture. 'Hannah's pregnancy suits you.'

'I can't believe how excited I am about this.' She smiles and then looks anxiously at me, peering at the dark circles under my eyes, pursing her lips in concern.

'But how are you, Fliss? I must say, you look tired.'

There's a sign up at work. 'Do you feel most of the following?' it asks. I ticked them off one by one.

Loss of energy? Yes.

Tearfulness? Yes.

Guilt? Yes.

'You could be depressed,' it announces happily at the end.

'Life is rather complicated at the moment,' I offer, but I'm not in the mood for a heart to heart, and Caro is far too intuitive to press for information at the wrong moment. Feeling comfortable enough to forget the excuse that I'm in a hurry, we take a jug of weak Pimm's out on to the lawn, and sit on wrought-iron chairs with pale yellow cushions under the shade of the wizened old apple trees, as we did earlier in the summer.

Distant memories.

Eric, released and watered, wanders round the vast lawn incredulously sniffing as though never having seen such exciting things as trees and grass before, lifting his legs in a very wobbly amateur way against anything upright, peeing as though he'll never get another chance.

'He's just been sprung from canine jail,' I explain to Caroline, who smiles indulgently, though whether at me or at Eric I don't know.

'Who'd have thought we'd have weather like this at the end of October?' she breathes happily. 'Especially as yesterday I was wrapped in my winter woollies toasting my toes on the Aga.'

She turns and puts a hand over mine, her blue eyes direct and warm with affection.

'I'm so glad you came, Fliss. Really I am.'

'So am I,' I agree, squeezing her hand. 'I think I've laid a few ghosts.'

'Well, I suppose that's better than laying the neighbours!' she laughs.

I finally head off just before midday, cruising fairly well down the M40, then crawling my way along the hideously busy M25 which is bumper to bumper with half-term holidaymakers, finally hitting the civilised beauty of Royal Tunbridge Wells just after three, hot, sweaty and ready for road rage or a large alcoholic drink, neither of which is a very good idea at the moment.

Ten miles on and things are getting pretty rural. The road I'm following is little more than a track; I have to stop every five minutes to open and close a gate or bump uncomfortably over a cattle grid. Eric thinks it's a great game to leap out of the car every time I do and let me chase him round the fields several times before we get back in again.

The dog obviously has a warped sense of humour.

I think I like it.

I reach my destination as the church clock strikes five. Bishops Cross is a tiny hamlet, hidden at the bottom of what is more of a bowl than a valley, surrounded by a mantle of woodland. It's a bit like driving over the horizon and into Brigadoon.

Apart from the church, which is situated in the grounds of Wakeley Hall, a well-known weekend retreat of one of London's most notorious backbenchers, there are a few stone cottages dotted around a handkerchief-sized village green complete with pond and obligatory ducks.

There is also a picture-postcard pub – Dad wouldn't live in a place that didn't have at least one of these – and a small post office selling everything from stamps to exotic spices, and hung with riotously coloured hanging baskets.

It's so gorgeously quaint I almost expect to see Noddy and Big Ears tootling down the main street in their little red car. It's the sort of place that instantly makes you feel better about the world. If it can house something so lovely then it can't be all bad, can it?

Florence's house used to belong to the Wakeley Estate. It's hidden away down some back lane that seems to wind on forever under a canopy of dark golden beech trees. Dad's directions were pretty hard to decipher, but I finally pull up outside Bluebell Cottage, only to find I can't get out of the car.

I'm tired, hot and thirsty, and highly relieved to have got here, but suddenly so nervous it's untrue.

So many emotions, so little time.

I'm suddenly a six year old again, and overcome with crippling shyness.

I manage to get out of the car only to sit on the bonnet for another ten minutes, trying to pluck up the courage to go and knock on the door.

What if I don't like the love of my father's life?

Worse still, what if she doesn't like me?

Bluebell Cottage is long and low, and made of crumbling yellow stone. Ivy crawls up its walls to tap at the bedroom windows with pointed fingers. A lone swift is catching the flies that hang in a cloud above me, no doubt regenerated by the sunshine. She swoops and snaps, flies away to disappear under the eaves, and moments later circles back to swoop and snap again, accompanied by another of her dark sleek ilk.

I look closer. There are several muddy brown upturned igloos nestled under the eaves.

'I see you're admiring my swifts? They're so graceful, aren't they? They come back to me year after year, my little friends, I should be quite lost without them.'

Florence walks towards me across the immaculate lawn.

It has to be Florence. Dad told me quite proudly that she is beautiful, and it would appear that he wasn't exaggerating the way you do when you're in love with someone, and everything about them, from their sparkling eyes to their habit of biting the skin at the edges of their toe nails, seems attractive.

The sun seems to follow Florrie across the garden, lighting on her white-blonde hair like a halo. She moves a little stiffly, yet gracefully. As she comes closer, I can see that she looks slightly younger than my father, that her face is lined, her smile easy, and her eyes the colour of a bluebell and as bright as the early-evening sky.

'They've normally left me by now, but perhaps they knew this glorious weather was on the agenda. You must be Fliss. Do you mind if I call you that? Your father talks of you so often, I feel as though I already know you.'

She extends a slim hand. She has long fingers devoid of any jewellery. Her nails are neatly manicured, and although her skin is soft, when I politely take her hand, I can feel the calluses of the keen gardener.

'You must call me Florrie. We're in the back garden, your father and I, making the most of this miraculous weather.'

She leads me across the lawn to a path which winds around the side of the cottage. The rear garden is a riot of autumn flowers, sadly battered by the recent storms but now recovering in the gentle Indian Summer sunshine.

Dad is seated at a white wrought-iron table, reading Dick Francis. Roger lies panting at his feet. Dad looks strong and

251

brown. Like a snake shedding its skin, the years have fallen away from him. He reminds me a little of the flowers, battered by a life with stormy, wintry Miriam and now being nursed back to health by sunny late-summer Florrie.

He gets to his feet when he sees me coming, a huge grin splitting his craggy face from ear to ear. He reaches out to me, envelops me in a long-armed hug, squeezes the breath from my body with pleasure.

'Darling! How wonderful to see you.'

He smells comfortingly of childhood memories, of pipe tobacco, spicy aftershave, and the distinctive smell of lamb's wool sweater. As he kisses me, his moustache tickles my face.

'What do you think to my daughter then, Florrie?' he proclaims proudly, releasing me from his bear hug and swinging me round to face her. 'Didn't I tell you she was beautiful?'

'He said the same thing to me about you,' I say shyly.

Florrie laughs. I can see her smiling at my father. Her eyes are coy, like a young girl in the first flush of love.

'He's an old flatterer,' she chides, but her voice is soft and full of affection. As she smiles the myriad fine laughter lines around her eyes deepen. She must laugh a lot.

'I hope you don't mind but I brought an extra guest with me,' I venture uncertainly.

'You did?' Dad is curious but unperturbed. 'A male guest perhaps?' he asks, voice full of innuendo.

'As a matter of fact, yes, he is,' I tease. 'He's waiting in the car. He's a little nervous, doesn't get out much, hasn't quite picked up the usual social skills . . .' I confide in a whisper.

Dad nods in understanding, and rubs his hands together briskly.

'Well, let's go and put the poor chap out of his misery then, shall we? The sooner introductions are over the better.'

We walk back around the house towards my car. Dad rests a hand on my shoulder.

'I must say,' he smiles happily, 'I'm rather glad you've found yourself another chap . . .' He stops as we reach the car.

Eric is leaning in friendly fashion out of the window.

'I'm really sorry to spring him on you unannounced, but it was a spur-of-the-moment thing.'

Dad starts laughing.

'Well, hopefully he'll be easier to train than a new man.'

252

'And more loyal,' I add.

Florrie treads softly up the path and joins us.

'What a lovely little chap,' she murmurs, stroking his head.

Eric closes his eyes and grunts in appreciation.

'I'd hardly call him little.' Dad wipes his eyes with his handkerchief. 'What is it, Fliss?'

'A dog,' I say defensively.

'Are you sure? He looks more like a pot-bellied pig to me,' Dad guffaws, then looks apologetically at my uptight protective expression.

'I don't know,' I mutter. 'Heinz probably.'

'Well, I think he's wonderful,' says Florrie, smiling reassuringly at me. 'Lovely nature obviously.'

I decide that Florrie has a lovely nature, too, as Eric rewards her with a curling kiss on the inside of her wrist.

'You don't mind me bringing him, do you?' I ask uncertainly.

'Well, we certainly don't, do we, darling?' Dad squeezes Florrie's arm. 'But what Roger will make of him, I do not know!'

We return to the back garden. Eric immediately introduces his nose to Roger's backside.

Roger delicately removes himself from Eric's nasal intrusion, circling him like a fat black vulture, thumping his tail slowly and warily.

'We'll take them for a stroll together,' Dad suggests. 'See how they get on. And I can show you round a little. Are you coming with us?' He turns to Florrie, who shakes her head.

'You go, I have dinner to see to.'

Dad and I go through a gate at the rear of the garden into the wood that surrounds it. We follow a twisting path strewn with leaves turning crisp as toast in the unusual warmth, and then walk through the beautiful parkland of the Hall.

Stately lawns, statuesque oak trees, sweeping vistas. It's all so beautiful. Dad proudly points out the local landmarks. The cottage where some well-known musician hides out on odd weekends, his presence heralded by the swell of loud rock music floating through the trees. The folly where the notorious back-bencher was caught with the well-known musician's girlfriend. The blood-stained flag stone where the musician hit the back-bencher full on the nose. He takes me to see the crumbling grey Bishop's Cross itself, erected in memory of an historical event not dissimilar to the one just described, but made infinitely more noble and romantic by the passage of time.

Dad doesn't press me for information or news from home, simply chats about our surroundings, about his new garden, about how happy Roger is to be living in the countryside. We need to talk, but I'm grateful for his intuition that now is not quite the right time.

We walk arm in arm back to the house as the sun is slowly sinking behind the trees, casting a soft warm orange glow over the green and russet leaves. Florrie's darting swifts have been replaced by bats swooping blindly overhead like little black shadows. The air is growing cool. We can see the lights of Bluebell Cottage blinking through the trees as we approach like the welcoming lights of a harbour across the sea.

Outside, Dad pauses and takes my hand.

'This place is more of a home to me than The Beeches ever was,' he says. 'Always remember, it's not the bricks and mortar, it's the people that make a place welcoming. Florrie and I want you to think of the cottage as a second home, Fliss.'

She is waiting with a welcoming smile. I'm still shy of her. We tread around each other, smiling, polite, unsure.

After dinner we sit drinking coffee around the open fire which is lit and casting dancing shadow-pictures across the walls. Mozart is playing on the old gramophone. Dad and Florrie keep trying to engage me in conversation but my brain and my mouth once again aren't functioning in anything remotely resembling harmony, and I've not even been drinking!

Roger is stretched out on the hearthrug. I am seated on the floor with my back against the floral chintz sofa, Eric stretched heavily across my legs, snoring quietly. Dad and Florrie are sitting together, discreetly holding hands, resting against each other like bookends with no books to support. When the small German clock atop the Adam fireplace finally strikes midnight, I suddenly realise how very weary I am.

I think of where I was this time four nights ago, and sigh heavily. If only I could jump through time at will I'd just keep going back to the same moment when I was lying naked in the arms of an equally naked Alexander Christian.

For some reason I think of Sash mouthing 'Phwoar' at me the first time she met him. I wonder where they all are now? What they are doing? Has she managed to tempt Niall out of his period of purdah with some edible massage oil and a naughty night nurse outfit? Is Richard at home with Sally-Anne or out on the tiles with the shitty Kitty Kat?

I tell myself to call them both in the morning, especially Sal, and make sure that everything's OK, but I know that I won't because I'm too scared of finding out that it isn't.

Dad is watching me intently.

'Are you all right, Fliss? There's something wrong, isn't there?' he probes gently.

'No, of course not,' I lie, scratching Eric behind his ears. 'I'm fine, just a bit tired, that's all.'

Dad shakes his head, not believing me.

'You can't pull the wool over my eyes. I'm still your father, remember. I've known you far too well for far too long not to know when you're upset about something. You've been so quiet all evening.'

'It's a man, isn't it?' says Florrie intuitively. 'It has to be a man, they seem to be the main source of misery.'

Dad raises his bushy eyebrows at her.

'Oh, yes? So that's what you think, is it?'

'Oh, and of course a source of infinite happiness,' she laughs. 'If one's lucky. Which I am.'

She squeezes my father's hand and they both smile indulgently at each other.

'Well, Fliss?' he asks in concern.

'Nothing's wrong, honestly, I'm just a little tired like I said. It's been a long day. Actually,' I yawn widely as if to prove my point, 'I think I might go up to bed.'

'Of course.' Florrie gets quickly to her feet. 'I'll help you take the rest of your things up.'

My room is a quaint little place tucked away under the eaves. Its sloping ceiling is too low for Dad to stand up straight, even at the highest point. It's painted a delicate rose pink, and the throw on the bed and curtains at the little paned window blinking blackly under its fringe of shaggy ivy, are tiny rose print.

A huge cream earthenware bowl full of meadow flowers sits on the tallboy, casting powdery scent across the room. The floor is of bare boards with a raffia rug of palest pistachio green thrown across.

'I hope you like it?' Florrie says anxiously. 'That's Elliot.' She indicates a huge shaggy brown bear seated on a Lloyd Loom chair in the corner. 'Drew thinks I'm daft, but I thought you might like the company.'

'Well, good night, dear.' Dad leans over, kisses my cheek and ruffles my hair like I'm a ten year old again. 'Sleep tight.'

A door at the other end leads into a tiny shower room, with just enough space for the shower cubicle, a loo, and a corner washbasin.

All I want to do is fall into bed and sleep, but I feel dusty and dirty and horrible so I drag my weary body under the shower. I wish I hadn't had to wash for the past four days. Not because I'm a disgusting tramp who likes to be stinky, but I hated washing away the smell and the touch of Alex from my body.

I haven't washed the pillow that his head lay against, though. It's faded, but I can still distinguish his scent on it.

I have a sad confession to make.

Ignoring my new suitcase, I head for the overnight bag on top of it and pull back the main compartment zip. Sitting inside, instead of the usual assortment of clothes, is that pillow. Carefully pulling it out, I press my face into the soft cotton, and breathe in heavily. I feel like a sad perverted knicker sniffer. And, yes, if I could have done, I would have kept *those* as well.

Unfortunately I think it might have looked a bit odd, him arriving home without any on, and an 'Oh, whoops, the rest of your clothes are on the floor where we dropped them but I appear to have lost your underpants' probably wouldn't have washed with Alex either.

To my chagrin, the small smile that this thought induces begins to wobble pathetically, and the next thing I know the tears begin to fall again.

The return of Fliss the Wuss.

I wake at ten the next morning, still hugging the pillow as though my life depends on it. I must have cried myself to sleep. I feel stupid and pathetic, but a whole lot better for being so stupid and pathetic.

I shower again, this time revelling in the sharp needles of water stinging my lethargic libido into action, then change and make my way downstairs. I can see Dad in the garden kneeling arthritically by a border dead-heading delphiniums in a masterly way that even Aunt Vera would approve of. I've never seen him look so happy and contented, especially not while gardening.

Back at The Beeches he used the garden as a means of escape from Mother; now his objective is pure pleasure.

I notice, happily, that there is no shed in this garden.

Roger is lying loyally and lazily by Dad's side. Eric is chasing Roger's tail, which is wagging slowly from side to side like a pendulum. Backwards and forwards, backwards and forwards he goes, never seeming to tire of his fruitless monotonous chase. I wish I had his energy.

Another beautiful day has dawned. The sun is streaming through the gauzy curtains, lighting on the old dark oak furniture which shines with warmth after years of being lovingly polished over and over again. On top of the baby grand piano that takes pride of place at the end of the room like a queen holding court are numerous framed photographs.

I wander over and pick up an old sepia-coloured print of a handsome laughing young man leaning against the bonnet of a vintage Morgan.

'That's my husband Alan. He died a long time ago.'

I turn. Florrie is standing behind me, looking over my shoulder at the photograph I'm holding.

'He was very handsome,' I say, studying the laughing eyes and the easy smile.

'Oh, the cream of the crop.' She smiles.

She reaches over and picks up another photograph, holding it out to me.

'That's my daughter Helen. My lovely grown-up daughter. Don't you think she looks like her father? It was taken on her thirtieth birthday last year. Her husband Peter, that's the lanky dark-haired chap behind her, well, he's American. They live in Florida so I don't get to see them very often at all.' Her voice is wistful, and then full of pride as she picks up another photograph of a very pretty child.

'And this beautiful young lady is my granddaughter, Abbie. She's four now.'

'You must miss them.'

'Oh, yes, very much. I haven't seen them since this photograph was taken, but Helen writes to me often. We have quite a correspondence going! I should have shares in the Royal Mail, the amount I pay each month for postage stamps . . .'

I pick up another photograph of a brown-eyed little girl with golden skin and hair. It takes a moment for me to realise that

I'm looking at a picture of myself. Next to this in a heavy silver frame is a picture of Dad, Sally-Anne and me. I think it was taken one summer in France. I was seventeen, with brown glowing skin, wild hair, and long lanky legs in cut-off jeans. Wow, was I ever that slim! Sally was just ten, small, slim and dark, huge eyes in a small pale face, but still as pretty and serene. Dad is standing between us. He has his arms around our shoulders and is grinning broadly. His already greying blond hair flops over his face, and he looks young and tanned and very handsome.

Beyond that is a photograph of me at my graduation, and one of a young Sally as an angel in a Christmas Nativity play. Then Dad proudly displaying the capture of a prize carp on the banks of the local river, and the three of us perched on a lion at the foot of Nelson's column.

They are all familiar scenes, but not familiar photographs. The only photograph ever to be displayed at home is of Sally and Richard, on their wedding day. It now takes pride of place on the mantelpiece in a new and very expensive frame. It's a very good shot of Richard in his penguin suit, but not a particularly good likeness of Sally whose pretty face is partially hidden by her veil. Mother polishes it every day. She'll have rubbed away the gilt in no time.

'You see, I know you all by proxy.'

Florrie watches me anxiously as I incredulously work my way through a photographic family history. She smiles affectionately, hesitantly, and I suddenly realise that she is as desperate for me to like her as I was nervous about her liking me.

'You've been rather like an extended family to me,' she says almost apologetically.

Florrie too has photographs of Sally's wedding. There's even one of me, as I predicted, all hat, lips and legs but fortunately no face.

'Your father got them for me,' she says wistfully. 'I would really have loved to have been there.'

'I wish you had been.' I turn and smile broadly at her. 'I could have done with a friend.'

'The sun's past the yard arm,' announces Dad, hauling his long frame from one of the low chintz sofas. 'Anyone for a jar?'

'Goodness!' Florrie looks up at the pretty grandmother clock

258

ticking quietly in the corner. 'Is it that time already? You two go, I must start lunch.'

'Are you sure?' I ask, aware that she has been deliberately fading into the background all morning so that I can be alone with my father. 'I'd like you to come.'

She looks pleased, but still refuses.

'Of course I'm sure. You two have some catching up to do.' She and Dad exchange a glance. In other words he is to have some time alone with me in order to attempt to worm out whatever terrible secret is making his elder daughter such a misery guts.

'We should stay and help you with lunch,' I say, not at all sure I'm ready for the third degree.

'Nonsense, you're a guest. Besides shelling peas keeps my fingers supple, it's good for my arthritis.'

'Well, why don't you come and join us when you're ready?' I reach out and touch her hand. 'Honestly, I'd really like you to.'

The White Horse is small and low, made of crumbling white lime with black beams holding it together like the whale bones in a corset pinioning a genteel old lady. As we duck under the low portal and enter the cosy, smoky gloom, Dad is hailed from all sides. He's obviously a regular. It's really odd to think that these people have known my father for over six years. He's an old friend to them, even though this part of his life is totally new to me.

'Hello, Evan,' Dad hails a short, swarthy, moustachioed man behind the bar. The landlord smiles broadly to reveal a row of beautiful white teeth, lined up in shell pink gums like little even tombstones.

'Afternoon, Drew, the usual?' Even though he looks like an extra from *The Magnificent Seven* his voice is low and local, a soft burr that's reminiscent of those wonderful bread ads with fields of golden corn waving like a crowd of football fans, and rustic old farmers leading shire horses across a pink sunseted horizon. He reaches for a bottle of whisky perched upon the top shelf.

'No Roger?' he queries.

'I've got better company today.' Dad smiles and squeezes my hand.

'So I see.' Evan turns his broad white grin on me. 'Aren't you going to introduce me then?'

'This is my elder daughter, Fliss.'

'Daughter? No! I don't believe you. How did a hoary old sod like you produce a beautiful young girl like this then?'

We take our drinks outside, and sit on one of the beer-stained benches overlooking the village green.

'Your health.' Dad raises his glass. 'Well, what do you think to my Florrie then?'

There's obvious pride in his voice and in that 'my' Florrie.

'She's lovely,' I reply, pleased and relieved that I can answer truthfully.

'I knew you'd like her.' He smiles in relief. 'She likes you too, you know, a lot, I can tell. I've been so happy since moving down here, my darling, it makes me wonder how I managed to stay with your mother for so long.'

I've often wondered that too.

I pull the lemon slice out of my G & T and suck the flesh, revelling in the sour taste. It matches my lingering sour mood. I've also recently wondered why Dad never felt he could confide in me about Florrie, and to be honest I feel a little hurt.

'Why didn't you tell me about her, Dad?' I ask hesitantly.

'Fliss, what's the matter?' He immediately picks up on the tension in my voice.

'Nothing, I'm happy for you, honestly I am, it's just . . .'

It's hard to explain how I feel. Being here in Dad's alternative life just brings it all home. Feelings surface that I've buried because I feel bad about feeling them, because I know what an awful loveless existence he's had to bear.

'I thought we'd gone through this. You said you understood, Fliss?' Dad looks hurt.

'I know, I do understand. I understand your reasons for wanting to leave a miserable existence with *her* . . .' I allude to my mother with about as much affection as a cow would award Ronald McDonald '. . . and gain happiness with someone who loves you. What I don't understand is why you never told me what was going on. Perhaps I'm not being fair, but I feel like you've deceived me. I thought we were so close, I thought you could tell me anything. So why didn't you tell me about Florrie before?'

He stares deep into his glass and nods his head.

'You're right, I should have told you, but I was ashamed of myself, Fliss. I mean, no matter what the circumstances, it's still wrong, isn't it? Having an affair? No matter how badly I got on with your mother she was . . . is still . . . my wife. It entails an awful lot of guilt.'

He's telling me! Guilt still flies in ever-decreasing circles around my head, the old ever-present vulture on the wing.

'You know, it's such a relief to get everything out in the open,' Dad continues. 'I still feel guilty about what's happened, but at least I'm not creeping around making excuses and lying to people about where I've been or where I'm going.'

I stay silent.

He sips his whisky, and opening a packet of plain crisps, begins to feed the ducks which have wandered over from the pond on the green in search of sustenance.

'How's your mother?' he asks, crumbling crisps on to the ground, not looking at me.

'Oh, busy making Sally's life a misery as usual.'

'Oh, dear,' Dad sighs.

'She won't leave them alone. Richard probably thinks he's married Sal and Mother, not just Sal. Love me, love my mother.'

'Oh, dear,' Dad repeats, taking another fortifying slug of his malt.

'The way things are going they don't stand a chance. I mean, things are ropey enough with this other business, they don't need Mother on their backs or in the spare room the whole time as well.'

'Other business? What other business?' His attention veers away from the pretty little mallard shovelling hopefully around his feet with its shoehorn bill.

It's my turn to say, 'Oh, dear.'

I put my hand over my mouth, like a schoolgirl who's just let slip a secret.

'Fliss?' He looks worried.

'I didn't want to say anything,' I mumble, going red.

'Fliss, if there's a problem I think I have a right to know, don't you?'

I nod my head slowly in agreement.

'You never know, I may be able to help.'

'OK,' I say reluctantly. 'I'll tell you. The problem is, where do I start?'

Chapter Twelve

'You see, if Alex and I . . . well, if he left Kat then there'd be nothing stopping her from running straight to Richard,' I finish lamely, and look from Dad to Florrie who has left the joint to roast and walked up to join us.

They look at each other. Dad shakes his head.

'Oh, Fliss,' he sighs, 'what a mess. If only I hadn't been so selfish . . . I should have stayed and made sure you were all right.'

'Don't be silly, Dad, none of this is your fault. Besides if you had have been there, what could you have done?'

'I could have kept your stupid mother from interfering in Sally and Richard's marriage for a start,' he says angrily, 'I might have known she couldn't leave them alone. I feel so guilty.'

'You're telling me,' I groan. 'I feel so rotten for poor old Sal. If it's anybody's fault then it's mine. When I left Richard I never even dreamt the consequences would be so awful.'

'You weren't to know what would happen,' Dad defends me quickly.

'Yes, but I knew about Kat and Richard's relationship before I . . . well, before Alex and I . . .'

I trail off, then try again.

'I mean, it's bad enough that Alex is *married*, let alone the fact that he's married to her! "Thou shalt not covet another man's wife", and all that. I could be really literal here and say that there is absolutely no mention of not coveting another woman's husband, but we all know the truth, don't we?' I sigh, resting my chin in my hands.

Florrie flicks her gaze over to Dad and then back to me. She looks embarrassed.

'I'm sorry,' I gasp as I realise what she may think I was implying, 'I'm not getting at you, honestly I'm not. I haven't offended you, have I? I really didn't mean to at all.'

'Of course not, Fliss,' she says quickly, 'I know you didn't mean it like that. Tell me about Alex. How do you feel? Do you love him?'

'Yes . . . no . . . I don't know. Yes, I do. I really think I do, but maybe it's best if I try not to think about that one at the moment.'

I rub my eyes. They ache. My head aches, my brain aches, although judging from recent events it's not from overuse.

'I'm so confused! All I know is I want to be with him, but I can't. I can't stop thinking about him. I want to be able to touch him, to hold him not just in my head and my heart but in my arms . . .'

I stop, suddenly very embarrassed.

'I'm beginning to sound rather Mills & Boon, aren't I?'

'The language of love is full of clichés, corn, and good old genuine horse manure,' laughs Florrie. 'It's the sincerity that counts.'

'We grow some of our most beautiful roses with the help of a little horse manure,' agrees Dad.

'So you sacrificed the man you love for the sake of Sally-Anne and Richard's relationship?' Florrie says quietly. 'It's a shame Richard isn't worthy of such magnanimity.'

'Oh, I didn't do it for him,' I say hastily. 'No way! As far as I'm concerned, he and Kat make a bloody good couple. They deserve each other. I did it for Sally, because she loves him and I don't want to see her get hurt.'

At least, I hope Sally loves him. She says she does. I've always found it very difficult to believe that somebody as infinitely sensible as she could love someone like him.

'Do you believe in love at first sight?' I ask Florrie, remembering Sally's words.

'Oh, I believe in love at first sight, but then again your father keeps telling me I'm the last of the true romantics. But I have to believe in happy endings. It's that belief that kept me going all these years waiting for Drew.'

'Why did you wait for him, do you mind my asking? I mean, you knew he was . . . I'm sorry, but it would really help if I knew, if I could truly understand.'

Florrie reaches out and touches my hand. My flesh is cold, hers warm. It's an intimate gesture, carrying genuine affection, and I appreciate it.

'I knew your mother didn't love him. If I'd thought she did I could never have taken him away from her. It's not a role I wanted to play Fliss, the "Other Woman", it just happened, I'm afraid. I fell in love with Drew. It's very hard to fight such strong feelings. I just knew I had to be with him, no matter what.'

'But Dad was so unhappy, and you loved him . . . why wait so long?' I turn to him. 'Like I said to you when you first told me about Florrie, I don't understand why you stayed with Mother for so long.'

'Duty, misplaced loyalty, sheer stupidity . . .' Dad shrugs and smiles ruefully.

'And he had you and Sally,' says Florrie softly. 'I know you were all grown up and had left home but when I first met your father, Sally-Anne was still only sixteen. When you're that age you feel awfully grown up, but really you're only a child still. If Drew had left then it would have torn her apart.'

'Florrie was my salvation,' Dad says, gazing lovingly at her. 'My light at the end of a very dark tunnel.'

He puts one arm around her waist and squeezes gently.

'I don't know what I would have done without her.'

Florrie rests her other hand on his knee and smiles up at him.

'I may never have met your mother, Fliss,' she says to me, 'but I think that I understand her. That may sound like an awfully arrogant statement, but I know Drew inside out, and through him I know your mother. I know what she did to him, Fliss, inflicting a loveless, lifeless existence, and I know what she did to you. She caused you all so much unhappiness, but sadly I think that only came about as an extension of her own discontent. I don't mean to sound patronising, but I really do feel sorry for her.'

I nod my head in agreement. 'So do I, but she's taught me a valuable lesson. I don't want to make the same mistakes as she did.'

'So what do you intend to do, Fliss?'

'You know, people keep asking me that and I haven't the faintest idea. All I know is that I'm trying to do the right thing. If I just stay out of everybody's way. Sally and Richard, Alex and Kat, well, they might all be able to sort themselves out. I'm just an added complication in an already disastrous situation.'

'Does Alex have any children?' asks Florrie.

'No. I don't see his wife as the mothering type at all, not

unless a child becomes the next ultimate fashion accessory.'

'You don't like her very much, do you?'

'Is it that obvious? No, I don't. I know I'm not exactly whiter than white in this whole thing, but as far as I can see she's playing a dangerous game that's messing up a lot of people's lives. But, like I said, who am I to talk? We all have our own private guilt, don't we?'

Dad and Florrie exchange a look.

'I think it would help if I knew what she wanted – Kat that is. If it's just one big ego boost or if she actually really loves Richard . . . look, I think I'm going to go out for a walk. Clear my head.' I stand up.

'Are you sure you should?' says Dad anxiously.

'Well, I'm allowed to cross the road on my own now. Honestly, Dad, I'll be OK. I just need to be on my own, to think . . .'

'OK, darling.' He nods. 'We'll see you back at home then. Just remember one thing, Fliss. As you grow older your perspective on life changes. You learn that sometimes trying to do something for the right reasons means you end up doing the wrong thing for everybody . . .'

The Wakeley Estate is a very good place for indulging in a little heartache. An hour later, an hour of wandering self-indulgently through lonely groves, of pressing my forehead against tree trunks, of sobbing dramatically against the statues that are dotted throughout the estate like mythical creatures hiding from the outside world, of pouting with Pan and petulance with Persephone, of aching with Aphrodite and . . . well, sitting down and feeling sorry for myself next to Zeus, I realise that I am lost.

Typical really.

Just when I thought my self-esteem could sink no lower, I have to lose myself.

The Bermuda triangle of Bishops Cross.

My father managed to disappear down here for years without ever being found out. Perhaps I should bring Kat here and set her free amidst the shrubbery, hopefully never to be seen again. Then Sally and Richard will be left alone, to get on with their marriage and make it work, which would also have the added advantage of a certain person being minus a wife.

Could bumping off Kat Christian be the answer perhaps?

Maybe I could train Eric to savage on sight. I doubt it, though. The only thing sweet-natured Eric ever sinks his baby teeth into is food.

I wish I had him with me now, he could probably sniff out home just from the smell of lunch wafting gently toward us on the breeze.

Where the hell am I?

I'm trying very hard not to cry again, I've really done far too much of that just lately. If I keep it up at the current rate my cheeks will begin to corrode from all the salt water running down them.

I swivel round like a satellite searching for radio waves, and sigh with relief as I finally spot a familiar landmark. I can see the church spire through the golden canopy of trees, guiding me like a beacon.

The interior of the church is cool and dark. It smells of incense and strong wood polish, of old damp hymn books and musty hassocks. I'm drawn inside by the magnetism of some higher perfect force that can forgive even when we can't forgive ourselves, that will love even when we don't love ourselves.

I walk up the aisle, running a cold hand along the smooth wood of each pew end.

The last time I was in a church, Sally was marrying Richard. I never thought I could be more unhappy, but here I am, misery personified.

I don't like living with myself at the moment, I hate being around miserable people.

Dear God, I pray, give me the strength to do the right thing, to resist temptation. P.S. Could I have a lot of strength, please, because my particular temptation is pretty bloody irresistible?

You know, I always thought that love was God-given, but I realise it's wrong for me to love a married man. It's very confusing. I suppose I ought to try to transfer my feelings for Alex on to a higher, more spiritual plane, but it's very hard to disassociate the mental from the physical where he's concerned.

My only consolation is that I've done the right thing.

The right thing for who? Whimpers my heart dejectedly.

I nearly jump out of my skin as the sombre silence of the old church is broken by the sound of my mobile phone, finally receiving a signal and trilling the arrival of a voice message. I relax a little when the first voice I hear is the happy upbeat tone of Sash.

'Hello, flower, it's Tuesday, it's midnight, and I just wanted to let you know that I'm sitting in bed in a torn naughty night nurse outfit, covered in half-consumed edible body lotion, and smoking my first ever cigarette. And what's even better is that the kids are at my mother's so as soon as Niall has woken up from the best night's sleep he's ever had, we're going to do it all again! Love ya! Hope you're OK. Tatty 'bye.'

Good old Sash.

Or should that be good old Sesh, 'cause she's finally had one?

I feel a huge sense of relief that she is happy. Let's just hope Niall can keep it up, in more ways than one!

I'm still giggling as the next message gets underway, but the smile's wiped straight off my face.

It's Sally-Anne.

She doesn't say much, just hello really, asks if I'm OK and then asks me to call her as soon as possible. But it's not what she says, it's how she says it.

She's normally such an upbeat person. You know, the sort of person you either really envy or could quite cheerfully slap because they always wake up smiling, even on a dark rainy Monday winter's morning.

Today she sounds like she's just discovered her first grey hair, her first cellulite dimple, and her first major wrinkle all at the same time.

Worried, I phone Sally-Anne's work only to be told that she's off sick.

Sal is *never* sick. She's far too healthy.

I can't sit down here, hiding away from everything, hoping it will all blow over and everybody will end up living happily ever after. It's not going to work like that. It can't in a situation like this. Somebody is going to get hurt.

I thought if I handled it the way I have been then I could limit that hurt just to me, but I see now that I can't. All I've done is left Sally-Anne to face everything alone.

I've got to go back.

I finally arrive back at Bluebell Cottage just as Dad, Roger and Eric are about to form a search party. They are sitting in a dejected row by the front gate, awaiting my return. Dad is looking at his watch, his face drawn and anxious. Roger's ears are pricked alertly listening for my footsteps. Eric is licking his own bottom, although the minute he spots me he attempts to transfer his tongue to my face instead, an affectionate gesture which although much appreciated is not accepted.

Lunch is a quiet affair.

I announce my intention of going home, and Dad and Florrie are united in their attempts to persuade me to stay. They're so keen in fact that I end up agreeing to stay until the following morning, instead of leaving this afternoon.

Once lunch is over, I volunteer for the washing up. Eric and Roger, the twin waste disposal units, sit at my feet, clearing scraps.

They have hit it off extremely well, best friends in less than twenty-four hours. Life is so much easier for a dog. Eat, sleep, walk, sniff, scratch, their five main senses, far more sensible and less complicated than human emotions.

The last plate dried and put away, I go out into the garden. The Indian Summer was perhaps only an Indian Summer's day; the brilliant sunshine is fading away like a false promise. It's four o'clock in the afternoon. The last rays of sun are only weakly warming, and the sky is already turning the palest dove grey.

There is a slight breeze blowing from the north, but protected by the house the south-facing garden is still relatively warm. I sit down on the bench at the far end. Through the French doors into the lounge I can see Dad and Florrie curled up on the sofa. They are idyllically happy together, and while the sight of them makes me incredibly happy, I can't suppress a slight pang of jealousy.

Still, Florrie had to wait nearly six years for her man. She deserves to be happy now. I really don't know how she managed to do it. It's only been four *days* since I last saw Alex and look what a sorry state I've been getting myself into.

A bee is droning drowsily in a lavender bush next to me, a quiet consistent buzz like the noise of Mother manically hoovering every Saturday morning. I'm enveloped in the soft heat, fanned by the slightest of breezes that whispers across my face, the birdsong a lullaby to my tired mind.

I close my eyes, the two bottles of wine we consumed with lunch helping me surrender to sleep. I can feel my mind slipping

269

away. Hazy, fragmented images flit and dart across my vision like the swifts.

A shadow falls across my face. I look up and smile sleepily at Alex who smiles tenderly back at me, his aquamarine eyes sparkling like the sun upon the sea. This is a lovely dream. It's so wonderfully vivid I can even smell the glorious heady tang of his aftershave.

'Hello, Fliss.' His voice is tender.

'Hello, gorgeous,' I murmur.

'Fliss?'

He leans down and touches my face, pushes the hair out of my eyes. His hand feels warm and solid. Blinking hazily, I reach out and touch the very substantial material of his jacket, and realise with a jolt that I'm no longer dreaming.

'Alex?' I sit bolt upright, shooting Eric, who had been resting once more across my knees, on to the grass at my feet.

'I think I prefer gorgeous.'

I rub the back of my hand across eyes.

'What are you doing here?'

'Well, that's a nice welcome. Aren't you pleased to see me?'

A dying man is pleased to see an oasis until he realises it's only a mirage.

Alex sits down on the grass next to me and starts to stroke a slightly disgruntled Eric who, giving me a dirty look, transfers the solidity of his large hairy body on to Alex's lap instead, and settles down with a contented sigh.

Alex looks tired. His beautiful eyes are shadowed, his hair is tousled, but as usual he is breathtakingly desirable.

I move away from him, breathing in so hard I think I might pass out, but there's no way I can touch him. I know what happens when I touch him, self-control loses it entirely; self-control trots off happily to that little grey Bermuda triangle in my head where decorum vanishes while I'm drunk.

Alex looks at me, silently, appraisingly.

'Well, aren't you going to ask me what I'm doing here?'

'What are you doing here?' I repeat blankly.

Distractedly he starts to scratch the rough hair on Eric's head.

'I told her,' he finally ventures.

'You told her what?' My voice is less than a whisper.

'That our marriage was a farce. That I'd fallen in love with someone else . . .'

He loves me.

A surge of hope, a fresh renewal of guilt.

Joy and pain, lovely mixture.

'But that I was prepared to make a go of things if she was. To try and set everything straight . . .'

Joy departs, pain remains and doubles in quantity and quality.

He's come to tell me that he and Kat are going to work at their marriage, that I should just forget about him. This is what I've been telling myself is the right thing to happen, this is what Saint Felicity had convinced herself she really wanted, so why does it hurt so much?

'Oh.' I sigh heavily, all the air released from my lungs like a punctured balloon.

'I'm really pleased it's all worked out OK for you both.'

'Honestly?'

'Honestly. I just want you to be happy, Alex.'

Well, that's true enough. Although it would be quite nice if I could be happy too. But that's what's been scaring me so much for the past few weeks, I don't know if I can be without him.

However, if you love someone, set them free. I used to think they were stupid lyrics, but Sting was spot on unfortunately. The best thing I can do is put on a smiley face and wish him well. The right thing to do is often the hardest thing to do. The smile is found weak and wanting.

'You *are* happy?' I have to ask.

'Oh, I think I will be, amazingly so.'

'Then I'm happy too,' I mumble, crossing the fingers of the hand furthest away from him. I force myself to look up at him. Look into those laughing eyes, at the person I've grown to love so deeply my gut twists with longing every time I think of him.

He certainly looks happy.

His eyes are shining so brightly he could do for Optrex what a dazzling smile does for toothpaste. A smile is playing about his lips, almost as though he could burst into laughter at any minute.

'You don't *look* very happy, Fliss.' His voice is teasing.

What does he expect?

Fireworks?

Tap dancing?

For him to make a go of his marriage really is laudable, but for

271

me it's not a cause for major celebration. I've lost someone I love. It's all too much. I wanted to be strong, I wanted to be pleased, I *am* pleased but . . .

I'm fighting, but I can't hold back the tears.

He stops smiling.

'Fliss.' His voice is low and uncertain.

He reaches out and touches my face, gently wipes away a tear with his thumb.

'Do you love me?'

I close my eyes. 'Thou shalt not covet' is battling desperately with 'Thou shalt not lie.'

'Do you?'

Covet loses a bloody fight.

'You know I do.' I'm almost whispering.

'Oh, Fliss, I'm so sorry.'

'Don't be, I'll get over it.'

Covet strikes back. Now I'm lying as well.

'Fliss, look at me.'

I look. He's smiling again, grinning in fact. I'm rather confused. He's not the sort of person to take pleasure in hurting others.

'I don't want you to get over it. I love you, Fliss.'

'But I thought . . . what about you and Kat?'

'Kat and I are finished. I'm sorry, I shouldn't have teased you. I did offer to make a go of things with her, but only because you wanted me to. I'd gladly have been as miserable as hell in order to make you happy, but thank God it never came to that. Kat finally took the advice of her solicitor and left.'

'Her solicitor?'

He nods slowly.

'Know any good solicitors?'

'No,' I reply fearfully, 'but I know a bad barrister. What happened, Alex?'

I'm trembling.

'Richard finally got what he wanted: Kat made a decision. It seems that his marrying your sister was the right move in their interminable game.'

'Oh, no.' I cover my mouth with my hand. 'Poor, poor Sally-Anne!'

'It's OK, Fliss, Sally's all right. She's upset, of course, but she's OK.'

272

'You've seen her?'

'Not exactly.' He shakes his head. 'You're not going to believe who came to see me this morning – your mother.'

'My mother?' I query incredulously.

He nods. 'Yes. You know, she actually wanted to apologise. She feels as if everything is her fault. She was the one who told me where I could find you. Apparently your father phoned her this afternoon to let her know you were here and to make sure that everything was OK with Sally and Richard, which of course it wasn't.'

'But surely she must have told him what had happened? Why didn't he tell me! He didn't say a word.'

'Because he knew I was on my way down here to see you. Miriam told him to try to keep you here until I arrived, thought it would be best if you heard it all from me. She gave me this to give to you.'

He hands me an envelope. I stare uselessly as it for a moment. My hands are shaking so much I tear the letter as I rip open the envelope. Mother's small neat handwriting is familiar and strangely reassuring.

Dear Fliss,

Well, what can I say? You were right and I was wrong. Richard has left Sally-Anne for another woman. I can't quite believe that they've been married for less than two months and are already heading for the divorce courts. Poor Sally is strangely calm about it, I really don't think it's sunk in yet, but after all it only happened yesterday. Please don't worry about her, though. I'll make sure that she's all right, I promise, it's the least I can do considering I am the major cause of this whole mess.

I'm sure that Sally really did love Richard, but I have to admit now that you were right, I shouldn't have pushed them into getting married so quickly. We obviously knew far less about him than we thought we did.

What makes me feel worse is that I think I actually wanted her to marry him for all the wrong reasons. For me, and not for herself. I think it was I who wanted the big white wedding, the successful husband, the beautiful apartment, the golden future. Well, I've certainly found out that all that glitters isn't gold, and Richard is a . . . well, you

273

know what he is, and now so do I. I just hope that in time Sally realises she's probably far better off without him too.

I'm taking her away for a week to try and help her get over the past few months. We both need a break. I've left details of where we're staying with Erica in case you need to contact us, but you'll have the opportunity to say 'I told you so' when I come back.

Please don't blame yourself for any of this, Fliss. Alex told me what you did to try and help them stay together, and I want you to know how proud I am of you for that. I really have no right to say this but Alex is a good man. But I'm sure as usual you've worked this out for yourself, and don't need me interfering in your life yet again.

With love,
Mother.

Alex waits for me to finish reading and then hands me another envelope.

'One last thing,' he smiles encouragingly at me, 'Sally asked if you could return the favour for her. She said you'd know what she meant.'

I open the envelope with shaking fingers, and tip the contents into the palm of my hand. Sally's wedding and engagement rings.

I instantly think back to the time when I asked her to return my engagement ring to Richard for me.

'Oh, poor, poor Sally,' I mutter again, scrubbing my eyes with my other hand.

'Don't worry, I have a feeling it will all turn out OK in the end, Fliss,' Alex says softly.

'You really think so? She must be devastated.'

'Well, she's certainly better off without him, and although that's probably the last thing she wants to hear right now, I'm sure given time . . . James was last seen harassing Erica for the name of Sally-Anne's hotel, then driving hell for leather up the M1.'

'James?'

He nods. 'Some flames never die.'

'Well, he swore to always defend and honour her,' I agree. 'I always said he'd be better for her than Richard.'

'He's in love with her, Fliss,' Alex murmurs. 'I always think

274

that's a good start to any relationship, don't you?'

Reaching out, he puts his hand under my chin and tilts my face upwards, forcing me to look at him.

'Now there are no more obstacles, do you think we might get to have a happy ending?'

Forbidden fruits taste sweet, but leave a lingering bitter taste of guilt. Alex's lips taste sweet, a lingering, delicious kiss, spoilt no longer by guilt but by the fact that although I feel like I've died and gone to heaven, I am still human after all and have to breathe.

Everyone in life is looking for something. The main problem is half the time we're never quite sure what that something is. It's taken me a long time to find the right path. Along the way I've detoured, backtracked, and finally almost broken down completely, but as Alex and I breathlessly, reluctantly, laughingly, break apart, I know that I've finally found what *I* was searching for.

It feels very strange letting myself into Richard's apartment once more. The place is silent. The sort of silence you can feel, cold and very empty. Even the ever-present, irrepressible Eric shudders and presses his furry body closer to my ankles.

Sally brought a warmth to Richard's life that he was a fool to give up, and he'd be a very lucky fool ever to find that again, especially with a cold fish like Katherine Christian.

I head straight for the bedroom, intending to leave Sally's rings in the same place I left my note and keys the night *I* walked out on Richard Trevelyan.

Kind of symbolic, I know, but it's with a great sense of sadness at the way it's happened, and also a great sense of relief, that I finally dismiss Richard the Turd from both our lives for good.

The wardrobes where Sally's clothes were kept are standing open. Where once was row upon row of neatly pressed, perfectly coordinated outfits, there is absolutely nothing. There are still some clothes in Richard's wardrobe, but something catches my eye on the other side of the bed.

Richard's side of the bed.

Skirting round, I find a large suitcase on the floor, an open suitcase, filled almost to overflowing with the contents of Richard's drawers: silk underwear, socks, handkerchiefs, sweaters.

Richard is in the process of moving out and moving on as well, a For Sale sign prominent in the window, obscuring the gorgeous panoramic view of the city of Oxford, the only thing of true beauty this spartan place possesses now that Sally has gone.

I'd kind of like to wait until Richard comes home to collect the rest of his belongings.

I think back to the fateful dinner party and Ethelred the Unready-cooked. Poor old lobster. Richard deserves Ethelred's end far more than Ethelred himself did. I have a lovely vision of holding Richard's head in an unlit gas oven, until his short stumpy legs stop kicking.

I shake my head and the picture clears.

It would be nice to see him suffer, but after spending the whole of the past week with Alex Christian, Holloway is no longer a tempting option as the place to spend the rest of my life. Besides I have a feeling Kat will make Richard suffer far more than I ever could.

I decide it's time for me to make my final exit.

Alex is waiting outside for me in the car. We're en route to a homecoming dinner at The Beeches with my Mother, Sally . . . and James.

Unfortunately, although *I'm* heading for the front door, it seems I have lost Eric. He's not hugging my heels as usual, and doesn't come when I whistle, so I head back to where I last saw him.

In Richard's bedroom.

I knew Eric was the right dog for me from the first moment I spotted him.

I push open the bedroom door now to find him squatting happily in Richard's open suitcase, his cute face a picture of strained concentration. I could almost swear he winks at me as he parks the remains of his lunch in a neat and stinking curl on Richard's favourite cashmere sweater.